Henry Edward Manning

The Life of Saint Teresa of the Order of our Lady of Mount Carmel

Henry Edward Manning

The Life of Saint Teresa of the Order of our Lady of Mount Carmel

ISBN/EAN: 9783337054151

Printed in Europe, USA, Canada, Australia, Japan

Cover: Foto ©Raphael Reischuk / pixelio.de

More available books at **www.hansebooks.com**

THE

LIFE OF SAINT TERESA

OF THE ORDER OF

OUR LADY OF MOUNT CARMEL.

EDITED WITH A PREFACE

BY HIS GRACE

THE ARCHBISHOP OF WESTMINSTER.

𝕾𝖊𝖈𝖔𝖓𝖉 𝕰𝖉𝖎𝖙𝖎𝖔𝖓.

DUBLIN:
JAMES DUFFY, WELLINGTON QUAY;
AND
LONDON: 22, PATERNOSTER ROW.
1867.

WYMAN AND SONS, PRINTERS,
GREAT QUEEN STREET, LINCOLNS INN FIELDS,
LONDON, W.C.

PREFACE.

—◆—

AMONG the accidental glories of the Blessed Mother
of God, the amplest and the most conspicuous is the
elevation of her daughters and their participation in
the service of her Divine Son. In the first Eve they
fell under the bondage of this world. In the second
Eve they are elevated to a supernatural life and grace.
In the midst of the degradations of the old world
there was a chosen line in which the types of Jesus
and of Mary were continually repeated. Noe, Abraham, Josue, and David, were ennobled by the typical
character they bore. Sarai, Rebecca, Judith, and
Esther in like manner rose above themselves, and
were arrayed in a dignity derived from her whom
they foreshowed. The shadow of the Mother of
Jesus yet to come cast a beauty upon them. But
if this was so even before she came, how much more
since her coming. Her example and her power with
God have, by His grace, raised her handmaids to the
knowledge and love of her Divine Son, and to a participation in the works of His kingdom. This is
verified in the sanctity of Christian women, in their
fortitude as martyrs, their fidelity as confessors, their
perfection as saints, their supernatural zeal as founders
of religious Orders, and as ministers of the works of

charity and mercy which cover the face of the Church.
There is, however, one other dignity which our Lord
has put upon them in honour of His Blessed Mother·
The Apostle legislates for the Church in saying, " I
suffer not a woman to teach, nor to usurp authority
over the man, but to be in silence."* Nevertheless
our Lord has constituted His Blessed Mother Queen
of Apostles, and has admitted certain of her daughters
to a share in the illumination and office of Teachers
and Reformers in His Church. To pass over many,
we may name S. Catharine of Sienna, whose illuminated judgment gave counsel even to Pontiffs ; S.
Catharine of Genoa, who has expounded the dogma
of Purgatory, as theologians have said, with a special
light of the Holy Ghost; and S. Teresa, who for her
singular illumination and treatment of mystical theology has been associated, by a graceful courtesy, with
the Doctors of the Church.

In the few words prefixed to this Life it is not
possible, nor would it be right, to attempt an analysis
or a synopsis of S. Teresa's works. What she has
contributed to the teaching of the Church will appear
in the Life itself. I cannot attempt to do more than
fix upon one point in her writings, which is also the
transcript of her own character. It gives the outline
and the proportions of her own mind and of all her
teaching, and can be expressed in no words better
than her own : " We must fix our eyes on Christ, our
only Good, and then we shall learn true humility. . . .
I said our understanding must be *ennobled*, and then

* 1 Tim. ii. 11.

the knowledge of ourselves will not make it base and cowardly;"* or, in other words, the knowledge of God ennobles the soul. The true nobility of the soul is to know and love God: to be ignorant of God is its true baseness. The knowledge of God is the condition to conformity to Him, and conformity to Him is the glory of the soul. The deformity of the soul is its own degradation, and ignorance is the chief cause of this deformity.

The life and writings of S. Teresa are a perpetual exposition of the words of S. Paul to the Ephesians :

That He would grant you, according to the riches of His glory, to be strengthened by His Spirit with might unto the inward man. That Christ may dwell by faith in your hearts : that being rooted and grounded in charity, you may be able to comprehend, with all the saints, what is the breadth, and length, and height, and depth. To know also the charity of Christ, which surpasseth all knowledge, that you may be filled unto all the fulness of God.†

Her single and unceasing aim was to unite herself to God, through His Incarnation, with the most expanded vision of her intelligence illuminated by faith, and the most intense union of her will inflamed by charity. This appears from the outset of her life. In childhood she was remarkable for her love of solitude, and her devotion to the Blessed Mother of God. At seven years old she used to pray to die that she might see God. She read in the lives of saints that the martyrs enter immediately upon the vision of God. She at once desired to be a martyr that she might imme-

---

* " The Interior Castle," c. xi. p. 13, London, 1852.

† Ephes. iii. 16-19.

diately see God. For this purpose she resolved to escape from her father's house, and find her way into Africa, that she might be martyred by the Moors. She secretly left her home, but was overtaken at some distance beyond the walls of Avila, and brought back to her parents. When asked why she had run away, she said, "I ran away because I want to see God, and I must die before I can see Him." This is the key of her whole life, for which the reader must be referred to the following pages. I must be content with touching a few points in her character as illustrating her great axiom, that the knowledge of God is the nobility of the soul.

1. The first great perfection which runs throughout her mind and words is an intense perception and appreciation of the perfections of God. His Purity, Truth, Justice, Unchangeableness, Mercy, Compassion seem to penetrate and to encompass her mind. She speaks of them as the motive and measure of her own conduct, as people of the world speak of its rules and laws. This is the true determining cause of great and little characters. God who created the soul in His own image and for Himself, has constituted Himself as the end of our existence, so that nothing but God or out of God is adequate and proportionate to the likeness which is in us. Everything but God, if loved without God, dwarfs, stunts, contracts the soul. Not sin only, or the perversion of the creatures, but creatures in their purest and most perfect state and use, out of God and apart from God, narrow the soul to their own dimensions, and by narrowing it draw it down. God alone enlarges, and by

enlarging elevates it; and by elevation, unfolds and perfects the soul with all the faculties of the intellect, all the affections of the heart, and all the powers of the will: and that because He is the proper end for which it was created. As the soul knows and is conformed to God, it ascends towards its perfection; and that perfection is not transient, as all out of God must be, but passes into the essence of the soul, and is eternal. The greatest man, according to the developments and powers of the natural order, is narrow compared with one who is thus elevated to intellectual and moral union with God. As they who inhabit mountains, and live in heights, and among the grandeurs of nature, are developed not only in sinew and strength, but in every sense and instinct, and possess an elevation of character, a simplicity and a dignity above other races; so it is with those who converse with God, and walk to and fro among the Divine perfections, inhabiting the high places, within the folds of the Presence of God. Such was eminently S. Teresa.

2. Another perfection of her character was a singular intensity in the perception of sin. She used to say, "Every sin we commit, we commit in God;" that is, not only in His sight and in His presence; but "in Him we live and move and are;" our vital powers are sustained and fed by Him; we could not subsist for a moment if the influences of His being were withdrawn; and all the activity of our soul with all its faculties and volitions, except so far as they deviate from His perfections, are sustained and empowered by Him. When we sin, therefore, we turn His image

consciousness, it may be called, of the presence, the
sanctity, the majesty of God, of the glory and perfection of the Sacred Humanity, of the sinless beauty
and nearness of the Heavenly Court, of the state of
souls expiating sin beyond the grave, caused her not
only to see all the contrasts to light and purity which
were in herself, but to conceive of herself as the
patriarch did of old in the light of the presence of
the Lord : " With the hearing of the ear I have
heard thee, but now my eye seeth thee. Therefore
I reprehend myself, and do penance in dust and
ashes."*

This she describes in the two following passages :—

O Thou Lord of my soul ! how shall I be able to express with
gratitude the favours Thou didst bestow upon me during these
years ? And how, at the very time I was offending Thee most,
Thou didst in a short time dispose me for a most profound sorrow,
that so I might enjoy Thy favours and consolations. The truth is,
O my King ! Thou didst adopt as one means, the most exquisite
and sharp kind of punishment which could be found for me : for
Thou knowest well what would prove most afflicting to me, viz.,
that my sins should be punished by receiving favours from Thee !
It is no foolish thing which I utter, though one should not be
surprised if I became foolish, when I recall the memory of my
ingratitude and wickedness against Thee. But it was much more
grievous for me to receive favours, when at the same time I was
committing great faults, than it would have been to have endured
severe punishments. Hence, *even one* of those favours received
seems capable of confounding and afflicting me, more than many
corporal infirmities and other troubles united. As to the latter, I
saw that I deserved them, and I thought I had made some satisfaction by them for my sins ; though all, indeed, were but little,

---

* Job xlii. 5, 6.

considering the multitude of my sins. But to see myself again receiving fresh favours, though I had made such a bad return for those I had received before, was a most terrible punishment for me : and I think it will be considered so by all who have any knowledge or love of God. Hence flowed my tears and came my indignation, seeing what I found in myself, that I was still on the point of falling again, though my desires and resolutions were then firm—I mean as long as the favours lasted. It is a great misfortune for a soul to be alone amidst such dangers ; and methinks if I knew any one to whom I could have spoken on these matters, it would have helped me from not falling again ; at least I should have been prevented through shame, even had I no shame in offending God.—*Life,* pp. 46, 47.

Again :—

True it is, that I am both the weakest and most wicked of all creatures ; but yet I believe, that whoever will humble himself— though he be strong—and not trust in himself, but in one who has experience in these matters, will not lose anything. Respecting myself, I am able to say, that if our Lord had not discovered this truth to me, and had not also given me means to treat, in a very familiar manner, with persons who were given to mental prayer, I should still have gone over—falling and rising—till I had fallen headlong into hell. For I had many friends who would have helped me to fall ; but in endeavouring to rise up again, I found myself so much alone, that now I am astonished I did not always remain in a fallen state. I praise the mercy of God, for He alone it was who gave me a helping hand : may He be praised for ever and ever. Amen.—*Ibid.* pp. 48, 49.

This vision of God, and of herself, and of herself in God, produced in her, as in the vision of S. Francis in Mount Alvernia, the perfection of humility which consists in the beatitude of the poor in spirit. It is the nearest approach to the filial fear of the Heavenly Court, and is to be found only in those whose charity has cast out fear, whose fear is purified of servile motives.

4. A fourth perfection conferred upon S. Teresa by this union of the soul with God, was an enlargement of the intellect. No one can read her writings without perceiving a breadth, strength, and subtlety of intellect which is more like the intelligence of a man than of a woman. It is in the moral and spiritual sciences as it is in the physical or the mathematical. We must have axioms to start with, and unless we possess certain principles of truth which are in themselves evident, and anterior to all reasoning, we have no starting-points, and the mind is unable, not only to make progress, but even to set out on its activity. All the operations of a mind without first principles are confused, vague, and uncertain; and the mind itself becomes narrow and dwarfed. The knowledge of God gives the axioms of the spiritual life, and of the knowledge of self. The more fully God is known, the firmer and broader are the processes of the mind in all spiritual and moral science. The guidance of the Church, by its divine office of teacher, has elevated and enlarged the intelligence of Christendom; and all those who are conformed in heart and mind to the living voice of the Church, receive a strength and breadth, a clearness and a fulness of intelligence, which can in no other way be attained. To what but this can be ascribed the fact that the writings of S. Teresa, a Spanish lady of no more than common education, who entered early into a convent, and thereby lost the culture and development which the world confers upon many by contact and collision

with itself, should exhibit a justness of judgment, an exuberance of thought in the abstrusest matters of the interior life, with a perspicuity and force both of conception and language which it is hard to find among educated men? God had taught her to know Himself, and this science made her a teacher in His Church.

5. And, lastly, the knowledge of God conferred upon her an elevation and a force of will before which the trials of her life, great as they were, gave way. The will which at seven years old was so resolved as to leave her father's house in quest of martyrdom, expanded into a power which never sunk under the heaviest crosses, or gave back before the firmest assaults. The mistrust, calumny, abandonment, persecution she had to endure, might have broken down a strong man. But, woman as she was, she passed through all, and came out more than conqueror. She who was denounced as deceived and deceiving was recognized as a saint; she who was condemned as a visionary and hardly sound in faith, was listened to as a teacher; she who was rejected by her own sisters became the reformer, not of them alone, but of the Fathers of Mount Carmel; she who was barely suffered to remain within the walls of her convent founded thirty monasteries of strict observance, which the Catholic Church has recognized as the works of the Spirit of God. But, for such a life of forty years, nothing but a will conformed to the will of God, and confirmed by union with His power, could have sufficed.

In reading this life, we meet with many unusual

supernatural tokens and visitations of the presence and the grace of our Divine Lord. And we might be induced to think that the way in which He led S. Teresa is so far above the way we walk in, that it affords no example to us. In this we should mislead ourselves. The end of her life was indeed upon high places, where the clouds conceal the paths of the saints from the eyes of ordinary Christians. She entered into ways of prayer and was favoured with visions of the Sacred Humanity which we may hardly ask for, and perhaps may never attain; but though the ending of her spiritual life transcends our common lot, the beginnings did not. She is to us a direct and practical example, especially in the point of which I have spoken, the knowledge of God, and the nobility it confers upon the soul. She set out in her journey towards the mountain of the Lord as we all do. Her trials and probation were the same as ours. She passed through the same stages in attaining to the higher paths which wind out of sight in the mountain of perfection; and we must tread the same way if we would attain the vision of God in Eternity. That which was vouchsafed to her here is laid up, it may be, for us only hereafter. But the path is the same. I will therefore trace it briefly, and mark its chief steps.

The first degree of the knowledge of God in the order of grace of which we are speaking, is the illu-mination of faith which elevates the lights of nature to a supernatural perception of the being, perfections, character, and operations of God, one in Nature, three in Persons, our Creator, Redeemer, and Sanctifier. This is in every one who is baptized; but in some it is developed more than in others. It pervades the intelligence and the conscience with a kind of sense or consciousness of God, of His presence and moral judgment of our actions. In those who faithfully correspond with this light, it continues to increase in clearness and in constraining power. It becomes the motive and the measure of their actions, and is the basis of all perfection. "Walk before me, and be perfect," * was the command of God to Abraham. To live under the consciousness of God, in His sight and in His hearing, so to speak, is the highest and deepest motive to obedience. Such is the outset of our Christian life. It is to be doubted whether the light of faith once infused be ever altogether extinguished. "The devils believe and tremble." The baptized infidel may reject Christianity, but he retains the Theism both of nature and of revelation. He may lose his faith, but he does not therefore lose his reason; nor does his reason, we may believe, lose the intellectual consciousness of the Creator and Judge which baptism imparted to it.

The second degree is the knowledge of the heart, that is, of faith working by hope and by charity; by hope maturing into confidence, and by charity uniting the soul to God by the union of love. The effect of this knowledge which comes by love is two-fold. First, its essential effect, which is obedience, conformity of will, fervour in its true sense of punctuality, regularity, and exactness in the fulfilment of duties,

* Gen. xvii. 1.

generosity in serving God, promptness in doing or
suffering His will. All this is called *effective* love,
which may be in a high degree of perfection in souls
which are placid and calm by absence of emotion, or
even dark and dry by reason of aridities and derelic-
tions. The other effect is a certain emotion of joy
and sweetness in the knowledge and love of God,
which moves the heart with lively feeling, and is
therefore called the *affective* love. This latter operation is not essential. Many who are high in the
effective love have little of the affective. Nevertheless it produces its chief effects in the soul, which
are assimilation with God and sympathy with the
Sacred Heart in its sorrows, intentions, and interests.
This second degree is the state in which many truly
Christian souls live and die.

The third degree is the knowledge of experience;
and this is learned partly by the Holy Sacraments of
Penance and of the Altar, and partly by the Providence whereby God is pleased to visit and to dispose
of us. Just as we learn to know a friend by living
with him and making trial of his character by personal experience, so it is between the soul and God.
The events of life, joy and sorrow, sickness and
recovery, changes and crosses, bring out His tenderness, watchfulness, compassion. Selfish and unloving
natures live among their kindred and friends without
appreciating or knowing them. All their affection
and self-denial is taken for granted, exacted, and
forgotten. Nothing is appreciated but the last disappointment, or the inevitable crossing of some
unreasonable or hurtful wish. So the unworthy

children of the noblest parents, and the heartless companions of the most generous friends, live and die in profound unconsciousness of the love and care which have been lavished and wasted upon them. But higher and better natures discern and appreciate the actions and characters of those who love them; they perceive their motives and intentions; and the more delicate and nobler they become, they ever imagine for those who love them higher and more perfect thoughts and aims than they really have. So it is with those that love God, only they can never imagine for Him any perfection of love and tenderness which goes beyond the truth, or even reaches towards the exceeding depth of His compassion. To those who love Him God is a perpetual object of loving contemplation; and as He is contemplated, He is more and more perfectly known with the knowledge which comes by the heart. It is this the Holy Ghost intends in the words " Gustate et videte quoniam suavis est Dominus." " Taste and see that the Lord is sweet." We see by the intellect and taste by the heart; but the heart gives back a new and further light to the intellect, so as to see not only that He is love, but that He is sweetness. This is what S. Paul intends by the words "that, being rooted and founded in charity, you may be able to comprehend with all the saints what is the breadth, and length, and height, and depth, to know also the charity of Christ, which surpasseth all knowledge, that you may be filled unto all the fulness of God." *

* Ephes. iii. 17, 18.

b

It is a new faculty opened in the soul. As Aristotle, in the *Ethics*, says of the just man who acquires even in the natural order a discernment, and a knowledge of moral truths which others have not because "an eye grows upon the soul"—ὄμμα τι τῇ ψυχῇ προσ-φύεται—so it is with those who, knowing God by faith and by the heart, make trial of His goodness and His sweetness by experience. The three chief ways of this experience are prayer, the Holy Sacraments, and intelligent submission to God in His providence. By prayer is meant, not vocal prayer only, but the prayer of the mind and of the heart sustained habitually by recollection of the presence of God, and articulated often by desires, aspirations, momentary petitions in the actions and trials of the day, the renewal of intentions in our words and works, and a consciousness of His personal relation to us and of ours to Him as our Father and our Lord. By the Holy Sacraments as a means of knowledge is meant chiefly those of Penance and of the Altar. Frequent confession and frequent communion are the two fountains of the knowledge which comes from the experience of the love and tenderness of God in Jesus Christ. And lastly, by intelligent submission to His providence is meant a recognition of the sovereign will of God in all things, and a conviction that our actual lot, excepting only our sins, which are a depravation of our lot, is a revelation of the will of God concerning us. The converse of the soul with God, and the conscious union of our intelligence with His intelligence, and of our will with His will, converts our life into an intelligent moral government and probation, the reasons and issues of which become at once, in the main, evident. S. Hilarion on his deathbed said to his soul, " Go forth, what fearest thou ? Go forth, O my soul ! why dost thou doubt ? For nearly seventy years thou hast served Christ, and dost thou fear to die ? " which words breathe the internal personal knowledge which a faithful servant had of a loving master by the long experience of His goodness.

The fourth degree of knowledge is more simply supernatural than the last, and comes by an infusion of grace. S. Paul speaks of knowing " the charity of Christ which surpasseth knowledge," which must needs therefore be a knowledge above nature. The Psalmist describes it when he says, " The light of Thy countenance is signed upon us." * This describes a special revealing or manifestation of Himself, as when the sun rises on the earth, or comes forth from behind a cloud. It is an action of God superadding to the lights of nature and of reason, of faith, of charity, and of experience, a further light of direct effusion in reward of the fidelity of the soul. And this is distinctly promised by our Divine Lord through His Apostles to all the faithful.

If any one love Me he will keep My words, and My Father will love him, and We will come to him, and will make Our abode with him.

He that hath My commandments and keepeth them, he it is that loveth Me. And he that loveth Me shall be loved of My Father : and I will love him and will manifest Myself to him.†

---

* Ps. iv. 7.   † S. John xiv. 23, 21.

This special abiding or special manifestation of Himself to the faithful is something over and above His inhabitation in all the regenerate, and the ordinary illumination of faith. It signifies a special grace vouchsafed to the soul in the maturity of its obedience and union with God. It includes two things—a new and fuller objective manifestation of Himself, and new and deeper subjective faculties in the soul to perceive it. "The eyes of your understanding being enlightened," as S. Paul says: "the nobler way of knowing God," as S. Gregory calls it: or as S. Teresa describes it, after telling us how a picture of our Lord, with the crown of thorns and the purple robe, one day in the forty-third year of her life pierced her heart—"From that time," she says, "I opened a new Book, that is, I began a new life. That which I had lived hitherto was my own: but that which I have lived since, I may say, has been God's; for it seems to me God has lived in me." "O wonderful goodness of God!" she says in another place. "How changed does the soul come forth, by having been only for a short time (never, in my opinion, a full half-hour) immersed in the greatness of God." * It is as if the presence, nearness, majesty, and spirituality of God had become so vast and so immediate that all things pass out of sight and out of consciousness.

The last degree of this knowledge is purely supernatural, and comes by a sovereign favour of God; namely, a vision of His presence. The latter years

---

* "Interior Castle," Fifth Mansion, c. 11, p. 73.

of S. Teresa's life were full of it. She describes it as follows: "It is as if a person were in the dark, and saw not another who stood near him;" that is, by a consciousness which depends on no sense. "Our Lord's presence is represented to the soul by a sign clearer than the sun itself; and yet no sun or brightness is seen, but only a certain light which, without our seeing it, illuminates the understanding." Again, in another place, she says it is like "a fragrance rising from a brazier in the dark." Now, by this she does not mean only the consciousness of which I have already spoken, nor the instincts by which S. Paschal Baylon, S. Francis Borgia, S. Colette, and many more, could follow and discover the presence and the place of the Blessed Sacrament. She intended a certain kind of vision granted to her by the direct action of God. This she carefully distinguishes into its several kinds —intellectual, spiritual, imaginary, and sensible. She says that she saw our Lord "neither with the eye of the body nor of the soul, because it was no imaginary vision;" that is, it was not represented to her under any image, but by the supernatural sense of His nearness. At another time she describes a vision which assumed the form or the true image of the Divine Humanity.

Being one day in prayer, it pleased Him to show me His sacred hands, and they were so excessively beautiful that I am not able to describe them. But this sight gave me great fear, as indeed every new sight does in the beginning of any of those supernatural favours which our Lord is pleased to show me. Within a few days after, I saw His Divine face, the sight of which ravished me with delight. I could not conceive why our Lord showed Himself thus to me, by little and little, since afterwards He resolved to do me the favour that I should see His whole person, till I came to reflect that He was pleased to conduct me according to my natural weakness. (P. 47.)

Again, she says—

On the feast of S. Paul, while I was hearing Mass, the most Sacred Humanity of Christ was fully represented to me, as it is painted after His resurrection ; but with such great beauty and majesty that I can only say, that if there were nothing else in Heaven to delight our eyes but the excessive beauty of glorified bodies, the bliss would be immense, especially the sight of the Humanity of Jesus Christ our Lord. And if His Majesty be so great, even when It is represented to us in this world, according to that proportion which our misery can bear, what will it be when we shall wholly enjoy and possess such a happiness ? This vision, though represented to me by the way of a mental image, was never seen by me with the eyes of my body ; nor was any other, but only with the eyes of my soul. They who understand these things better than I do, affirm that this kind of vision, which is purely intellectual, is of a higher and more perfect kind than those which are seen with the bodily eyes. (P. 47.)

This is, in fact, the same vision of Jesus which was vouchsafed to S. Stephen in his martyrdom, S. Paul on his way to Damascus, S. Thomas of Canterbury at Pontigny, S. Ignatius at La Storta; but in the life of S. Teresa was so frequent and so abiding in its effects as to give a habitual elevation and nobleness to her mind. She describes the glory and beauty of these visions as follows :—

It is a sight, the clearness and brightness of which exceeds all that can possibly be imagined in this world. It is not a splendour which dazzles, but a sweet lustre ; nor does that light offend the eyes whereby we see this object of such divine beauty. It is a light so different from that of this world, that even the brightness of the sun itself which we see is dim in comparison with its brightness. It is as if we beheld very clear water running upon crystal, with the sun's rays reflected upon it, and striking through it, in comparison with other very muddy water seen in a cloudy day, and running upon an earthy bottom. This is a light which never sets, and has no night; but as it is always light, nothing disturbs it. Indeed, it is of such a nature that no understanding in this life, however sublime, would be able adequately to conceive it. (P. 48.)

One more quotation must be added. S. Teresa had ascended through the Sacred Humanity into an almost habitual consciousness of the Presence of the ever Blessed Trinity, which she describes in words which will better express than any of mine what I have endeavoured to trace as the knowledge of God by intuition.

The Three Persons of the most Blessed Trinity manifest themselves to this soul in such a manner, that she understands them all to be of one substance, one power, and one wisdom; to be, in short, one God. So that what we know in this world only by faith, that soul, one may say, knows by sight: not that she sees anything with her bodily eyes, nor even by her interior sight. . . . . But the Three Adorable Persons communicate themselves to that soul, speak to her, and make her to understand these words in the Gospel : *If any man love Me, he will keep My commandments; and My Father will love him, and We will come to him and dwell in him.*

O my God, what a difference there is between these words striking upon our ear, or even believing them, and understanding them in the manner which I have described! Since that soul has received this favour, it seems to her that those Divine Persons have never quitted her. She sees clearly that They are in the very inmost depth of her soul, as if in a deep abyss. Being an unlearned person, she cannot say what that abyss may be, but only that there she finds herself in that Divine Company. (P. 164.)

For general readers into whose hands this book may pass it may be well to add, what for Catholics is needless, namely, that in S. Teresa's mind two things, which are sometimes thought to be incompatible, are to be found not only in combination but in their highest perfection, that is, spirituality and common sense. The mystical elevations, and the obscurity which comes from the splendour of the subjects of which she speaks, may lead those who are not familiar with the science of the Saints to imagine that hers was a dreamy, unpractical nature, unbalanced in its judgments, fanciful, and impulsive. Nothing can be more contrary to the fact. S. Teresa was the reverse of all this. Throughout her long life common sense in dealing with men and things was supreme. Even her running away to be martyred, that she might see God, is the common sense of the Sermon on the Mount. The Founder of thirty monasteries, and the Reformer of Mount Carmel, both of men and of women, had the broad common sense, calm judgment, and balanced mind of a legislator or a ruler. In fact, S. Teresa is an example of a great moral truth, namely, that spirituality perfects common sense: forasmuch as it is a part of the nobleness and perfection of the soul which comes by the knowledge of God. "God is a Spirit, and they who adore Him must adore Him in spirit and in truth." Spirituality is the perfection of the reason and the will, the sanity of the whole intellectual and moral nature in all its instincts and operations. God is not glorified by diseases of the imagination, nor by the imbecilities of the mind. Wheresoever God abides in the soul He perfects it. The Seven Gifts of the Holy Spirit, to Whom S. Teresa had an especial devotion, perfect both the intellect and the will: the intellect in its speculative and practical faculties, and the will in its rectitude and power. In truth, the soul cannot be conformed to God without growing in what is called common sense, which does not consist, as the world would have it, in conformity to its own public opinion, or to the customs which reign among the majority, but in conformity to wisdom and prudence, to the will of God which is the universal rule of right, and to the common instincts and judgments of those who are united with Him. The common sense of a soul full of God may be opposed to the common sense of the world full of itself. But "the foolishness of God is wiser than men."

Such, then, are the five degrees of the knowledge of God, which are illustrated in a luminous distinctness in the life of S. Teresa, namely—the knowledge of faith, of love, of experience, of infusion, and of intuition, or of vision. And it is this knowledge of God which expanded and ennobled her soul to a capacity of the Divine Presence hardly to be surpassed in the examples of the Saints.

And with this one axiom of the spiritual life and of S. Teresa's theology, that the knowledge of God is the nobility of the soul, I commend this book, beautiful and simple both in its thoughts and in its expressions, to the devout reading and the meditation of all who desire to know and to love God.

✠ HENRY EDWARD MANNING.

Feast of the Nativity of the Blessed Virgin, 1865.

CONTENTS.

CHAPTER V

CHAPTER VI.

CHAPTER VII.

CHAPTER VIII.

CHAPTER IX.

CHAPTER X.

1561.

CHAPTER XI.

1561, 1562.

CHAPTER XII.

1562—1567.

CHAPTER XVI.

1571—1574.

CHAPTER XVII.

1574.

CHAPTER XVIII.

1575, 1576.

CHAPTER XIX.

1576 –1579.

CHAPTER XX.

1578, 1579.

CHAPTER XXI.

1579.

CHAPTER XXII.

1580.

CHAPTER XXIII.

1580, 1581.

c

INTRODUCTION.

It has been often said that when God raises up one
of His chosen champions to do great things in His
Church, He places a woman by his side to be his
helper, and to bear her part in the work; that as
Mary stood by the Cross of Jesus, uniting her sacrifice with His, her daughters may not be deprived of
their share in carrying out the great work of redemp-
tion.

The two Saints in many instances work together,
as S. Francis and S. Clare, S. Benedict and S. Scho-
lastica, S. Francis of Sales and S. Jane Frances de
Chantal; in others they are unknown to each other
by face, and labour in their several spheres apart, the
woman carrying out in silence and in prayer the
ministry which calls forth all the active strength and
intellect of the man.

Thus, in opposition to the great Protestant delusion,
God raised up two instruments, most unequal, according to man's judgment, to cope with the gigantic
powers of Luther. They were indeed, like him, endowed with extraordinary intellectual gifts; yet what
power but His Who sent David to fight against Goliah
with a shepherd's sling and stone, could have enabled

a Spanish soldier and a Spanish woman to cope with
the apostate friar and learned theologian of Witten-
burgh ?

It is a stirring tale, which tells us how Ignatius
fought and conquered; how the hard-won victory first
gained over his own iron will gave him a mastery,
perhaps unequalled, over the wills of other men, and
how his whole after-life was a carrying out of his own
meditation upon the two standards, a close following
of his Leader's footsteps in the conflict with the armies
of Lucifer. But while he was thus fighting in the
plain, there was one upon the mountain holding up
her hands in prayer, to whom no less a share of
the victory is to be assigned; one who like himself
had been cradled in ease and splendour, and had left
all to share the poverty of her Lord; one endowed
with all the gifts of person, fortune, and intellect which
could make this world alluring ; with a woman's quick
and sensitive affections, joined to the intellect of a
highly gifted man, and who yet buried all these in a
Carmelite cell, finding no better way to slake her
burning thirst for the glory of God and the salvation
of men than to gather together a few poor women like
herself to labour with her in perfecting their own
souls, that so God might hear the prayers they offered
night and day for others.

There is a resemblance in the characters of the
two Saints, no less than in the aim they set before
themselves; arising partly, no doubt, from the identity

of their country and their class. Human nature no-
where seems to have worn a nobler aspect than in
the Spanish hidalgos of their day, and in the Spanish
peasants of our own. The national character has all
the fire of the South and all the calm steadfastness of
the North; it is cast in a heroic mould, and, when
touched by fire from above, moves heavenward with
a free unfaltering step like that of Ignatius Loyola
and Teresa d'Ahumada.

But besides what is common to them as Spaniards,
there is a peculiarity in the character of both, which
forms another point of resemblance. S. Ignatius,
even in the dazzling light of the abundant revelations
vouchsafed to him, is remarkable for nothing more
than for his calm practical wisdom and deep insight
into the souls of other men; and the seraphic S.
Teresa, the highly favoured spouse of Christ, the great
teacher of mystical theology, is no less distinguished
as the *Saint of common sense.*

It is this which makes her life of such practical
utility as an example, not only to those who are called,
like her, to seek after perfection in the observance of
the counsels, but to the great multitude of Christian
people, who have to sanctify their souls in the tangled
and cumbered paths of ordinary life. For them, as
well as for the solitary dwellers on Mount Carmel,
this great contemplative Saint has a lesson, which,
if faithfully carried into practice, will enable them to
attain to the only perfection of which a creature is

capable—conformity to the will of its Creator. She
has a lesson, too, for all, whether religious or secular,
in times full, like ours and like her own, of distress
and perplexity, when the enemies of the Church are
active and mighty, and the love of too many of her
children waxes cold. Their hearts often faint within
them when they look out on the wide harvest-field
and ask in vain for the reapers. They have neither
power nor vocation, it may be, to enter it themselves; they are women or unlearned laymen; how
shall they cope with the hideous shapes of sin and
blasphemy which choke the air of England, or answer
the sophistries of modern rationalism? S. Teresa
will teach them—by sanctifying their own souls and
the souls of those under their immediate influence.
This was her weapon against the Antichrist of her
day: this must be ours against the Antichrist of our
own. What instrument could have seemed more
powerless than a lonely nun in a relaxed convent to
work that greater wonder than the conversion of
sinners—the awakening of the lukewarm and the
self-indulgent? Yet she accomplished the task which
holy and learned prelates had essayed in vain. She
made the Order of Mount Carmel once more the glory
of the Church; and by the prayers of her daughters
and the heroic labours of her sons, made ample
reparation to the Sacred Heart of her Divine Spouse
for the desolation of His vineyard by the Lutheran
and the Huguenot. Still does she speak to the

weakest amongst us those great words of hope and promise :—

> Let nothing disturb thee,
> Let nothing affright thee ;
> All passeth away :
> God only shall stay.
> Patience wins all :
> Who hath God needeth nothing,
> For God is his all.*

The materials for the following life have been furnished by the Saint's own history of her life and foundations (in the translations of Père Bouix and Canon Dalton) ; her *Letters*, with the valuable notes of Père Bouix, and an Italian *Life*, in four volumes, published at Rome 1837, by il Padre Federigo di S. Antonio, of the Order of Mount Carmel, derived from the contemporary histories of Ribera and Yepez, both confessors of S. Teresa, the chronicles of the Order, the acts of her canonization, and other authentic sources.

P. Federigo tells us in his preface that he does not write for learned men or religious alone, but for all kinds of readers, to whom S. Francis of Sales, in his *Introduction to a Devout Life*, especially commends the history of S. Teresa, as a mirror in which they may behold the perfect reflection of the Christian life.

To *him* and to *her* we commend this attempt to

* Lines written by S. Teresa in her Breviary.

throw the light of heroic sanctity upon ordinary life, praying them to obtain for us the grace which shall raise our low aims and bring down our proud wills, that so our dear country (once the *Island of Saints*) may recover its lost inheritance of sanctity.

LIFE OF SAINT TERESA.

———◆◇◆———

CHAPTER I.

1515–1530.

S. TERESA was born in the ancient and beautiful city
of Avila, in Old Castile, whose inhabitants had been
long distinguished for their nobility of character and
their love for the holy Church of Jesus Christ. They
were no less remarkable for their refinement of
manners, and for the grace and beauty of the Castilian idiom, which they spoke in all its purity. Avila
was called of old, from the chivalrous bearing of its
people, "the city of knights," an appellation which,
when it became the birthplace of Teresa, and the
cradle of her reform, gave place to the higher and
holier title of "the city of Saints."

The parents of S. Teresa—Alonzo Sanchez de
Cepeda, and Beatrice d'Avila d'Ahumada — sprang
from two of the noblest houses of Castile, and were
not less eminent for their virtues than for their proud
descent.   Alonzo Sanchez was, we are told by his
daughter, a most pious and devoted Christian, full of
charity to the poor and to the sick, and so compassionate towards slaves that he could never endure to
have one in his service, and on one occasion, when a

B

female slave belonging to his brother happened to stay
in his house, it was observed that he treated her with
the same charitable and fatherly kindness which he
would have shown towards a daughter of his own.

Never was an oath or a word of deceit or of detraction heard from his mouth. His favourite recreation was the study of devout books, with which his
house was abundantly supplied. He was in fact the
very model of a Christian nobleman—

> A very perfect gentle knight.

Doña Beatrice was endowed by God with many excellent gifts of mind and person ; she was especially
devout to our Blessed Lady, and carefully instilled this
devotion into the minds of her children ; she was
remarkable for her modesty, and (though she died at
the early age of thirty-three) for her singular prudence.
S. Teresa, in one of her ecstacies, had the happiness
of seeing both her parents in bliss enjoying the vision
of God.

Teresa d'Ahumada, as she was generally called
(according to the Spanish custom), after the family
name of her mother, was born in 1515. It was in
this year that Luther first began to publish his heresies. Little did he dream that an infant born in the
far distant Spain would perhaps win more souls to
God than he would be able to destroy.

She was baptized immediately after her birth in the
parish church of S. John, by the name of Teresa,
which, if the Greek derivation assigned to the word
be correct, means " wonderful ; " a more suitable name
could scarcely have been assigned to her.

From her very earliest years Teresa was remarkable
for her singular beauty of countenance and her sweet
and gentle modesty. She gave indications also of a
mind of no common order. With the graceful play-

fulness of a lively child, there was mingled something which attracted grave and thoughtful persons to converse with her, and before she could be said to have attained the age of reason, she had acquired amongst her mother's friends the name of the "wise and discreet matron." Above all, it appeared that Divine grace was sowing deep within her soul the seeds of what was one day to prove such a rich and abundant harvest. There arose within her a deep disgust for the world and all its pomps, a longing after solitude, and an early tender devotion to the most holy Mother of God.

Her favourite pastime was to read or hear the histories of the Saints. From the reading of these lives, so intense a desire arose within her soul to behold the face of God, that at the age of seven years she earnestly prayed that she might die and go to dwell with His Saints before His throne for ever. So deeply was she impressed with the thought of the exceeding glory and intense anguish of the world beyond the grave, that she would often exclaim, as if transported out of herself, " For ever, for ever."

These passages of her childhood S. Teresa thus described : " I had a brother (named Roderick) about my own age, to whom, though I loved all the others much,* and was much beloved by them, I bore especial affection. We delighted in reading the lives of the Saints together, and when we saw what tortures they endured for the love of God, it seemed to me that all this was as nothing to give for the enjoyment of Him ; therefore I desired to die in this manner, not so much moved thereto by the love of God as

---

* Don Alonzo de Cepeda was twice married, and was the father of twelve children. Teresa was the third of his nine children by the second marriage.

by the desire of soon entering upon the possession of
those great joys which, as we read, were to be found
in Paradise. My brother and I often discoursed
together upon the matter, and at last we agreed that
we would go into the country of the Moors, asking
alms for the love of God, that so we might come to be
beheaded; and it seems to me that our Lord gave us
in that tender age courage to suffer whatever might
have come upon us. But our parents being alive
seemed to us a great impediment. It terrified us
much to read and hear of eternal punishment and
eternal glory; hence it came to pass that we spent
much time in discoursing of such things, and delighted in repeating over and over again *For ever, for
ever.* Thus, by the repetition of these words, did the
Lord impress this truth upon my heart even in my
childhood."

The two children at last bethought themselves to
put their plan in execution. They took a few bits of
bread with them to serve for provision by the way;
and, escaping from their father's house, they resolved
to cross over to Africa, there to ask alms in the name
of Jesus Christ, and for the love of that blessed name,
so hated by the Moors, to lay down their innocent
lives. So rapid was their pace, that they had passed
the city gates and the bridge which crosses the river
Adagia before their flight was discovered. Their
mother was in anguish at the news of their disap-
pearance, fearing that they might have slipped into
a well, or that some other misfortune had befallen
them, and sent in search of them in every direction,
when Divine Providence, which had other enterprises
in store for the heroic child, so ordered that she
should be met by her uncle, Francis Alvarez Cepeda,
and brought back, together with her brother, to
their father's house. Being severely reproved by his

mother, poor Roderick, although the elder of the two,
threw the blame upon his sister, who, he said truly,
had persuaded him to the enterprise. Teresa's
apology bespoke the greatness of her courage. " I
ran away," said she, " because I want to see God,
and because I must die before I can see Him." She
was to die, not by the Moorish scimitar, but of the
lingering wound of Divine Love ; and this brother, so
dearly loved, who was to have been her companion in
martyrdom, grew up to be a valiant warrior, and at
last fell in battle with the enemies of the Church,
being honoured by his saintly sister as a martyr for
the faith.

Teresa was greatly disappointed, and shed many a
tear over the loss of her expected crown. She tried
to console herself by other exercises of piety ; as she
could not be a martyr, she resolved to become a
hermit. Roderick was again called into her counsels,
and together the two children erected little hermitages
in the garden, where they were to live like solitaries
in the desert. The hermitages, like all other creations
of young and inexpert hands, soon fell into ruin ; but
there was an earnest meaning beneath this childish
play, a presage of the solitudes which were hereafter
to be peopled by her daughters, as the victories of
the boy David over the lion and the bear prefigured
his future triumphs over the enemies of God.

At this early age the Lord began already to impart
to her some foretaste of that excellent gift of prayer,
by which she was hereafter to be such a light to His
Church. She had no one to teach her, but she would
gaze for hours upon a picture which hung in her
chamber of our Lord conversing with the woman of
Samaria, until an intense thirst arose within her to
drink of the living water, which had been promised
to her, and she would repeat over and over again,

" Lord, give me this water." To the exercise of prayer, Teresa joined other acts of piety and mercy. " I confess," she says, " that I gave alms to the best of my ability, but I had very little in my power. I stole away into solitude to recite various devotions, and especially the rosary, to which my mother was particularly devoted, and which I had learned from her to love. I took great pleasure, when I was with other children, in erecting convents and pretending to be nuns. I felt a great desire to be a nun, yet not so great as I had felt to be a martyr or a hermit."

Such were the holy images which filled the heart of Teresa in her early childhood. When she came to about the age of nine years, the enemy of souls spread a subtle snare before her, to arrest her onward progress. Encouraged by the example of her mother, and the sympathy and companionship of her faithful ally Roderick, she began to read the romances of chivalry, which were the darling amusements of her age and country. To this she attributed in after years, not only a decay of her childish fervour, but the introduction of a spirit of worldliness and frivolity, which led to an over-fastidiousness as to dress, personal appearance, and other vanities little thought of by the ordinary run of Christians, but seen in its true light by the spiritual discernment of the Saints.

" My mother," she tells us in her narrative of these early years, " was particularly fond of reading books of romance, though she did not imbibe so much evil by this entertainment as I did, because it did not hinder her usual work, but it made us omit many duties that so we might read these books. And perhaps my mother read them that thus her thoughts might not dwell on the great troubles she endured, and her children might so occupy themselves as not to fall into other more dangerous things. My father, however, was so particular on this point, that great care was taken lest he should know anything on the subject. But I continued in the habit of reading those books, and this slight fault of mine, which I perceived in myself, began to cool my good desires, and was the cause of my failing in other things. I fancied, however, there was no harm, though I spent many hours both of the day and night in so vain an exercise, unknown to my father. But I was so much addicted to this habit, that if I could not obtain some new book, it seemed to me I could not be happy.

"I began also to wear fine clothes, and to desire to appear handsome. I took great care of my hands and of my hair, and was fond of perfumes, together with all those vanities which I was able to obtain, which were many; for I was very curious in this respect. I had, however, no bad intention, because I did not wish any one to offend God on my account."

But an act of tender devotion towards our Blessed Lady exercised by Teresa in her twelfth year proves that her early piety, if weakened by these frivolous studies, was by no means extinguished. It was in that year that our Lord called to Himself the soul of her beloved mother Beatrice d'Ahumada. In the anguish of this first and most cruel bereavement, the orphan girl ran to an image of Mary, and with many tears, but with sincere and childlike confidence, besought the Queen of Angels to be to her not only an advocate, but in very truth a mother, like that beloved one who had just been taken from her. How graciously her prayer was accepted will appear in the sequel of this history. She tells us herself: "It seems to me that, though I did this in my simplicity, it has been of great use to me, inasmuch as whenever I have recommended myself to that sovereign Virgin, I have ever experienced from her the tender love of a mother, and she has finally brought me into her own house."

But Teresa was not yet weary of the vanities which had taken possession of her imagination, and a new temptation assailed her on the death of her mother. The strict decorum of her father's house forbade all familiar intercourse with any but near relations. On the plea of kindred, however, several of her cousins about the same age with herself were freely admitted. The conversation of these young men, who delighted in her beauty and vivacity, kept Teresa in a state of unhealthy excitement, which was still more dangerously worked upon by a kinswoman of light and worldly character, who, by professions of warm and sincere attachment, gained a most dangerous ascendancy over the deep and strong affections of the motherless girl. The very loftiness and purity of Teresa's mind, which suspected not in another the evil of which it had no consciousness in itself, gave this unprincipled young woman the greater advantage over her; and so far did the ill-omened friendship proceed, that she was beguiled into a secret contract of marriage with a stranger, introduced to her by this dangerous companion; so subtle a snare had Satan laid for her who was to be his deadly and victorious enemy.

CHAPTER II.

1530–1537.

SOME suspicion of his daughter's danger was conveyed to the mind of Alonzo de Cepeda, by the anxious care of her elder sister Doña Maria, whose approaching marriage with a nobleman named Don Martin de Guzman furnished a fitting opportunity for

placing Teresa in the safe keeping of some good
religious of the order of S. Augustine, devoted to the
education of young persons of quality.

Some days before she entered the convent, while
the nuns were saying office, a star-like light appeared
in the middle of the choir, and having circled round
the religious, seemed to disappear in the bosom of
Doña Maria Briceño, the mistress of the pensioners.
In after years the nuns recognised the meaning of the
vision, as betokening the brilliant light which was to
be entrusted for a while to the fostering care of Doña
Maria. Teresa's first week in the convent was troubled
by many unquiet memories of the vain excitement of
the last few months at home. The stillness of the
cloister and the calm faces of the nuns were felt at
first as an oppressive burden, but gradually our Lord
opened her heart to the quiet happiness around her;
it felt like balm upon her fevered and agitated spirit;
she began to love the house wherein she dwelt, and
to like conversing with the good religious, though she
felt an extreme repugnance to embrace the religious
state. But our Lord was gently drawing her to Himself. In this holy retirement she learned to understand the perils through which she had passed; and
while she shuddered at the recollection, she felt a
thrill of gratitude to that Divine Champion, who had
rescued her so gently and yet so mightily. She felt
moved to love Him ardently who had so deeply loved
her. "It seems," she says, "as if His Majesty had
gone on considering and reconsidering how He could
bring me back to Himself." She frequently approached
the Sacrament of Penance, communicated with sincere
and fervent devotion, resumed the saying of her rosary
which she had somewhat neglected, and the reading
of spiritual books, used many vocal prayers, and besought the nuns to obtain for her from God the know-

ledge of the state in which He would have her to serve Him.

Yet she shrank from the thought that the answer to their prayers might be a vocation to religion, so dark and cheerless did the life of a nun still seem to her. But the Lord had laid His hand on her, and He used the gentle persuasions and wise counsels of her mistress to dispel the clouds which darkened her mind.

" As I now began," says she, " to take delight in the good and holy conversation of this nun, I was pleased in hearing her speak so well on God, for she was a very pious and discreet person. As far as I remember, I was always pleased to hear her speak (on heavenly things). One day she began to tell me how she came to be a religious, which was by merely reading these words of the Gospel : ' Many are called, but few are chosen.' She spoke to me on the rewards our Lord will give those who leave all things to follow Him. Her good company soon began to banish all the habits evil company had led me into, and to bring back to my mind the desire of eternal things ; and also, in some degree, to divest me of that aversion I had to become a nun, which once was so very great. But now, if I saw any one shed tears at her prayers, or perceived that she possessed other virtues, I envied her extremely, though, in this respect, my heart was so very bad, that were I even to read the whole history of our Saviour's passion, I could not shed a tear : this gave me a great deal of pain."

Before she had been a year and a half in the convent, Teresa had made up her mind to be a nun, but not in that house. In the year 1533, she was attacked by a serious illness, which obliged her to return to her father's house. She partially recovered, and Don Alonzo next sent her to visit her sister, Doña

Maria, by whom she was tenderly loved. On her
way thither she visited her uncle, Peter Sanchez de
Cepeda, a widower, who spent great part of his solitary life in prayer, and who, by his pious conversation, helped to confirm his niece in her holy resolution. Thence she went to the house of her sister, by
whom, as well as by her husband, she was most
cordially welcomed. On her return home, Teresa
endured a terrible struggle of mind between her new
convictions that God was calling her to religion, and
the obstacles which arose to bar her way, especially
the pain which she must give her father should she
carry these convictions into effect.

She thus describes this conflict. " I was three
months debating with myself, and urging myself by
reasons like these : ' The labours and sufferings of
religion cannot be worse than the pains of Purgatory,
but I have well deserved Hell ; it will be no great
thing then for me to pass this short life in Purgatory,
with the hope of passing from it direct to Heaven.' I
think I was moved to choose the religious state
rather by a certain kind of servile fear than by love.
The devil then represented to me that, having
been so delicately nurtured in ease and luxury, I
should never be able to bear the austerities of
religion ; but I warded off this assault of the enemy
by the consideration of the sufferings of Christ, and
said to myself that it was no great thing to endure
somewhat for His love which He would not fail to
give me strength to bear ; great was the conflict
which I endured in those few days. It brought on an
attack of fever, with frequent fainting fits, for I had
always been weak in health. I was consoled by
reading good books, for which I had a great affection. I read the Epistles of S. Jerome with singular
pleasure, and derived such courage therefrom that I

determined to tell my design to my father, which was
as much as to put on the habit, so punctilious was I
as to keeping my word, that when I had once said a
thing, no power on earth would make me unsay it.
But he loved me so much that it was impossible to
obtain his consent; and the entreaties of several other
persons, who at my desire spoke to him on my behalf,
were equally unavailing. The utmost that could be
obtained was that after his death I should do as I
liked. I was afraid of myself and my own weakness,
lest it should make me swerve from my purpose, so
that I determined not to wait for so long a time, but
to find out some other way of accomplishing my
desire."

Teresa chose the Carmelite Convent of the Incarnation, just outside the walls of Avila, for the place of
her rest. Her attention seems to have been drawn to
this house by the fact of her intimate friend, Jane
Suarez, being already there; from her report, as well
as from the general estimation in which the convent
was held, she judged that there she should be able to
serve God with the perfection to which she aspired.
A prophecy had preceded her thither as well as to her
former convent. An unknown man came seeking
treasure throughout the vast plain which surrounds
the city of Avila, and when he came to the convent
walls, he said to those who stood round him, "A
Saint shall come to dwell in this house whose name
shall be Teresa." When told of the prediction, she
said playfully to another nun of the same name:
"Which of us two shall be the Saint?" Little did
the humble novice dream when she asked the question, that the Church of God should one day ring
with the answer.

The time was now come for Teresa to put her
purpose into execution. She had made known her

intention to her friend Jane Suarez, who prepared the
nuns to receive her; and then, under the protection
of her brother Antony, who, by her advice, was himself on the point of consecrating himself to God in
the order of S. Dominic, she left her father's house
very early in the morning, a few days before the feast
of All Saints, in the twenty-second year of her age,
and took refuge in the Convent of the Incarnation.

What she suffered in the separation from her
beloved father, and the rest of her kindred, she tells
us in her own forcible words. "I remember well,
and can affirm with truth, that when I left my
father's house I felt such sorrow, that I do not think
that the pains of death can be greater. It seemed as
if my very bones were disjointed by the anguish
I endured." But the love of God within her heart
was stronger than death or Hell, and no sooner was
she within the sacred enclosure than the storm passed
away, having served but to make the sunshine of her
first days in religion brighter. Her father's anger,
too, was appeased as soon as he was convinced that
her vocation came from God, and he gave his free
consent to her receiving the holy habit on the Feast
of All Souls, 1536, the very year in which Henry VIII.
of England began his impious work of destruction,
wherein many Carmelite houses perished in the
universal wreck of religious foundations in England.

No sooner had Teresa assumed the habit of her
Heavenly Mother than all her difficulties and repugnance to the religious life seemed to vanish. The
austerity and stillness of the cloister, from which she
had shrunk at a distance, were now sweet and
welcome. The fervent novice made use of this time
of freedom and joy of spirit to correspond most
diligently with the graces bestowed upon her. She
made great progress, and so deeply was her heart

moved by meditation upon the perils of the world, and the exceeding love which had delivered her from them, that she obtained in that early period of her religious life a large measure of the gift of tears.

She was most exact in all the duties of regular observance, and especially in the ceremonies of the choir, and she practised all the austerities permitted by obedience and the still delicate state of her health. But beyond all her other virtues, a prompt and tender charity towards her neighbour was conspicuous. No office was either too great or too little for her to render joyfully to her sisters. Whether it were to fold up their choir cloaks, to light them to their cells, or to perform for the sick—offices from which even the older and more experienced religious shrank—the young novice was ever first. We read that the lifelong sufferings which she endured from illness were a reward, asked and granted, for the heroic charity of her noviciate.

One of the nuns had suffered for many years under a sickness so dreadful that it was hard to find any one charitable enough to remain with her. Teresa entreated to be allowed to nurse her, and watched over her as long as she lived with the love of a daughter.

Our Lord rewarded this exercise of charity by the infusion of a larger measure of the same grace; from admiring the patience of the sufferer she came to feel a holy envy of her sufferings, and a generous desire to have always something to suffer for God; and rising from desires to prayers, she besought Him to give her either the very sickness of this patient sister, or whatever other sufferings He should see fittest to send her.

The Lord granted the prayer which He Himself had inspired, and from that day forward Teresa was visited by various and acute bodily maladies, added to overwhelming spiritual desolation, which now took the place of the bright springtide of her early days in the convent. To all this was soon added a very trying kind of petty persecution on the part of some of the sisters. Ignorant of the supernatural source of the tears which she shed so abundantly, they accused her of melancholy and discontent; others took umbrage at her ready courtesy and eagerness to help her sisters in their labours, which they set down to officiousness or eccentricity.

This was a new trial to Teresa, who had been the darling and admiration of the loving hearts at home, and of the simple Augustinians, among whom she had dwelt so happily. It was a *hard* trial too to her, for her heart seems to have been peculiarly open to kindness, and, as a necessary consequence, alive to coldness and contempt. At first it was all she could do to bear these false accusations silently; but here again God gave grace for grace, and she soon learned to rejoice in them as another means of bringing her nearer to Him. She went on with a light heart in her course of devotion and charity; but the devil had sharper weapons in store wherewith to shake her constancy. As the time of her profession drew near, he took advantage of a season of interior desolation, to suggest to her that she had made a great mistake in choosing the religious life, which, if persevered in, would be fatal to both body and soul.

He represented to her that her continued attacks of sickness were a token from the hand of God that she was not in the position for which He intended her. It had never been so when she was at home, and he brought before her the brightness and energy of spirit for which she had been remarkable in times gone by, and compared it with the oppressive feeling

of languor and depression which she now carried with
her through all her convent life. Clearly she was out
of her place, and our Lord was denying her the
strength to bear a burden which she had laid un-
bidden upon her shoulders. And then she thought of
the holiness of many a happy mother in the world, of
her own, so fondly and reverently remembered, and of
her sister, so much better in her peaceful and
honoured home than she with her high aspirations
and sad shortcomings. Many nuns lost their souls
after all, and who so likely to do so as she? And so
all this suffering would be thrown away. But here
the tempter overreached himself. If Teresa's weakness had lent him arms against her, her love of
suffering had raised a shield in her defence. Better
were it, said the heroic heart within, to suffer with
and for her Lord, even in darkness and uncertainty as
to the issue, than to choose the bright things of this
world, in which He had dwelt as a sufferer and a way-
farer. To be despised and neglected was to be near
to Him; nor could she feel that she had come un-
bidden into His company, when she remembered how
He had drawn her against her will into a state of life
to which she had felt the greatest natural repugnance.

The enemy, baffled of his aim, left her soul at last
in peace, and Teresa made her solemn profession on
November 3, 1537, with such overflowing joy and
consolation as never left her memory all the days of
her life. "I know not how to contain myself," she
writes in her life, addressing herself to our Lord,
"when I remember the day of my profession, the
freeness of heart with which I made it, the consolation which I felt, and the espousals which your
Majesty then contracted with me."

CHAPTER III.

1537–1557.

For nearly twenty years after her religious profession, Teresa's desire of suffering was fulfilled by an almost uninterrupted course of sickness and pain. She became so ill immediately after she made her vows that, at her father's earnest desire, she was allowed to leave the convent, with her chosen friend Jane Suarez, to be placed under the care of a woman who was supposed to have great skill in the treatment of difficult cases. The custom of the time (abolished a few years afterwards by the Council of Trent) permitted nuns to leave their cloister upon occasions like this. Teresa at this time visited her sister, and the pious uncle whose conversation had before been of so much use to her. During this second visit he lent her a book by F. Francis Ossuna, a Franciscan, from which she derived great spiritual profit. She began to give herself to the exercise of the Presence of God, following the rules laid down in this book. It was at this time that our Lord first began to give her short glimpses of the supernatural states of prayer, which afterwards became habitual to her, and of which she discourses so admirably in the writings which have become a text-book with mystical theologians.*

The remedies used by the old woman had no other effect but to aggravate the sufferings of the patient, who was at last reduced to such a state of exhaustion that Don Alonzo, fearing to trust her any longer in

* *See* Note A, at the end of volume.

c

such hands, removed her with her companion to his
house, and called in the aid of several skilful physicians, by whom her case was pronounced to be
hopeless.

This was about the middle of the month of August,
1539. As the Feast of the Assumption was approaching, Teresa earnestly begged that a confessor might be
sent for, both to dispose her for a due celebration of
that great festival of her Blessed Mother, and to
prepare her for death. But her father, wise and
prudent man, and fervent Catholic though he was,
overcome by his fond affection for his child, refused
to send for the priest for fear of agitating and
fatiguing her. He soon, however, repented of his
over-caution, for on the very night of the feast Teresa
was seized by a mortal paroxysm which lasted for
four days. The unhappy father could not forgive
himself for having refused the entreaty of his dying
child, who was now incapable of receiving any sacrament but extreme unction. She was, indeed, supposed to be dead, and her grave was actually prepared
in the Convent of the Incarnation, and stood open for
a day and a half. Her funeral oration was even
pronounced in the church of the Carmelite Fathers,
and some nuns from the Incarnation came, according
to the custom of the time, to fetch home the body
of their sister. They would certainly have buried
her alive had not Don Alonzo interfered; he knew
by feeling her pulse that life had not yet departed,
and said authoritatively, " My daughter shall not be
buried yet."

She had nearly, however, been brought to her
grave by another accident. Laurence de Cepeda, her
brother, of whom we shall hereafter have to make
honourable mention, was left to watch by her one
night. He fell asleep ; and the flame of the candle

catching the bed-curtains, produced such a suffocating smoke as awoke him just in time to extinguish the fire before it reached his sister, who would else have been stifled or burnt without waking from her death-like trance.

At the end of the fourth day Teresa came to herself, and like one awaking from a deep sleep, looked at her weeping father and brother, and said, "Why did you call me? I was in Heaven, and I have also seen Hell. My father and Jane Suarez will be saved. I have seen the monasteries which I am to found. Many souls will be saved through my means. I shall die a Saint, and my body will be wrapped in a covering of brocade."

Those who were present gazed at her in amazement, as on one returned from the dead to reveal the secrets of the world beyond the grave, and the eternal doom of those yet dwelling upon earth. Joy and wonder for a while kept them silent, but when they found words to speak, they repeated to the Saint, now fully restored to the use of her senses, what she had spoken in her ecstacy. A faint colour overspread her cheek at the thought of what had escaped her, and she tried to make light of it, as the wandering of delirium; but she afterwards acknowledged to her confessor, and to some of the most trusted of her daughters, the reality of the vision, the truth of which, in its principal details, was proved by after events.

But though restored to life, Teresa had three years more of severe suffering before her. She had patiently endured all the remedies pressed upon her, but now even her father was compelled unwillingly to acknowledge that human skill was unavailing for her relief, and he yielded to her earnest entreaty to be allowed to return to her convent. The religious who had come to carry home her corpse took her back more dead than alive; and for three more years she suffered under a complication of maladies, which made her a spectacle of compassion and admiration to all the community, so excruciating were her sufferings, and so wonderful was the patience with which they were endured.

What human remedies could not effect was given to the intercession of S. Teresa's chosen Patron, the glorious S. Joseph; and the health and vigour thus regained were devoted, next to the service of God and our Blessed Lady, to the promotion of the honour of the Foster Father of Jesus.

Doubtless this devotion has lain deep in many a faithful heart from the first dawn of Christianity; for who could meditate upon the house of Nazareth, or worship the Babe of Bethlehem, without a gush of filial love towards him who shared the watching of Mary and guided the first steps of Jesus? But as an object of public and popular devotion, S. Joseph was little known until S. Teresa testified to the prevailing might of his intercession, and pointed him out as the ready helper in the homeliest necessities of human life, as well as the guide and companion of the sublimest flights of contemplation, the especial Saint and Patron both of the common and the hidden life.

Teresa had desired to be restored to health, chiefly that she might have greater facilities for prayer and recollection than she could enjoy amidst the distractions of the infirmary; and yet, strange to say, no sooner was she free to give herself to solitude and recollection, than she relaxed in her practices of devotion. The frequent intercourse with seculars is the cause to which she herself attributes this decay of fervour. An undue licence in this respect prevailed at that time in the convent. The elder nuns were little restricted in their visits to the parlour, and Teresa, from the high opinion entertained of her wisdom and prudence, was allowed to indulge in the same freedom. It was thought that the visitors could do her no harm, and might derive great good to their own souls from conversations, which were at first chiefly upon spiritual subjects, and which, though they slid insensibly into a lighter tone, never degenerated into levity or detraction. There was a charm in Teresa's conversation which attracted those who had known and loved her in the world ; and even strangers who knew her only by report came to pay her long and frequent visits ; and her own openness of heart, and free and gentle courtesy, made her loth to place any restraint upon what was after all permitted by the custom of the house, and sanctioned by superiors and directors.

But capacious as was the heart of Teresa, it was not large enough to hold creatures and the Creator, and when she turned to her Lord in prayer, she found that there was a veil between her soul and Him. Instead of removing the occasion of this estrangement, she withdrew in false humility from the Divine Presence, and discontinued the practice of mental prayer as something too high for her present state.

" This," says the Saint, " was a most subtle snare of the devil, who persuaded me that it was not for such as I was to approach so near to God, and that I had better go the common road, and content myself with saying vocal prayers, and reciting the Divine office. The effect of this false humility was most pernicious, for, as long as I used mental prayer, if I offended God one day, I came to see that I had done so, and accused myself of it before Him on the next."

And yet the picture drawn by the Saint of herself in those days of tepidity, over which she afterwards mourned so bitterly, might put many a Christian soul, whether religious or secular, to shame. She was most regular and prompt in observing the minutest point of rule, humble and gentle towards all with whom she conversed, and an enemy to every form of detraction; she was so ready to do acts of kindness to her sisters as to be greatly beloved in the community. Although she had herself laid aside the exercise of mental prayer, she was most anxious to promote the practice in others, as if she desired to provide other worshippers in her stead; and many a soul derived much benefit from her advice and instructions, even in this period of comparative distance from God.

She received a visit at this time from her pious father, who had been her disciple in the exercise of contemplation. He came to ask her to solve some difficulties which had occurred to his mind on the subject. With her wonted frankness, Teresa acknowledged that she no longer practised what he had found so profitable to his soul, adding (what was doubtless true) that in the state of her health she found the exercises of the choir a sufficiently heavy burden. Don Alonzo does not seem to have questioned the sufficiency of her reasons. He was deeply grieved to find that she was still suffering so much, but after remaining a very short time in the parlour, he left her with words which, from the lips of so loving a father, could not fail to sink into her heart : "to talk longer together," said he, "would be a loss of time." He had touched unconsciously the real cause of her neglect of prayer.

She received a still plainer lesson to the same effect from her Heavenly Father. As she was talking idly one day with an acquaintance at the convent-grate, she had a vision of our Lord bound to the pillar and covered with wounds. He looked at her with a sad and reproachful countenance, which pierced her to the heart ; she would fain have broken off at once the intimacy which she felt to be displeasing to Him, but she wanted resolution, and was persuaded by the enemy of souls to attribute this vision, which she mentioned to no one, to his own agency. It was, however, so deeply imprinted on her mind, that twenty years afterwards, on the foundation of her first monastery at Avila, she caused an exact representation of it to be made, a copy of which was afterwards placed in the Convent of the Incarnation, on the exact spot where our Lord appeared to her, as a warning both to nuns and seculars, of the reserve and moderation in speech to be used by and with the spouses of Christ.

Our Lord failed not to add internal remorse of conscience to the supernatural warning which was thus suffered to pass unheeded, in order to awake His servant from her lethargy, and arouse her to begin at once that high and generous course of perfect detachment from creatures, to which it was His divine purpose to bring her in the end. She would often return to her cell after a prolonged conversation with seculars at the grate, and pour forth bitter tears over her weakness and irresolution. The death of her pious father was the means of finally dispelling the illusion which had enthralled her so long. Don Alonzo de Cepeda died the death of the just. His daughter, who in spite of her feeble health, hastened to his bedside and tended him with dutiful affection, has left us an account of his last moments.

"This was indeed a death for which to give thanks to God. I cannot express his willingness to die, or repeat the wise counsels he gave us. After receiving extreme unction, how he charged us to recommend him to God, and to implore pardon for him, never to slacken in the service of God, and to remember that *all things will have an end.* He told us with tears how it grieved him now that he had not served our Lord better; and how he wished that he had entered some strict religious order. I believe, assuredly, that God had revealed the day of his death to him a fortnight before it took place; for, before that time, he never seemed to think himself ill, but afterwards, although his physicians assured him that he was getting better, he paid no heed to them, and attended to nothing but the affairs of his soul. His principal ailment was a most acute pain in the shoulders. I said to him one day that, as he had always been so devout to the mystery of our Lord bearing His Cross, His Majesty had been pleased to give him some small portion of the pain which He had suffered therein, and this consideration so affected him that he was never afterwards heard to utter a complaint. He was three days delirious, and then the Lord restored his senses to him, so that we all marvelled, and as he was reciting the creed he expired. His face was beautiful after death as that of an angel, and it seemed to me that such also was his soul and its dispositions. I know not why I have written this, except it be to condemn my own perverseness, that, having seen such a death and known such a life, I have never learned to grow better by the example of such a father. His confessor (F. Baron), a very learned man of the order of S. Dominic, who had directed him for many years, and knew the purity of his conscience, felt assured that he went straight to Heaven."

The consideration of the holiness attained by her father in his secular state, with its lower graces and lighter obligations, incited Teresa to attempt in good earnest to follow his example. She made her confession to his director, who discovered and exposed to her the snare of false humility in which she had been entangled, and which had caused her to lay aside mental prayer. "The soul," said he, "which neglects prayer in the midst of the darkness of this life, is like a man, who, travelling by night on the edge of a precipice, should put out his lantern or depart from his guide. When our Lord bade us to pray always and not to faint, He laid down the importance of prayer for all states and conditions of men." Teresa, in obedience to the counsels of this experienced director, at once resumed the exercise of mental prayer, and persevered in it with unflagging patience and courage, through every vicissitude of painful aridity and overflowing consolation, until the day of her death.

She was now about thirty, and for the next twelve years her life is described by one of her confessors as a long struggle with temptations, arising partly from the consequences of the exterior conversations in which she had for a time indulged, but still more from a fiery trial by which the Lord was pleased to purify her soul. She had turned away at last from creatures, and now it seemed that the Creator was turning Himself away from her. Many and many a time, as she tells us herself, had she to drag herself to the oratory, feeling that no torture or martyrdom would be so hard to her as prayer. She would gaze wearily at the hour-glass, and long for the appointed time to be over. But she faltered not, she remained motionless as a statue in her Lord's presence, waiting till He should breathe the breath of life into her soul. She knew, as she says herself, that He alone could give her this life, that she could do nothing of herself to obtain it, and that He who alone could give it had every reason in the world to withhold it from her, seeing that He had so often drawn her to Himself, and she had so often resisted His attractions. This desolation of spirit, although the consequence of her unfaithfulness to grace, became also its remedy, and laid the foundation in that heroic soul of a perfection in patience, resignation, poverty of spirit, and detachment from all consolation, whether human or Divine, which has made her the teacher and the model of all who since her day have trodden the steep way of the perfect life. To throw her more absolutely upon His own all-sufficient guidance, the Holy Spirit seems to have withheld from her confessors the light needful for directing such a soul, so that they became the instruments of some of her severest sufferings. And all this mental anguish was endured by a frame weakened by illness, and worn by continual pain; for although, by the intercession of her glorious Patron S. Joseph, she had been so far restored to health as to be able to rise from her bed and follow the ordinary exercises of the community, she remained subject till the very end of her life to many distressing ailments, amongst the rest to an habitual sickness every morning, which prevented her taking food until late in the day.

In the face of all these obstacles, Teresa steadily pursued her upward way, taking the most scrupulous care never to offend the God whose face was still hidden from her, and observing with the greatest exactness every most minute point of the rule. She tells us herself that she was never weary of speaking of God, or of hearing others speak of Him; and she eagerly seized every opportunity of hearing His holy word even from the lips of preachers from whom others thought that they could gain no benefit. He rewarded her fidelity by fresh infusions of grace, by the light of which she grew daily in self-knowledge and humility; recollection became more easy to her, solitude more delightful, and her desires after Divine things more eager and efficacious, till she attained at last to that perfect conversion of which we have now to speak.

CHAPTER IV.

1557.

IT was in the year 1557, and in the forty-third year of her age, that our Lord was pleased to reward the patient fidelity of Teresa under this long trial of bodily suffering and spiritual desolation, by raising her to that state of supernatural prayer and close union with Himself, in which she persevered, in ever increasing perfection, until death.

It happened one day, as she entered the convent chapel, that her eyes fell upon a picture which had been lent for the celebration of some approaching festival. It represented our Divine Lord as He was presented by Pilate to the enraged populace, wearing the crown of thorns and the purple robe. An intense feeling of sorrow and compunction thrilled through Teresa's heart at that woeful spectacle. "My heart," she writes herself, "seemed breaking at the sight of these wounds, and at the thought of how evil a return I had made for so much love. Casting myself at the feet of our Lord, I besought Him with an abundance of tears to give me grace never more to offend Him." She turned to S. Mary Magdalen, to whom she had a special devotion, and whose conversion had long been a frequent subject of meditation with her, particularly before holy Communion : " O blessed penitent,"

she cried, " your sins were light in comparison with
mine. You were a sinner in the city amongst sinners;
I have been a sinner in the convent amongst Saints.
You offended Him Whom you knew not ; I have
offended the God Who has heaped favours upon me.
You were called but once, and you instantly obeyed
the call ; I, heedless both of favours and chastise-
ments, have daily and with increasing stubbornness
resisted repeated invitations. I cry to you for help.
Oh ! be you my protectress." Then turning in utter
self-distrust, and strong confidence in Him, to her
Divine Spouse, she said : " Lord, I will never leave
Thee till Thou hast granted me the favour I implore."

From that day, she tells us, her soul began to
amend.

Her courage and compunction were increased by a
remarkable providential circumstance which shortly
afterwards occurred. The Confessions of S. Augustine,
which she had never before seen, were given to her
to read, without her having asked for or thought of
them. As she read, her heart seemed changed within
her, while the very conflict she was experiencing in
herself was presented before her, as in a mirror, in
the example of the Saint whose intercession she now
began most earnestly to implore. At last she came
to the passage in which he relates his conversion at
the sound of the voice which called him while he was
sitting under a tree. The same words seemed now to
echo within the heart of Teresa : " *Take and read,
take and read.*" She melted into tears, and began to
repeat over and over again those touching words of
Augustine, " *How long, O Lord, how long ? To-morrow,
O Lord ? Why not to-day ? Why should not to-day put
an end to my baseness ?* " Such was the internal conflict and agony which she endured at this time, that
on looking back upon it in after-years, she wondered

how she had ever survived it. But the death-struggle issued in a new and victorious life. From that moment, fresh fervour and a more intense desire of perfection were impressed on her soul. She grew in love of retirement and of the holy presence of God, spending long hours in prayer, and scrupulously avoiding the slightest offence against Him. In the same measure as she increased in the knowledge and love of God did she descend deeper and deeper into the sense and detestation of her own sinfulness and misery. She believed that she was unworthy even to tread the earth, and that all creatures ought to arm themselves against her, to avenge their insulted Creator. No penance seemed adequate to expiate her offences; she could only offer herself to her offended God, and ask Him to inflict upon her such vengeance as she deserved.

Teresa, be it observed, according to the testimony of the directors of her conscience, had never committed a mortal sin. The intensity of this anguish and remorse was excited simply by an aroused consciousness of the guilt and ingratitude of her want of correspondence with grace. Neither was it an exaggerated view of the case. The Spirit of Truth, from whom such convictions of sin proceed, shows the awakened soul nothing more than the truth; a truth which seems exaggerated to us, only because it is mercifully veiled from eyes not sufficiently pure and single to behold it without despair.

From this crisis in her spiritual life, Teresa arose another being from her former self. She seemed to herself to dwell in another world, and to live a new life, with a new understanding and a new will. The love of God, wherewith she was now inflamed, was something unprecedented and extraordinary. " From this time," she writes in the history of her life, " I opened a new book, *i. e.* I began a new life. That which I had lived hitherto was my own ; but that which I have lived since, I may say, has been God's ; for, as it seems to me, God has lived in me. It would have been impossible for me to deliver myself in so short a time from so many evil works and sinful habits. May our Lord be praised, Who has delivered me from myself ! For as I began to remove the occasions of sin, and to give myself more earnestly to prayer, our Lord began to bestow more graces upon me as He saw me more willing to receive them. His Majesty now began to give me almost always the prayer of quiet, and sometimes that of union, which would continue for a considerable space of time together."

The sweetness of these Divine consolations was attended, however, by a new form of suffering, a horrible dread lest she should be under a diabolical delusion. Several causes concurred to suggest this fear to her mind. First, her humility, which led her to account herself a most unlikely subject for super-natural favours. Secondly, the mode of these celestial communications, during which the operations of the understanding remained suspended, the soul being wholly absorbed in the contemplation of heavenly things. This she feared might be an artifice of the devil, seeking to turn her away from her habitual meditation on the Passion of our Lord. Her fears were aggravated by the fact that several poor miserable women had been lately thus deluded, amongst others a certain *Magdalen of the Cross*, whose case had inspired her with great terror.

As long as she continued in prayer she was free from these perplexing thoughts, but no sooner was she engaged in exterior occupations of any kind than they returned to overwhelm her. She looked round

in vain for some one well versed in the spiritual life,
to whom she might unburden her trouble. The
Fathers of the Society of Jesus had lately founded a
house at Avila, but she would have accounted it to be
a singular boldness and indiscretion in a weak and
sinful woman like herself, to seek counsel or guidance
from men so learned and so saintly as they were held
to be. She set herself first then to the task of cor-
recting her slightest faults, aiming at an exceeding
purity of conscience, removing the least remaining
attachment to earthly things, and bringing into a
severe captivity the most innocent impulses of her
heart. And so with a courageous humility she held
on her unaided course. " If this spirit be of God,"
said she to herself, " it is clear that it can bring me
nothing but good ; if it be from the devil, so long as
I can please our Lord and keep clear from offending
Him, it can bring me little harm, or rather the evil
one will have the worst of it."

Still, as the Divine favours continued to increase in
measure and in frequency, Teresa's anxiety returned,
and she determined to seek a director. With this
view she consulted a kinsman of her own then living
at Avila, a pious layman named Don Francis Salcedo,
whom she was accustomed to call " the holy knight,"
and who, although married, led such a life in the
secular state as to prove that perfection is not confined
to the cloister.

" This gentleman," says S. Teresa, " was married,
but his life was so exemplary and virtuous, and so
charitable was he and given to prayer, that all men
admired his goodness and perfection ; and with reason,
because many souls obtained great good through his
means. He had an excellent understanding, and was
mild and kind to every one ; his conversation was never
wearisome, but so sweet and agreeable, as well as just

and holy, as to delight all who spoke with him; he
directed all things for the greater good of those souls
with whom he conversed; and, indeed, he seemed to
have no other aim or desire but to do good and give
pleasure to every one by all the means in his power.
Now I do believe that this holy and blessed man, by
his care and attention, was chiefly instrumental in the
salvation of my soul. I am astonished at his humility
in wishing to see me, for I think he had spent little
less than forty years in the practice of mental prayer,
and he led a life of the highest perfection possible in
his state of life. His wife was also a great servant of
God, and so charitable that she was a help rather than
a hindrance to him. Indeed, it seemed that God had
chosen her for his wife as one whom he knew to be a
fit companion for so great an example of fidelity in
His service. Some of his kindred were married to
relations of mine."

Don Francis recommended Teresa to consult a
priest of great reputation for sanctity and learning,
named Gaspar Daza, who, although he declined to
undertake the office of her confessor, gave her such
advice and instructions as he deemed suited to her
case. The event proved, however, that whatever may
have been the amount of Gaspar Daza's spiritual discernment, it was not equal to the direction of such a
soul as Teresa's. He was for making her a saint in a
moment, and freeing her at once from all the imperfections which, in the transparent simplicity of her character, she unfolded to him. The remedies he proposed
to her were hard, and indeed, impracticable. "I soon
found," she says, "that the mode of cure which he
pointed out to me was not suited to my malady."
Such a method of treatment was indeed calculated to
do such a soul more harm than good, as it seemed
only to discourage her. "Indeed," she continues, "if

I had never been able to consult any other director, I
think I should never have gained any benefit to my
soul, because the grief which I felt at finding that I
did not, and could not, do as he enjoined me, was
enough to cause me to lose all hope, and give up
everything as useless."

Her good friend, Salcedo, did what he could to
comfort and encourage her under the rigorism of her
director, and his visits were at this time her only
earthly consolation—a consolation, however, which she
was not long to enjoy. Our Lord would have His
faithful servant to find comfort in Himself alone.   As
Don Francis came to know more of the extraordinary
favours vouchsafed to her, and heard at the same time
of the many imperfections of which, in her humility,
she believed herself guilty, and which, with her accustomed candour, she fully detailed to him, the good
knight took alarm, and came to the same conclusion
with Gaspar Daza, that such graces and such imperfections could scarcely coexist together, and therefore
that the supposed illuminations must be delusions of
the enemy of souls.

Being, however, sincerely desirous of giving assistance and consolation to her troubled spirit, he suggested to her to put in writing a succinct account of
the extraordinary graces which she received in prayer,
as well as of her mode of making it, that he might
show it to Master Daza, and that thus they might be
able to weigh the subject more maturely and at leisure.

This was a fresh trouble to Teresa, who being
wholly unversed in the language of mystical theology,
had no words to express the wonders wrought within
her.   Divine Providence, however, threw at this time
in her way a book called the *Ascent to Mount Sion,*
written by a Franciscan lay-brother, in which she
found described the very method of prayer which she

was accustomed to exercise, especially that *suspension of the understanding* which had given such umbrage to her advisers. Greatly relieved to have found such a full description of what she had herself been unable adequately to express, Teresa underlined the passages which bore upon her case, wrote as clear a statement as she could of her faults, together with a short narrative of her life, and sent the paper and the book to Salcedo, begging him to lay them before Master Daza, and to give her the result of their united judgment.

She awaited their decision with no little anxiety, earnestly beseeching the Lord in the meanwhile to give them light to see the truth. Having conferred long and seriously on this perplexing matter, the two judges came to the decision that all these extraordinary things were wrought by the devil, with intent to delude Teresa herself, and all who should give credit to her words. They gave their decision with all earnestness, and with a sincere desire for her spiritual good; nor did they lack reasons of apparent weight to support it. In the first place, the statement of Teresa herself, which dwelt so fully and emphatically upon her defects, and so coldly and cursorily upon her virtues, would have led any one who had not fathomed the depth of her humility to a very mistaken estimate of her character. Secondly, there was the noted example of the miserable *Magdalen of the Cross* to scare well-regulated pity from all extraordinary ways. And, thirdly, there was a certain holy woman in those days at Avila, by name Maria Diaz, to whose mode and measure of sanctity Teresa's two friends clung with pertinacious and somewhat superstitious admiration. Maria Diaz gave all her substance to feed the poor. Maria Diaz found her only consolation in the presence of the Blessed Sacrament, her *Neighbour*, in her own quaint and sweet words. Maria Diaz lived a most

pure and holy life, in the midst of the dangers of the
world; yet Maria Diaz received no extraordinary
graces, was favoured by no supernatural gifts of
prayer. Was it likely that one so full of imperfections
should be preferred before Maria Diaz? Alas! for the
human prudence even of good and spiritual men, when
it takes to gauging and measuring the gifts of God,
and marshalling the rank and order of His servants
by the narrow rules of its own heraldry! How many
of its decisions will be reversed at the Great Day,
when account will be taken not only of the fruit which
has been visible to the eye of man, but of the patient
toil of the husbandry which produced it; a labour
known only to Him by whose grace the work has been
carried to perfection!

Salcedo brought Teresa the heavy tidings that both
the examiners agreed in the opinion that she was
labouring under a diabolical delusion. They added
one wise suggestion, that she should make a full and
minute statement of her case to some member of the
Society of Jesus, who were held to have deep experience in spiritual matters. She was advised to make a
general confession to one of these Fathers, that by
the grace of the Sacrament of Penance, he might receive greater light and knowledge for her direction.
The anguish of Teresa's mind may be conceived at
hearing the united judgment of two men whom she so
highly respected, but it can scarcely be duly estimated
except by souls endued with love like hers. That she
should have been the sport of a lying spirit, while her
most inward convictions attested that she was following the guidance of the Spirit of Truth, was grievous
and heart-breaking to hear; and yet her humility
forbade her to question their decision.

In this strait, when she could find no help from
man, our Lord Himself came to her assistance. As

she was reciting her office, when she came to this verse of the 118th Psalm, "*Just art Thou, O Lord, and right is Thy judgment,*" she began to consider how it was that the Lord, who is most right and just in His judgments, came to bestow such graces and favours upon her, which He did not vouchsafe to other souls far more faithful to him. Our Lord then, for the first time, was pleased to speak to her by an interior voice : " Serve thou Me," said He, " and seek not to inquire into these things." " These were the first words," continued the Saint, addressing our Lord, " which I ever heard Thee speak to me, and I was greatly astonished thereat." The consolation, however, equalled her amazement, and was increased shortly afterwards by reading the following words in a spiritual book : "*God is faithful, and will never suffer any soul that truly loves Him to be deluded by the devil.*" Teresa felt in her inmost heart that she truly loved God, and had placed her whole trust in Him. How could she fail to be comforted by these words ?

CHAPTER V.

1557.

In order to free herself from the fears and perplexities which returned ever and anon to disturb her peace, Teresa at last overcame her repugnance to ask aid of the sons of S. Ignatius. So great was the reputation of the new order for sanctity, that she not only accounted it a presumption to intrude herself upon such holy men, but dreaded that it should be known to her sisters in religion, fearing lest they should conceive a high idea of her holiness were they to know that she was in communication with the Fathers of the company of Jesus. When therefore her good friend Francis de Salcedo had obtained a Jesuit confessor for her, the Portress and Sacristan were strictly charged to say nothing to any of the religious of his coming. Her precautions were, however, in vain, for it so happened that a single nun was at the door when F. John Pradanos entered it; and, as her biographer drily remarks, "it was enough that one nun knew that Doña Teresa wished to speak to a Jesuit for all the rest of the community to know it immediately."

The strength and consolation which Teresa derived from the counsels of this good Father abundantly compensated for this little vexation. He encouraged her to perseverance, and to grateful correspondence with the Divine favours bestowed upon her, adding with something of a prophetic spirit: "Who knows but that God designs to make use of you for the spiritual good of many?" He bade her give herself more assiduously than ever to penance and mortification, and directed her to meditate daily upon some point of the Passion of Christ, and never in her prayer to lose sight of His Sacred Humanity. He also directed her to resist with all her might the sweetnesses and consolations which she experienced.

Overjoyed at having at last met with a guide who could understand and direct her, Teresa set herself with the whole ardour of her generous soul to carry out his directions to the letter. She felt the same ardent desire which in her childhood had impelled her to seek martyrdom, to shed all her blood for Him who had shed all His for her; and finding no persecutor's sword to immolate her, she made a living victim of her body by the use of the severest macerations. Notwithstanding the extreme delicacy of her health, she wore at this time a rough hair shirt, and disciplined herself with bunches of nettles, and often with heavy iron keys. She strewed her bed with thorns; such indeed was her thirst for suffering that, we are told, she would have torn herself to pieces had God permitted it. There was only one part of the instructions of her confessor which she found it difficult, or rather impossible, to put in practice—his injunction to resist the Divine favours which were showered upon her.

"After this confession," she tells us, "my soul became so tractable, that it seemed to me there was nothing which I was not ready to do; and so I soon began to change in many things, though my director did not press me much, but rather seemed to make little account of everything. This treatment had the more effect upon me, because he guided me by the way of the love of God; leaving me at liberty, and under no constraint but that of love. In the meantime, I continued for almost two months using every means in my power to resist the favours and caresses of God. A change was perceptible in my outward conduct, because our Lord already began to give me courage to do certain things, which those who knew me, and especially the religious of the convent, considered excessive; and they were right, considering what I was before, though I still fell far short of what my habit and profession required of me. By resisting the caresses of our Lord, I learned an excellent lesson from His Majesty; for before this time I always thought that to prepare myself for receiving these favours in prayer, I must shut myself in a corner, as it were, so that I dared hardly stir. Now, however, I perceived that this was of little importance, for the more I endeavoured to resist, the more did our Lord overwhelm me with sweetness and

overshadow me with His glory. I took so much
pains in resisting that it was quite a torture to me;
and yet the more I resisted, the greater favours did
our Lord bestow upon me, and the more clearly did
He manifest Himself to me, during those two months,
in order that I might understand that it was not in
my power to resist Him. And now my love for the
most Sacred Humanity of our Lord began to revive;
and my prayers began to attain solidity, like a building
which rests upon a strong foundation. I also felt
more inclined to do penance, which I had neglected
on account of my infirmities. But this holy confessor
told me that some penances would do me no harm;
that God had perhaps afflicted me so much because I
did not wish to afflict myself. He commanded me
also to perform certain acts of mortification, which
were not at all to my taste, still I performed them
all, knowing that our Lord Himself had commanded
them by His minister; and His Majesty gave him
grace so to direct me that I felt it easy to obey Him.
My soul now began to feel every offence, however
small it might be, which I committed against God;
and this to such a degree, that if I wore anything
superfluous about me, I was unable to recollect myself
until I had cast it off. I prayed much to our Lord
that He would keep His hand upon me, and that
since I conversed with His servants, He would not
permit me to fall back again, for I thought that would
indeed be a great offence, and that they might lose
their good name on my account."

Soon after her interview with F. Pradanos, Teresa
was permitted to lay open the state of her soul to
S. Francis Borgia, who some years before had abandoned the world and resigned the dukedom of Gandia
to enter the Society of Jesus. Her confessor, and
also Don F. Salcedo, wished her to speak to this

father, and give him an account of her manner of prayer, knowing that he was already far advanced in the spiritual life. " When Father Francis," says the Saint, " had heard me, he told me that my prayer came from the Spirit of God, and that it was his opinion I should no longer resist His favours, though till then he thought I had done right in so doing. He recommended me likewise always to begin my prayer by meditating on some part of the Passion, and that if afterwards our Lord should raise my soul to a supernatural state, I should not resist, but suffer His Majesty to carry it away, provided, however, I did not endeavour to procure the rapture. Being far advanced himself in this way, he gave both medicine and advice; for in such matters experience is very important. He told me also that it would be an error to resist any longer. These words consoled me greatly, as well as the gentleman; for he rejoiced exceedingly to hear Father Borgia say that my prayer came from God, so he continued to assist me, and gave me advice to the best of his power, which was very great."

F. Pradanos was shortly afterwards removed by his superiors, to the great affliction of his penitent. " It troubled me much," she says, " for I thought I should become wicked again; and it seemed impossible to find another like him. My soul appeared to be dwelling in a desert; so very sad and fearful was I, I knew not what to do with myself." But our Lord had provided a substitute. A relation of Teresa, whose house was near that of the Jesuits, took her home with her, in order that she might find another confessor belonging to the Society. " She induced me," says the Saint, " to confess to her own director " (F. Balthasar Alvarez), " and I remained for some days in her house, for she lived near me. I

was delighted to be able often to converse with those
fathers, for the mere knowledge of the sanctity of
their conversation was a great advantage to my
soul." Teresa thus describes the gentle and prudent
direction of this holy man. "This father began to
put me in the way of greater perfection, telling me
that I should omit doing nothing by which I might
give the greatest pleasure to God. This he told
me with great prudence and sweetness, for my soul
was not yet strong in anything, but very tender,
especially in giving up certain friendships which I
had then formed; for though I did not thereby offend
God, yet the affection I had for the persons was very
great, and it seemed ungrateful in me to break off
their friendship, and so I told him that since our
Lord was not offended thereby, I did not see why I
should become ungrateful. He replied, that I should
do well to recommend the matter to God for some
days, and to recite the hymn *Veni Creator*, that so
the Holy Ghost might enlighten me to do what was
best. Having then one day prayed for a long time,
and humbly besought our Lord to help me to please
Him in all things, I began to recite the hymn; and
while I was saying it a rapture came on me which
almost carried me out of myself. It was sudden, but
so manifest that I could not doubt it; it was also the
first time our Lord granted me this favour; then I
heard these words: '*I will have thee no longer to
converse with men, but with angels!*' I was much
amazed at this occurrence, for the commotion of my
soul was great; and these words were spoken to me
in the very interior of my heart, so that they made
me afraid, though, on the other hand, they gave me
great consolation, which remained with me after my
fears had left me; and this fear had, in my opinion,
been produced by the strange novelty of the ecstacy.

These words have been strictly accomplished; for never afterwards have I been able to form any friendship, nor to feel any consolation, or particular love for any one, except for those persons who I knew ardently loved God, and strove generously to serve Him. Nor is it now in my power, neither does it matter whether any of these be friends or relations; for if I find that this or that person is not a servant of God, and not given to prayer, it is a heavy cross for me to speak with him. This is the very truth, as far as I can judge. From that day I have remained full of courage and resolution to abandon all things for God, as if He had been pleased in that moment (and it seemed to be no more than a moment) to make His servant become quite another creature.

"Thus there was no longer any necessity to command me in this respect; for when my confessor found me at first so determined, he did not venture expressly to tell me I should do it. He waited till our Lord should be pleased to do it Himself, as He did indeed. And never did I imagine I should succeed; for already I had used some endeavours for this purpose, and so great was the affliction I endured therein, that I resolved to give up the attempt as inexpedient. But now our Lord gave me both liberty and power to put it in execution. This circumstance I told to my confessor, and I gave up everything as he had recommended me. It did him no little good, whom I had consulted, to behold what a resolution I had taken. May God be praised for ever, who gave me in a moment that power and liberty which before I had not been able to procure with all the diligence I had used for many years, for I had so often exerted all my strength, that my health was thereby much injured. But as He has accomplished it, who is all powerful and truly the Lord of all things, I now suffer no pain whatever."

It was at this time that S. Teresa, having broken through so many bonds which attached her to earth, formed a holy and enduring friendship with another penitent of Father Alvarez, Doña Guiomar d'Ulloa. This holy woman was descended from one of the most noble and pious families of Toro. Her parents were Peter d'Ulloa, governor of that city, and Aldonza de Guzman d'Avila.

Her holy mother, who early became a widow, educated her with the greatest care. She was married to Don Francis d'Avila, of the noble house of Sobralejo; but God, who had a higher vocation in store for her, quickly freed her from this tie by the death of her husband. It seems as though such a loss might have revealed to her at once the vanity of all passing things, and have separated her for ever from the world. Such, however, was not the case. Possessing those exterior attractions which the world loves and admires, she delighted to appear in society, where she shone as one of its most brilliant ornaments., It was left for Balthasar Alvarez to draw the veil from her eyes, and to show her the nothingness of all things here below. Under his direction she at once renounced worldly vanities, dress, and society, and gave herself up entirely to the service of our Lord.

Despising from this time all luxury and outward show, she retained only such servants as were absolutely necessary, and led a simple and retired life, consecrating her days chiefly to prayer and good works, and thus merited to obtain from our Lord those higher graces which He bestows on those who, for love of Him, cast away as worthless all the joys and pleasures of this world, and find their happiness in Him alone.

Father Balthasar Alvarez, who now undertook the guidance of S. Teresa, continued to direct her for seven years of the most important and trying period of her life, comprehending the four years preceding the foundation of S. Joseph's at Avila, and the three which immediately followed it. It was during this time that the Saint received the greater part of those marvellous graces which she relates in her life.

Whilst occupied in laying the foundation of the reform of Carmel, the encouragement and sympathy of Father Balthasar were a great support and comfort, in the midst of the storm which in consequence raged around her; nor was this all, he helped her also in the formation of the constitutions which she gave to her religious. Indeed, the Saint said of him, " In this world, Father Balthasar Alvarez is the person to whom my soul owes the most, and who has been the greatest help to me in advancing on the road to perfection."

It pleased our Lord to reveal to her the treasures of grace with which He had enriched the soul of this holy man. One day she saw him at the altar with a crown of glory surrounding his head, a symbol of the burning love with which he was offering up the Sacred Victim. This supernatural knowledge of the Saint led her to write of him in these words : " God gave him a special grace to discern the truth of every matter, and I am convinced that it was from the Blessed Sacrament of the Altar that he imbibed this wonderful light."

Her Divine Master not only showed S. Teresa the holiness of His servant whilst on earth, but also revealed to her the glory he would one day enjoy in heaven, and it was His will that she should make known to the holy man the certainty of his eternal salvation.

One day when Father Balthasar Alvarez was much agitated by a grievous temptation, a doubt as to his final perseverance and the salvation of his soul, S. Teresa, who knew by a supernatural light what was passing within him, threw herself at the feet of our Lord, imploring Him to come to the aid of His servant. Her Divine Master granted even more than she asked, revealing to her, not only the salvation of Father Alvarez, but also the glorious place prepared for him in heaven, making known to her that he was elevated to such a height of perfection, that at that time there was no soul on earth which surpassed his in holiness ; and that the glory which he would one day enjoy in heaven would be in proportion to his high perfection on earth. After this she told Father Balthasar Alvarez that he might be comforted, because the Lord had revealed to her the certainty of his salvation.

And yet the very virtues of Father Alvarez, and the low estimation in which he held his own judgment and discernment, served to increase and prolong the sufferings of his saintly penitent. The storm, which had been laid for awhile by the favourable decision of S. Francis Borgia, soon swelled again in its former fury. Father Alvarez, whether, as she afterwards understood, in order to try her, or because our Lord suffered him, for her greater perfection, to fall into perplexity with regard to the truth of the revelations vouchsafed to her, took counsel with five or six other highly esteemed servants of God. The result of this consultation was a decision that all the extraordinary graces bestowed on Teresa were the work of the devil, and an injunction from her confessor to refrain from frequent communion, to avoid solitude, and to do everything in her power to distract her mind from these supernatural communications.

The report that she was a prey to diabolical delusions spread rapidly from mouth to mouth, with the envenomed addition that such a fearful visitation had doubtless befallen her as a chastisement for secret sins hidden under the fair semblance of a spotless life. A heavy cross to bear for one whose exceeding purity of soul had been conspicuous even in the days of her worldly vanity—a bitter mortification for Castilian pride, if a vestige yet remained to wince under the loathsome touch of such a slander !

If she turned from the hard judgments of men to the God of all consolation, even here she was pursued by the sentence which debarred her from mental prayer, restricted the frequency of her communions, and permitted her only the use of vocal aspirations.

But a bitterer trial than men could impose was now laid upon her by Him for whom she had suffered all that went before. A darkness fell upon her, so deep and desolate that it seemed as if God had forgotten her, and as if she had forgotten that He had ever been on her side. The evil one took advantage of the horror which oppressed her to increase it by many a fearful suggestion, persuading her that she was already forsaken of God, and inflicting upon her tortures that she could only liken to those of the lost in hell. If she tried to persevere in vocal prayer, she hardly understood the words which she recited.

She suffered equally in conversing with her sisters in religion, and more severely still in the solitude of her cell. To these mental sufferings were added at the same time severe bodily pains.

As the only possible relief to her sufferings, she sought to occupy herself, as far as possible, in exterior works of charity, and in frequent and fervent acts of hope in Him who never forsakes those who trust in Him. She faithfully obeyed every command

of her director, submitting not only her judgment to
his, but the very experience of her senses. She
thus became daily more pleasing in the eyes of God,
who, in return for an obedience and humility so excellent, seemed to seek her in the same measure as
she withdrew from Him. If she kept away from
the Oratory to avoid those sweet colloquies with
Him which she was forbidden to enjoy, He met her
in the cloister, or pursued her even to the recreation
room. She thus describes the hushing of the tempest
at His sovereign command, and the restoration of
such a calm to her troubled spirit, that she, who had
been afraid to remain in a room by herself, was
strengthened to defy all the powers of hell :—

"I could have no comfort in any way when I
thought it was possible that the devil had often
spoken to me ; but as I now spent no more time in
solitude and in prayer, our Lord gave me the gift of
recollection, even when I was engaged in conversation, and this without my being able to avoid it ;
and He said to me what He pleased, though it
troubled me to hear Him. Being once all alone,
without having any one near to console me, I could
neither pray nor read, but was like one amazed at my
great tribulation, and I was also terrified by the consideration that perhaps the devil had received power
to deceive me. And being thus harassed and fa-
tigued, not knowing what to do with myself, for
never before (as I thought) had I been in such great
trouble, I remained four or five hours in this state ;
and there seemed to me no comfort for me, either
on earth or in heaven, in the midst of the sufferings
in which our Lord left me, and under the fear also
of a thousand dangers. But, O my Lord ! how true
a friend art Thou, and how powerful ! What Thou
wilt Thou canst effect, and Thou never dost forsake

or cease to love those who love Thee! May all
creatures praise Thee, O Lord of the world! Oh
that I could cry out loud enough to proclaim throughout the universe how faithful Thou art to Thy
friends! All things fail; but Thou, the Lord of
them all, dost never fail. How little is that which
Thou allowest those who love Thee to suffer! O
Lord, how delicately, how wisely, and how sweetly
dost Thou treat such souls! Oh that I had never
loved any but Thee! It seems, O Lord, that sometimes Thou triest severely those who love Thee,
that so, by the excess of their affliction, they may
understand the better the far greater excess of Thy
love. Oh that I had understanding, and learning,
and new words, that I might be able to proclaim
Thy works, as my soul knows them!

"Alas! I have none of these, O Lord; but at least,
if Thou wilt not desert me, I will never forsake Thee.
Let all the learned men in the world rise up against
me; let all creatures persecute me; let the devils
torment me, if only Thou, O Lord! wilt not forsake
me; for I know well by experience how mightily
Thou deliverest all those who put their trust in Thee
alone! When I was in this great trouble (even before
I had begun to have any visions at all), these words
alone were sufficient entirely to free me from all
troubles: 'Fear not, daughter, it is I; I will not
forsake thee; do not fear.'

"It seems to me that, considering what I was then,
a long time would have been necessary to bring peace
to my soul, and that no one would have been able to
comfort me, so great was my anguish; and yet I was
at once consoled by these words alone, and endued
with such strength, courage, confidence, tranquillity,
and light, that I could have maintained fearlessly
against the whole world that these words came from

God. Oh! how good is God! Oh! how good and
powerful is the Lord! He gives not only counsel, but
remedies also. *His words are works.* How admirably
does He strengthen our faith and increase our love!
I often called to mind how our Lord, when a tempest
had risen at sea, commanded the winds and the waves,
and there came a great calm; and I used to say then,
Who is this whom all the powers of my soul obey?
and who in an instant brings such dazzling light out
of such deep darkness, and makes that heart become
soft which seemed before to be hard as a stone? and
who gives the water of sweet tears, where before
there had been so long and great a drought? Who
inspires these desires? and who gives me such
courage? Such were the thoughts which now arose
in my heart. Of what am I afraid? What is this?
I desire to serve this Lord, and I wish for nothing
but to please Him. I renounce all pleasure, and
ease, and every other good, save only the doing of
His will. Of this I am sure, as I can fearlessly
affirm. Since then this Lord is so powerful, as I see
He is, and since all the devils are His slaves (and of
this I can have no doubt, since it is of faith), what
harm can they do me, who am a servant of this Lord
and King? Why may I not have strength enough to
fight with all the powers of hell? Thus I spoke. I
then took a cross in my hands, and it really seemed
to me that God gave me in a moment such courage
that I should not have been afraid to encounter
all the devils in hell; I felt that with that cross I
could easily overcome them all, and thus I challenged
them: "Now come all of you, for, being a servant of
God, I wish to see what you can do to me." It is very
certain I thought they were afraid of me, for I remained so quiet and so fearless of them all, that even
till this day all the fears I entertained are now entirely

removed. And though I have sometimes seen them, yet I never feared them again; rather, it seemed, that they were afraid of me. I have a certain dominion over them, given to me by the Lord of all creatures, so that I make no more account of the devils than so many flies; and they seem to me to be so cowardly that, when they see little notice is taken of them, they have no strength or power whatever. These enemies can only attack those who give themselves up to them, unless it be when God permits them to tempt and torment some of His servants for their greater good. I would that it might please His Majesty to make us fear that only which we ought to fear, and to make us understand that *we receive greater harm from one venial sin than from all the powers of hell combined.*"

CHAPTER VI.

1558.

ALTHOUGH Teresa's own fears and scruples were thus in a great measure laid to rest, she had still great troubles to endure from the doubts and anxieties of her spiritual advisers.

"I continued," she says, "in great affliction and trouble (on account of these doubts and suspicions), and at the same time many prayers were offered for me to the Lord, that He would be pleased to conduct me by another way, since this was thought to be so suspicious. But true it is, that though I earnestly begged this favour from God, yet, considering how evidently my soul was improved by the other way, I could never find it in my power to desire it heartily, though I did desire it in some degree at times when

I was harassed and distressed by what I was told, and by the fears with which my confessors filled me. I saw that I had now become quite another creature, and all I could do was to put myself into the hands of God, beseeching Him that, since He knew what was fit for me, He would be pleased to dispose of me absolutely according to His holy will. I saw clearly that, by this way, my soul was going to Heaven, which formerly was on the way to hell: why, therefore, should I desire to take another path, or believe that the devil had brought me into this? It was not in my power to force myself into such an opinion. Still I did what I could to desire the one and to believe the other; but, as I have said, it was not in my power. I offered for this object a few poor works which I performed, if indeed I have ever done any good at all. I became devout to some of the Saints, that by their means I might be delivered from the devil. I performed novenas, and I recommended myself to S. Hilarion, and S. Michael the Archangel, for this purpose; many other Saints also I importuned, that by their prayers our Lord might show me the right way. At the end of two years, which both myself and others spent in prayers that our Lord might either conduct my soul by some other way, or show me the truth of this, the following circumstance happened to me. Being one day in prayer, on the festival of the glorious S. Peter, I saw standing very near me, or, to speak more properly, I felt and perceived, for I saw nothing at all either with the eyes of my body or my soul, that Christ our Lord was close by me, and that it was He who spoke to me, as I thought. Having been up to this time extremely ignorant as to whether there could be any such vision as this, I fell at first into so great a fear, that I could do nothing but weep; but presently our Lord gave me comfort, by speaking only one word; and I found myself, as I was wont, very quiet, with great delight and without fear. It seemed to me that Christ walked always by my side; but the vision not being *imaginary*, *i. e.*, represented in any form to the imagination, I perceived not in what shape He was, though I found and felt very sensibly that He was always at my side; that He witnessed whatever I did, and that if I were recollected even in a small degree, or rather unless I was very much distracted, I could not help being conscious that He was near me.

"I went immediately to my confessor, though I was much grieved that I was obliged to tell him what had happened. He asked me under what form I saw our Lord? I told him I did not see Him. My confessor then inquired how I knew it was Christ? I answered I knew not how, but that I could not help perceiving that our Lord was close by me, for I knew and felt clearly that so it was; that the recollection of my soul in prayer was far greater and more continual; that the effects also were very different from those others which I formerly experienced. In a word, the thing appeared to me very certain and evident. I made use of several comparisons, whereby to make myself understood, and yet, in my opinion, there is none which properly explains this vision, for as this is one of the highest kind according to what that holy and spiritual man, Father Peter of Alcantara, told me, as well as other great and learned men, so one cannot find words in this world to express it; at least, we who know so little cannot, though learned men may make themselves better understood. But if, as I say, I saw our Lord neither with the eyes of the body nor of the soul, because it was no imaginary vision, I may be asked how I can understand and assert more clearly that He was near me, than if I had actually seen

Him ? I answer that it is as if a person were in the
dark, and saw not another who stood near him, or as
if the person were blind. This is something of a
comparison, though not very exact, for even if a
person were blind, he might know another to be
present by his other senses, because he could hear
him speak or move, or he might touch him. But
here there is nothing at all of this, nor is there any
darkness ; but our Lord's presence is represented
to the soul by a sign clearer than the sun itself,
and yet no sun or brightness is seen, but only a certain light, which, without our seeing it, illuminates
the understanding, that so the soul may enjoy so
great a good. This vision brings also great benefits
with it."

The Saint proceeds to describe the blessed and
salutary effects of thus literally walking with God,
and doing every action under the consciousness that
His Divine eyes were resting upon her, even as they
rested on Peter on the water and on Martha and
Mary in the house of Bethania, thus making another
paradise of the cloisters and the orange gardens of
that Convent of the Incarnation.

" This vision continued for some days together, and
it was so profitable to me that I never omitted prayer ;
and besides, whatever I had to do, I took care that it
should be done in such a manner that it might not
displease Him, whom I evidently saw to be there, as
a witness of all that passed ; and though sometimes I
feared on account of what I was told, still my trouble
did not last long, because our Lord comforted and
encouraged me.

" Being one day in prayer, it pleased Him to show
me His sacred hands, and they were so excessively
beautiful that I am not able to describe them. But
this sight gave me great fear, as indeed every new

sight does in the beginning of any of those supernatural favours which our Lord is pleased to show me.
Within a few days after, I saw His Divine face, the
sight of which ravished me with delight. I could not
conceive why our Lord showed Himself thus to me,
by little and little, since afterwards He resolved to do
me the favour that I should see His whole person, till
I came to reflect that He was pleased to conduct me
according to my natural weakness. May He be blessed
for ever, since such great glory so base and wicked a
creature as myself could not have endured ; and therefore, our merciful Lord, who knew this, disposed things
thus tenderly.

" It may, perhaps, be imagined that there was not
any need of much strength to behold hands and a face
so beautiful. But such is the beauty of glorified
bodies, that the sight of them quite amazes and dis-
tracts the soul ; and thus I was so frightened at first,
that I fell into great trouble and disorder, though
afterwards I gained certainty and security, with other
such effects, that fear quickly vanished away. On the
feast of S. Paul, while I was hearing mass, the most
Sacred Humanity of Christ was fully represented
to me, as it is painted after His resurrection ; but
with such great beauty and majesty that I can
only say that if there were nothing else in Heaven
to delight our eyes but the excessive beauty of
glorified bodies, the bliss would be immense, especially the sight of the Humanity of Jesus Christ
our Lord ; and if His Majesty be so great, even
when it is represented to us in this world, according
to that proportion which our misery can bear, what
will it be when we shall wholly enjoy and possess
such a happiness?

" This vision, though represented to me by the way
of a mental image, was never seen by me with the

eyes of my body, nor was any other, but only with the eyes of my soul. They who understand these things better than I do, affirm that this kind of vision, which is purely intellectual, is of a higher and more perfect kind than those which are seen with the bodily eyes; for these latter, they say, are of the lowest kind, in which the devil can more easily introduce his delusions; though at that time I could not understand any such thing, but rather desired that when I was to receive any favour of this nature I might see it with my corporal eyes, that my confessor might not tell me I only fancied things. ·And so it often happened to me that as soon as it was past (and this was in one instant) I began to think I might perhaps have only fancied the vision, and I was thus somewhat troubled at having told my confessor, thinking whether or no I had deceived him. This was the cause of another trouble, and so I went to him and told him of it. He asked me whether I had really thought that things were as I described them, or if I had a desire to deceive him? I told him truly that I had spoken in all sincerity, because as far as I can judge, I had no wish to tell a lie, nor did I intend to do such a thing, nor would I have done so for the whole world. This he knew very well, and so he did his best to comfort and calm me. But I felt so unwilling to trouble him with these matters, that I know not how the devil could have made me fancy I had feigned anything or deceived my confessor: this he did to torment me." She proceeds to describe, after the best of her power, the exceeding glory of the vision. "It is a sight, the clearness and brightness of which exceeds all that can possibly be imagined in this world. It is not a splendour which dazzles, but a sweet lustre; nor does that light hurt the eyes whereby we see this object of such divine beauty. It is a light so different from that of this world, that even the brightness of the sun itself which we see is dim in comparison with its brightness. It is as if we beheld very clear water running upon crystal, with the sun's rays reflected upon it, and striking through it, in comparison with other very muddy water seen in a cloudy day and running upon an earthy bottom. This is a light which never sets and has no night, but as it is always light, nothing disturbs it. Indeed it is of such a nature that no understanding in this life, however sublime, would be able adequately to conceive it. Still I was continually assured that these things came from the devil, or that I only fancied them, for as there were some very holy persons in that place (compared with whom I was but misery itself) who were not guided by this way, they immediately began to fear that my sins were in all probability the cause of these effects, and so the report went from one to another in such a manner, that many became acquainted with these secrets of mine, though I spoke of them to no one but my confessor, or those to whom he commanded me to mention them. I said to them once, that if they who spoke thus to me should assert that some person with whom I had just been talking, and whom I knew very well, was not that person, but that I only fancied him so to be, I should have more easily believed them than myself. But if that person had left some jewels with me, and they remained still in my hand as pledges of the great love he bore me; and if I now perceived that I was rich, whereas I was very poor before, I should not then be able to believe them, however much I might desire it, especially since I could show these jewels to others, for all who knew me saw clearly that I had become quite another person, and so my confessor also told me, for the

difference was very great in every respect, and plainly
visible. Having been so wicked before, I used to say
I could not believe that the devil did this to deceive
me and send me to hell, which had so greatly served
to root out vices, and to plant in me spiritual strength
and every kind of virtue; for I perceived very clearly
that one of these visions was alone sufficient thus to
enrich me. My confessor was very discreet and
very humble; and yet this humility cost me many
troubles, for though he was a learned man, and a
man of prayer, yet he did not trust in himself, as our
Lord did not lead him along this road. He was much
troubled on my account in many ways. He was
even warned to beware of me, lest the devil might
deceive him, by inducing him to believe what I told
him; and to prove their point, those who spoke thus
adduced the example of other persons. All this gave
me trouble enough, for I was afraid I should have no
one to hear my confessions, but that every one would
fly from me; and so I did nothing but weep. It was
a mercy of God that this Father still continued to hear
me; but he was so great a servant of God that for
His sake he was willing to expose himself to everything; and so he bade me not to offend God—not to
depart from the directions he gave me; he also bade
me not to fear his leaving me. He always comforted
and encouraged me, and commanded me never to
conceal anything from him. And should I observe
this command, he told me that, though the devil were
the cause of these visions, he would not be able to do
me any harm, but rather that our Lord would draw
good out of the evil which he wished to do to my
soul. He thus tried to lead me forward to perfection
in all things to the utmost of his power, and I being
in such fear, obeyed him in everything, though imperfectly. He had a great deal of trouble with me for

more than three years, during which I confessed to
him in the midst of these afflictions and great persecutions which I endured, for our Lord allowed people
to form a bad opinion of me, and these afflictions
came (many of them at least) from no fault of mine,
so that I was always coming to the Father, and he
was blamed on my account, though he was not in any
fault whatever.   I think it would have been impossible for him to have endured all these troubles so
long had he not been a man of great sanctity; but
our Lord encouraged him and enabled him to bear so
much, for he had to answer every one who thought I
was a lost soul, though they believed him not; and,
on the other hand, he had to calm my mind, and to
deliver me out of the fears in which I lived.   He had
also to satisfy me in another respect, for after every
new vision our Lord permitted me to be in great terror.
All this came from my having been and being still so
great a sinner.   Still he comforted me with much
compassion, and had he followed his own opinion, I
should not have suffered so much, for God enabled
him to understand the truth in all things; and it was
I believe from the Sacrament of the Altar that he
derived all his illumination.   Those other servants of
God, who could not be satisfied that I was in a safe
way, often conversed with me; and when I spoke to
them with openness and simplicity, they would often
misunderstand my words.   Now one of these (Don F.
Salcedo) I loved much, for my soul was exceedingly
indebted to him, and he ardently desired my perfection, and prayed to God to enlighten me.   I was
much troubled to see that I could not make myself
understood by him.   And so when I used to speak
thus frankly to these friends, it seemed to them to be
a sign of little humility in me; and when they saw me
commit some fault (and they might have noticed

many) they at once condemned me altogether. Sometimes they asked me some questions, and I answered them with candour and without reserve, then they thought I wished to teach them and that I considered myself very wise, and accordingly they would go to my confessor to complain, because they certainly wished me well, and he reprimanded me. This lasted a long time, amd I was afflicted in many ways; but as I received many favours from our Lord, I was able to endure every trouble."

The Saint proceeds to describe more particularly the visions with which she was favoured, and the prolonged vexations and persecutions which they brought upon her.

"In these visions our Lord almost always represented Himself to me as risen again, and the same in the Sacred Host; except that sometimes, in order to strengthen me when in tribulation, He showed me His wounds as on the cross, or appeared in agony as in the garden; and on some few occasions I saw Him with His crown of thorns, and at other times carrying His cross. By mentioning these things I drew upon myself many affronts and vexations, and great persecutions and fears. People were so certain that I was under the influence of the devil, that some wished me to be exorcised. This, however, gave me very little trouble; but what I felt the most was, to see my confessors afraid of hearing my confessions, or when I came to know that tales were told to them about me. Still, on the whole, I know not how to be sorry for having seen these heavenly visions; nor would I exchange any one of them for all the goods and pleasures of the world, for I always consider these visions to be great favours from our Lord, and I esteem them as most precious treasures, and our Lord Himself has often assured me that such they are. I also observed that thereby I began to love our Lord the more, and to Him I went to complain of all my troubles, and always came forth from prayer both with comfort and with new strength. As to these persons, I did not presume to contradict them, for I saw it would make things worse, as they would have thought it a want of humility; I spoke only to my confessor, and whenever he found me in affliction he always consoled me greatly.

"As my visions began to increase, one of those who used before to assist me, and sometimes hear my confessions when my ordinary confessor was not in the way, began to tell me that I was evidently deluded by the devil. He commanded me (since there was no other means of resisting him) always to be crossing and blessing myself when I saw any vision, and to use some sign of scorn, because it was certainly the devil, and by this means he would come no more, and that I need not fear, but God would preserve me, and deliver me from him. This command was very painful to me, because as I could not help believing my visions came from God, it was a terrible thing for me to use any act of contempt to Him; neither could I desire that these things should be taken away from me: still I did all that was commanded me. I earnestly besought our Lord to free me from being deceived; and this I did continually, and with abundance of tears: I also prayed to S. Peter and S. Paul; for as I had the first vision on their Festival, our Lord told me that they would take care of me that I should not be deceived; and accordingly I have often seen very clearly, though not by the way of any *imaginary* vision, these two glorious Saints on my left hand, as my good Patrons.

"But this command to make signs of contempt gave me excessive trouble, when I saw this vision of our

Lord; for when I saw Him present before me, I could not be induced to believe it was the devil, even though I should have been torn in pieces, and therefore it was a severe kind of penance. But in order that I might not be so perpetually blessing myself, I took a cross in my hands; and this I did almost always. But I did not use the signs of scorn so often, because this would have afflicted me too much, for I remembered the injuries the Jews inflicted on our Lord, and so I besought Him to pardon me, since I acted in obedience to those whom He had appointed in His own stead, and not to blame me, since they were the ministers whom he had placed in His church. He then said to me, *Be not troubled at this, for thou dost well in obeying them, and I will make known the truth.* But when they forbade me the use of mental prayer, our Lord appeared displeased, and told me to tell them *This was tyranny.* He also gave me reason to understand that I was not deceived by the devil.

"When once I was holding in my hand the cross which was at the end of my rosary, He took it into His Hand, and when he returned it to me it consisted of four great stones, incomparably more precious than diamonds, for there is nothing here below that can equal the supernatural: a diamond is but an imperfect kind of stone in comparison with those jewels. They had on them the five wounds wrought in a most curious manner. And our Lord told me I should see the cross thus thenceforth, and so I did: and now I no longer saw the matter of which the cross was made, but only these precious stones: no one saw them thus but myself.

"When I was commanded to make these trials, and to resist the favours, they increased much more: and though I might wish to turn my mind to something else, yet my prayer was so continual that it ceased not even in sleep. I felt that the love of our Lord was increasing more and more, and I would then utter loving complaints to Him of the state of thraldom in which I was held; nor was it in my power, though I had desired it, to leave off thinking of Him : still I obeyed as well as I could, though I was able to do little or nothing therein. Our Lord never freed me from the obligation of obeying my confessors; but though he commanded me to do as they bade me, He gave me confidence on the other side, and taught me what I should say to them : giving me (as He does now) such convincing reasons as to make me feel wholly secure.

" Not long after this, His Majesty began to perform what he had been pleased to promise me before—to assure me more strongly that it was He; for there grew in me so great a love for God, that I knew not who infused it into me, for it was of a very supernatural kind : nor had I done anything to procure it. I felt as if dying through a desire of seeing God, and I knew not how or where to seek or find this life, but by the way of death."

Our Divine Lord was pleased to convince one of the Saint's confessors (probably the same who had given her so much trouble) of the *possibility* of the appearances vouchsafed to her by his own experience. As this priest was one night alone in his chamber, to his great astonishment our Lord suddenly stood before him. The next morning he hastened to S. Teresa to tell her what he had seen. "Father," replied she, "do you mean that Christ really appeared to your paternity ? Impossible ! I cannot credit it !" The confessor did his best to convince her of the reality of his vision, and received for answer : "Your paternity will now be pleased to understand that as certain as you are of your vision, so sure am I of those which I have related to your reverence."

CHAPTER VII.

1559.

WE are told by S. Teresa's holy son, S. John of the Cross, that our Lord never confers any supernatural favour on the body without having previously bestowed something greater on the soul. S. Teresa herself has described to us the wonders of the celestial flame which was consuming her soul in anticipation of that piercing of her heart by the fiery dart of the Seraph which conformed her to the passion of her Lord. The following is her own relation of the miracle :—

"Our Lord was pleased that I should have repeatedly the following vision. I saw an angel very near me on my left side, in a corporeal form, which is not usual with me; for though angels are often represented to me, yet it is only by that kind of intellectual vision of which I have already spoken. He was not tall, but rather low of stature, and very beautiful; his face was so luminous that he seemed to be one of those glorious spirits who appear to be all on fire (with divine love). He might be one of those who are called Seraphim, for they do not tell me their names; but I see clearly that in Heaven there is so great a difference between some angels and others, that I am not able to express it. I saw that he had a long golden dart in his hand, and at the point there seemed to me to be a little fire : I thought that he pierced my heart with this dart several times, and in such a manner that it went through my very bowels : and when he drew it out, it seemed as if they were drawn forth with it, and I remained wholly inflamed with a great love of God. The pain of this wound was so intense that it forced deep groans from me; but its sweetness was so excessive, that I could not desire to be free from it, nor find content in anything but God. This is not a corporeal but a *spiritual* pain, though the body in some measure, yea, in a great measure, participates in it. It is so delightful an intercourse between the soul and God, that I beseech His goodness to give some taste of it to him who may imagine I do not speak the truth."

The reality of this marvellous infliction was attested after the death of the Saint by various credible witnesses, who declared that the lance had not only wounded the heart, but actually pierced it through and through, and that the edges of the wound bore the marks of having been burnt. Still more solemn evidence of the miracle was brought to Rome and printed there in the year 1726, on the petition of the Carmelite Order for permission to keep a festival in its honour. Proof was then brought by the testimony of eye-witnesses, and the declaration upon oath of two physicians and a surgeon, that the heart of the Saint remained up to that time incorrupt, and bore the marks of a wound produced by some sharp instrument piercing it through from side to side, the edges also indicating the effects of fire.

The life of S. Teresa for the three-and-twenty years during which she survived this supernatural infliction, was a physical miracle, no less astonishing than the spiritual wonders by which it was accompanied. It appears, moreover, that the infliction was several times repeated, the scars of several smaller wounds besides the principal one being visible on the heart.

The venerable Anne of Jesus, one of the best be-loved of her daughters, relates that on one occasion, when she was sleeping in a cell over that of the Saint, she heard her utter deep sighs and groans. She went to see if she needed anything, and was answered: "Go, go, my child, I would that the same thing might happen to thee."

Well may our Saint bear the name of the Seraphic Virgin; well may the Church salute her in her Vesper Hymn as the victim of charity, *O charitatis victima,* for assuredly the burning dart of the Seraph which pierced her material heart did but symbolise the fire of Divine charity which inflamed her soul.

Even after death her heart seemed to be still on fire with love. The precious relic was no sooner enclosed in a crystal reliquary, that it might be visible to the faithful, than the crystal was broken, as if by a fire within it. In vain was one crystal placed over another. They were all successively broken, until the expedient was adopted of leaving an aperture at the top of the reliquary, by which the flame of that burning heart might escape.

The miraculous wound in the heart was followed by a succession of extraordinary raptures in which the Saint was frequently raised from the ground, and that (to her great confusion) very often in the presence of others. But the most conspicuous proof of the ardent love to which she had now attained was the sublime vow which, in the same year, she was inspired and permitted to make, always and on all occasions to do that which is most perfect, hereby imposing upon herself a new and most arduous kind of mortification, even the perpetual bondage of her free-will. By this promise she bound her soul, under the pain of mortal sin, to observe with the utmost possible perfection, not only the precepts of the

F

Gospel, but the rules and constitutions of her religious state, which ordinarily are understood not to bind under sin; and, moreover, all the commands, counsels, and directions of superiors, or spiritual guides, or devout books. In all cases, wherein she would otherwise have been free to choose, she thus bound herself by an irrevocable engagement to do the most perfect thing possible.

For this vow, which could be exonerated from the guilt of presumption only by the inspiration of Him who moved her to make and enabled her to keep it, S. Teresa prepared herself by trying her strength in the fulfilment of a simple resolution to the same effect; then, under the sanction of her director and the " guidance of God," *a Deo edocta*,* in no blind presumption, but with consummate prudence and most ardent love, she offered her great vow to God.

In this act S. Teresa has been followed by some others of the Saints, as S. Jane Frances de Chantal, and the B. Margaret Mary Alacoque; but her biographer tells us that, to the best of his knowledge, she was the first to set the example of this heroic sacrifice. Of the fidelity with which she was enabled to accomplish it, we may judge by her own words in the sixth chapter of her life, written some years afterwards: "Whilst I am now writing these lines, it seems that I may say by Thy favour and mercy what S. Paul said: 'I live now, yet not I, but Christ liveth in me,' though not with the same perfection as he did; and according to the experience which I have now had for some years, Thou still keepest Thy hand over me, and I find myself filled with desires and resolutions not to do anything against Thy will, however small it may be, though I know I must

---

* Bull of canonisation.

commit many offences against Thy Majesty without knowing it. And it also seems that nothing could be proposed to me which I would not resolutely perform for the love of Thee; and in some things Thou hast so assisted me that I have succeeded in them. I care not for the world, nor for the things of the world, and I find that nothing gives me pleasure but what comes from Thee, and that everything else is but a heavy cross."

That the Saint persevered in her heroic purpose to the end of her life, through a period of two-and-twenty years, we know by the evidence of her spiritual directors, and by the testimony of the acts of her canonisation. The following are the words of the Sacred Congregation of the Rota: *Quod et Deo fideliter reddidit, præ nimio amore quo illum propter seipsum prosequebatur, ut totius vitæ ipsius cursus probat.*

Teresa's anxieties and perplexities still continuing, it pleased our Lord to send her relief by the hands of His holy servant S. Peter of Alcantara. Her faithful friend Guiomar d'Ulloa was the medium of communication between these chosen souls. S. Teresa thus relates the circumstances of their first introduction to each other, and of the benefits conferred upon her soul by the counsels of the aged Saint.

" Our Lord was pleased to remedy a great part of my trouble, and for that time all of it, by bringing to Avila that blessed man, F. Peter of Alcantara, so wonderful for his austerities. Among other things I was assured that for twenty years he continually wore a garment of iron plate in the form of a hair-cloth. He is the author of certain little books of prayer, in Spanish, which are now much used; for, as he was well versed in prayer, he wrote very profitably on it, and gave excellent instructions to those who practised

it. He observed the first rule of S. Francis in all its
rigour." S. Peter was the founder of that reform of
the Franciscan Order, the members of which are
known in Spain by the name of Alcantarines, in Italy
of Riformati, and in France of Recollets.

"A certain widow lady," continues the Saint,
"who was a great servant of God, and a particular
friend of mine, came to know that this holy man was
then at Avila. She was also aware of my troubles
(for she had witnessed my afflictions, and had comforted me on many occasions, because her faith was
so great, that she could not help believing I was
directed by the Spirit of God, though all others
thought I was deceived by the devil); she had likewise a very good understanding, and was very
cautious in her words, and knew how to keep a
secret, and to her our Lord was pleased to show great
favours in prayer, and to give her a knowledge of
many things, of which even learned men were
ignorant. My confessor, therefore, gave me leave to
treat with her on various spiritual matters, for she
understood them well, having herself enjoyed some
of those very favours which our Lord had bestowed
on me; for He sent her, through me, certain instructions and admonitions, which were very profitable to
her soul. Without saying anything to me, the lady
obtained leave from my provincial for me to remain a
week in her house, in order to be able the better to
consult this holy man; and so, both there and in
several churches I spoke to him often, on this first
occasion of his coming to Avila; and afterwards I
corresponded with him on many occasions. Having
given him a short account of my life and manner of
prayer, with the greatest possible clearness, I found
almost at the very first that he was enabled to understand me by his own experience, which was indeed

the only thing I stood in need of at that time, for I
could not then well understand those things, at least
not so far as to be able to express them. I have
always endeavoured, however, to treat in truth and
sincerity with those to whom I committed the care of
my soul; I have always wished also to make known to
them the first motions of my heart; and, as regards
those things which might be in any way doubtful or
suspicious, I was wont to discuss them with strong
reasons against myself. I therefore laid open my
soul to him without any disguise or duplicity. Since
that time, our Lord has been pleased to make me
understand, and has enabled me to express the
favours which His Majesty bestows upon me; but at
that time I needed a person who had experienced
those things perfectly to understand me, so as to be
able to declare to me the meaning of everything.

"The good Father gave me very great light, for I
could not by any means understand what those intellectual visions meant, nor even those imaginary visions
which I saw only with the eyes of my soul; for those
only which were visible to the corporeal eye seemed
to me to be of any value, and of these I received none
at all. But this holy man enlightened me in everything, and explained all things to me, and bade me
not to be troubled, but to bless God, and be assured I
was directed by His Spirit, and that next to the
verities of the faith there could be nothing more
certainly true, nor worthy of more entire belief. He
seemed to feel much consolation in being with me,
and he showed me every courtesy and kindness, and
ever afterwards took great care of me, and communicated his most inward thoughts and purposes to
me. Finding that I also had the same desires which
he had already carried into effect, and that I was likewise full of courage (for our Lord had given me great

resolution), he took particular pleasure in speaking with me. Whenever our Lord brings anyone to this state, there is no pleasure or comfort which can be equal to that of meeting with such another person, to whom our Lord has given some beginnings of this same disposition; for then I had not much more than a beginning, by what I can remember, and God grant that I may have it now. He had also very great compassion for me, and he told me that one of the greatest afflictions of this life was that which I endured, viz., *the contradiction of good men;* and that there was still a great deal for me to suffer, because I should always have need of help, and there was no one in that city who understood me. He promised to speak with my confessor, and with one of those also who gave me the most trouble, and this was that married gentleman (Don F. de Salcedo) of whom I spoke before; for because he had a great esteem for me, he disturbed me the most. He was a man of a tender and holy soul, and knowing how wicked I used to be, he could not rest satisfied or secure. The holy man did as he said, for he spoke with those two persons, and gave them reasons and proofs to show they need not be uneasy, and that I ought not to be harassed any more. My confessor needed few reasons, but that gentleman so many that these were not altogether sufficient, though still they served to deter him from terrifying me so much as he did before. It was agreed between this holy religious and me that I should send him an account of my progress from that time forward, and that we should frequently recommend one another to God; for so deep was his humility that he set a little value even on the prayers of this miserable creature, and this gave me great confusion. He left me in possession of very great comfort and joy, and told me to continue my prayer in security, and to make no doubt that it came from God ; but that whenever I was in any doubt, I should for my own greater security mention whatever happened to my confessor, and that then I might consider myself safe. But notwithstanding all this, I could not rest so entirely secure because our Lord was still pleased to conduct me by the way of fear ; so that I was inclined to believe my prayer came from the devil when people told me that it did, and thus no one was able to give me either so much fear or so much security as to make me give more credit to either of these feelings than our Lord was pleased to infuse into my soul ; nevertheless, I enjoyed much comfort.

"I could not then satisfy myself with giving thanks to God and to my glorious Father S. Joseph, who, I thought, had brought the good Father to Avila, for he was commissary-general of the guardianship* of S. Joseph, to whom, as also to our blessed Lady, I used frequently to recommend myself."

The following paper was drawn up at this time by S. Teresa, as a full manifestation of her spiritual state to S. Peter of Alcantara. It has been happily preserved, and affords us an insight into the state of that saintly soul at this period of her life, when, after the fiery spiritual trials through which she had been brought to so great a height of perfection, she was standing almost on the threshold of the great work for which they had been sent to prepare her :—

"JESUS.

"May the grace of the Holy Spirit be with you, my reverend Father.

"This is my manner of prayer at the present time. I am seldom able to exercise the understanding

---

* A certain number of houses, not sufficient to form a province.

therein, because at the very beginning of my prayer, my soul enters into a profound peace, or into a rapture which entirely deprives me of the use of my senses ; so that if I am spoken to I only hear the sound of the speaker's voice, but without understanding what is said to me.

" This is what often happens to me. At times, when I am occupied with other things, without intending to think of God, or when my soul is in such great dryness and my body so overwhelmed with suffering that it would seem impossible to me to pray, however great a desire I might feel to do so, I feel myself suddenly and irresistibly plunged in this state of recollection and this elevation or rapture of spirit ; and I find myself in a moment enriched by those spiritual treasures which are the consequence of favours of this kind. And this befalls me without any previous vision or illumination of the understanding, and without even knowing where I am ; only it seems to me as if my soul was lost in God, and in that state it seems to make greater progress in a moment than it could do by any effort of its own in the course of a year. At other times I am irresistibly seized with such great transports of the love of God that I seem to be dying of the desire to be united to Him. I cry aloud to my God as if I were at the point of death. The vehemence of these transports is very great ; sometimes I cannot remain sitting and suffer a pain so delicious that I would never wish it to cease. This pain arises from my very ardent desire to depart from this life, from the thought that there is no other remedy for my suffering but death, and that I am not permitted to inflict it upon myself. Thus it seems to me that everyone else is joyful, and I alone afflicted ; that everyone else finds consolation and relief in sorrow, and that I alone am comfortless.

At this thought the grief which overwhelms me is so great that it seems to me as if I must die of it but for the raptures by which my Divine Master quiets all my trouble, and infuses peace and happiness into my soul by the marvels which He reveals to me.

"At other times I am filled with desires to serve God, so impetuous, and so full of trouble at finding myself so useless to His glory, that I can give no idea of their intensity. It seems to me then that there is neither pain nor torture, nor death nor martyrdom of any kind, which I would not joyfully endure to prove my love to Him. This also happens without any previous consideration; it is something sudden which wholly carries me away, and I know not whence I derive such great courage. I would fain, as it seems to me, lift up my voice to make all men know how much it imports them not *to content themselves with doing little for God*, and what wonderful blessings He is ready to bestow upon us, if only we would prepare ourselves to receive them. These desires seem inwardly to consume me. I desire to do what I cannot do. I find in this body of mine a chain which hinders me from rendering the slightest service to God or my neighbour; had I but the power, it seems to me that I would do great things. And thus when I feel myself powerless to serve God, I feel an anguish which words cannot express. This trouble is lost at last in the delight and consolation with which He overwhelms my soul. Sometimes, when transported by these desires to serve God, I would fain do severe penance, but I have not the power; it would be a great relief to me, if I may judge by the consolation I feel in the practice of the little which my bodily weakness enables me to perform : indeed, if I were left to myself I believe that the ardour of these desires would lead me to excessive austerities.

" It is often a great trouble to me to be obliged to converse with others, and sometimes an occasion of many tears. This arises from my thirst to be alone ; for even when I am neither praying nor reading, I feel an inexpressible delight in solitude. Intercourse with my neighbour, especially with my relations, is a heavy burden to me, unless they be persons with whom I can speak of prayer and spiritual things, for this is a consolation and a joy to me; sometimes, however, even these conversations weary me ; I would fain go where I should see nobody, and be quite alone. But I seldom feel this with regard to persons of this kind, still less with regard to my spiritual directors, who always give me consolation. From time to time I feel it a great trouble to be obliged to eat and sleep, especially to find that I am less able than other people to do without these things. I submit to this necessity for the love of God, and offer to Him the pain which it gives me.

" The time which I spend in prayer passes so quickly that I seem never to have enough, for I should never be tired of conversing alone with God. I always wish to find time to read, for I have been always very fond of reading. I read very little, however ; for I have no sooner opened a book than I fall into a state of profound recollection, and so my reading is changed into prayer. But even time thus spent seems too short for me because of my many occupations, which, although they are good, do not give me the same satisfaction as I should receive from reading and prayer. But I cannot help grieving that I have not so much time as I desire.

" Our Lord has given me these desires, and greater virtue than I had before, ever since He has favoured me with that prayer of quiet, and those raptures of which I have spoken ; and I find myself so much changed for the better, that I seem to have been formerly imperfection itself. These raptures and visions have produced this admirable effect upon my soul, and if there be any good in me, it has come therefrom.

"God has inspired me with so firm a resolution never to offend Him even by a venial sin, that I would rather endure a thousand deaths than commit the slighest sin deliberately. And farther, whenever a thing appears to me to be more perfect and more pleasing to God, and as soon as it is commanded me by my director, I feel myself so resolved to execute it, that for no suffering and for no reward would I omit it. Were I to act otherwise, I should not, methinks, have the boldness to ask anything of the Lord our God, nor to address any prayer to Him. Nevertheless in all this I commit many faults and imperfections.

"My obedience to my confessor is no doubt imperfect, nevertheless when I understand that he commands or wills anything, it seems to me, according to my interior disposition, that I should not fail to do it, and were I not to do it, I should consider myself to be greatly deluded.

"I love poverty, but not as much as I ought to do. It seems to me that if I were rich, I would not reserve any revenue, nor keep any money for my private use, but would content myself with what is barely necessary. I feel, nevertheless, that I possess this virtue very imperfectly, for if I desire nothing for myself I I should not be sorry to have something to give away.

"I have seldom had any vision which has not left me with a greater degree of virtue than I had before. I leave my confessors to judge whether there be any delusion of the devil here.

"All the beauties of earth, waters and fields, and

flowers and perfumes, and music, and all other things which the world calls delightful, are so little to me in comparison with those presented to my soul by my ordinary visions, that I desire to have neither eyes to see, nor ears to hear them. Thus they affect me very little, exciting but a momentary impression; to my eyes all these are but dust.

" When duty obliges me to speak with seculars, even when the conversation turns upon spiritual things, if it be unnecessarily prolonged, I am obliged to do violence to myself to overcome the pain which it gives me. As to conversations of simple amusement, in which I once delighted, or on worldly subjects, I feel now so great a disgust to them that they are perfectly intolerable to me. Those desires which now consume me of loving, serving, and seeing God, are not excited, as formerly, by considerations which kindle great devotion, and cause me to shed many tears; they arise from an interior fire, and a fervour so intense that it would soon deprive me of life, were it not that God comes to my aid, by one of the raptures of which I have spoken, in which He seems to quench the thirst of the soul.

" When I see persons advanced in the ways of God, who have these firm resolutions of which I have spoken, who are detached from all things and full of courage, I cannot help loving them much, and desiring greatly to hold communication with them, because their example seems to strengthen me. The sight, on the contrary, of those timid people who go so sluggishly about what they might reasonably undertake for the service of God, saddens and grieves me. I call the great God to their aid, I implore His help, and that of the Saints who wrought with such courage those very things which now affright us. It is not that I am good for anything, *but it seems to me*

*that God helps those who for His sake undertake great
things, and that He never fails those who put their trust
in Him alone.* Thus I desire to find souls who will
confirm me in this thought, and who will help me to
have no further care for food and raiment, but to leave
all this to the Providence of God. By leaving all to
God, I do not mean that I am not to take the ordinary
care to procure the necessaries of life, I mean only
that I am to do it without disquietude. And since
our Lord (I think about a year ago) gave me this interior liberty, I find it well to follow this course, and
I try to forget myself as far as I can.

" As to vain-glory, I have, thanks be to God, as far
as I can judge, no ground for it. I see clearly that I
contribute nothing to the favours which my Divine
Master bestows upon me. It has even pleased Him
to give me thereby a deeper sense of my misery; and
in fact I feel that by no effort of thought which I
could make during my whole life, could I arrive at the
comprehension of one only of those great truths of
which I receive the knowledge in a rapture.

" In time past I have often felt great confusion when
the graces which God bestows upon me have become
known to others; but for some time past I have
ceased to feel this. I speak as easily of them as if
they related to some other person, because I do not
think myself on this account better than I was before.
On the contrary, I think myself still worse ; and that
profusion of graces of which I have made so little
use, makes me believe, without hesitation, that there
has never been in this world a soul worse than my
own. Therefore it seems to me that, while I do
nothing but receive favours, others, by their virtues,
acquire greater merits; and that God will give them,
in one moment in Heaven, what He is pleased to give
me here below; this thought makes me beseech Him

with all my heart not to give me my reward in this life. Thus I believe that it is because I am so weak and so wicked that God has led me by this way.

" When I am in prayer, I could not, even if I would, desire any rest, nor ask it from our Lord, because I see that He never had any upon earth, but that He passed His life in continual sufferings. I pray Him therefore not to spare me, but to give me grace to bear them.

" All things of this kind, even those of the highest perfection, present themselves to me in prayer, and make so vivid an impression upon my mind, that I am lost in astonishment at their greatness. These truths are shown to me with such clearness, that the things of this world seem to me but folly. By this light I see that it is madness to make any account of the losses and sorrows of this life, or to be inconsolable at the death of friends. Nevertheless, when I consider what I have been, and how sensible I used to be to all these things, I see that I have great need to watch over myself, lest I relapse into the same weakness and imperfection.

" If I observe in any persons things which visibly seem to be sins, I cannot make up my mind to believe that they are thus offending God, because it seems to me that every one must desire like myself to please Him. He has bestowed on me this signal grace, never willingly to fix my thoughts on the defects of others when presented to my mind. Instead of thinking of them, I immediately begin to consider what there is good in those persons. Thus nothing afflicts me but public sins and heresies; and by these I am often so deeply moved, that it seems to me to be the only trouble we ought to feel. I am sometimes sad, it is true, when I see spiritual persons fall back and

neglect prayer; but this trouble is not great, because
I try not to dwell upon it.

" I have far less curiosity than I used to have, although I do not always practise entire mortification
in this respect, but only sometimes.

" What I have just described, and an almost continual attention to the Presence of God, is, as far as
I can judge, the present state of my soul. Thus,
when I am occupied with other things, I seem to be
aroused, I know not by whom, to renew that attention. This does not happen always, but only when
the affairs in which I am engaged are important; and
even then, thank God, these affairs do not occupy my
whole mind, except for a few moments at a time.

" There is a state of soul which comes upon me,
though rarely, for three, four, or five days together:
fervour visions; in short, all good things are not only
taken away from me, but so entirely effaced from my
memory, that I could not, if I would, recall to mind
the slightest good there has ever been in me. All
appears to me a dream; at least, I cannot remember
anything; my bodily infirmities almost overwhelm me;
my mind is troubled; I cannot form a thought of
God; I seem not to know under what law I am living.
If I read, I understand nothing of the book. I find
myself full of imperfections, with no courage for virtue; and the great courage which I usually have so
entirely disappears, that I should be incapable, as it
seems to me, of resisting the slightest temptation, or
bearing a single word which the world might say
against me. Then it comes into my head that I am
good for nothing, that it has been a mistake to bring
me out of the common way. I am troubled by the
thought that I am deceiving all those who think well
of me. I want to go and hide myself in some place
where nobody could see me. It is not from virtue

that I then desire solitude, but from cowardice. Lastly, I feel interiorly moved to illtreat all those who attempt to contradict me. But God bestows this grace upon me, that in the midst of this conflict I do not offend Him more than usual. Far from asking Him to deliver me from this torture, I am ready to suffer it even to the end of my life; and I accept it with all my heart: I beseech Him only to support me with His Hand, that I may not offend Him. Nay, I consider it a very great favour that He does not leave me always in this state. One thing which astonishes me at these times, is, that one only of those words which I am accustomed to hear, or a vision, or a recollection, lasting only for the space of a 'Hail Mary,' or the first step towards the Altar for Holy Communion, suddenly changes and purifies my soul, even restores health to my body, fills my understanding with light, and gives back to me my ordinary spiritual strength and desire after God. I have experienced this many times; and for the last six months I have always felt great relief to my corporal infirmities when I communicate. The raptures also sometimes produce the same effect. Sometimes this bodily relief lasts for three hours, and sometimes for a whole day. I do not think there is any delusion here, for it is a fact which I have often carefully observed. Thus when I am in this state of recollection, I have no fear of any illness, but when I pray after my former manner, I do not experience this improvement in my health.

"All these effects which I have described, make me believe that these things come from God. When I remember what I was, I feel that I was in the way to perdition, and in a short space of time, these favours have so changed me that I can hardly recognise myself. I find within my soul virtues which astonish me, as I know not how they came there. I see that this is a pure gift, and not the fruit of my labours. That which I understand in all truth and clearness, and in which I know that I am not deceived, is, that God has not only used these means to draw me to His service, but also to deliver me from hell, as those of my confessors know who have heard my general confession.

" When I meet with persons who know something of the great graces which God has bestowed on me, I wish that I might be allowed to tell them the whole history of my life ; for my only joy is that our Lord should be praised, and all the rest is nothing to me. My adorable Master knows this well; and I am sure of this also, that in all things I seek His glory alone, and that besides that glory, neither honour, nor life, nor glory, nor blessings of soul or body, nor any personal advantage has any charm or attraction for me.

" I cannot believe that the devil would have procured for me such great benefits in order to draw me to him, and then destroy me; I cannot suppose him so stupid. Besides, although I have deserved by my sins to be deceived and deluded by his artifices, I cannot believe that God has rejected all the earnest prayers which so many fervent souls have offered for me during the last two years, for I have never ceased to beseech them to pray that of His goodness He would make known to me whether or not I am in the right way; and that if I am going astray, He would be pleased to bring me back into it. No, our Divine Master would never have permitted all this, if what passes within me did not come from Him.

" Whilst on the one hand the solid arguments of so many holy and learned men whom I have consulted on this subject, and the sight of my own misery terrify me and make me fear I am deluded ; on the other, when I am in prayer, and on the days when I enjoy that sweet tranquillity in which I think only of God, though the most holy and saintly men in the world were to combine together to convince me that I am in error; though they were to inflict upon me all imaginable tortures to compel me to believe it, and though, on my side, I were to endeavour with all my power to agree with them, it would be impossible for me to persuade myself that the inestimable favours I receive from God come from the devil.

"It is true that at one time, when they have tried to persuade me of it, I have been agitated by many fears; considering on the one side the merit and sincerity of those who undertook to prove it, and on the other that my unfaithfulness well deserved such punishment. But at the first word, the first vision, the first moment of recollection, all the fears which they had sought to instil into me were dispelled, and I felt more confirmed than ever in the belief that what passes within me comes from God.

"Sometimes, it is true, certain things which come from the devil may be mingled with these favours, but the effects produced by these illusions are so different from those which arise from graces received from God, that I cannot believe that a person with any experience could be deceived by them. Yet notwithstanding my full persuasion that what passes within me proceeds from God, I would not for the world do the slightest thing without the approbation of my spiritual guide, who serves our Lord better than I do. Of all the words which have been spoken to me, there has never been one which has not commanded me to obey him, and to conceal nothing from him, and which has not taught me that this is my duty.

"I am often reproved for my faults, and in such

sort as seems to pierce through my very soul. The sins of my past life are brought before me so vividly that my heart is wrung with grief. At other times, I receive important counsels showing me the danger that there is, or may be, in some matter which I have in hand.

"Although I have written at great length, it seems to me that I have not said enough of the great spiritual benefits which I find within me after prayer. But this does not prevent me from being full of imperfections, very useless, and very miserable. Perhaps from not understanding good things I am deceiving myself; but that which leads me to judge as I have done is the manifest change in my life.

"I can, I think, assert that I have truly felt all that I have said. Such are the graces which our Lord has wrought in this miserable and imperfect creature. I submit it all to your judgment, for you now know fully the state of my soul.

"Your unworthy servant and daughter,
"TERESA OF JESUS."

CHAPTER VIII.

1560.

THE consolation which S. Teresa derived from the encouragement given her by S. Peter of Alcantara was soon disturbed by fresh assaults of the enemy of souls, who was now permitted to scare her by horrible visions, and even to inflict severe blows upon her; his fury being especially excited by the extraordinary effect of her prayers in delivering sinners from his power.

" I was once in a certain oratory," says she, " when he appeared to me on my left side, in a horrible shape. I observed his mouth in particular while he spoke to me, and it was most terrible ; for it seemed that a very great flame came out of his body. He told me, in a fearful voice, that though I had escaped his hands, yet he would bring me back again. I was exceedingly terrified, but I blessed myself as well as I could, and he vanished away : but presently he returned again. This happened to me twice, and I knew not what to do. But as I had some holy water near me, I threw it towards the place where he was, and he returned no more. Another time he tormented me for five hours together with terrible pains, joined with such interior and exterior disgust, that it seemed impossible for me to endure it. The sisters who were then with me were astonished to see what passed ; but they knew not what to do, nor could I help myself. My custom is when any corporal sickness or pain is very intolerable, to make certain acts of resignation within myself, as well as I can, beseeching our Lord, that His Majesty may be pleased to give me patience, and that I may so suffer, if He please, even until the end of the world. Whenever then I found myself in this state of suffering, I helped myself by making some such acts and resolutions, that so I might bear it the better.

" Our Lord was pleased I should understand that I was tempted by the devil, for I saw near me a very horrible little negro, gnashing his teeth like one raging mad, as if he had lost something which he had hoped to gain. As soon as I saw him, I laughed, and showed no fear at all ; but the sisters who were near me knew not what to do with me in this case, nor what remedy to apply to so great a torment, for the blows he made me give myself were very severe, and I had no power

at all to resist him : and what was still worse I felt
so great inward disquiet, that I could in no way find
any rest : neither did I dare to ask for holy water lest
I should terrify those who were present, or let them
know who was the cause of the mischief. I have often
found, by experience, that there is nothing from which
the devils fly more quickly, and that not to return,
than from holy water ; they fly also from a cross, but
return again immediately. Certainly the power of
holy water must be great ; for my part, my soul feels
a particular comfort in taking it ; and very generally
a refreshment and interior delight which I cannot
express, and which comforts my soul. This is no
fancy, or a thing which has happened to me only
once ; it has happened very often, and been observed
by me with great attention. It is as if a person,
suffering from heat and thirst, should drink a glass of
cold water, which would greatly refresh him. I consider also, that whatever is ordained by the Church is
of the greatest importance ; and it is a matter of great
joy to me that those words which the Church uses
when she blesses the water, should be so powerful
in making such a difference between blessed and
unblessed water. I told those who were present, as
my torment did not cease, that if they would not laugh
at me, I would beg some holy water of them. They
brought me some, and sprinkled me with it, but it did
me no good. I sprinkled some myself in the place where
the devil was, and in an instant he departed, and all
my pains went away also, as if some one had removed
them with his hand, except that I felt as much tired
as if I had been severely beaten. I afterwards considered that if the devil, when our Lord permits him,
is able to do so much mischief to us in body and soul,
even when we are not his, what will he do to them
who shall fall entirely into his power ? This consi-

deration gave me fresh desires to be free from such ill company.

" Another time I was in the choir, when I fell into a state of deep recollection, and I went away lest others might perceive it ; but all the nuns who were near heard great blows struck in the place from which I had retired. I also heard persons talking near me, as if they were contriving some plot, though I understood not the conversation, for I was so fixed in prayer that I understood nothing, neither had I any fear. This used to happen almost every time that our Lord did me the favour to confer a benefit on some soul by my advice. An ecclesiastic once came to me who had lived about two years and a half in a most grievous mortal sin ; and during all that period he neither confessed it nor reformed himself, but yet he presumed to say Mass. And though he confessed his other sins, yet respecting that one he used to say to himself, ' How can I ever confess so foul a crime ? ' Still he was desirous of freeing himself from it, but he knew not how. I took great compassion on him, and was grieved to see God offended in such a way. I promised him to beg God to grant him some remedy, and that I would prevail on others to do the same, who were much better than myself. I accordingly gave him a letter to a certain person which he was to deliver himself ; and it so happened that he was thus led to confess his sin, and thus God was pleased by the prayers of these very holy persons (I also, miserable sinner that I am, not failing to beg that favour to the best of my power), to extend His mercy to this soul. The ecclesiastic wrote to tell me that he was already so far reformed, that some days had passed in which he had not returned to the sin, but that the torment which the temptation caused was so great, that he seemed to be in hell, and therefore that I must still recommend him to God. Upon this I once more commended him to my sisters, by whose prayers our Lord was pleased to grant this favour, for they took the matter exceedingly to heart. None of them knew for whom they were praying. I also besought the Lord to put an end to his torments and temptations, and to suffer those devils to come and torment me, provided that I might not be led to offend our Lord in anything. And it is quite true, that shortly after this I had to endure most grievous torments for the space of a month. But our Lord was pleased as I have since learned, that the devils should not afflict that person any more; his soul was strengthened, and became quite free, so that he could not be satisfied with giving thanks to our Lord, and to me also, as if I had done anything; the conviction, however, which he had that our Lord sometimes bestowed favours on me, might have been of some benefit to him. He used to say that when he found himself greatly assaulted, he was accustomed to read my letters, and that then the temptation immediately left him. He was much amazed to hear what I suffered, and how he came himself to be free. May our Lord be praised by all men; for the prayers of those who truly serve Him, as I believe my sisters do in this house, can do much; but because I had procured those prayers, the devils were exasperated against me, and our Lord permitted it for my sins.

" Another time I saw a multitude round about me ; but it seemed to me that I was encompassed with a great light, which did not allow them to approach me. I understood by this, that our Lord kept them from coming near me, so that they might not make me offend God. Now, therefore, I do not fear them at all, for their strength is a mere nothing, unless they find the souls they attack to be cowardly, and that they yield to them; then, indeed, they show their power. Sometimes in the temptations I have already mentioned, it seemed that all the vanities and weaknesses of my former life revived in me, so that I had great need to recommend myself frequently to God; then I was presently tormented with the apprehension that all that passed within me came from the devil, till at last my confessor comforted me; for it seemed to me that even the first motion of an evil thought ought not to be entertained by any one who had received such great favours from our Lord. At other times I am tormented to see myself so much esteemed, and especially now, that eminent persons should esteem me so much, and speak such good things of me. In this I have suffered, and still suffer much; and presently I consider the life of Christ and of the Saints, and methinks I walk in a way very contrary to theirs, because they endured nothing but contempt and injuries. This consideration makes me so fearful, that I scarcely dare raise up my head, and would be glad not to be seen. This does not happen to me when I am suffering persecution, however much I may be afflicted in body or mind; for then my soul seems to be mistress in a way that I do not understand; she then seems to be in her kingdom, and to tread all things under her feet. This state of fear sometimes lasted many days; and it appeared to me to be virtue and humility, but now I am sensible it was a temptation; as a Dominican father, a very learned man, showed me very clearly. When I thought that those favours which our Lord was pleased to show me would be publicly known, it was so excessive a torment to me, that it troubled my soul exceedingly. I thought I could more willingly have consented to be buried alive; and so when I began to have those very great recollections and raptures, in such a way that it was impossible for me to resist them, I remained afterwards so confounded with shame, that I wished to be where no one could see me.

"Being once extremely afflicted at this, our Lord said to me : ' Of what art thou so much afraid ? Only one of these two things can happen: either they will find fault with thee, or they will praise Me'—meaning that they who believed it would praise Him, and that they who did not believe it would condemn me, without any fault of mine ; and that as both these things would prove an advantage to me, I had no reason to be thus troubled. These words comforted me very much, and do comfort me still whenever I call them to mind. The temptation went so far, that I was desirous of leaving the convent in which I was, and of retiring to another much more strictly enclosed, and in which great austerities were practised. I was the more drawn to that house because it was very far off, so that I might have hoped in that place to remain unknown ; but my confessor would never give his consent. These fears greatly deprived me of liberty of spirit, and afterwards I came to understand that this was no good humility, since it gave me so much disquiet ; our Lord then taught me this truth, that if I were convinced and assured I had no good whatever in me, but that it all came from God, it would follow that just as I was not sorry to hear other persons praised, but was rather glad and greatly comforted that in them God manifested Himself, so neither should I be sorry that His works should be shown also in me." .

The last revelation recorded by S. Teresa as preceding those relating to the foundation of her reform, is that terrific vision of hell, which, when she wrote of it six years afterwards, still chilled her blood with fear, and which still thrills with terror all who read it.

"After our Lord had bestowed those favours upon me which I have already related, as well as many others, which were very great, He was pleased that one day, while I was at prayer, I should find myself (without knowing how) in a moment lodged in hell. I understood that our Lord was pleased to let me see the place which the devils had prepared for me there, and which I should have deserved by the sins into which I should have fallen had I not changed my life. This vision lasted only for a very short time; but yet, if I should live many years, it seems impossible that I should ever forget it. The entrance seemed to be like a long close alley, or rather like a low, dark, and narrow cavity; and the ground appeared to be like mire, exceedingly filthy, and having a horrible stench, and full of a multitude of loathsome vermin. At the end of it there was a certain hollow place, as if it had been a kind of little press in the wall, into which I found myself thrust, and closely pent up. All that I have yet described might pass for delightful, in comparison with what I felt in this press; the torment was so dreadful that no words can express the least part of it.

"I felt a fire in my soul, which I cannot express or describe, as it was in reality. All those other most grievous and almost insufferable torments which I have endured by the shrinking up of all my sinews, and in other ways (which in the judgment of physicians, were the greatest that could be suffered, in a corporal way, in this world), and some also which were caused by the devil, were all a mere nothing in comparison with what I suffered there, joined with the dismal thought that all this suffering was to be without end or intermission. And even this is still nothing, if compared with the continual agony the soul suffers; that pressing, that stifling, that anguish so exceedingly sensible, together with such desperate torturing discontent and disgust, that I cannot express it. To say it is a butchering or rending of· the soul, is to say little; for this would seem to express a violence, used by some other agent to destroy her. But here she is her own executioner, and even tears herself in pieces. I saw not who it was that tormented me; but I seemed to be both burnt and cut in pieces, and in so dreadful a place there was no room for the least hope of ever meeting with any comfort or ease; neither was there any room to sit or lie down. Thus was I thrust into this place like a hole in the wall; and these walls, which are also most horrible to the sight, press in upon their prisoner, so that she is choked and stifled. There is nothing but thick darkness, without the least glimpse of light; and yet, I know not how it is, though there is no light, yet all that can afflict the sight is visible.

"Our Lord was not pleased that I should see any more of hell at that time. But afterwards I had another vision of most terrible things, as punishments inflicted for certain particular vices; and these, as far as I could judge of them by the sight, seemed to be more hideous than the former. But as I did not feel the pain, they did not so much affright me as the first vision. Our Lord was pleased that I should really feel those torments and that affliction of spirit, as if my very body had been suffering them. I knew not how all this could be; but I understood very clearly that it was a great favour, and that our Lord was pleased that I should see, by the sight of my own eyes, from what a place His great mercy had delivered me. It is nothing to have heard people

talk of hell, nor to have meditated on various kinds
of torments; all is nothing to this, since it is quite a
different thing: and, indeed, the torments of this
world are no more than a mere picture; and the
burning here in this life is but a trifle in comparison
with the fire of hell. I was so astonished and amazed
at this sight (and so I am even now while I am
writing, though it happened six years ago) that at the
thought of it my blood seems to be chilled in my
veins through fear. And whatever troubles or pains
I now suffer, if I do but call to my remembrance what
I then endured, immediately all that can be suffered
in this life seems to be nothing at all. I therefore
say again, that this was one of the greatest favours
which our Lord has ever shown me; for it has been of
very great benefit to me, both in making me lose all
fear about the tribulations and contradictions of this
life, and giving me strength to bear them; and also in
teaching me to give thanks to our Lord, for delivering me (as I may now believe) from those dreadful
and never-ending torments.

" Since that time all seems easy to me, in comparison with one moment of such suffering as I then
endured. I wondered, that having so often read
books which give an account of some of the torments
of hell, I yet feared them so little, and did not regard
them as I ought to have done. Considering in what
state I once was, I was also astonished to see how it
was possible for me to take pleasure in anything that
was likely to bring me at last to so bad a place. Be
Thou eternally blessed, O my God! For how well
hast Thou made it appear, that Thou didst love me
incomparably better than I loved myself! How often,
O Lord! hast Thou delivered me from that dark and
horrible dungeon! And how often have I returned
to cast myself into it again, even against Thy will!

This vision caused me to feel very great pain on account of the many souls which are condemned to this prison, especially the Lutherans, because they had once been members of the Church by their baptism. It was followed also by strong impulses to do good to souls; so that it seems to me very certain, that for the delivery of any one of them from such excessive torments, I could very willingly suffer many deaths.

" I consider that if we see a person in this world, whom we love dearly, in any great pain or affliction, it seems that our natural disposition invites us to compassion. And, therefore, to see a soul which is for ever to endure that supreme affliction, and misery of all miseries, who shall be able to bear it? Surely, no heart can endure it without great grief. And since in this world we are moved to so much compassion for those whose misery at the farthest is to end with their lives, I know not how we can be at rest, considering what a vast number of souls the devil daily takes with him to hell.

" This also makes me desire most intensely, that, in a business of so great importance, we should not be satisfied with less than doing all we can on our part, and leaving nothing unattempted; and I beseech our Lord to give us His grace for this purpose. When I consider that although I was formerly very wicked, yet I was somewhat careful to serve God; nor did I then commit certain sins which are swallowed down by the world as if they were nothing; and though I had endured most dreadful sickness with much patience which our Lord gave me, and also I was not inclined to murmur, or to detract, or to speak ill of anybody; nor was I covetous or envious, as far as I can remember, in any way, so as grievously to offend God, for though I was so wicked, I usually had the fear of God before me; yet, notwithstanding all this, I see where the devils had provided me a lodging : hence I conclude, that it is a dangerous thing to be contented with slight efforts when eternity is at stake ; and, above all, that a soul ought to know neither peace nor rest, which is falling at every step into mortal sin."

———•>•- - -

CHAPTER IX.

1560.

It was while the terrors of this vision were full in the mind of S. Teresa, and the woeful tidings of the loss of souls by the Lutheran apostacy were still ringing in her ears, that the idea of her great reform was first divinely impressed upon her mind. * Not that she then dreamed of such a work as she was eventually enabled to carry out, in the restoration of the Order of Mount Carmel to its primitive perfection. But her heart was consumed by the love of Jesus, and the love of the souls for whom He died ; her eyes had been opened to behold the anguish of hell, and the bliss of Paradise, and to measure the length and depth of that dread *for ever*, the thought of which had haunted her when a child. What could she do for Jesus, what could she do for souls ?

The course she adopted seems strange to the wisdom of this world, for it cut her off from many apparent means of spiritual usefulness; these were indeed already restricted by her sex and her position ; she could not preach to perishing sinners, or argue with obstinate heretics. Nevertheless the unrestrained intercourse with externs, and the freedom of egress from the convent, permitted in the then relaxed state of the rule, afforded many opportunities of doing good to souls of which her past experience must have shown her the value; neither could she be ignorant of the influence for good which she possessed over all who came within the sphere of her attraction, for she tells us that, by the special favour of our Lord, she was always loved by those amongst whom she was placed.

What then was the motive which impelled her to bury all her gifts and powers within the narrow boundary of a strictly cloistered convent? We shall find it in the vow she had made to God to do always the most perfect thing in His sight. Her perfection as a Carmelite nun must consist in the perfect observance of her rule, and by that perfect fulfilment alone could she render to God that "greater glory" for which He had created her, and give that efficacy to her fervent intercession for sinners which belongs to the prayers of those who do His will. And herein is this exalted Saint a pattern to the feeblest and the least amongst ourselves. That she gave herself to a life of prayer belonged to her high vocation as a contemplative nun; that she gave herself to it as the duty of her state of life belonged to that calling which she shares with all baptized believers in Him, who said to the mixed multitude of his disciples: "Be ye perfect," and who has made the efficacy of our prayers and our labours for the souls of others, so awfully dependent upon the faithful keeping of our own.

On the evening of July 16, 1560, a loving band were gathered together in Teresa's cell to keep the festival of our Lady of Mount Carmel. There was the Saint herself with her burning heart so lately pierced by the Seraph's lance, and her deep eyes "beautiful with

gazing upon God." There was her faithful friend
Jane Suarez, the first link in the providential chain
which drew her to Carmel, now in the decline of life,
and approaching the predestined glory which had
been long before revealed as hers to her saintly companion; and in company with the two holy nuns were
five young maidens, still in the secular state, all kinswomen and spiritual children of S. Teresa, under whose
care they had been brought up in the Convent of the
Incarnation, all hereafter to be religious of her reform.
Mary of Ocampo and her sister Eleanora, nieces of
the Saint; Isabella de Cepeda, her great niece; and
Agnes and Anne de Tapia, her cousins. The conversation had turned upon the hindrances to a life
of strict retirement and recollection in a community
consisting of one hundred and ninety nuns, exposed
to constant intercourse with externs, and harassed
by continual anxiety about temporal matters, arising
from the insufficiency of means for the support of so
large a number of religious. It was a theme ever
present to the thoughts of Teresa, who, as we have
seen, had been strongly tempted to escape from the
trials of her present position, by taking shelter in
some distant and strictly enclosed convent.

She thus describes the conflict which had long
distracted her mind upon this subject:—

"Having now seen all these great things, and having
heard many secrets which our Lord through His mercy
was pleased to show me, concerning the glory which
is prepared for the good, and the torments prepared
for the wicked; and desiring, therefore, to find out
some way and method whereby I might do penance
for all the sins I had committed, and be enabled to do
something towards obtaining so great a glory, I was
desirous of flying from the world, and avoiding once
for all the company of men. My heart could find no

rest; but this restlessness was not troublesome to me, but sweet and delightful. It was evident that it came from God, and that His Majesty had given heat enough to my soul for digesting other stronger meats than she had before eaten. And now I began to consider what I could do for God; the first thing I thought of was to follow the call which He had given me to a religious life, and to observe my rule with the greatest possible perfection. And though there were in the house where I lived many servants of God, by whom He was greatly served, yet as they were in great want of temporal means, many of the nuns were often obliged to go abroad to seek assistance; though they did so with all due decorum and piety; and, besides, that house was not founded according to the first rigour of the rule, but that rule only was observed which was conformable with the practice of the rest of the Order, according to the Bull of the Pope granting a relaxation. There were also some other inconveniences. It seemed to me, that the place was too good, as the house was large and pleasant; and the evil practice of leaving the monastery had become very troublesome to me, for it affected me more than others, because some persons, whose wishes the superior could not refuse, were pleased that I should accompany them when they went out, and the superiors being importuned by them, commanded me to do so: and thus I grew accustomed to remain but seldom in the monastery."

Such had long been Teresa's anxious communings with her own heart. But it was not her voice which now gave them utterance. Perhaps they lay too deep for words.

It was Mary d'Ocampo, the most thoughtless, as it seemed, of the party, who first clothed in words the idea which had so long been deeply cherished. This young maiden had for some time past been a source of

no little anxiety to her holy kinswoman, who seemed
to see her own days of youthful vanity rise once more
before her in the person of her beautiful and gifted
niece.   Notwithstanding all her careful convent
training, Mary of Ocampo at seventeen was as full of
the love of pleasure, as careful in the adornment of
her person, as much attached to all the refinements of
life, as Teresa d'Ahumada had been when she reluctantly entered the Augustinian convent thirty years
before.   But if she resembled her aunt in this passing
season of worldliness, she resembled her also in the
truth and purity of her nature, as she was to resemble
her in the supernatural life of grace ; and it was with
an intense energy like her own that the noble-hearted
girl exclaimed: "Well! then, let us all who are here
assembled go hence and lead a solitary life like the
hermits of the desert; if you have the courage to live
like the discalced Franciscans there will be no difficulty in founding a convent."

The words fell like a spark of fire upon the long-
smothered hopes of the Saint: this her own cherished
child was then to lay the first stone of her reform;
for, when something was said of the difficulty of
finding means for the foundation, Mary cut short the
discussion by promising a thousand ducats of her own
property for the purpose. It was a generous offer, and
it was made to One Who has never yet suffered Himself to be outdone in generosity; on that very night
our Lord appeared to her and testified His acceptance
of her gift, rewarding it by the inestimable grace of a
vocation to Carmel.   Six months after the foundation
of the first convent of the reform, she received the religious habit, with the name of Mary of John Baptist,
and became afterwards, as prioress of the Convent at
Valladolid, one of the Saint's most efficient fellow-
labourers in the formation of her religious.

Teresa, seeing the way thus opened for the execution of her long-cherished purpose, took counsel with her faithful friend, Guiomar d'Ulloa, who eagerly proffered her aid in a work which promised to bring such glory to God. They both recommended the matter fervently to our Lord, from Whom Teresa soon received an express command to proceed to the work without delay.

" One day after I had communicated, His Majesty earnestly commanded me *to endeavour to accomplish His object with all my strength,* promising me at the same time, *that the monastery should certainly be established, and that He would be greatly served in it ; that it should be called by the name of S. Joseph; that He Himself would guard us at one gate, and His Mother our Lady, at another ; that He would continue with us, and that the place would become like a star, which would shine with great splendour; and that though other convents were then relaxed, yet men must not think He was but little served therein : and what would become of the world, were it not for religious orders?* I was told to inform my confessor of all that had been said to me, and that our Lord wished him not to oppose my design, nor to put any obstacle in the way. This vision was followed by such great effects, and the words used therein were uttered in such a manner, that I could not possibly doubt of their having come from God."

In spite of this conviction, the devil contrived to stir up a thousand doubts and fears within the heart of Teresa to hinder the execution of the Divine command. Never had the home, in which she had now dwelt for four-and-twenty years, seemed so lovely in her eyes, as now that by her own act she was about to sever herself from it for ever. The Convent of the Incarnation, which remains to the present day much

as it was in the time of S. Teresa, is surrounded by
every natural beauty, which could lay hold on a heart
alive like hers to all that is glorious in the works of
God and man. It is described by F. Bouix, who
devoutly visited it, as standing at a little distance
from the city of Avila, in a delightful valley. "It
contains," he says, "a fine church, magnificent
cloisters, and a spacious garden and orchard, watered
by a clear and abundant stream."

Amongst the hundred and ninety religious with
whom she had lived so long, there were many, no
doubt, whom she loved, and who loved her, with that
deep enduring affection, passing even the love of natural
kindred, which our Lord sometimes gives, over and
above His own, to those who have left all for His sake,
as a part of the "hundredfold" promised them in this
life. But more than all, it was here that she had
dwelt all those years with Him; here that He had
knocked so long and so patiently at the door of her
heart; here that, when it was at last opened, she in
her turn had waited so penitently and so patiently for
Him, through the long night of dreary desolation
which had given place to so glorious a morrow. In
those cloisters and gardens she had walked side by
side with Him. Here had her heart been enkindled
by the Seraph's dart with that burning love which
could find relief only in the sublime vow which bound
her freewill as a perpetual holocaust to His altar, and
was now urging her once more to leave her kindred
and her Father's house (her spiritual kindred and the
house of her Heavenly Father) to go she knew not
whither, save that it was into a land which He would
show her. It was a rending asunder of her whole
being, perhaps more painful than the struggle which
preceded her first entrance into religion. All the trials
and difficulties which would beset the undertaking

before her were also vividly represented to her mind, so that, as she tells us, she " experienced the greatest affliction."

" I considered how extremely happy I was in my first house ; and that though I had long ago begun to think about this matter, it had not been with any determination nor with any certainty that it would succeed. It seemed, however, that the reward I should have for accomplishing it was placed before me, yet when I foresaw what great trouble the undertaking would give me, I began to doubt what I should do. But our Lord again spoke to me so many times on the subject, and represented to me so many reasons for undertaking it, that I saw clearly it was His will I should do so, and I thought of nothing else but of acquainting my confessor with the matter, and I gave him in writing a statement of what had taken place."

F. Alvarez was unwilling to contradict his holy penitent, or absolutely to forbid the prosecution of her design, which seemed to him in the highest degree difficult, if not impracticable. He therefore got rid of the responsibility of giving a decision, by referring her to that of her Provincial, which he probably thought would put an end to the matter. Before applying to the Provincial of the Carmes, Teresa took counsel of the two great lights of the orders of S. Francis and S. Dominic, then in Spain, S. Peter of Alcantara, and S. Louis Bertrand, the Apostle of the Indies. The reply given by both these holy men was in the highest degree encouraging. The letter of S. Louis contained moreover a prophecy ; the exact fulfilment of which was brought forward in the process of his canonisation. It is as follows :—

" MOTHER TERESA.

" I have received your letter ; and because the matter concerning which you have asked my opinion so greatly concerns the service of God, I desired to recommend it to Him in my sacrifices and in my poor prayers (for which reason I have thus long delayed my reply). Now I bid you, in the name of our Lord, to take courage and go forward in your glorious enterprise, for He will help and prosper you. And on His part I assure you that before fifty years are passed, your Religion shall be one of the most illustrious in the Church of God. May He have you in His holy keeping, &c.

" Br. LOUIS BERTRAND.

" From Valentia."

The approbation most necessary to the work, that of Angelo Salazar, Provincial of the Carmes, was now alone wanting. The Saint had never conferred with him on the affairs of her soul, or on the revelations which she had received concerning the establishment of her reform : and fearing that he would pay little heed to the suggestions of a poor, solitary, and (as he might probably think) visionary nun, she employed Doña Guiomar to open the matter to him. " The lady," says S. Teresa, " spoke to him, and told him that she wished to erect a new monastery. The Provincial very readily gave his consent, for he was a friend to all religious orders ; and so he gave her all the liberty and power that were necessary, and told her that he would accept the house. They then settled the revenue that it should have, and that the community should not consist of more than thirteen religious, to which number we had always wished to limit it, and that for many reasons."

The Provincial having been found so favourable to the design, F. Alvarez also gave his consent, to the great joy of the Saint, who was now in perfect peace and tranquillity, seeing that her great design was approved, not only by our Lord Himself, but by His ministers on earth.

All things seemed now ready for execution, and measures were taken secretly for the purchase of a small house on the site of which the present Convent of S. Joseph stands. The legal instruments were in preparation, and several religious from the Convent of the Incarnation were waiting to accompany Teresa to the new foundation, when a storm burst forth which threatened destruction to all her hopes.

" As soon," says she, " as our intention began to be known in the town, there instantly arose such a violent storm of persecution as cannot be described in words. The scoffs, the jeers, the laughter, the exclamations that it was a ridiculous, silly undertaking, were more than I can describe. They 'said that I was mad to think of leaving a convent where I was so well off; but they persecuted my companion to such a degree that she could hardly bear it. As to myself, I knew not what to do ; for they had some apparent reason for what they said. In this distress I recommended myself to God, and then His Majesty began to comfort and encourage me, and told me that now I might see through what difficulties those saints had passed who had founded religious orders in the Church ; and that I was to suffer many more persecutions than I could imagine, but that I must not be troubled at them. He told me also some things which I was to tell my companions ; and that which astonished me most was, that we were instantly consoled respecting what had passed, and encouraged to bear up against all trials that were to come. I am quite certain that there was hardly any person in the town, even of the devout sort, who did not oppose us, and look upon our undertaking as a ' great folly.' "

To such a height was the persecution carried, that absolution was refused to Doña Guiomar by more than one priest, " until she should remove the scandal which she was occasioning in the city." Neither she nor her holy companion, however, wavered in their conviction that the work was of God, and that in His own good time He would bring it to pass; but in order, if possible, to quiet the tumultuous opposition which had been excited in the city, they resolved to consult F. Peter Ibañez, reader of theology in the Convent of the Friars Preachers, who was accounted the most learned man at that time in the city of Avila, and highly esteemed also for his sanctity.

S. Teresa thus relates the circumstances of this appeal and its results :—

"My companion went, therefore, to a very learned man, who was a great servant of God, and belonged to the order of S. Dominic, and told him all that had passed, stating that the revenue she had intended to settle on the convent came out of her own estate, and that she wished he would assist us, because he was the most learned man in the town at that time; indeed, there were few so learned in the whole Order. I told him likewise all that we intended to do, and gave him some reasons for the undertaking; but I did not mention any of my revelations; I only dwelt on those natural motives which struck me, because I wished him not to give any opinion but what was conformable to them. He answered, that he wished to have eight days to consider the matter; he also asked us whether we were determined to do whatever he should tell us, and I assured him we were. But though I said so much, and methinks I would have done as I promised, yet never did I lose the confidence that the convent would be established. The faith and confidence of my companion were still greater than my own, for whatever people might say to her, she was resolved never to give up the project. But, though I considered it to be quite certain that the work would be accomplished, so deeply was I convinced that the revelation concerning it was true (supposing it to contain nothing against Holy Scripture, or the decrees of the Church, which we are bound to observe), yet if this learned man had told me that we could not effect our design without offending our Lord, and going against a good conscience, I think I should instantly have abandoned it, and have sought for some other means of serving our Lord. But he gave me no other light at that time. This servant of God told me, sometime afterwards, that he had carefully considered the matter, and had come to the resolution of doing all in his power to induce us to abandon the undertaking, because the opposition of the people had already come to his ears, and also because everyone considered it to be a foolish thing. And a certain gentleman, as soon as he heard that we intended to speak with this Father, had sent word to him, and advised him to consider well what he did. But now when he began to consider what answer he should give, and to reflect seriously on the matter, and upon our intention, and the regularity and devotion which we intended to introduce into the convent, he came to the conclusion, that its establishment would tend much to the honour of God, and that we should on no account abandon our project; and hence he advised us to make all possible haste to bring the matter to a conclusion, and he gave us his own opinion as to the best method we should adopt; and told us, that though the revenue was small, God was to be trusted, and that whoever opposed the design should be sent to him, for he knew well what answer to give them.

"From that moment he has never ceased to assist us. With these words we went away much comforted, and we found that some holy persons who had before been opposed to us, were now not only much more satisfied, but were ready to help us. Amongst them was that devout knight (Don Francis Salcedo) who, knowing that our work aims at great perfection (as indeed it does, because it is wholly founded on prayer) gave us his opinion, that however difficult its accomplishment seemed to be, having no apparent probability of success, yet it might well be an undertaking inspired by God. Now our Lord may have disposed him to be of this mind, and the priest also (Master Daza), that servant of God whom I had consulted long ago, who is a pattern for all the town, and one whom God has visibly placed there for the advancement of many souls. He now came forward to assist me in the business.

"We had thus so far succeeded, by the help of many prayers, for we bought a house, though a small one, in a good part of the town; but its smallness did not trouble me at all, for our Lord had told me before that I should take possession as well as I could, and that afterwards I should see what His Majesty would do; and this promise I have strictly performed. And thus, though I found we had but little means, yet I believed our Lord would so arrange matters that we should be assisted in other ways."

Great was the consolation which the Saint derived from the encouragement of so holy and learned a man as F. Ibañez; greater still perhaps her satisfaction in the heart-felt sympathy now shown in her undertaking by her two old and faithful, though somewhat trying friends, Francis Salcedo and Master Daza; but worse troubles were to come. The day before the purchase of the house was to be completed, Doña Guiomar went to ask the Provincial for his promised licence for the foundation; well did F. Salazar remember the pledge he had given, nor could he in conscience and honour withdraw it; on the other hand, he was terrified at the tumult in the city, and the great discomposure of his subjects, the nuns of the Incarnation, who looked upon the attempt to found a reformed convent as a slight upon themselves. He bethought himself, therefore, of a middle course, whereby, without the shame of breaking his word, he might soothe all these perturbed spirits. He told Doña Guiomar that the endowment which she proposed to make was insufficient, and that he could not permit the foundation.

Here was a new affliction for our Saint, to which her confessor soon added a still keener trial. As soon as F. Alvarez heard of the Provincial's refusal to accept the house, he felt justified in his own unfavourable views of the project, and wrote to her with no little severity, bidding her to lay aside at once an idea which she must now see to have been simply the offspring of her own imagination, to consider the scandal she had thereby occasioned, and never again to contemplate any such foundation.

" By this refusal of the Provincial," says the Saint, " all the former objections were confirmed, namely, *that the project was the foolishness of women,* &c. ; and I had to bear all these complaints and murmurs, though up to this time the Provincial had sanctioned the work. In the meantime, I was in very bad odour in the house where I was, because I wished to establish one more strictly enclosed, they said, *I affronted them* (*by my new project*) ; *that there was nothing to hinder me from serving God as well there as in another place; that there were persons there much better than myself; that I had no love for the convent; that I should have done much better to procure revenues for that house than for any other place.* Some even said that I ought to be thrown into prison; some few there were who feebly took my part.

"I saw clearly that those who opposed me had reasons for many things they said, and sometimes I tried to explain things to them; though as I could not tell them the principal motive (which was the command of our Lord), I generally held my peace, not knowing what to say. Our Lord granted me one great grace, that all this affair of the monastery troubled not my peace, for I gave it up with as much pleasure and facility as if it had cost me nothing. But this no one could believe, not even those persons of prayer with whom I used to converse, for they thought I was still full of trouble and shame; even my confessor could hardly believe the contrary. But, as I thought I had done all that lay in my power to fulfil our Lord's command, it seemed to me I was no longer obliged to do anything further. I remained in the house, where I was quite content and at my ease, but I could never help believing that, though I neither knew how nor when, the work would certainly be accomplished."

The severe reprimand of her confessor was the only part of the present trial which disturbed the tranquillity of the Saint. She had borne the clamours of the city, and the still more trying censures of her sisters in religion, with an equanimity which edified all who witnessed it, and astonished F. Alvarez himself; but his letter troubled her greatly.

"This letter, I confess," says she, "gave me greater pain than all my other troubles put together, because

I then began to think whether I might not have been the cause of all the evil, and whether I had not committed an error whereby God might have been offended ; nay, I even began to fear whether my visions might have been illusions, and my whole course of prayer have been from the devil ; and whether, in a word, I were not then in a state of error and perdition. These thoughts so overpowered me that I fell into the most profound grief and trouble. But our Lord, who was never wanting to me in all my afflictions, now comforted and strengthened me. He told me that *I should not trouble myself; that I had served Him well, and had not offended Him in this matter.*

"In the meantime, He told me that I should do what my confessor commanded me, by keeping silence, till a fit time should come to resume the matter. After this, I felt so much contentment and consolation that the afflictions which came upon me seemed to be a mere nothing. Hereby our Lord showed me what an immense benefit it is to endure troubles and persecutions for His sake, because so much had the love of God increased in my soul, as well as other virtues, that I was amazed at it, and this is why I cannot help desiring afflictions.* In the meantime, other persons thought I was quite dejected with what had happened ; and this, indeed, would have been the case, had not our Lord been pleased to support and favour me with such extraordinary graces. It was at this time that greater impetuosities of divine love, and greater raptures than any which I had before experienced, began to befall me, though I did not mention them to any-one, nor the benefit which I derived from them."

* "Aut pati, aut mori !"—"To suffer, or to die !"—her favourite aspiration.

CHAPTER X.

1561.

WHILE S. Teresa remained thus perfectly passive in obedience to the command of her confessor, F. Peter Ibañez and Doña Guiomar d'Ulloa, who were under no such restraint, took vigorous measures for the prosecution of her design. They determined to have immediate recourse to the Holy See, whose decision would overrule all the objections of subordinate authorities. A letter was therefore written to Rome, asking permission to found the proposed convent, in the name of Doña Guiomar d'Ulloa, and of Doña Aldonza de Guzman, her mother, whose interest in the work seems to have nearly equalled her own. This appeal to Rome had been commanded, and even the minutest circumstances relating to it, marked out to the Saint by our Lord Himself, who also made known to her His will that the new foundation should be placed under the jurisdiction of the Bishop of Avila. This was a severe sacrifice to Teresa, who clung with loyal affection to the superiors of her order, hostile as they had now shown themselves to her work ; and our Blessed Lady was pleased to comfort her by a vision, in which, on the Feast of the Assumption, she appeared to her in company with S. Joseph, and told her that it pleased her well to see her so devoted to him. "Our Lady told me," adds the Saint, "that our Lord, and she herself and S. Joseph would be devoutly served in that monastery ; that though the obedience under which I should be placed might not be agreeable to my inclinations, they themselves would protect us, and that her Son had already promised to remain with us."

Three days before this vision was vouchsafed to S.

Teresa, on the Feast of S. Clare, that Saint had appeared to her radiant with glory, bidding her go on
fearlessly with the work she had in hand. "She
promised," says S. Teresa, "to assist me, and well
has she kept her promise, not only by aiding us by
the alms of one of her houses, which is near our convent, but also, which is far better, by obtaining for us
the grace to live in a poverty like her own. We no
doubt owe it to the prayers of this Blessed Saint that
our Lord is pleased, in His fatherly kindness, to provide us with all necessary things without our having
to ask them of anyone."

While Teresa was calmly waiting the issue of the
application to Rome, "the devil," she says, "began
to make known (one person talking of these things to
another) that I had had some revelation on the matter.
Upon this some came to me in great fear, to tell me I
had better look well to myself; that the days were
evil, and that perhaps men might lay things to my
charge and complain even to the inquisitors. These
fears made me laugh, for in this matter I never had
any fears, because I knew well that in all things relating to the Catholic faith, even to the least ceremony
of the Church, or for the truth of any doctrine in the
Holy Scripture, I was ready to die a thousand deaths.
I therefore desired those persons not to fear for me,
and that my soul would indeed be in a miserable
condition if anything could be found in it to make
me afraid of the inquisition; that if I thought there
were any grounds to fear, I myself would be the first
to go before the inquisitors; and that if any charge
were brought against me, our Lord would deliver me
from it, and that I should be the gainer thereby."

S. Teresa was not to be thus a gainer, for the
threatened accusation was not brought against her.
The apprehension of it, however, induced her to lay

open the state of her soul to the learned Dominican,
F. Ibañez, to her great spiritual consolation, and his
still greater spiritual benefit.

"I spoke," says she, "on this matter with the
Dominican Father, who, as I have said, was so learned
a man, that I could confidently rely upon whatever he
said. And on this occasion I told him, with all the
clearness I could, of all the visions I had received, and
of the kind of prayer I used, and of the great favours
our Lord had been pleased to show me, and I begged
him to consider all these things well, and to let me
know if they were in any way against Holy Scripture,
and give me his opinion thereon. This he did, and
so he made me very secure in my mind, and I also
thought he himself derived some advantage from this
matter; for though he was before an excellent religious, yet from that time he devoted himself more
entirely to prayer, and entered into a monastery of his
own Order, which was a place of great solitude and
silence, that he might give himself the better to recollection. There he remained about two years, and
then he was removed by obedience, much to his
sorrow. But his superiors stood in need of such
a man. I was much grieved myself when he left me,
because I wanted such a person, though I knew he
would be the gainer. While I was in trouble about
his departure, our Lord told me to be comforted, for
that he went under the direction of a good guide.
And, indeed, he returned afterwards with his soul so
much improved in spiritual matters, that he himself
told me on his return, he would not for anything in
the world have neglected making the journey. I
also might say the same thing, because as he formerly
consoled and encouraged me only by his learning, he
was now able to do the same, by the great experience he had acquired in supernatural things. Our

Lord was also pleased to bring him back at the time when His Majesty saw we stood in need of him, to assist His work concerning this monastery, which it was His will should be established."

Such was the benefit derived by F. Ibañez from his diligent examination of the spirit of Teresa. The Catholic world owes him a debt of gratitude for the obedience which he was the first to lay upon her to write her life. It might have seemed that the temporary removal of this religious from Avila would be a serious hindrance to the foundation of the reform; but God, who was to be its principal promoter, came to its aid when matters seemed most discouraging.

About the end of the year 1560, or the beginning of the year following, the Father Rector of the Jesuits' college at Avila was removed, and Father Gaspar de Salazar appointed in his place. It now appeared that the somewhat narrow and timid mode of direction, which Father Alvarez had lately adopted towards his spiritual daughter, arose rather from the perfection of his obedience, than from any deficiency either of light or of judgment. His superior disliked his conversing with women about visions and revelations, and laid such restrictions upon his method of dealing with his penitent, as proved a martyrdom to them both. "Being one day," says S. Teresa, "in great affliction because I thought my confessor did not believe me, our Lord told me not to be disquieted thereat, assuring me that all my troubles would soon be at an end. At these words I rejoiced, thinking I should soon die, and I felt a thrill of joy whenever I remembered them. But I clearly perceived afterwards, that they related to the appointment of the new Rector, of whom I have spoken, because from the time of his coming all my great trouble ceased. He was in no way opposed to the Sub-Rector, who was my confessor; but rather

I

he told him to console me, and assure me that there was no reason for me to fear; and bade him not to conduct my soul by such strait and narrow ways, and with such restrictions, but to allow the Spirit of God to work freely in me.

"Sometimes it seemed, by reason of these great impetuosities, that my soul had scarcely room to breathe. I went to visit this Rector, and my confessor commanded me to speak to him with all candour and clearness, though I felt the greatest difficulty in doing so. I no sooner entered the confessional, than I felt in my soul an indescribable consolation which I never remember to have experienced before or since. I cannot tell how it was, nor can I explain it by any kind of comparison, because it was a spiritual joy and a conviction in my soul, that the soul of this man would be able to understand me, and that his judgment and mine would agree, although (as I have said) I knew not *how* this would be. If I had spoken with him before, or if others had told me something great about him, it would not have been very surprising if I rejoiced when I heard he was to hear me. But neither of us had ever spoken to each other, nor had anyone ever given me any account of him. Since that time, however, I have clearly seen that my soul did not deceive me, for, by speaking with him, I have derived great advantage in every way, because his method of direction is very profitable to those persons whom our Lord is pleased to advance (in the road of perfection), for He makes them *run*, and not walk step by step. His method is entirely to disengage them from all creatures, and to exercise them by mortifications; and in this respect our Lord has given him very great illumination, as well as in many other things. As soon as I began to speak with him, I immediately understood his method, and saw I had met with a holy and pure soul, and that our Lord had given him a particular gift for discerning spirits. He consoled me exceedingly. Soon after I had spoken to him, our Lord began to press me to resume the business of the monastery, and bade me declare both to my confessor and to this Rector the many reasons why they were not to oppose my design : some of these reasons made them quite afraid to delay the work, for the Father Rector never doubted but that it was inspired by the Spirit of God, since he 'beheld and considered with great care and attention all the effects produced on my soul by this revelation."

Our Lord vouchsafed by a special inspiration to reassure the timid conscience of F. Alvarez on this matter. " Bid thy confessor," He said one day to Teresa, " to meditate to-morrow on this verse :—*Quam magnificata sunt opera tua, Domine ! nimis profundæ factæ sunt cogitationes tuæ.*" * O Lord ! how magnificent are Thy works ; very deep are Thy thoughts. As the father, in obedience to the Divine command, was meditating upon these words, he was enlightened to see how far the ways of God are above the reach of human reason, and to recognise His hand, which was now making use of a poor weak woman to work out His sovereign will. He lost no time in signifying to Teresa his full consent and approbation of the immediate commencement of her work.

"Yet I clearly foresaw," she says, " what trouble the undertaking would give me, because I was quite alone, and had very little power to do anything. We determined that the matter should be carried on with great secrecy, and therefore I prevailed on a sister of mine, who lived elsewhere, to buy the house with money, which our Lord found means in a wonderful way to give me for the purchase."

* Ps. xci.

I 2

This sister was Jane d'Ahumada, the youngest of the children of Alonzo de Cepeda, and especially beloved by S. Teresa, under whose care she had been educated in the convent of the Incarnation. Doña Jane was married to a gentleman named John of Ovalle and Godinez, of one of the noblest houses in Salamanca, who had served with distinction in the wars of Charles V., and was no less zealous in the service of his Heavenly Master, as he proved by leaving his home at Alva, and removing to Avila, in order to aid his holy sister in the arduous and troublesome work of her first foundation. It was of essential importance that until the arrival of the expected brief from Rome, the destination of the house, lately purchased in the name of Doña Guiomar, should be kept secret. Don John d'Ovalle and his wife therefore, at the request of S. Teresa, took up their abode at Avila, and superintended the necessary alterations, as if to prepare it for their own residence. The money furnished by Doña Guiomar proved, as often happens in such cases, insufficient for the expenses required, so that, as we learn from the Saint's narrative, she was often in great perplexity how to proceed with the building. "It would be too long to mention," says she, "how our Lord continued to provide for us. In procuring money to make the bargain and fit up the house, I endured many troubles; and some of them all alone, though my companion did what she could. But this was little, so very little that it was next to nothing; all she did was to lend her name and support to the undertaking, all the rest fell upon me, and that in so many ways, that I now wonder how I was able to endure it. Sometimes when I was thus in affliction, I said, 'O my Lord! why dost Thou command things which appear impossible? Though I am but a woman, yet, if I had liberty, something might perhaps be done; but being bound in all directions, without money, and without knowing where to get any, to pay either for the brief, or for anything else, what can I do, O Lord?' Being one day in great want, and not knowing what to do to pay the workmen, S. Joseph, my true Father and Patron, appeared to me, and told me not to fail to make the agreement, and that I should not want for money. Accordingly, I made the bargain without having any money, but afterwards our Lord provided some by such wonderful ways as amazed all who heard of it."

Amongst these "wonderful ways," in which our Saint received help from her beloved Father S. Joseph, may probably be numbered an unexpected and very considerable supply of money, sent her by her brother Laurence, then far distant in Peru, who could by no natural means have been informed of her need.

Her letter of thanks, dated December 30, 1561, is especially interesting, as showing the warmth and freshness of the sisterly affection, which had been neither dimmed by an absence of twenty years, nor swallowed up by the absorbing interests of her supernatural life and divinely inspired work. S. Teresa was assuredly one of those Saints, of whom S. Paul has been said to be the type, who have been not *unclothed, but clothed upon;* all that was tender and beautiful in their natural character being, not absorbed, but transfigured, by the rays of Divine glory which fall upon it from on high. There is nothing more saintly, and nothing more frequently disregarded by good people who are not Saints, than considerateness in little things. That S. Teresa should have cared and prayed for her brother's soul, and rejoiced to hear of its welfare, is what we should all have expected; but perhaps we should hardly have looked for the refined and graceful courtesy with which she acknowledges his bounty; the tender sympathy with which she writes of the temporal necessities of the widowed sister, who had been like a mother to her; the exulting fondness with which she notes the virtues and the happiness of the younger, who had been to her as a child, and who with her husband was now aiding in the foundation of her great work, or the loving mention of the sister-in-law and her little boy, and of the beautiful image sent by her, "which, had I received it at the time I wore gold, I should very likely have kept, for it is exceedingly pretty." No one who reads the letter from which the following passages are extracted will share the wonder of the Saint, *why people loved her so much.*

" Jesus.

" May the Holy Ghost ever dwell in your heart, and reward you for coming so quickly to our relief. I trust in God, you will gain great merit by so charitable an act, for it is certain you bestowed your charities just when they were wanted; and all those to whom you sent the money stood so much in need of it, that it has been a great consolation to me. As for a poor little nun like myself, who considers it an honour to wear a patched habit, I believe God inspired you to send me so great a sum; for what I received from John Peter d'Espinosa and Varron (such I think was the name of the other merchant) was quite enough for my necessities for a long time to come. I have spent the money in a matter, which, as I told you some time ago, I could not help undertaking for several reasons, but chiefly for this, because God had given me so many strong inspirations to begin the work. I dare not trust things of this nature to a letter; I can only tell you that learned and holy people assure me I ought not to be timid, but that I must do all I possibly can for this undertaking, namely, to found a monastery, in which there are to be thirteen religious, and no more, who will be bound to live in strict enclosure, and can therefore never go out. They will never be able to see anyone except with their veil down ; their chief duties being to devote themselves to prayer and mortification, as I have told you before at greater length. I will give you more information when Antony Moran departs. Doña Guiomar, who is also writing to you, is of great service to me. She is the widow of Francis d'Avila, of the house of Sobralejo ; I know not if you remember this family. It is nine years since her husband died ; he was a very rich man ; she now enjoys his property, besides the money she has inherited from her own family.

"Although she was left a widow at the age of twenty-five, she refused to marry again, and has given herself entirely to God. She is a very pious person. It is now more than four years since we have contracted so close a friendship, that I love her as if she were my own sister. But though she assisted me in the foundation, by giving me a good part of her income, she cannot now relieve me, as just at present she has no money at her disposal. With regard to the purchase of the house, I must do this with ready money, by the Divine assistance. I have already received (though the monastery has not yet been opened) the dowry of two young ladies. By help of this money I have secretly purchased the house, though I have not money enough to remodel it for a convent. But I have great confidence in God's assistance, knowing that it is His will that the thing should be done. I have engaged the workmen, though it may have seemed very foolish to do so.

But His Majesty took care of us all, and moved you to come to our assistance. What surprises me the more is, that I was in want of just the forty crowns which you sent. I think that S. Joseph (who is to be the patron of the house) has assisted me by your means. I am sure he will repay you. Though the monastery is very poor and small, the view from it is good, and I think we shall have room enough. We have sent to Rome for the Bulls; for though the house will be of the Order of Mount Carmel, it will be under obedience to the Bishop. I trust in our Lord, that all things will prosper for His greater glory, if we should succeed in the undertaking (as I think we certainly shall), because those who are to enter the house are chosen souls, fitted to be very great examples of humility, penance, and prayer. I beg of you to recommend the matter to God. I hope, by the help of His grace, that everything will be finished before Antony Moran goes away.

" He came here, and I had great comfort in seeing him. He seems to be a trustworthy and judicious man. He gave me every particular about you. I think that the greatest favour our Lord could bestow on me was to give me to understand by what he told me, that you were convinced of the vanity of the world, and had made a resolution to retire from it altogether, and live in repose and quiet. If you do so, I think you will be walking in the road to heaven. This is what I wanted most to know, for till then I had been rather uneasy. Glory be to Him who doth all things.

" May He give you grace to advance more and more in His service; for since the reward will be unbounded, we ought not to linger on the way, but daily advance (though it be but little every day) with

such fervour, that we may never cease from our warfare until we have gained the victory.

.   .   .   .

"My sister Mary sent me this letter yesterday to
be forwarded to you. She tells me she will write to
you again as soon as she has received the rest of the
money you sent her. The first sum came very oppor-
tunely.

"She is a very good Christian, whom the death of
her husband has left in great trouble.*

"God has given John d'Ovalle a very perfect wife.
The goodness of my sister Jane is something to
praise God for; she has the soul of an angel. I am
the worst of the family, and so degenerate that you
would hardly own me for your sister. I know not
why people love me so much. I say this in all
sincerity.

"I am now staying at the house of Doña Guiomar,
and find great comfort in being among persons who
often speak to me of you. I shall remain here till the
Provincial orders me elsewhere, and I hope he may
allow me to remain here for some time, as I should
thus be better able to manage the business which I
have mentioned.

"Now to speak of my dear sister Jane.† Though
I name her the last, she does not hold the last place
in my heart, for I assure you I pray to God for her
with as much affection as for you, and I love her as
much as yourself. All I can do for her is frequently to

* Doña Mary de Cepeda, daughter of Alonzo de Cepeda by his
first marriage, had been lately left a widow by the sudden death of
her husband, Don Martin de Guzman.

† Jane Mary de Fuentes y Guzman, the wife of Laurence de
Cepeda, a woman of great piety and virtue.

recommend her and her little boy to God. I have recommended him particularly to the holy friar, Peter of Alcantara, who promised to pray for him, and also to the Fathers of the Society of Jesus, and several others, whose prayers I hope God will hear. May His Majesty be pleased to make him better than his parents! I do not mean that you are not good, but I want him to be still better. I pray you always tell me of the love and contentment in which you both live together, for I receive great pleasure therefrom.

"I thank my sister a thousand times for the beautiful image she has given me. Had I received it at the time I wore gold, I should very likely have kept it, for it is exceedingly pretty. I beg of God to keep you both in health for many years. This wish comes at the right time, for to-morrow is the eve of the year 1562.

"I wish to tell you that some very holy persons, who know all the particulars of my undertaking, account it to be a miracle that you sent the money just when I wanted it. I hope in God that, if I should want any more, He will put it into your heart to help me, whether you wish it or not.

"Your very loving sister,

"Doña Teresa d'Ahumada."

The sudden death of Don Martin Guzman had left him no time to receive the last sacraments. "I was exceedingly troubled," says the Saint, "because he had no time to confess. I was told in prayer that my sister should die in the same way, and that therefore I should go to her and exhort her to prepare for death." This warning having been several times repeated, S. Teresa obtained permission to visit her widowed sister, to whom she gradually unfolded the revelation which she had received concerning her. The warning was piously and submissively taken, and the advice which accompanied it carefully followed. " I persuaded her," says S. Teresa, " to confess often, and above all things to take care of her soul. As she was very pious, she did so, and four or five years afterwards, having taken very great care of her conscience, she died without seeing anyone, or being able to make her confession. Happily she had been to confession only the week before. I was exceedingly glad when I heard of her death; she was a very short time in Purgatory; it was not, I think, quite eight days afterwards, when one morning, after Communion, our Lord appeared to me, and I saw Him conduct her to glory. During all those years, up to the very moment of her death, I never forgot what had been said to me, nor did my companion, who, upon the unexpected news of her death, came to me quite amazed to see how punctually our Lord's words had been fulfilled. May He be blessed for ever who takes such care of souls that they may not perish ! Amen."

During the time which S. Teresa was now spending out of the convent, for the prosecution of her work, she was called upon to endure one of those trials from the " contradiction of good men," of which S. Peter of Alcantara had forewarned her. She went one day with her sister Doña Jane to a church, when a sermon on mental prayer was preached for her especial edification, by a divine, whose zeal greatly outran his discretion and his charity. So vehement were his invectives against the Saint, whom he only just stopped short of pointing out by name, that stronger language could scarcely have been found to describe some notorious sinner in the city, or to unmask some fanatical impostor who had been practising upon the

credulity of the faithful. Teresa listened to the tirade
with undisturbed equanimity. Not so Doña Jane,
whose indignation would scarcely permit her to
remain quietly in the church, where such an indignity
had been offered to one whom she so deeply loved
and venerated.

The heat of the opposition raised by the citizens of
Avila (who had certainly, in thus warring upon women,
somewhat forgotten their chivalrous character) had
now, in a great measure, died away. The enemy
of all good betook himself to a more direct method of
attack, whereby, as is happily his wont, he overreached himself, by giving occasion for the exercise of
the Saint's heroic constancy, and for the manifestation of her extraordinary power with God.

While the workmen were busy in raising the walls
of the new building, Gonzalez d'Ovalle, a beautiful
boy of five years old, the only and darling child of
Doña Jane, was playing about among them. Suddenly, and without any apparent cause, a large
fragment of the wall was detached from the rest, and
fell upon the child, who was drawn forth lifeless from
the ruins. The bystanders, dreading to carry such
evil tidings to the mother, ran to the house of Doña
Guiomar to make the fatal accident known to Teresa.
The two friends hastened to the spot. Doña Guiomar,
that woman full of faith, who knew full well the
power of the Saint with God, took the child up in her
arms. "Sister," said she, turning to Teresa, "this
boy is dead; but God, whose power has no limit, can
easily restore him to life. See what a reward your
sister and your brother-in-law have reaped for the
pains they have been at in this building! Think
how sad and comfortless they will return to their
childless and desolate home, and ask God to give him
back to them alive!"

The Saint took the boy in her arms, just as the cries of the unhappy mother at the tidings of her child's death broke upon her ear. She held him upon her knee, and moved by an interior inspiration, she bade her sister and all those who stood around to be still; then dropping her veil and bowing her head over the lifeless child, she breathed, in the silence of her heart, an intense and prevailing prayer that his life might be restored to him again. God heard the voiceless entreaty; and infused once more into that cold form the breath of life. Gonzalez, as if just wakened from a refreshing sleep, stretched out his little hands to his aunt, and stroked her face. Teresa gave him into his mother's arms, saying: "Take your boy, alive and well, for whom you have been grieving thus bitterly." Great was the astonishment of the witnesses of the miracle, who were so many in number, that this fact is one of the most fully attested of all that were brought forward in the process of canonisation. Teresa herself could not deny it, but, when questioned by one of her friends, only smiled and was silent. Gonzalez was wont from that day forward to follow her about and play round her, after embracing and caressing her, as if in token of gratitude. As he grew to riper years, he had other and more serious thoughts of his marvellous restoration to life, and would often gently reproach his holy aunt for depriving him of the assured beatitude which would have been his lot, had she not recalled him to this life of trial, telling her that she was bound to shield him by her prayers from the danger of a worse death than that from which she had raised him. Teresa failed not to intercede continually for this precious soul, which departed from this world three years after her own death, bearing every token of a fitness to be with her in Paradise.

About a month after the miraculous resurrection of Gonzalez, Jane d'Ahumada gave birth to a second son, whom she called *Joseph*, in honour to her sister's devotion to that glorious Saint. Teresa, as she held the new-born babe in her arms, said ; " I pray God, my child, that if He sees that thou wilt one day leave His service, He will take thee even as thou art, in thine angelic innocence, to Himself."

Before the end of three weeks the child was attacked by a mortal sickness. Teresa, seeing that our Lord was about to call him to Himself, took him in her arms and gazed intently upon him. The poor mother, whose eyes were fixed upon the Saint, saw her face suddenly become bright and beautiful as that of an angel; at that moment the infant expired, and Teresa, wrapping it round, would have left the room with it, in order to prepare the mother for the blow ; but Jane, deriving supernatural strength from the thought that her child was with God, said to her sister, "Do not go; I see plainly that my little Joseph is dead." The Saint, still enraptured with the glories which she had seen, answered with a heavenly smile, " Oh ! how can we refrain from praising God when we see such a multitude of angels come to carry home the soul of one of these little children who are so like themselves ? "

So signal a miracle as the restoration of Gonzalez to life, wrought at her intercession, failed not deeply to impress the minds of men with reverence for her, who had been so long an object of distrust and suspicion. The devil had made one great mistake, and he very soon fell into another. The workmen had completed a wall, which, though strong, well-cemented, and built in accordance with all the rules of art, was found the next morning level with the ground. Great was the amazement of all concerned,

and very great the wrath of John of Ovalle, who had
so anxiously watched the building, and who had
narrowly escaped paying for it with the life of his
only child.

Attributing the accident to the carelessness of the
workmen, he was for compelling them to rebuild the
wall at their own expense; but Teresa, who better
knew at whose door lay the blame of the mischance,
said to Doña Jane: "Tell my brother not to deal
hardly with the poor men. It is no fault of theirs
that the wall has fallen down, but of the devils who
have combined together to overthrow it. Let him be
quiet, and give them money enough to rebuild it."
And she added, "We may see by the pains which the
devil takes to destroy this work that he knows it will
do him no good." The shock which overthrew this
massive wall shook for a moment the long-tried constancy of Doña Guiomar. "Surely, dear sister," she
said to her undisturbed companion, "the fall of
so strong and well-built a wall must be a token that
it is not the will of God that we should proceed with
this work." "If the wall has fallen down," answered
Teresa, quietly, "it must be built up again;" and
she immediately took measures for procuring money
to rebuild it. Doña Guiomar, at her desire, wrote to
her mother, who was then at Toro, to ask for thirty
ducats for this purpose. She wrote with very little
hope of obtaining what she asked, but was assured by
Teresa, two or three days after her letter had been
sent, that the money had been already counted out by
Doña Aldonza, and delivered to the messenger who
had been sent with the letter from Avila. On his
return it was ascertained that he had received the
required sum at the very time and place thus super-
naturally revealed to Teresa.

CHAPTER XI.

1561, 1562.

NOTWITHSTANDING all the prudent precautions which had been taken for its concealment, the real destination of John of Ovalle's supposed residence had become known to so many, that S. Teresa was in continual fear of a mandate from the Provincial to stop all further proceedings before there should be time for the expected permission to arrive from Rome. It may be imagined with what anxiety she watched the daily progress of the work, and how reluctantly she removed from the spot in obedience to an order of F. Angelo Salazar, the Provincial, which she received on Christmas Day, 1561, bidding her to repair at once to Toledo, to give consolation to one in deep affliction, who had earnestly entreated this favour of the Provincial of the Carmes. Louisa de la Cerda, sister of the Duke of Medina Cœli, had been just then left a widow, by the death of her husband, Don Arias Pardo, one of the greatest nobles of Castille. The poor lady's health was sinking under the extremity of her sorrow. She had heard of the holy nun of Avila, and knew that she was at times permitted to leave her convent for the help and consolation of those who needed her aid. She therefore assailed the Provincial with such repeated and passionate entreaties as he was unable to withstand, and the result was an obedience to the Saint to undertake the office of charity required. Great was the consternation of all concerned in the new foundation at the prospect of her absence at so critical a time. They would fain have persuaded her to address a humble remonstrance to F. Salazar, and meanwhile to remain where she was till she could hear from him again. The obedience was most painful to her, not only because it would remove her from the work which she was so anxiously superintending, but because it sent her into the midst of the world, and amid the splendours of a court, for the princely magnates of Spain, such as those of the house of Medina Cœli, kept little less than regal state. It sorely wounded her humility too, that she should have been so spoken of abroad as to induce people to send for her to heal their sorrows. But Teresa had but one will to consult, and heeding neither the remonstrances of her friends, nor the reluctance of her own heart, she went straight to our Lord and asked counsel of Him. "It gave me much trouble," she says, "to see that they were resolved to take me away, as if they saw some good in me, for knowing myself how wicked I was, I could not endure the journey; and so recommending myself earnestly to God, I remained during the greater part of the time of Matins in a rapture. Our Lord then told me that I must not fail to undertake the journey, and that I was not to listen to the opinion of others, for few would think they could advise me to go without rashness; but, that however painful the journey might be to me, He would be greatly served thereby; and that it would also be proper to absent myself from the monastery till the brief should arrive, because the devil had devised a great plot when the Provincial should come, but that I must be afraid of nothing, for He would assist me in the business. These words strengthened and comforted me exceedingly, and I mentioned all to the Rector, who told me that I must go by all means.

"But others said I ought not to go, and that it was only a stratagem of the devil, in order that some evil might happen to me, and that my best plan would be to write to the Provincial. But I obeyed the Rector, and considering also what had happened in prayer, I began my journey without fear, but yet not without extreme confusion at the thought of their sending thus for me, and finding how much they were deceived, it made me importune our Lord the more not to forsake me. But I was comforted to know that in the place whither I was going, there was a college belonging to the Society of Jesus, and by obedience to all their commands, I thought I should enjoy some security."

S. Teresa began her journey to Toledo on January 1, 1562, accompanied by another religious, and under the escort of her brother-in-law, John of Ovalle. Great was the joy occasioned by her arrival.

" When I arrived there," she tells us, " our Lord was pleased to give the lady so much comfort, that an improvement in her health immediately began to be visible, for she became daily better and better. This was the more remarkable, because her grief had reduced her to a most deplorable state. But our Lord no doubt granted her ease on account of the many prayers which certain holy persons whom I knew had offered in her behalf. She was full of the fear of God, and so good that her deep piety supplied for what was wanting in me. She conceived a great affection for me, and in return for her goodness I conceived the same for her; but still all was a cross to me, for the attention which I received was a great torment to me, and caused me to fear exceedingly.

" I was obliged to watch continually over my soul, for fear I should lose sight of it for a moment, and our Lord also was not unmindful of me; for while I was there He bestowed on me exceeding great favours; and these gave me such liberty of soul, as made me despise all the esteem in which I was held there, and the more honour I received the more I despised it, so that I failed not to converse with those great ladies with as much liberty as if I had been their equal, though they were of such exalted birth, that I might, without any dishonour to myself, have been their servant. I derived great advantage from all this, and so I told this lady. I saw that she was a woman subject to weakness and passions like myself, and that she had little reason to value her dignity and power, which, in proportion to its greatness, brings with it so much the more trouble and care. For so careful are these great people to live in a manner conformable to their rank, that they cannot rest a moment in peace; for they eat out of the proper time, and out of order, because everything must be done in accordance to their station, and not with regard to their health and constitution; and sometimes even they must eat such things as are more agreeable to their greatness than to their taste; and thus I abhorred the idea of being a great lady : may God deliver me from such a dangerous state. There are few, indeed, more humble and affable than she of whom I am speaking, though she is one of the principal ladies in the kingdom ; but still I feel great compassion for her, to see how she sometimes acts, not in conformity with her own inclinations, but to comply with the rules of her state. This high station is indeed a slavery; and one of the greatest lies which the world tells, is to call such persons as these lords and ladies. To me they seem to be nothing more than slaves a thousand times over. Our Lord was pleased, while I remained in this lady's house, that her servants should greatly improve in serving His Majesty, though I was not free from some troubles, and some persons even envied me on account of the great affection which she bore me. They

might, perhaps, fancy that I had some personal interest in what I did; and so our Lord permitted
them to give me some little trials, both in this and
other ways, in order to prevent me from being in-
toxicated by the kindness and attention that were
paid me on the other side. But from all these
troubles He was pleased to deliver me, to the great
benefit of my soul."

Marvellous indeed was the change wrought on the
household of Doña Louisa by the presence of the
Saint; frequent confession and communion and liberal
almsgiving became the practice of the house; great
was the reverence borne by its inmates to the holy
guest who lived among them in such humility and
simplicity; little suspecting that, with a pardonable
curiosity, they contrived to watch her in her retirement, and often saw her in ecstasy, radiant and
glorious as an angel. The affection of Doña Louisa
for her who had been sent to heal her broken heart
and shield her from temptations to despair, was
grateful and enduring, and she proved her gratitude
to both her Divine and human consolers, by the
foundation, six years afterwards, of a Carmelite convent on her own estates at Malagon. But this dreaded
visit to Toledo won a more saintly soul for Heaven,
and gave to Teresa a child who was one day to be (in
her own words) the *dearest friend of her heart*, and one
of the chief pillars of her reform; who, of all her
daughters, was to bear the heaviest cross, and drink
deepest of the chalice of suffering and humiliation
long after her own entrance into bliss.

Amongst all the letters of S. Teresa to her spiritual
daughters, there are none more full of interest and
edification, none in which her whole heart and soul
are poured forth with a freedom betokening such full
sympathy with her correspondent, as those to Mary

of S. Joseph, first prioress of the convent at Seville, whose long life of heroic conflict in the establishment of the reform was crowned by a saintly death, followed by a succession of miracles. All this array of graces and glories was little dreamt of, when S. Teresa entered the palace of Doña Louisa, by the young kinswoman who eagerly welcomed her as the bringer of peace and consolation to the broken-hearted widow. Mary of Salazar was then about two-and-twenty, richly endowed, both in mind and person, with all that this world could offer at her command. But she had learned a lesson from the stroke which had desolated her princely house. It had taught her not to set her heart upon earth, and Teresa came to teach her to fix it upon Heaven. By her advice, Mary de Salazar made a general confession to one of the fathers of the Society of Jesus, under whose direction she devoted herself to the exercises of the interior life, in preparation for the day when she should be free to consecrate herself to God in religion. Her patience and constancy were, however, to be tested by a probation of six years, at the end of which time she received the habit of Mount Carmel from the hand of S. Teresa in the new convent founded by Doña Louisa at Malagon.

During her six months' sojourn at Toledo, Teresa renewed her long-suspended intercourse with the holy Dominican, Father Baron, her father's confessor, under whose direction, nearly twenty years before, she had resumed the practice of mental prayer, and entered once more upon the narrow way of perfection. As she was one day hearing mass in the Dominican church, which was close to Doña Louisa's house, she saw and recognised this religious, and felt immediately inspired with a great desire to know the state of his soul before God, and the degree of perfection to which, in the long years which had elapsed since their last

meeting, it had attained. She resisted this interior
impulse for some time as a movement of idle curiosity;
but finding it too strong to be overcome, and believing it to be a Divine inspiration, she made herself
known to F. Baron, and, at his urgent desire, unfolded
to him in the confessional the marvellous history of
her own spiritual life since they had parted at what
seemed to have been its turning point. The priest
begged her to recommend him to God; but there was
little need of such a request, for it was Teresa's wont,
whenever she saw a soul which seemed capable of
doing great things for God, to beseech Him fervently
that He would be pleased to enable it to fulfil its vocation. Perceiving now in the soul of this religious
far greater powers and capabilities for the service of
God than she had observed him to possess in times
past, she set herself earnestly to implore her Lord,
that, good as he now was, He would be pleased to
make him still better. Having persevered for several
hours together in this petition, she fell into a rapture,
in which she thus spoke in the freedom of her love:
" O Lord, do not refuse me this favour; consider that
this good man is worthy to be numbered among our
friends." " O! how great," she continues in the fervour of her affection, " is the goodness and kindness
of our God. He does not consider so much our words
as the desires and affections with which they are
spoken, or how could He have allowed such a miserable creature as I am to speak to Him with so much
boldness? May He be blessed for ever and ever!"
This bold and fervent entreaty for the soul of another
was followed by a thrill of exceeding terror regarding
her own. " There came upon me that night a great
affliction—a doubt whether or not I was in favour
with God—and I desired not so much to know this,
as to die, rather than continue in such a life, wherein

I could not be sure whether I was dead or no, for I could not endure a more cruel death than to think I had offended God. Being thus transported with love, and shedding a torrent of tears, I entreated His Majesty not to permit it ; and then I came to understand that I was in a state of grace, because such a love for God and such favours from His Majesty were not compatible with a state of mortal sin."

Teresa felt also assured that her prayer for F. Baron was granted. "Our Lord," she says, "told me to say certain words to him. But this command troubled me much, because I knew not how to utter them ; for to carry a message to a third person in this way always greatly afflicts me, especially when I know not how it will be received, or whether I shall not be laughed at for my pains. At last, on account of the great confusion I was in, I wrote down the words and delivered them to him." So wonderful was the change effected in the soul of this holy man by the Divine communications vouchsafed to him through the medium of our Saint, that she was filled with gratitude and amazement. She thus writes, about a year after the occurrence of these events : " Whenever this holy man speaks to me it lifts me almost out of myself ; for had I not seen it with my own eyes, I should have doubted whether, in so short time, so many favours could have been bestowed upon a creature ; and these keep him so occupied with God, that already he seems not to live for anything in this life. May His Majesty take him by the hand, for if he should continue to advance in this way (as I trust in our Lord he will), his soul being so deeply rooted in the knowledge of himself, he will become one of the most eminent of God's servants and will do great good to many souls, on account of the deep experience he has acquired, in a short time, of spiritual things."

It was during her residence in the splendid palace of the Dukes of Medina Cœli, that S. Teresa first fully realized the principle which was to form so prominent a feature of her reform, and which led to the foundation of its houses in absolute poverty. Her original idea had been to endow the proposed Convent of S. Joseph with such a moderate provision as should relieve its inmates from anxiety regarding the necessaries of life. Gradually, however, the longing arose in her soul for a poverty which should more perfectly conform her to the image of our Lord. In a manifestation of the interior dispositions of her soul, addressed to one of her confessors, about a year later than that sent to S. Peter of Alcantara, she depicts just such a mode of life as she was eventually enabled to realize.

" With regard to poverty, God has been very gracious to me. He has not only made me willing to depend upon alms for the necessaries of life, but He has given me an ardent desire to live in some house entirely dependent on charity. It seems to me that I cannot so perfectly follow the counsels of Jesus Christ, or so fully observe my vow of poverty, in a house where I am assured that I shall want neither food nor clothing, as in one in which, being without endowment, I may come to be in want of something. The blessings of perfect poverty are to my mind so great, that I am most anxious not to lose them. My faith in the infallible fulfilment of the words of Jesus Christ is so vivid that I cannot believe that He will ever forsake those who serve Him faithfully."

Teresa, when she wrote this, was not aware that the ideal of perfect poverty, after which she yearned, was contained in the primitive rule of Mount Carmel, which she was destined to restore. She was enlightened upon this point during her stay at Toledo by a great servant of God, Mother Mary of Jesus, who had

received a command from our Lord, in the same year
and month as herself, to erect a reformed house of the
Order. She was now returning from Rome, whither
she had travelled barefoot to obtain the brief for her
foundation, and she remained for a fortnight at Toledo
to confer with S. Teresa.

"She showed me," says the Saint, "the despatches
which she brought from Rome; and during the fortnight that we lived together, we arranged the plans
according to which we should establish our monasteries. Till I had consulted with her, I never knew
that our rule, before it was mitigated, forbade our
having property. I was unwilling to found the house
without revenue, because I wished to avoid harassing
ourselves with the care of providing what was necessary for our support, not reflecting on the many cares
which property brings along with it. But as our
Lord had taught this blessed woman, she knew well,
though unable to read, that of which I, with all my
study of our constitutions, was yet ignorant. When
she told me this I was glad, though I was afraid the
superiors would not give their consent, but that they
would say, I attempted extravagant things, and that I
should not undertake what might make others suffer
on my account. Had it concerned myself only, I
should not have hesitated a moment to found the
house in poverty; nay, I felt great pleasure in thinking
that I was to observe the counsels of Christ our Lord,
because His Majesty had already given me strong
desires exactly to follow His counsels.

"Thus, for my own part, I made no doubt but that
it was for the best, for long before I had wished, had
it been suitable to my state, to go begging for the
love of God, and to possess nothing, neither house
nor anything else. But I was afraid that if our Lord
did not give the same desires to others, they might,

perhaps, be discontented ; and also I was afraid lest it might be a cause of distractions, for I saw some poor monasteries not very recollected, not considering that their poverty came from want of recollection, and not their want of recollection from their poverty. Solicitude makes not religious the richer, and God is never wanting to those who truly serve Him. In a word, my faith was weak, but not so that of this servant of God. Though I asked the opinion of many on this matter, yet hardly any one was for this project, neither confessors, nor the learned theologians whom I consulted.

" They gave so many reasons against it, that I knew not what to do; for, when I understood that the rule enjoined it, and that it tended to promote greater perfection, I could not be persuaded to admit revenues. And though I sometimes found myself convinced by their reasons, yet, when I afterwards returned to my prayers, and beheld Christ so very poor and naked, I could not have the patience to be rich; and so I begged of our Lord, with tears, that He would so order things that I might find myself poor as He was. I discovered so many inconveniences in having revenues, and I saw that so many troubles and distractions would arise from them, that I did nothing but dispute with the learned."

In this perplexity the Saint applied once more to F. Ibañez, who at first strongly opposed her design.

" He sent me," she says, " in writing, two sheets of objections and theological reasons against the project, assuring me that he had deeply studied the matter. I answered that I would not make use of theology to obtain a dispensation from following my vocation, and observing my vow of poverty, and the counsels of our Saviour, in all perfection ; nor did I

wish that he would assist me in this point with his
learning. If I met with any one who took my part, or
was of the same mind as myself, I rejoiced greatly.
The lady with whom I was living assisted me in this
matter very much. Some told me at first they liked
the project very well ; but, considering the matter
afterwards more carefully, they found so many difficulties in it, that they laboured all they could to
dissuade me from it. My answer was, that since
they had changed their mind so suddenly, I was
resolved to follow the opinion which they gave me
first."

Our Lord was pleased to send a faithful counsellor
to Teresa in this great perplexity in the person of
S. Peter of Alcantara, perhaps, next to his great
father S. Francis, the most perfect follower of the
poverty of Jesus whom the world has ever seen.
Doña Louisa had an earnest desire to see the aged
Saint, and, at the request of S. Teresa, he consented
to visit her at this time ; our Lord, no doubt, so disposing events for the assistance of His servant in her
present difficulty, as well as for the consolation of her
friend.

" About this time it happened," writes the Saint,
"that as this lady had never seen the holy man, Peter
of Alcantara, our Lord was pleased, through my entreaties, to bring him to her house. And, as he was
a true lover of poverty, having observed it for many
years, he knew well what riches were to be found
therein, and accordingly he was of great assistance to
me, and he commanded me, on no account, to desist
from my design. Thus, with his opinion and approbation, being one whose judgment on account of his
long experience was worth far more than that of others,
I resolved to proceed no further in asking any other
opinion."

To the approbation of this great servant of God, our Lord was pleased to add the assurance of His own.

"Being one day in prayer," says S. Teresa, "earnestly recommending this matter to God, our Lord said to me, 'By no means neglect to found the house in poverty, for this is the will of My Father and Mine ; I will assist thee.' These words were said in a rapture, and such was their effect, that I could not possibly doubt of their coming from God. Another time He told me that with revenues would come confusion, with several other things in praise of poverty, assuring me that *whoever should serve Him should not want necessaries ;* and of this want (as I said), for my part, I was never afraid. Our Lord also changed the mind of the Dominican, who had formerly written to me against founding the house without revenue. I was now exceedingly delighted at having heard this from our Lord, and having had the opinions of other persons ; and hence by resolving to live upon alms, I thought I already enjoyed all the wealth in the world."

For some reason which does not appear, probably for the satisfaction of some of her timorous friends, S. Teresa thought it advisable to depart in one instance from her determination to ask no further advice upon the question of endowments after having received the decided opinion of S. Peter of Alcantara. She wrote to a pious priest at Avila named Gonzalez d'Aranda, asking him to obtain for her the opinions of various learned men upon the subject. Gonzalez showed the letter to S. Peter of Alcantara, who was then at Avila, and who wrote as follows to Teresa :—

"May the Holy Spirit fill your heart !

"Señor Gonzalez d'Aranda has shown me a letter from you, and I am much surprised that you should ask the opinion of learned men concerning matters which do not belong to their province. If some case of conscience or question of casuistry were at issue, you would do well to consult jurists or theologians, but where the question relates to the life of perfection, those only should be consulted who practise it, and for this reason, that men generally measure their conscience and their good feelings by the standard of their good works. Neither is it lawful to ask the opinion of others as to whether the Evangelical Counsels are to be followed or not, for this were a kind of infidelity. The counsel of God cannot fail to be good, nor is it difficult to follow, except to the unfaithful, and to those who trust but little to God, and are guided only by the dictates of human prudence, forasmuch as He who gave the counsel, can and will give the power to observe it. If you are willing to follow the counsel of highest perfection given by Jesus Christ, follow it with good courage, for it is not given to men more than to women, and you shall have good success, as all those have had who have followed it faithfully. But if you choose to depend upon the counsel of learned men, who are devoid of the spirit of perfection, you may then obtain abundant revenues, and you will see what good the learned men and the revenues will do you, and whether you would not have done better to give them all up and keep to the counsel of Christ. Moreover, if we daily see imperfections in monasteries of poor nuns, it is because they are poor against their will, not in order to follow the counsel of Christ, but because they cannot help it. I do not simply praise *poverty*, but only that poverty which is patiently endured for the love of Christ our Lord, and still more that which, for this same love, is not only embraced, but desired and sought after ; for were I to feel or believe otherwise I should not hold myself to be secure in the faith. In this as in all other things, I believe Christ our Lord, and hold most firmly that His counsels, being the counsels of God, are the best ; and I believe that though they do not oblige under sin, they do render the man more perfect who follows them than the man who does not oblige himself to do so. I hold that if they do not oblige, they at least make him more perfect, more holy, and more pleasing to God. I account those to be blessed according to the words of our Lord, who are poor in spirit, that is, who practise voluntary poverty, and I have proved it well myself, although I trust more to the words of God than to my own experience. I hold that all those who, by the grace of God, live in willing poverty, lead a blessed and happy life, such a life as is led by those who love, hope, and trust in God. May His Divine Majesty enlighten you to understand this truth, and to carry it into execution ! Do not attend to those who tell you the contrary, for they thus speak either from want of light, or from want of faith, or because they have never tasted how sweet the Lord is to those who love and fear Him, and who renounce for His love all un-necessary things ; they thus speak because they love not to bear the cross of Christ, and believe not in the glory which flows from it. May the Lord infuse such light into your heart, that you may neither doubt nor waver in the knowledge of this most certain truth ! Ask advice only of those who follow the counsels of Christ, because, although others shall be saved, if they observe those things which are of obligation, men have seldom light to judge of any works higher than those which they practise themselves ; and even sup-posing their counsel to be good, that of Christ our Lord is infinitely better ; for He knows well the meaning of His own counsels, He will help us to fulfil them, and will eternally reward those who trust not in earthly things, but in Him alone.

" Your humble chaplain,

" B. PETER OF ALCANTARA.

" Avila, 14th of April, 1562."

During her stay at Toledo, S. Teresa completed the first narrative of her life, which she had begun at the desire of F. Ibañez.

The time was now approaching for her return to Avila. After an absence of some months, she received a letter from the F. Provincial, requiring her to return thither, in order to be present at the election of the prioress, which was soon to take place, leaving her free in the mean time either to return home at once, or to remain a little longer with her friend. The mention of the election threw the Saint into great uneasiness. She immediately guessed the motive of her Superior in fixing that period for her return. " I was informed," she says, " that many intended to give me this office (of prioress), the mere thought of which so afflicted me, that I resolved to endure any torment for God's sake with joy, but that no one should prevail on me to accept this dignity; for, in addition to the trouble, which was great, the nuns being very numerous, together with other motives, I never loved to be in office, but always refused it, thinking it would be very dangerous to my conscience, so that I thanked God I was not there. I wrote to my friends, begging them not to vote for me. Being very much pleased to be out of the way of this disturbance, our Lord said to me, ' Do not neglect, on any account, to go; and since thou desirest a cross, there is a good heavy one prepared for thee; do not refuse it, for I will support thee; go immediately.' These words afflicted me extremely, and I did nothing but weep, because I thought the *cross* was the office of prioress; and this I could not persuade myself would be good for my soul in any way, so I knew not how to resign myself to it. I mentioned the matter to my confessor, who commanded me to depart immediately, for that this was clearly the way of greater perfection; but because the heat of the weather was then excessive, he allowed me to remain a few days longer, lest the journey might injure me, for it was sufficient if I arrived in time for the election. But our Lord having ordered things otherwise, I wished to obey His command instantly, for I was so extremely disturbed in my mind, that I could not pray, and I thought I was wanting in obedience to our Lord's commands: and that being treated there kindly, and made much of, I was unwilling to go away and expose myself to suffering. It seemed to me that all I gave to God was but words; and I asked myself, since I could please our Lord better by returning immediately, why did I delay? Were I to die on the way, let me die. To this was added a heaviness of soul, and such weariness of prayer, that life was a burden to me. I therefore begged of the lady to allow me to depart, for my confessor seeing me in this state, had already told me to go, God having moved him as He had moved me. She felt my intended departure so much, that this proved another affliction to me, for she said it had cost her much trouble and many importunate requests to prevail on the Provincial to allow me to come here. I considered it very extraordinary that she consented, on account of the great grief she felt; but as she feared God, and as I told her my departure would tend greatly to the Divine honour, besides giving her many other reasons, and holding out some hopes that she would see me again, she consented with much difficulty. As for myself, I now felt no sorrow at all about my departure, because when I understand that anything tends to promote greater perfection, and to give greater glory to God, I am contented; and the joy I found in pleasing Him, took away the grief I felt in leaving this lady (who I perceived regretted my departure exceedingly), and in leaving others also, and especially my confessor, from whose direction I derived great benefit. But the greater were the consolations which I gave up for God, the greater was my joy in losing them. I could not understand these two contrary sentiments of joy and sorrow, and of gladness springing out of grief. All my trouble had fled; I was serene and joyful, and able, without effort, to spend many hours together in prayer, and yet I saw that I was about to cast myself into a fire, our Lord having already signified this to me, by telling me that I was to endure a heavy cross (though I never thought it would prove so heavy as afterwards I found it); still, in spite of all these things, I departed cheerfully, and was even impatient to begin the battle immediately in which it was our Lord's pleasure that I should engage, and for which His Majesty gave such strength to my weakness."

Teresa left Toledo with a light and resolute heart, ready most cheerfully to suffer whatever our Lord should be pleased to send her; and not many days after her arrival at Avila, it was made clear to her why He had so urgently pressed her return at this time. She reached home about the middle of July. On the very evening of her return, the brief for the foundation arrived from Rome. It was addressed to the two noble ladies, Aldonza de Guzman and Guiomar d'Ulloa, her daughter, in whose names it had been asked, and they being both absent from Avila at the time, it happened, by the disposition of Divine Providence,

L

that the person most deeply interested in the matter should be there to receive it; so that both the Saint and all who knew the circumstances of the case were astonished to see how necessary her return at that particular moment was to the establishment of her work.

Another favourable circumstance was the presence of S. Peter of Alcantara, who was then staying at the house of Don F. Salcedo, and by whose persuasions the Bishop of Avila was induced to accept the foundation.

Before applying to that prelate, Teresa made one more attempt to obtain the sanction of the Superiors of her Order. Concealing the fact of her having obtained a brief from Rome, she once more besought F. Angelo de Salazar to receive the proposed foundation. The Provincial might probably (now that the storm was laid, in fear of which he had withdrawn his previous consent) have yielded to her repeated solicitation, but a new feature had been introduced into the plan, which drew from him a peremptory refusal; the idea of founding a house in absolute poverty he would not tolerate for a moment. The holy foundress, and all concerned in the work, gave thanks to Him who had commanded them to have recourse to the Holy See, without whose concurrence, it was plain, they would have been powerless to effect anything.

Though the Provincial refused his assistance or sanction to the work, he aided it unconsciously and indirectly, by the permission which he gave to S. Teresa to remain for a while out of her convent, in order to attend her brother-in-law, John of Ovalle, in a severe illness with which he was attacked at this time. And here, again, we see the hand of God, sweetly and mightily ordering all things for the good of His Church and the benefit of His elect. John of Ovalle having occasion to return to his house at Avila, whither his wife had gone about the middle of June, went first to Toledo to take leave of S. Teresa. As he passed through Avila on his return, he was struck down by a severe attack of fever, and laid up in the house which he had so long been preparing for her use. He lay thus for the space of a fortnight, and on the return of the Saint to Avila, he asked and obtained the permission of the Provincial that she should tend him in the absence of his wife. The illness lasted just so long (and no longer) as the necessities of the new foundation required. Ovalle himself saw the hand of God in his indisposition, and said to his sister when matters began to look brighter, " Señora, there will be no need for me to be ill much longer." And accordingly, as soon as the matter was concluded, the invalid was restored to health.

In the mean time, S. Teresa was secretly arranging the business of the foundation with S. Peter of Alcantara, who wrote, and at last went himself to the Bishop of Avila, to induce him to receive the proposed convent under his jurisdiction.

Alvarez de Mendoza, Bishop of Avila, was a good man, and in after years a most devoted friend of S. Teresa ; he also proved himself a faithful protector of her reform. She thus writes of him after the foundation of S. Joseph's at Avila :—" What has happened since has shown me of what importance it has been to us to place ourselves under obedience to the Bishop, Don Alvarez de Mendoza. But I did not know him then, nor what a superior we should find him to be. It has pleased our Lord, not only that he should be full of goodness towards us, but that he should possess such qualities as have enabled him to carry our little vessel through the tempests of which I have had

to speak, and to bring it to its present condition."
The white marble tomb which faces the high altar in
the Convent Chapel of S. Joseph, covers the mortal
remains of Alvarez de Mendoza, who chose to be
buried there rather than in his own cathedral, in the
hope, which was not destined to be realized, of thus
resting near the Saint.

At the time, however, of which we now speak, the
Bishop of Avila viewed with no greater favour or
confidence than the Provincial of the Carmes the proposal of so great a novelty as the foundation of a
convent to be totally dependent upon alms. He
yielded at last to the arguments of S. Peter of Alcantara, supported as they were by the evidence of his
experience and the weight of his sanctity ; and, after
an interview with S. Teresa herself, was so completely reassured by her consummate prudence and
manifest illumination that he not only accepted the
foundation, but became the beneficent protector as well
as the ecclesiastical superior of the infant community.

Peter of Alcantara, having thus removed the last
obstacle to the beginning of so glorious a work,
departed from Avila, and soon afterwards passed to
his eternal reward, to aid it still more effectually by
his prayers. "It seems," says S. Teresa, "that our
Lord preserved him till he had finished this business, for he had been ill for a long time (I think for
more than two years), and soon after it was concluded
our Lord took him to Himself."

There was only one thing now needed, and this
was to give the house, which had been so long in
course of preparation, the exterior form and order of
a convent. It was very small ; so small that the
Saint had at one time a great desire to purchase
another adjacent to it to serve as a chapel, but our
Lord reproved her for this over solicitude. One day,

after Communion, He thus spoke to her: "I have already, told you to enter as best you can;" adding, as if in astonishment, "Oh! the covetousness of mankind! why are you afraid of wanting a little earth? How often did I sleep in the open air, not knowing where to lay my head!"

In this little house, fit cradle of the new reform, a small but very neat chapel was prepared, where the religious might hear Mass behind a strong double wooden grate. A narrow corridor led from the nuns' apartments to the chapel, and over the doors at either end was placed an image of our Blessed Lady and of S. Joseph, in accordance with the promise of our Lord that they should be special guardians of this new *Paradise of His delights.* A little bell, of no more than three pounds weight, was hung in a hollow of the wall to summon the community to mass and office. This poor little bell was removed in 1634 to the Convent of the Carmelite Friars at Pastrana, by command of the Superior General of the discalced Carmelites in Spain, in order that the general Chapters, which were usually held at that monastery, might be called together by the bell of their sainted foundress, and so be continually reminded of the sublime poverty which she had left them for an inheritance. The simplicity and poverty of the dwelling of the nuns, their cells, furniture, habits, and food exceeded, if possible, that of their chapel. It would need a heart full of love as Teresa's in any adequate degree to enter into her joy when she first knelt to adore our Lord, present on the poor altar which He had chosen for His dwelling-place, and presented to Him the four poor orphan girls who were to be the first fruits of the renewed glories of Carmel. No pen but her own must attempt to trace the emotions of that long-looked-for day.

"Everything being now prepared, our Lord was pleased that, on the feast of St. Bartholomew, some ladies should take the habit, and the most Blessed Sacrament was then placed in our Church; and thus with full license and authority this monastery of our most glorious Father S. Joseph was established in the year 1562. I was present to give the habit to the novices, together with two other nuns from the monastery of the Incarnation. I had done nothing without the advice of learned men, lest in any point I should offend against obedience. For these persons, seeing that, on many grounds, the monastery tended to the reputation and advantage of the whole Order, told me that I might proceed in the business, even without the knowledge of my superiors. Had they seen the slightest imperfection in thus acting, I would have given up not this only, but a thousand monasteries; this is very certain. For though I was desirous to separate myself entirely from the world, and to follow my profession and vocation with the greatest perfection, and in the strictest enclosure, yet I submitted my desire entirely to the good pleasure of God; and if I had seen that it would tend more to His honour to abandon all this, I would have done it with tranquillity and cheerfulness, as I had already done once before. I seemed now to enjoy a foretaste of heavenly glory; to see the most Holy Sacrament on the Altar, and shelter given to four poor orphans (for they were admitted without dowry), who were great servants of God; for it had been intended from the beginning that such persons should be first received, as their example might prove a firm foundation to the new building, and enable us to attain our object of leading a life of great perfection and prayer. I saw at last the accomplishment of a work which would, I was confident, contribute to the glory of our Lord and to the honour of the habit of His glorious Mother, for this was my sole desire. Besides, it gave me great consolation to behold the fulfilment of that which our Lord had so strictly commanded me to effect, and to see the first church opened in this place, under the invocation of my glorious Father S. Joseph. Not that I seemed to have done anything in this matter myself, for I never had, nor have I now, any such thought, because I ever knew it was our Lord who did everything; and what little I may have done towards it was attended with so many imperfections, that I find I rather deserve to be blamed than to be praised. But I was even overwhelmed with joy to see that His Majesty had made use of me, though so very wicked, to be the instrument of so noble a work; and I was, as it were, carried out of myself and absorbed in profound prayer."

There was one circumstance connected with the ceremonial of this happy day which must have given especial consolation to the heart of S. Teresa, so long wearied by *the contradiction of good men.* The necessary faculties for all the solemnities were granted by the Bishop (probably designedly) to Master Gaspar Daza. It was his hand, rather than that of Balthasar Alvarez, or Gaspar Salazar, or Peter Ibañez, or S. Peter of Alcantara, which was to place the Lord of Glory on His lowly throne, and give the habit of His Blessed Mother to the first four daughters of Teresa. It must have been a refreshing sight, a glimpse of that far country where it has been said *Christians shall never misunderstand one another;* and we can forgive the good priest his long-continued and vexatious opposition to the Saint, in consideration of the magnanimous humility wherewith he that day testified in the face of the city, of which he had been so long deservedly the oracle, that he had made a great mistake.

The habit given by S. Teresa to her daughters was of rough serge; a veil of coarse unbleached linen covered their head, and their feet were bare. Two religious of the convent of the Incarnation, Agnes and Anne of Tapia, cousins-german of S. Teresa, were present at the ceremony, as were also Gonzalez of Aranda; the holy Priest, Julian of Avila, brother to one of the novices; Francis of Salcedo, with John of Ovalle, and Jane of Ahumada, who had toiled and suffered so generously in the preparation for the work now thus happily begun. Guiomar d'Ulloa, whose absence had been judged necessary at this time, was in spirit by the side of her friend, and S. Peter of Alcantara, Peter Ibañez and Balthasar Alvarez, representing the three orders of S. Francis, S. Dominic, and S. Ignatius, offered the Holy Sacrifice in thanksgiving at their respective altars for the blessed work begun that day.

Of the four maidens chosen by S. Teresa as the first pillars of her reform, the first was Antonia of Enao, a cousin of her own, and the spiritual daughter of S. Peter of Alcantara, whose blessing and approval S. Teresa accounted to be the wealthiest dowry which her first novice could bring with her. She bore in religion the name of Antonia of the Holy Ghost, and was remarkable for her exceeding purity and child-like simplicity. S. Teresa was wont to say of her that the devil could do nothing with Antonia, because of her obedience to her spiritual directors. The second was a poor girl, named Mary de la Paz, who had been adopted by Doña Guiomar d'Ulloa, and placed by her under the spiritual direction of her own confessor, F. Balthasar Alvarez. S. Teresa gave her the name of Mary of the Cross, and bore her an especial affection on account of her perfection in obedience. The habitual ejaculation of this holy child of God was *Tibi soli peccavi*. The third retained in religion the name which her parents had given her in baptism— Ursula of the Saints ; for no holier name, in the judgment of S. Teresa, could be found for her.

Ursula had lived much in the world and loved its vanities, but happily had fallen under the guidance of Gaspar Daza, who disentangled her from its snares and taught her to fix all the affections of her strong and generous heart on God alone. She died in the Convent of S. Joseph ; and S. Teresa, being then at Alva, saw her at the moment of her death ascend in a glorified form to Heaven. The name of the fourth was, in the world, Mary of Avila, in the cloister, Mary of S. Joseph. F. Ribera in his life of S. Teresa records that she was still living when he wrote, in the convent at Avila, *in great sanctity and edification*.

S. Teresa at this time altogether laid aside the use of her family name, by which she had hitherto usually signed her letters, for that of *Teresa of Jesus*. She is said to have been the first to extend the pious practice of thus exchanging the secular for a religious name to a whole Order or Congregation. It had been frequently adopted by individuals, but she seems to have set the example of a custom, now almost universally adopted in the religious Orders and Congregations of the Church. The contrary practice previously in use sounds strangely in our ears, when, in the stately Castilian fashion, so great a lover of simplicity as S. Peter of Alcantara addresses a letter of spiritual direction to a Carmelite nun under the high-sounding title of *The very magnificent and most religious lady Doña Teresa d'Ahumada*. At the same time she exchanged the seal bearing the device of a skull which she was accustomed to use, for one engraved with the

sacred name of Jesus. In a letter to her brother
Laurence from Toledo, she begs him to send her this
seal, which she had left at Avila, "because I cannot
bear now to seal with that death's head, but only with
that which I would to God were engraven on my
heart, as it was on that of S. Ignatius."

Thus, then, was laid the first stone of that work of
reparation which Teresa of Jesus was to offer to the
outraged heart of her Divine Spouse. It is remarkable that in the very year, 1562, in which the Blessed
Sacrament was placed on the altar of S. Joseph,
a convent of Carmelite friars of the strict observance
was dismantled, in the island of Cyprus, by the fury
of the Turks. In this very year too, and, as some
say, on this very Feast of S. Bartholomew, a church in
France was for the first time desecrated and turned
into a stable by the Huguenots. The thought of the
terrible evils which heresy was inflicting upon that
unhappy country was one of the motives which had
stirred up the spirit of S. Teresa to attempt the work
of her reform, and, in the judgment of more than one
Catholic historian, the assuaging of the floods of
heresy in the reign of Louis XIV. was due rather to
the prayers of her children than to the arms or the
policy of that mighty monarch. "These Teresians,"
said the Huguenot Governor of the city of Tours,
"will make Papists of us all, whether we will or no."

CHAPTER XII.

1562–1567.

THE sacred functions were over, and Teresa was left
in the long-desired place of her repose. All the
cherished wishes of her heart had been granted far
beyond her expectation or her hope. Yet there fell

now upon her soul a mortal agony, such as in all her previous experience of trial and conflict it had never known before. The serpent had entered with her into her chosen paradise, and, baffled as he had been in all his exterior attacks, he threw himself now with more intense and envenomed hatred upon the citadel itself, the strong fortress of that holy woman's faith and constancy. He had chosen his time well, for truly he has had long experience of our variable and complicated nature, and has observed it well. He knows better than we do how, after long tension of body and spirit in the pursuit of any object very near our heart, the powers of both will suddenly flag and fail, and leave us only tears to welcome its attainment. He knows, for he has once tasted the joys which are at God's right hand, the insufficiency of any other to satisfy an immortal spirit; and he knows too, for he has watched every child of man from his cradle to his grave, that our fallen nature, even in the might of its regeneration, is no longer strong enough to bear without faltering such a weight of heavenly glory as had now been laid upon the soul of S. Teresa. So he waited his time, and on the evening of that glorious Feast of S. Bartholomew he drew near to tempt her.

"I think," she says, "it was some three or four hours after all was finished that the devil attacked me in the following manner :—He represented to me that what I had done had perhaps been ill done, and suggested whether I had not acted contrary to obedience by attempting to found the monastery without a command from the Father Provincial, for I imagined he might take some offence at my subjecting it to the Bishop before I had acquainted him of my intention, although as he was himself unwilling to admit the monastery, I thought he would not be displeased. The devil also suggested to me, whether those sisters who were to live here in such austerity would be contented; whether they might not sometimes come to want food; whether the whole idea of the foundation had not been a folly; had I not a monastery of my own in which to serve God? In a word, the command our Lord had given me, the opinions of so many others whom I had consulted; the prayers which I had offered up without ceasing almost for two years—all these things had now escaped my memory as completely as if I had never entertained the thought of them. The project seemed to be all the offspring of my own fancy. All virtues, and even faith itself, seemed then to be suspended within me, so that I had no power to exercise one of them, or to defend myself from the blows of the devil. He also represented to me the folly of attempting to keep enclosure in so strict a house, and that, being afflicted with so many infirmities, I should never be able to endure such penance, after having left so spacious and delightful a convent, where I lived so happily and had so many friends. That, perhaps, the sisters would not prove to my liking; that I was binding myself too strictly; that possibly I might fall into despair; and that perhaps the devil had instigated me to this to deprive me of my peace and quiet, and that, being thus disturbed, I should be unable to continue my practice of mental prayer, and might in the end lose my soul. With thoughts of this nature he so filled my mind, that I had no power to think of anything else; and all this was accompanied with inexpressible affliction, obscurity, and spiritual darkness. In this state of desolation I went to visit the most Blessed Sacrament, though I was unable to recommend myself to our Lord, being in an agony, like the agonies of death. I dared not mention my state to any one, because I had not a confessor appointed for me. O my God! what a miserable life is this, in which there is no secure contentment, nor anything without change! A very short time before I was so happy, that I thought I would not have changed my condition with any one on earth, and in a moment the very same thing that had given me such happiness so tormented me that I knew not how to bear it. Oh! did we but carefully observe the events of our life, we should learn by our own experience how little we ought to esteem either its joys or its sorrows. This certainly seems to me to have been one of the sharpest attacks I ever had to endure during my whole life, my soul seemed then to have a presentiment of all it was hereafter to endure, though this suffering, had it lasted, would have far exceeded anything which afterwards came upon me."

Teresa knelt thus before the Blessed Sacrament, in anguish, which was a faint shadow of the agony of Gethsemane, and she was comforted, not by the ministry of an angel, but by the strong consolation of Him Who endured that agony that He might be able to succour those in all ages who in their degree should be called to suffer the like. "Our Lord," she continues, "did not abandon His poor servant, for He has always supported me in every tribulation, and so He did in this, for He gave me a ray of light to understand that all those thoughts came from the devil, and that he suggested them to terrify me with his lies. Then I began to remember the strong resolutions I had made to serve our Lord, and the desires I had felt to suffer for His sake; and I considered that if I intended to carry them out, I must not seek after ease; that if I should meet with troubles and labours, there would be the greater merit therein; and that if I bore them to honour God, they might serve me instead of Purgatory. What was I afraid of? If I desired crosses, these were good heavy ones, and the more opposition, so much the more gain; and why did I want courage to serve One to whom I was so much indebted? With these and other considerations, doing violence to myself, I promised before the most Holy Sacrament to do my utmost to obtain leave to come and dwell in this house, and in case I could do so with a good conscience, here to vow perpetual enclosure. As I was forming this resolution, the devil immediately vanished, and left me quiet and content, and so I have continued ever since. All that is observed in this house respecting enclosure, penance, and other matters, have become extremely pleasant to me, and seem to me a very light yoke; the delight which we experience therein is so very great, that sometimes I think I could not have chosen in the whole world any sweeter life. This may be the reason that I now have better health than ever I had before; or else because there is now both reason and necessity that I should be able to do what all the rest do, our Lord has perhaps been pleased to give me this consolation, and has enabled me, though with difficulty, to follow the community life; and this strength of mine all wonder at who knew my infirmities. Blessed be He who gives every gift, and who can do all things by His power! I was very weary and much exhausted by this conflict, but I laughed to myself at the devil when I saw clearly it came from him; I believe our Lord permitted it (for during twenty-eight years and more since I have worn the habit, I have never known, even for a moment, what sadness meant), in order that I might understand what a favour He had therein bestowed upon me, and from what a torment he had preserved me; and also, that in case I should see any of the sisters in the like state, I might not be perplexed, but rather compassionate her, and be enabled to console her."

Foiled in his direct attack upon the faith and hope of Teresa, the enemy betook himself to the Convent of the Incarnation, already greatly disturbed by the tidings of the new foundation. He represented to the troubled minds of the nuns the disgrace and ridicule which would be brought upon their ancient and venerable house by the erection of this miserable hovel, in which a spirit of vanity and ambition had led their misguided sister to take up her abode. The Prioress was assailed by clamorous remonstrances and entreaties for the immediate recall and summary punishment of the refractory religious.

Nothing, certainly, but such a Divine command as Teresa had received, could have justified her in acting without the knowledge and consent of her immediate superior; and it can be no matter of surprise or censure that a command should have been sent to the Saint and her two kinswomen, Agnes and Anne of Tapia, to return immediately to their convent. Teresa received the obedience just as she had laid down, after her poor meal, to take a little rest after the fatigues of the preceding day, and the exhaustion of the night of anguish which had followed it. She obeyed without remonstrance or delay, leaving her four novices motherless on this their first day in religion.

"As soon," says she, "as I received the message of the Prioress, I went immediately, leaving my novices very unhappy. I saw I should now meet with many troubles; but as the house was established, I did not disturb myself much about them. I gave myself to prayer, beseeching our Lord to help me, and begging my father, S. Joseph, that he would bring me back again to his dear house, and I offered up to him whatever I was about to suffer. Being exceedingly desirous of an opportunity of suffering something for his sake, and in his service, I went in great joy, thinking they would certainly put me into prison. This I thought would be a great comfort to me, for there I should have no one to speak to, and should be able to repose a little while in solitude, which was very necessary for me ; for, by conversing with so many people, I had been, as it were, ground to dust.

" As soon as I arrived, I gave an account of myself to the Prioress, which somewhat pacified her. But the community sent for the Father Provincial, that the cause might be heard before him.

" As soon as he came, I was summoned to appear before him, and right glad was I to suffer something for the love of our Lord ; without having, in this case, offended His Majesty, or done anything against my conscience or my Order, for I had endeavoured, on the contrary, to promote its interests with all my strength, and for it I would willingly have died, my sole desire being that its rule should be observed in all its primitive perfection. I called to mind the sentence passed on our Lord, and saw how little in comparison was that which awaited me.

" The Provincial blamed me very sharply, for I acknowledged my fault to him as if I had been very guilty ; yet he did not reprove me so severely as the offence, as represented to him by so many, deserved.

" I did not attempt to excuse myself, because I was resolved to suffer ; but only desired him to pardon and punish me, and not entertain any angry feelings against me. In some things I saw clearly that they condemned me wrongfully ; for they said I had begun this work to obtain for myself a name and reputation, and so forth. But in other things I was convinced that what they said was true ; as, for instance, that I

was the worst of all the nuns; that, not having observed the rule in force in that house, it was presumption to think of subjecting myself to one of greater
austerity. They said also that I gave scandal to the
people, and thought of nothing but introducing novel-
ties. These accusations did not give me any trouble
or pain, though I took care not to seem to disregard
what they said to me. At last, the Father Provincial
having commanded me to declare there before the
nuns my reasons and intentions in what I had done,
I was obliged to obey. As my soul was at peace,
and our Lord assisted me, I so explained my reasons
that neither the Provincial nor the nuns present
found any cause to condemn me. I spoke afterwards
to the Father Provincial alone, and informed him
more in detail of the progress of the affair. He was
quite satisfied, and promised that he would give me
leave to remove to the new house, if I could find
means to appease the tumult in the city, which was
very great."

Peace having been now restored to the heart of S.
Teresa, the anger of the nuns of the Incarnation
appeased, and the F. Provincial satisfied, the author
of discord had betaken himself once more to the
citizens of Avila, and stirred up such fear and pertur-
bation amongst them as would hardly have convulsed
the City of Knights, had an army of infidel Moors
suddenly appeared at its gates. It was no vulgar
clamour, but a panic which had seized all the authorities of the city, ecclesiastical as well as civil. At the
end of three days, which had been spent in the consideration of this weighty affair, the governor called
together a council, consisting of the magistrates and
some members of the cathedral chapter; a decree
was passed, in accordance with the excited spirit of
the assembly, to the effect that the new convent should

M

be suppressed, and that on no account whatever should the safety of the commonwealth be thus risked by the caprice of a woman.

The governor repaired in person to the convent, and in great wrath commanded the four novices to depart immediately, threatening that, unless they instantly obeyed, he would cause the Blessed Sacrament to be consumed, break down their doors, and drag them by main force out of the cloister. But the novices answered, with a courage worthy of their mother, that they would not come forth except at the command of him who placed them there; that their superior was the bishop, not the governor, and that he had better take care how he broke the doors and removed the Blessed Sacrament, because he would find that he had a judge on earth, even the king, and another in Heaven, even God. The courage of the angry governor quailed before this calm reply, and he retired to ponder over a more legitimate mode of effecting his purpose.

On the following day he reassembled the council, and to give greater solemnity to its decision, he summoned two grave and learned religious of every Order in the town, to assist at its deliberations. The governor addressed the assembly with great vehemence, stating first, that this foundation was a novelty, and therefore to be suspected; secondly, that the foundress was a woman given to private revelations, which made it much more to be suspected, seeing that in those times so many of her weak sex had been carried away by notable delusions; that the city of Avila was already sufficiently provided with convents both for men and women; and therefore that the erection of another was simply superfluous and burdensome; fourthly, that the one in question was rendered much more burdensome by the fact of its being without any provision for the support of its members, which would fall as an additional tax upon the citizens ; fifthly and lastly, he complained that the monastery had been founded without his knowledge, and without the consent of the city having been asked.

Such were the politic reasons adduced by the governor against the new foundation ; the greater part of his hearers blindly assented, without giving themselves the time or the trouble to weigh their worth. Some perhaps, though unconvinced, wanted resolution to oppose the stream. One man alone had zeal and courage enough to enter the list in defence of the forlorn cause of Holy Poverty. This was F. Dominic Bañez, of the Dominican Convent of S. Thomas.

Modestly apologizing for his boldness in opposing so many and such grave personages, he set himself to answer, one by one, the objections of the governor. Not every novelty, he said, is blameable, otherwise no religious Order could ever have arisen in the Church, for every religious Order must have been at one time new, adding that the faith of Jesus Christ Himself once bore the character of novelty ; moreover, he denied that the foundation of Mother Teresa was a novelty at all. "That which is introduced," said he, "for the greater glory of God, and for the reformation of manners, should not be called a novelty or an innovation, but rather a renovation of virtue, which is always ancient." He went on to refute the other objections, acknowledging that he himself was of opinion that it would be more expedient for the monastery to possess revenues, but that this, as it seemed to him, was a point of minor importance. As to the convent having been erected without the consent of the city, it had been founded by the authority of the Holy See, and with the approval of the Bishop, who was the sole judge in such cases. The assembly was greatly amazed

at the holy courage of Bañez, and even those who
were most bitterly opposed to the reform, felt that
they dared not attack it without further reflection.
Bañez himself has left us a memorial of this fact in
the following lines written with his own hand in the
margin of the original life of S. Teresa, preserved in
the library of the Escurial : "This was in the year
1562, and this opinion was given by me, Father
Dominic Bañez."

And as a witness in the process of canonization he
thus deposes :—" In her first foundation she had to
endure great contradiction from the city and from the
religious Orders. I alone at that time took her part.
For though I did not then know her, even by sight, I
defended her, because I considered that she had not
erred, either in her intention or in the means which
she had adopted for the foundation of this monastery,
since she had done everything by direction of the
Holy See." S. Teresa herself thus writes : " This
religious of the Order of S. Dominic was of great use
to us, for judging by the fury which possessed the
city, it was a great marvel that the monastery was
not destroyed."

Father Dominic Bañez was one of the most celebrated theologians of his day. Three years after the
foundation of S. Joseph's, S. Teresa chose him for
her confessor during the eight succeeding years which
he passed at Avila. It was by his command that she
wrote her *Way of Perfection.*

Meanwhile the tumult in the city waxed more furious
every day. "The excitement of the people was so great,"
says the Saint, "that no one talked of anything else, and
all condemned me, running first to the Provincial and
then to my monastery : " adding, with the sweet and
noble candour which always marked her judgment of
her adversaries : " They gave their reasons and showed

great zeal, and thus, without offending God, they made me and all who were favourable to the foundation endure great persecutions. I was no more moved," she continues, "by what they said against me, than if they had said nothing, but the fear lest the monastery should be dissolved, and the knowledge of what affliction they who assisted me endured, and that they were losing credit on my account, grieved me exceedingly. As to what was said about myself, I was rather glad of it, and if I had had a little more faith, I should not have felt the least disturbance. But even a slight defect in any one virtue, is sufficient to lay asleep all the rest. During the two days in which the meetings were held in the city, I was very much troubled; but when my sadness was at its height, our Lord said to me, ' Dost thou not know that I am all-powerful? Of what then are you afraid?' And He assured me that the monastery should not be dissolved. These words consoled me very much.

" In the mean time, the authorities of the city carried the matter before the king's council, whence came an order that a full account should be drawn up of the foundation of this monastery. Here, therefore, arose a great difficulty, for as on the part of the city some had gone to the court, it became necessary that others should go on the part of the monastery; but we had no money, and I knew not what to do. Our Lord so ordered that the Provincial never commanded me to desist from prosecuting the business; for he is such a friend to any good work, that though he might not assist us in the matter, he would not put any obstacle in our way. Still he would not grant me leave to remove to the new house till he should see what the result would be. Those servants of God (the four novices) remained there alone, and did more by their prayers than I with all my labours, though I was obliged to use my utmost endeavours. Sometimes all seemed lost, especially one day before the arrival of the Father Provincial, when the Prioress commanded me not to do anything in the matter, which was in fact to give up everything. I then went to our Lord, and said to Him, 'This house is not mine, it has been established for Thee alone; and since there is no one to conduct the case, be Thou pleased to undertake it Thyself!' Having spoken those words, I felt as perfectly at peace and as entirely free from care as if I had all the world to labour for me; and I immediately considered the success of our cause to be certain. A priest (Gonzalez d'Aranda), who is a great servant of God, and zealous for every kind of perfection, and who had always befriended me, went to court to defend our cause, and was exceedingly earnest in promoting it; and that devout gentleman (Francis de Salcedo), whom I have often already mentioned, laboured exceedingly in the matter, and did all he could to favour us; not, however, without bringing upon himself many troubles and persecutions. I always esteemed him, and do still esteem him, as our father. Our Lord, indeed, inspired those who assisted us with such zeal and fervour, that each took up the business as if it had been his own private affair, and as if his life and honour had been at stake; their only motive being, however, the conviction that this work would tend to the glory of God. Our Lord vouchsafed especial help to a certain holy priest (Gaspar Daza), who was of great assistance to me in this affair; for in another great assembly held in the city, he appeared in behalf of the Bishop, and stood alone against every one. He at last appeased them by proposing certain expedients, which sufficed to calm their fury, and delay the design of dissolving the house. But nothing would induce them wholly to desist; for they soon returned to the charge, and seemed willing to lose their lives if only they could destroy the monastery. This opposition lasted for nearly half a year; and to relate all the great afflictions I endured during that time would be too tedious. I was astonished to see what a storm the devil was able to raise against a few poor women, and how he contrived to persuade all the people that twelve women and a prioress, for they were not to exceed this number, could prove so injurious to the city, especially as they were to lead such a very austere and retired life; for, supposing there were any evil therein, it would all fall upon themselves, and the city would not suffer any loss; but these good people fancied so many misfortunes would happen, that they opposed the foundation with a good conscience. At length they came to the conclusion, that in case the monastery were endowed, they would be content that it should go on. I was now so wearied out with seeing the trouble of all those who assisted us, that, more for their sake than my own, I began to think that it would not be wrong to receive revenues till the storm should be over, and that afterwards I might refuse them. And sometimes I also imagined (like a wicked and imperfect creature as I am) that this might perhaps be our Lord's pleasure, since, without this concession, it seemed impossible that the house should be founded, and I was on the point of consenting to this agreement; but the night before it was to be concluded, our Lord said to me, in prayer, 'My daughter, make no such agreement, for if once you begin to admit an endowment, the people will not afterwards allow you to refuse it;' adding, also, other things.

"The same night there also appeared to me the holy friar, Peter of Alcantara, who died a short time before. He had written to me before his death (having heard of the opposition and persecution we endured), that he was glad the house was founded in the midst of such great opposition, for it was a sign that our Lord wóuld be truly served and honoured therein, since the devil laboured so much to hinder it, and that I should not by any means consent to have it endowed. He repeated this two or three times over in his letter with great earnestness, assuring me that if I continued firm, all would succeed as I desired. I had already seen him twice since his death, and observed the glory he was in, and so I was not at all frightened, but rather rejoiced, for he always appeared like a glorified body full of light, and it gave me the greatest delight to behold him. I remember, the first time I saw him, he told me, amongst other things, of the great bliss he enjoyed, and how blessed was that penance whereby he had obtained so high a reward.

" This time, however, he showed a little severity, and only told me by no means to accept revenue. He asked me why I had not followed his advice, and immediately vanished, leaving me greatly amazed. Early in the next day I acquainted the above-named gentleman (Don F. Salcedo) with what had happened, and told him not to consent in any way to an endowment, but to carry on the suit. He was overjoyed to hear this, for his firmness was greater than mine, and he afterwards told me how unwilling he had been to make the proposed concession."

The dispute between the civil authorities and the poor foundress of S. Joseph's had dragged on for nearly six months, and seemed as far as ever from an adjustment. Teresa's heart sank within her at the proposal of one whom she calls "a holy servant of God," to submit the question of its endowment to the decision of learned men, for she well remembered the warning of S. Peter of Alcantara not to ask counsel

concerning the way of perfection except of those who
follow it. Just at this moment of need, our Lord once
more sent her an efficient helper in the person of
Father Peter Ibañez, who, hearing by apparent accident of the destruction which threatened her work,
came to Avila on purpose to give her his assistance.

The force of his arguments, and the influence exercised by his character, both for learning and sanctity,
at last brought the men of Avila to reason, and induced
them to lay aside the senseless opposition by which
they had for more than two years striven against
the blessing which God was about to bestow upon
their city.

A second brief, which arrived from Rome on
December 5, authorizing and enjoining the establishment of the new foundation in strict poverty, overruled
the last ground of objection by the supreme authority
of the Holy See ; and there was no obstacle now to the
return of Teresa to her deserted children but the
extreme timidity of the good Father Provincial, who
still delayed from day to day to give his promised
consent till urged by the necessity of the case, and
the great injury inflicted upon the novices, left thus,
month after month, without the care of their mother
in religion, the Saint exclaimed, with holy indignation: " Remember, Father, that we are resisting the
Holy Ghost." These words, and the tone of inspiration with which they were uttered, at last put an end
to the irresolution of Father Angelo Salazar, and he
not only gave permission to the Saint to return to
S. Joseph's, but allowed four religious from the Incarnation, who desired to embrace the reform, to
accompany her.

For six long months the four novices had persevered in their forlorn condition, in the practice of all
the virtues of the religious life, under the never-failing

guidance of the Spirit of God, but destitute of any
human direction but that which they received from
the good priest Gaspar Daza, to whose care they had
been committed by the Bishop of Avila. Ursula of
the Saints, by the direction of S. Teresa, held the
office of superioress.

Having no one to instruct them in the recitation of
the Divine office, the little community said that of the
Blessed Virgin in choir. They ceased not, with
many tears, to beseech our Lord to restore their
beloved mother to them; and at last, in the latter
part of December, 1562, they had the unspeakable
happiness of receiving her once more amongst them.

She came accompanied by the four fervent souls
who had volunteered upon this service of suffering
and of glory, and bringing with her, as her only
portion, a pailliasse, an iron chain, a discipline, and an
old patched habit, having left behind her an acknowledgment in her own handwriting, that she accepted
all these valuables simply as a loan from her former
convent.

Before she entered the enclosure she remained for
awhile in prayer with her four companions in the
chapel, pouring forth the gratitude of her full heart
before the Blessed Sacrament. Here, falling into
an ecstasy, our Lord was pleased to assure her of
His gracious acceptance of all that she had done
and suffered for the Order of His Blessed Mother.
"He placed," she says, "a glorious crown upon my
head, and thanked me for what I had done for His
Mother."

Teresa now set herself to the joyful task of establishing regular discipline in the little community,
and of instructing the docile novices, who had so
ardently longed for her holy teaching, in all things
belonging to the perfection of their state. She began

her lessons by setting an example of profound humility
in appointing two of the religious who had accompanied her from the Convent of the Incarnation to be
Prioress and Sub-Prioress. This appointment was
overruled by the Bishop, at the earnest petition of the
community, and Teresa was compelled to fill the
place of Prioress. She contrived, however, to neu-
tralize what she dreaded as the effects of this com-
pulsory elevation, by using her authority to monopolize
for herself all the most distasteful and humiliating
employments in the house. Under the rule of such a
superioress, the Convent of S. Joseph's speedily
became a model of sanctity, and an example of the
ancient Carmelite perfection. All those points of the
rule which had come to be considered impracticable
even for strong men, were cheerfully followed by these
young and feeble women, some of whom had but
lately left comfortable homes and secular lives, whilst
others, like the holy foundress herself, were so delicate
in health, as apparently to want strength for the observance of a far milder rule. They practised (except
in case of sickness) perpetual abstinence from flesh-
meat, rigorous silence and retirement, and a fast of
eight months in the year. To these mortifications,
prescribed by the original Carmelite rule, the Saint,
with the approbation of the Bishop of Avila, added
others admirably well adapted to promote its more
exact and perfect fulfilment. The linen worn at
the Convent of the Incarnation was exchanged at
S. Joseph's for a coarse woollen serge, the shoes for
sandals, the comfortable mattresses gave place to a
single pailliasse, or rather sack of straw, and the
abundant and well-served table to a dinner of coarse
bread and common vegetables. Matins were recited
in choir three hours before midnight, because, as the
traditions of the Order say, no other religious insti-

tute is at that hour offering praises to God. After
Matins followed the examination of conscience, the
points were read of the following morning's meditation, and the sisters retired to rest at about an hour
before midnight. The convent and all its arrangements
embodied and symbolized the spirit of holy simplicity
and poverty which dwelt in the hearts of its inmates ;
there were no needless ornaments, no wide cloisters,
no roomy cells, for S. Teresa was wont to say that it
was not fitting that the houses of the poor should
make a great noise when they fall at the day of judgment. The religious were not permitted to sleep in a
common dormitory, nor to labour in a common work-
room, lest the silence and recollection, which were to
be the principal means of attaining the end of their
institute, should be infringed.

The chief aim of S. Teresa in all her regulations was
to establish a fervent, assiduous exercise of mental
prayer and interior recollection, as the principal
means to attain the perfection aimed at in the Order
of Mount Carmel. She therefore forbade her daughters to go to the grate, except on very rare occasions,
teaching them to find their only pleasure in conversing with God; and for this purpose she caused little
hermitages to be constructed in the garden, to which
they might retire for long and fervent prayer. Were
not these the realization of those which she and her
brother Roderick in their childish play had erected
long ago in their father's garden! She caused a
religious to be elected under the name of "Zelatrix,"
whose office was to give notice to the sisters in the
refectory, after supper or collation, of any slight failings
which she might have observed during the day which
had escaped the notice of the superioress. She was
most anxious to banish idleness from her community,
and therefore earnestly impressed upon the sisters

the duty of unremitting occupation. She forbade the practice in use in the Convent of the Incarnation and in other religious houses of the time, of giving to the sisters the name of "Doña," or "Lady," and ordered that they should call each other "Sister," or "Your Charity," and that the Prioress should be distinguished by the sweet name of "Mother," and honoured only by the title of "Your Reverence."

For herself—foundress, superioress, and legislatrix, as she was, she would accept no pre-eminence, except that of being chief in labour and humiliation. She was the first and the busiest in sweeping the house, washing the dishes, serving in the kitchen and in the infirmary. In the week when the cook's office fell to her share, she fulfilled it with such care and attention, as if the whole power of her strong will and rare intellect were concentrated upon the work in hand. And as an illustration of the true nature of devotion, on those days she would not allow herself to remain in the choir with the other sisters for their accustomed long devotions after Communion; but leaving them to enjoy the Presence of our Lord, she returned, after a short thanksgiving, to the kitchen to serve Him in this lowly ministry to the necessities of His spouses. The example which she set of all other virtues was no less bright than of this her great humility; she was uniformly sweet and gentle to her daughters, austere only to herself. Though worn with pain and sickness, she relaxed nothing of the severity of her penances, treating her feeble and sensitive body as if it had possessed the insensibility of a stone. It was the belief of her confessors that, but for the prudent restraint which they laid upon her austerities, she would, in the excess of her love for her crucified Lord, and her desire to render to Him suffering for suffering, have shortened her life by the rigour of her penance.

The first daughters of S. Teresa were worthy of their mother. In the beginning of her book of Foundations, she thus writes with a holy wonder and enthusiasm of the heroic virtues of these first fruits of her reform :—

"I lived five years in the Convent of S. Joseph at Avila after it was founded; and it appears to me now that these were the most quiet years of my life; the tranquillity and calmness of that happy time my soul has since oftentimes longed for. During this period several young ladies received the habit, whom the world, to all appearance, seemed likely to hold captive, to judge by their fine dress and frivolity; but our Lord soon removed them from these vanities, by drawing them to His house, and endowing them with such great perfection, that I was even ashamed to live amongst them. Their number soon amounted to thirteen, which I had determined not to exceed. It was very sweet to live amongst such pure and holy souls, for all their care was to serve and praise our Lord. His Divine Majesty sent us there everything that was necessary for us, without our asking for it; and whenever we were in want (which was but seldom), their joy was the greater. I praised our Lord at the sight of such heroic virtue, and especially of their indifference about everything relating to the body. Even I, who was their superioress, never remember to have been troubled with any care in this matter, because I firmly believed that our Lord would not be wanting to those who had no other wish but to please Him, and if, sometimes, when there was not enough for all, I said that those only who stood most in need of it should partake of what food we had, each one considered herself not to be in need, and thus the food remained till God sent sufficient for all.

"With regard to the virtue of obedience—which I

valued so much (though I knew not how to practise it
till these servants of God taught me; for if I possessed any virtue I should never be ignorant of it)—I
could mention many things which I here saw in them.
As for instance: one day in the refectory a few
cucumbers were given to us at our meal; a very
small one, which was rotten inside, fell to my share.
Appearing not to be aware of this, I called one of the
sisters who had more judgment and talent than the
others, Mary of S. J. Baptist (in the world, Mary of
Ocampo), and to try her obedience, I told her to go
and plant the cucumber in a little garden that we had.
She asked me whether she should plant it upright or
downwards. I said downwards, and immediately she
did so, without the thought once occurring to her that
it must wither immediately, for her esteem for obedience so brought her natural reason into the captivity
of Christ as to make her believe the thing was quite
proper to be done.

"I once imposed on a sister at one time six or
seven incompatible offices, which she undertook without saying a word, thinking it possible to perform
them all.

"We had a well containing very bad water (according to the report of those who had tried it), which I
wished to have conveyed by a pipe to our house;
thinking that if the water could once be made to flow,
it might serve for us to drink; but this appeared to
be impossible, as the well was very deep. However,
I called in some skilful workmen, to see what they
could do; but they laughed at me as if I had wished
to throw money away. Thereupon I asked the sisters
what they thought of the matter? The same sister
said that the work should be attempted, adding 'our
Lord is obliged now to give us water from without,
and moreover, wherewithal to pay those who bring it

to us. It will cost His Majesty less to give it to us in our house, and assuredly He will not fail to do so.' Seeing the great faith and resolution with which she spoke, I considered the matter quite certain, and therefore, contrary to the wish of the person I employed (who knew what kind of water was in the well), I ordered the work to be done, and our Lord was pleased that we should obtain a current of good water, sufficient for our wants, which we drink at this day.

"I am not citing this as a miracle, for many such things could I relate, but only to show the great faith of these sisters.

"I lived, then, amongst these angelic souls, for such I knew them to be, because they concealed no imperfection from me, however interior it might be; and the favours, the ardent desires, and the detachment from worldly things which our Lord gave them, were very great and wonderful.

"Solitude was their joy, and they have accordingly assured me that they were never tired of being alone, and that it was quite a torment to them when any one, even their own brothers, came to see them. She who had the most time to remain in a little hermitage we had in the garden, esteemed herself the happiest."

Such was the blessed community to which our Divine Lord had given the name of the *Paradise of His Delights,* and over which S. Teresa saw our Blessed Lady spreading her mantle in token of her special protection.

The prejudice and opposition of the citizens of Avila melted away before the fervent prayers and the saintly lives of those whom they had sought to banish, as the consumers of their substance, and the troublers of their peace; and Teresa was left undisturbed to *sing the mercies of the Lord,* and to thank Him for

the holiness of her children. She pondered in grateful
wonder over the treasure which He had placed in
her hands, marvelling how she should lay it out to
the best account for His honour and glory. "When
I was considering the great value of these souls, and
the courage which God gave them beyond that of
women, to suffer and to serve Him, I thought many
times that the riches with which our Lord endowed
them were given for some great end; *that*, however,
never came into my thoughts, which afterwards happened; for then it appeared to me a thing impossible,
as I could see no grounds even to imagine what was
to come; and in the meanwhile, as time went on,
my desires increased more and more to be instrumental in doing some good to any souls. And thus
it appeared as if my soul was bound: and often I
seemed like one that had a great treasure to guard,
and who was desirous that all should share in it; and
yet my hands seemed tied, so as to prevent me from
distributing it : thus my soul seemed bound, for the
favours which God bestowed on me in these years
were very great, but being concentred in myself, they
appeared to be ill bestowed. But I endeavoured to
please the Lord with my poor prayers, and always
exhorted the sisters to do the same, and to be zealous
for the good of souls and for the extension of the
Church : and whoever conversed with them was always
edified; so my desires to labour for the glory of God
continued to increase."

How vividly does this union of Apostolical zeal and
fervent contemplation remind us of that great Saint,
whom of all others S. Teresa perhaps most closely
resembles, both in the intense energy of her natural
character, the depth of her human affections, and the
fervour of Divine charity which consumed her whole
being as a holocaust to God; of him who had been

N

caught up to Paradise to behold "the joys which are at God's right hand," who thus knew what it was "to depart and be with Christ, and yet could choose to be absent from Him, for his brethren's sake—for the sake of the souls for which He died!"

It was revealed on one occasion by S. Teresa after her death, that, for her fervent love of souls, our Lord had committed to her patronage the conversion of heretics. Surely such an office must place her throne in the kingdom of God not far from that of the Apostle of the Gentiles.

So the fire waxed hotter and fiercer within her, till at last her Divine Master showed her to what end He had kindled it.

"After four years," she says (after the foundation of S. Joseph's), "or it may be a little more, a religious of the Order of S. Francis, lately returned from the Indies, came to see me: his name was F. Alphonsus Maldonado, a great servant of God, having the same desires as I had myself for the good of souls, but having the power also to accomplish them, for which I envied him extremely. As he had lately come from India, he began to tell me how many millions of souls were lost in the countries whence he came for want of instruction, and he preached us a sermon on the subject, exhorting us to do penance; and so departed. I was so much afflicted at the loss of all these souls that I could not contain myself, and I went to one of our hermitages, and there, with many tears, cried to our Lord, beseeching Him to give me the means whereby I might be able to gain some souls to His service, since the devil was robbing Him of so many, and that He would make my prayers of some avail, since I could do nothing for them but pray. I envied those greatly who, for the love of God, were able to spend themselves in this work, though they should suffer a thousand deaths. Thus, when we read in the Lives of the Saints how they converted souls, this thought excites within me more devotion, more tenderness and envy, than all the tortures endured by the martyrs; and by this feeling with which our Lord has inspired me, I see that He values one soul which we gain through His mercy, by our prayers, more than all the other services we can render Him.

"One night while I was in prayer (in this great affliction), our Lord presented Himself to me in His accustomed manner; and, showing me much affection, as if He wished to console me, He said : ' Wait a little while, my daughter, and thou shalt see great things.' These words remained so fixed in my heart, that I was unable to drive them from me ; and though I could not conjecture nor see any ground to imagine what they meant, yet I was greatly consoled, and felt certain the words would come true, but by what means never entered my imagination to conceive, and thus another year passed."

The means by which "the great things" promised by our Lord were to be brought to pass remained still a mystery, but the end before her gradually assumed a more definite shape in the mind of S. Teresa.

In the foundation of the Convent of S. Joseph, her only thought had been to found a retreat, in which she, and others likeminded with herself, might perfect their own souls in the strict observance of their holy rule, and offer fervent prayers for the souls of others ; but in her ascent of the heights of perfection, one mountain range after another opened on her view ; and now, as she pondered over those words of her Lord : "my daughter, wait awhile, and thou shalt see great things," she beheld the wide extent of Carmel covered with convents, both of men and women, singing the praises of God, and labouring for the souls for which He died, under a rule of primitive austerity.

There is no Order in the Church whose traditions are so majestic and so full of sacred poetry as the Order of our Lady of Mount Carmel, reaching back, as it does, nine centuries before the birth of our Divine Lord ; carrying on its succession from the elder to the later Church, and tracing its descent from him who stood alone, the Prophet of the Lord, when all the people of Israel, save the seven thousand known only to the eye of God, had bowed the knee to Baal.

It claims as its founder that wondrous Saint who, with his mysterious companion, is even now waiting in his mortal body, in some unseen abode, some far-off hermitage within the limits of this visible creation, the hour when a greater and more fearful apostasy shall call him forth to witness once more for God.* The founder of the Order of Mount Carmel is the founder of the religious life in its earliest cremitical type, and, in his mysterious and silent vigil of nearly 3,000 years, he symbolizes, in his own person, the hidden and solitary life which is the portion and the privilege of his children.

Nor is it only the awful and venerable forms of Elias and Eliseus, which haunt and hallow the steeps of Carmel. The Carmelite Order is the Order of the Mother of God ; *her* peculiar heritage who, though in a most true sense the mother of all Christians, and the most loving mother of all the spouses of her Son, we may believe, has a special affection for the offspring of her own land and her own people. The true Esther forgets

---

* A constant tradition in the Church teaches that Enoch and Elias are to reappear before the second advent of our Lord.

not her brethren when she stands before the King. "The Glory of Carmel," the royal daughter of Juda, remembers the caves and grottoes in the rocks of Carmel and Horeb where her kindred dwelt, and worshipped the God of their fathers in purity and peace,* and views with a peculiar complacency those who have inherited that name, and carried the tradition of that life into the new creation of her Son.

The Carmelites of the first ages of the Christian Church led a life closely resembling that of their fathers of the elder dispensation, as solitary dwellers in the desert. They were first formed into a community about the year 1210, when they received a written rule from S. Albert, then Patriarch of Jerusalem, which, amongst other regulations, enjoined them to abide in their cells day and night, unless otherwise occupied, as becometh hermits, in assiduous prayer; to fast, except on Sundays, from the Feast of the Exaltation of the Cross until Easter; to observe perpetual abstinence from flesh; to employ themselves in manual labour, and to keep silence daily from Vespers until after Tierce on the following day, &c.

The disasters which befell the Christian arms in Palestine obliged the Carmelites to seek refuge in Europe about the year 1238. Here the Order spread with marvellous rapidity; and some points in the original rule of S. Albert having been found unsuited to the nations of the West, it was submitted for revision by our countryman S. Simon Stock, elected General of the Order in 1245, to Pope Innocent IV., then presiding at the General Council at Lyons. The necessary corrections and adaptations having been made by authority of the Holy See, the rule, thus ex-

---

* See the Revelations of Catherine Emmerich concerning the ancestors of the Blessed Virgin.

plained and perfected, has been ever since received in the Order as the primitive rule of Mount Carmel. It was the aim and the mission of S. Teresa to restore it to its first perfection.

The lapse of time, and the downward tendency of human infirmity, gradually introduced declensions from a standard so far above its ordinary attainment ; and superiors were driven from time to time to ask the Supreme Authority of the Church for mitigations of a rule whose requirements they were no longer able to enforce. The declension of fervour was moreover aggravated by the breach of unity in the Order consequent upon the great western schism, in which the General, Bernard Ollery, unhappily espoused the cause of the anti-pope, and was deposed in consequence by Urban VI. Many houses of the Order still continued to acknowledge his authority, and to resist that of his legitimate successor ; and the consequent loss of unity brought with it, as usual, loss of grace and decay of discipline.

The Carmelites, or White Friars of England, in consequence (we may hope) of the severity of their northern climate, were the first to ask for a dispensation of that point of the rule which forbade the use of flesh meat. This indulgence was granted to them, in the year 1396, by Boniface IX., and was extended by Eugenius IV., together with other mitigations of the original rule, to the whole Order in the year 1432. By the Bull of Eugenius, the religious of Mount Carmel are relieved from three of the principal austerities of their institute. 1. The perpetual abstinence from flesh-meat is no longer required of them. 2. The daily fast, enjoined from the Exaltation of the Holy Cross till Easter, is restricted to three days in the week. 3. The strict retirement in the cell, so strongly enforced by the rule, is mitigated, the religious being permitted, at suitable hours, to converse together at their pleasure in the cloisters, or other parts of the monastery.

Such was the prevailing practice of the Carmelite Order when S. Teresa was professed in the Convent of the Incarnation.

At different times, and in various places, fervent souls had risen here and there, to attempt a return to the ancient ways. Amongst these, the most illustrious was the Blessed John Saret, elected General in the year 1451, who, with the approval of the sovereign Pontiff, erected several convents of strict observance, both for men and women; but notwithstanding the influence of his personal sanctity and the authority of his position, he was unable to effect anything more than a partial and temporary renovation. Many subsequent attempts at reform by other holy men and prelates of the Order resulted, like this, in the establishment of isolated communities (such as was S. Joseph's at Avila at its first foundation), whose inmates, having sanctified their own souls in prayer and penance, went to their reward, leaving no visible impression upon the face of their Order.

The Lord's time was not yet come. He was to save His people once more " by the hand of a woman," the restored beauty of Carmel was to be the work of a humble and solitary nun, that "all men might see the glory of the Lord, and the beauty of our God."

The way was at last opened for the great things of which our Lord had spoken, by the arrival in Spain of the Father General of the Carmes, John Baptist Rossi, " a man," says S. Teresa, " much and deservedly esteemed in the Order." He had been summoned to Spain by King Philip II., who, being anxious for the restoration of discipline amongst the religious of his kingdom, had earnestly invited the

prelates of the different Orders to make a visitation of
their convents. At the command of Pope Pius IV.,
Rossi set forth on his journey to Spain in the beginning of the year 1566. On his arrival at Madrid, he
was most graciously received by the king, who promised his assistance and protection in all that he
should do for the reform of his Order. The General
proceeded to Seville, and on September 20, of the
same year, he assembled a Provincial Chapter, which
was attended by more than two hundred religious,
whom he laboured very zealously to rouse to the
ancient fervour. He enacted various new constitutions, omitting nothing which he judged likely to
promote regular discipline.

He next visited the whole province of Andalusia,
whence, in the beginning of the year 1567, he
returned into Castile. Here he found that the mind
of Philip II. had been poisoned against him by some
of the religious of Andalusia, so that he refused to
admit him to an audience. Upon this the General
proceeded to Avila, where he assembled another
solemn Chapter, in which Father Alonzo Gonzalez was
elected Provincial; and here he had the happiness to
meet S. Teresa, in whom he was to find an instrument
for introducing a reform of far higher perfection than
it had ever entered into his mind to conceive.

Teresa had heard of the General's expected arrival
at Avila with no little anxiety, "for," as she tells us,
"I feared two things: the first, that the General, not
being fully informed of all that had passed, would be
displeased with me (as he justly might have been) for
having subjected the house to the Bishop instead of
to the Order; the other, that he would command me
to return to the monastery of the Incarnation, which
would have been a great affliction to me. But our
Lord directed this matter better than I imagined, for

the General, who was a man of great virtue and rare prudence, thought that I had done nothing wrong, and showed no displeasure with me. On his arrival at Avila, I prevailed on him to visit St. Joseph's, and the Bishop wished that the same attention should be paid to him as to his own person. I gave him an account of the foundation with all truth and simplicity, because it is my desire thus to act with my superiors, come of it what may, since they stand in the place of God. I do the same with my confessors, for if I did not, I think there would be no security for my soul. And thus I gave him an account of the monastery, and also of my whole life, though it has been so wicked. He consoled me greatly, and assured me that he would not command me to remove hence. He was very much pleased to see our way of living, which was an image, though imperfect, of our Order at its commencement, and how the primitive rule was here observed in all its rigour, which was not the case in any other monastery of the whole Order. As he had a great desire that this beginning should be carried on, he gave me several letters-patent for the erection of more monasteries, with an injunction that none of the provincials should prevent me. I had not asked these letters of him, but he knew my manner of prayer, and the great desire I had to be the means of enabling souls to approach nearer to God. Still it appeared to me madness to imagine that a poor weak woman, like myself, without a shadow of authority, could do anything. But when these desires come into a soul, it cannot reject them; but faith and love, and the burning desire to please God, and confidence in His Divine Majesty, make those things possible which seem impracticable to natural reason. Thus, when I saw the great desire of our very reverend Father General, that more monas-

tories should be founded, it seemed as if I saw them
already established; and remembering the words our
Lord had spoken to me, I now perceived some beginning of that which before I could not understand.
Therefore, when he was about to return to Rome, I
was very much grieved; for he had shown me the
greatest affection and favour, and I had a high regard
for him, and felt very desolate at his departure.
Whenever he was disengaged, he used to come and
converse with us on spiritual things, for he was one
on whom our Lord had bestowed great favours, and
on this account it was a great comfort for us to hear
him."

In one of these confidential conversations, the
Father General, soon after his arrival at Avila, inquired of S. Teresa what had first moved her to
attempt a work which God had so signally blessed.
"Most reverend Father," she replied, "I had no
other motive than charity towards God, charity towards myself, and charity towards the Church."
And then with her wonted transparent simplicity, she
told him of her vow to do always that which is most
perfect; of the too great ease of her life at the Incarnation; of the glory which might redound to the
Church by the restoration of the Carmelite rule to its
primitive perfection; of her hope that the prayers of
these her sisters might avail to stay the headlong
progress of heresy; and how she had been moved by
all these thoughts to the foundation of that poor
house of S. Joseph's. The good Father General, as
we have seen, entered warmly into her design of
extending her foundations; but though he readily
granted permission to multiply reformed convents for
women in Castile, he was by no means prepared to
grant, what was now the wish dearest to her heart,
and to sanction the like foundations for men.   S.

Teresa ventured to lay this proposal before him ; but the recollection of the factious opposition which he had met with in Andalusia to far milder measures of reform than she suggested, was so fresh in his memory that he gave a decided negative to a scheme which, however desirable, appeared to him absolutely and hopelessly impracticable. Teresa dutifully desisted from any further importunities ; but the Bishop of Avila, supported by the opinions of Master Daza, Francis of Salcedo, Julian of Avila, and other holy men, both religious and secular, endeavoured to obtain for her what she ceased to ask herself.

The Bishop's interference in her behalf was the more generous, inasmuch as the visit of the Father General to Avila had brought him a severe disappointment. There was but one point in the foundation of S. Joseph's which was unacceptable to the superior of the Carmelites, and that was the subjection of the convent to the Bishop instead of the Order. This arrangement had been made, as we have seen, in obedience to a direct revelation from our Lord as a means of protection to the infant community, but it was not to be permanent. The fairest offshoot of Carmel was one day, as we shall see hereafter, to be reunited to its parent stem. The General was still more displeased to find that the obedience of Teresa herself, and of the religious who had accompanied her from the Convent of the Incarnation, had been transferred from the Order to the Bishop. He observed certain informalities in the brief by authority of which the exchange of jurisdiction had been effected, and moreover assured the Saint that he possessed ample faculties, not only as General of the Carmes, but as Apostolic Visitor, for restoring her, should such be her desire, to the obedience of the Order. Teresa desired nothing better : it had not been at her

own wish, but simply in obedience to the Divine
command, that she had separated herself from the
superiors of her Order; and no sooner was the way
opened for her once more to place herself under their
jurisdiction, than she willingly and thankfully embraced it. The General, on his side, assured her that
he would never command, nor consent that any other
prelate of the Order should command her to return to
the Convent of the Incarnation.

The joy of S. Teresa on this occasion was qualified
by the pain which she felt in grieving the good
Bishop, who, in a few gentle words, expressed his
sorrow that she should have withdrawn herself from
his obedience. To Teresa's sensitive and grateful
heart, this was one of the severest mortifications of
her life. She bore it, however, calmly, patiently, and
humbly, until Alvarez de Mendoza came to see that
he had no just cause for displeasure, and showed himself ever afterwards a no less faithful and generous
protector of the reform than he had been at the first
foundation of S. Joseph's. Thus he now used his
powerful influence with the General of the Carmes
in behalf of the foundation of convents of discalced
friars in his diocese.

"Before the Father General departed," says the
Saint, "the Lord Bishop, Don Alvarez de Mendoza,
who loved much to assist all those whom he saw
endeavouring to serve God with greater perfection,
sought from him a license to erect in his diocese
some monasteries of barefooted friars of the primitive
rule; others also made the same request. The Father
General was himself desirous of effecting this object;
but as he feared some opposition to it in the Order,
he deferred his assent for the present, lest he might
cause some disturbance in the province.

"A few days after his departure from Avila, when

considering how necessary it was that, if I erected
convents for nuns, there should also be some monasteries for men observing the same rule; seeing also
how few houses of the Order there existed in this
province, after having earnestly recommended the
matter to our Lord, I wrote a letter to our Father
General, entreating him, as well as I could, to be
favourable to this design, giving him reasons to prove
that great honour would result therefrom to God;
and at the same time showing that the difficulties
which might arise were not sufficient to hinder so
good a work.   I likewise placed before him the
honour which would result to our Blessed Lady, to
whom he was exceedingly devout.   She it was, I
doubt not, who managed this matter; for the Father
General, having received my letter when he was at
Valencia, sent me from thence a license to found two
monasteries of discalced friars, thus showing his desire to advance the greater perfection of the Order.
And that there might be no opposition, he committed
the execution of the matter to the Provincial then in
office, and to the late Provincial (whose consent would,
I know, be very difficult to obtain); but as I saw the
principal point was gained, I had great hope that our
Lord would also do the rest; and so it happened, for,
by the kindness of the Lord Bishop, who managed
the business as if it were his own, both the Provincials were brought to give their consent."

The Father General, before his departure from
Spain, went to Madrid to take leave of the king, who,
being now better informed as to what had taken
place in Andalusia, received him graciously, and
listened with great interest to his report of the steps
taken for the reform of the Order.   De Rossi spoke
with great enthusiasm of Mother Teresa of Jesus, and
of the great perfection of her institute.   It was not

the first time that her name had reached the ears of Philip II., and he now besought the General to commend himself and his kingdom to her prayers and the prayers of her sisters.

The General failed not to comply with his wishes; and Teresa read the letter in which they were conveyed in full community, charging her daughters never to forget to pray for their king. It is manifest from her own letters to Philip, that she bore him respect and affection in a degree somewhat surprising to such as have formed their estimate of him from the testimony of Protestant historians.

Teresa had now seen the dawn of the "great things" promised by our Lord, but difficulties seemingly insurmountable lay in the way. "I was much consoled," she says, "at having obtained the license, but greatly troubled because there were no friars in the province that I could hear of to begin the work, nor any secular priests willing to embrace such a life. In this difficulty I could do nothing but beseech our Lord that He would be pleased to raise up at least one such person. I had neither house, nor means to purchase one. Here was a poor barefooted nun, without any one to help her but our Lord, furnished with plenty of letters-patent and good desires, without any possibility of putting them in execution. But neither my courage nor confidence failed me; for when I considered that our Lord, having granted one thing, would certainly grant the other, everything appeared to me possible, and so I began to set to work.

"O great God, how marvellously dost Thou show forth Thy power by giving courage to such an ant! No, my Lord! it is no fault of Thine that those who love Thee do not great things for Thee; the fault is in our own cowardice and fears, because we never do anything for Thee without mingling with it a thousand apprehensions and human considerations! And therefore, O my God, Thou displayest not Thy wonders and the greatness of Thy power! Who is more disposed to give than Thou, were there any to receive? Who more bountiful than Thou in rewarding our poor services? Oh! that I may have done Thy Majesty some service, and not, rather, have the heavier account to give for all that I have received."

S. Teresa's history of her life and the *Way of Perfection* were both written during the five years succeeding the foundation of S. Joseph's at Avila.

CHAPTER XIII.

1567.

THE time was not yet come for the erection of a house of reformed friars; and Teresa, keeping the design close in her heart, set her hand to the work for which the General had left her not only a permission, but a command—that of extending her foundations for nuns.

She chose for the site of her second convent the ancient and wealthy commercial town of Medina del Campo, being attracted to that place chiefly by the fact that the fathers of the Company of Jesus were established there, and in great repute amongst the citizens; the rector of their college being Father Balthasar Alvarez, who had been her guide and confessor through so many trying and eventful years. "I wrote to him," she says, "and told him what our General had permitted me to do, and he replied that he and all the other members of his college would help me to the best of their power." She wrote at the same time to Father Antony of Heredia, formerly Prior of the Carmes at Avila, now superior of the Convent of S. Anne at Medina, to procure her a house. Father Alvarez lost no time in seeking the necessary license for the foundation, to which great opposition at first arose. The old objections were renewed, which had been worn threadbare at Avila, against new foundations, above all, foundations without re-venues; and the old accusations against the foundress, of ambition, imprudence, and feminine love of novelty, were repeated over and over again. Happily the same champion who had defended her at Avila was at hand now. Father Dominic Bañez lent his powerful support to the arguments by which F. Alvarez sought to reassure the troubled minds of the authorities, ecclesiastical and secular, of Medina del Campo, and their consent was at last obtained for the foundation.

The next step was to obtain a house. "I had no house," said the Saint, "nor a farthing to buy one, and how could a poor stranger, as I was, have pro-cured credit or trust, had not our Lord assisted us ? He so ordered, that a very virtuous lady, who had been unable to obtain admission into S. Joseph's Convent for want of room, hearing that another house was to be established, should come to me, and ask to be admitted into it.

"She had some money, and though it was not sufficient to purchase a house, it enabled us to hire one, and helped to pay the expenses of the journey. And so a house was hired; and without any other assistance but this, two nuns of S. Joseph's and myself, with four from the Convent of the Incar-nation, set off for Medina del Campo, together with our father chaplain, Julian d'Avila. When the matter was known in the city, there was great murmuring; some said I was a fool; others, that they waited to see the result of such madness. The Bishop also, as he afterwards said to me, thought it a very foolish undertaking, although he did not then tell me so, not wishing to hinder me, because having a great regard for me, he would not give me any uneasiness. My friends also spoke enough to me on the matter, but I took little notice of what they said, because that which they considered very doubtful, appeared to me so easy that I could not be persuaded it would prove a failure."

Meanwhile the good Father Prior had, with no small difficulty, secured a house for the new foundation.

" He treated on the matter with a lady who esteemed him much, and who had a house at her disposal, which, with the exception of one apartment, was almost in ruins. This lady was so kind, that she promised to sell it to him, and without requiring any security beyond his word ; which, if she had insisted on, we should have been unable to make the purchase. But it was our Lord Who disposed everything for us. The walls of this house were so decayed, that we were obliged to hire another whilst they were being repaired, for there was much to be done."

The following is the account given by Ribera of the manner in which S. Teresa performed her journeys.

She never, except in case of necessity, took with her any religious but those who desired to accompany her, and testified in the most gracious manner her pleasure at their willingness to do so. On the day of their departure the whole party communicated.

In order to secure greater recollection, and to avoid interruption from strangers in the public vehicles, she travelled in a private carriage, which was often nothing better than a covered cart. During the journey the religious followed exactly the exercises of the community. A little bell marked the beginning and the end

o

of each, their duration being measured by an hour-glass: silence was kept at the appointed hours. The friars and priests, and even the drivers or other servants who might be of the party, kept it also, and the Saint was accustomed to reward the latter for the unusual restraint by some addition to their meals, or a trifling sum of money. When she was herself obliged to break the silence, it was in few words, and with such sweetness and brightness of manner as cheered her companions under the weariness of the way. Recreation was held at the usual hour, and with the same holy cheerfulness as in the convent. When they left the carriage, the religious put down their veils, that they might not be seen, even by women. In the morning the Saint was the first to rise to awaken the rest, and the last to retire at night. The little colony was always accompanied by a priest, who heard their confessions, said Mass for them, and gave them Holy Communion.

Julian of Avila, or Gonzalez of Aranda, usually acted as their chaplain. Teresa never failed to take holy water with her, and generally an image of the infant Jesus, which she carried in her arms, and one of S. Joseph. During all her distracting journeys she remained in a state of profound recollection. With her, the exercise of the presence of God was of a most special and exalted nature. She felt in the depths of her soul the presence of the Three Divine Persons, and remained continually in their company. Thus she was never for a moment alone, and would never willingly have spoken to others or have been diverted for a moment from that sweet and divine converse. Yet when duty compelled her to speak, it was with a sweetness, brightness, and celestial grace which delighted all who heard her, and which, once heard, could never be forgotten.

The Saint herself thus describes this wonderful grace: " The Three Persons of the Most Blessed Trinity manifest themselves to this soul in such a manner, that she understands them all to be of one substance, one power, and one wisdom ; to be, in short, one God; so that what we know in this world only by faith, that soul, one may say, knows by sight; not that she sees anything by her bodily eyes, nor even by her interior sight . . . But the Three Adorable Persons communicate themselves to that soul, speak to her, and make her to understand those words in the Gospel: *If any man love Me, he will keep My commandments; and My Father will love him, and We will come to him and dwell in him.*

" O my God, what a difference there is between these words striking upon our ear, our even believing them, and understanding them in the manner which I have described! Since that soul has received this favour it seems to her that those Divine Persons have never quitted her; she sees clearly that They are in the very inmost depth of her soul, as if in a deep abyss. Being an unlearned person, she cannot say what that abyss may be; but only that there she finds herself in that Divine Company.

" It may seem to you, my daughters, that a soul in such a state must be so absorbed as to be unable to occupy herself in anything. You are mistaken; she gives herself, with greater ease and fervour than before, to everything that is for the service of God ; and then, as soon as her occupations leave her at liberty, she remains in that Blessed Company."

S. Teresa left Avila on August 13, 1567, having a great desire to begin the foundation at Medina on the Feast of our Blessed Mother's Assumption. She took with her Mary of S. J. Baptist (Mary of Ocampo), Agnes of Jesus, and Anne of the Incarnation (Agnes and Anne of Tapia). Before her departure she went to one of the little hermitages in the garden, on the wall of which she had caused to be painted a representation of our Lord fastened to the pillar, according to the vision which had so powerfully affected her heart when, five-and-twenty years before, that woeful spectacle had aroused her from her state of torpidity. Prostrating herself before it, she implored Him so to watch over her children during her absence, that she might find no decay of fervour amongst them on her return. Our Lord was pleased in the fullest measure to grant her petition, and to bestow abundant graces upon the young religious whom she left to fill her place.

Mary of S. Jerome (in the world Mary of Avila) was a niece of S. Teresa; another member of that remarkable family, in which both saintliness and strength of character seem to have been hereditary gifts.

Her father had been commonly called *Don Alonzo the Saint;* her mother was also remarkable for her piety. Mary was early left an orphan; and God, who intended her to do great things for His service, bestowed on her with a lavish hand those external gifts which she was either to sacrifice or to consecrate to Him. She had scarcely attained her nineteenth year when, after a sharp conflict with the grace which was calling her to religion, the beautiful and wealthy heiress, whose Castilian pride had rejected the noblest suitors in the *City of Knights* as unworthy to match with her, to the amazement of the good people of Avila, humbly sought admission into the poor Convent of S. Joseph's two years after its foundation, and received the habit of Mount Carmel from the hand of S. Teresa.

"Mary of S. Jerome," writes her holy kinswoman,

"is a fertile mine, daily yielding a treasure of virtues and good works." Soon after her profession, she was appointed Sub-prioress and mistress of novices; and, having filled the place of S. Teresa during her absence at Medina del Campo, she was elected Prioress of S. Joseph's, when, in consequence of her frequent journeys for the foundation of her various convents, the Saint resigned the superiority of that house.

On their first day's journey from Avila, the Saint and her companions reached the town of Arévalo late at night, where they met a priest, who had provided a lodging for them in the house of some devout women.

"He told me in private," continues she, "that we could not have the house which had been hired for us, because it stood near the monastery of the Augustinians, and they greatly opposed our entrance there, and that, therefore, we should be forced to have a lawsuit about the matter. But, O my God, when Thou art pleased to inspire us with courage, how powerless are all contradictions! I was only the more animated and encouraged by the consideration that, as the devil began to raise disturbances and difficulties, it was a sign that our Lord would be served in this monastery. However, I desired our friend to say nothing, in order not to disturb my companions, especially the two nuns of the Incarnation; as to the rest, I knew they would endure any trouble for my sake. One of the religious from the Incarnation was the Sub-prioress of that monastery, and both of them were of good families, and both had come with me against the wish of their relations, who were greatly opposed to their departure, for all considered the undertaking very foolish, as, judging according to human reason, it certainly was."

Whilst S. Teresa was anxiously considering what

was the next step to be taken in the perplexing state
of her affairs, she received the welcome news that
Father Dominic Bañez was at Arévalo, and immediately applied to him for counsel and assistance.
"What I was about to undertake," says she, "seemed
not to him so difficult as it did to others, for the more
we know of God, the easier of accomplishment
appear the works which we undertake for Him. It
seemed the more possible to him, on account of
certain favours which God had vouchsafed to me, and
of what he had seen himself in the foundation of
S. Joseph's. He gave me great consolation whenever I saw him, because by his advice I believed
everything would succeed well. As soon as he came
to us, I told him very privately all that had passed.
His opinion was that we might soon settle the affair
of the Augustinians; but to me all delay was a
tedious matter, not knowing what to do with so many
nuns; and thus we all passed the night in trouble, for
the affair was soon told to every one in the house.

"Early in the morning Father Antony de Heredia
came to us, and told us that the house which he had
agreed to purchase was habitable, and that it had
a hall which we could convert into a little church by
adorning it with pieces of tapestry. This we resolved
upon; at least, I thought it would do very well, and
that the more haste we made, so much the better
it would be for us, considering we were out of our
convent; and as there was also some opposition to be
feared (for I had learnt a lesson from the first foundation), I was very anxious to take possession before
the matter became known. And to this Father
Dominic Bañez likewise consented. We arrived at
Medina del Campo on the eve of the Assumption
of our Lady about midnight; and to avoid all disturbance we alighted at the monastery of S. Anne,

and thence we went on foot to our house. It was a great mercy of God, that at such an hour we met no one, though it was the time when the bulls were brought into Medina for a bull-fight on the following day. I thought of nothing, on account of the terror and amazement we were in. But our Lord, who takes care of those who desire to please Him, preserved us; for we truly had no other object in view but His glory in this matter. Having come to the house, we entered into a court, the walls of which seemed much decayed, as I saw more plainly afterwards, when it was daylight. It seems to me that our Lord was pleased this good father should be so blind as not to perceive there was no proper place there for the Most Blessed Sacrament. When I saw the hall, I perceived that there was much rubbish to be removed, and that the walls were not plastered: the night was far advanced, and we had only brought a few hangings (three, I think), which were nothing for the whole length of the hall.

"I knew not what was to be done, for I saw there was no proper place for erecting the altar. Our Lord was, however, pleased that the house should be founded immediately, for the steward of the lady had in the house several pieces of tapestry which belonged to her, and also a piece of blue damask, and she had told him to give us whatever we wanted, which was very kind of her. When I saw such good furniture, I praised our Lord, and so also did the other nuns. But we knew not what to do for nails, and that was not the time to buy them; we began, however, to search for some on the walls, and at length with difficulty we procured abundance; and then some of the men began putting up the tapestry, whilst we swept the floor; and we made such great haste, that by break of day the altar was ready, a bell was put up, and immediately Mass was said. This was sufficient for taking possession; but we did not rest contented till we had the Most Blessed Sacrament placed in the tabernacle. We heard Mass through the chinks of a door that was opposite the altar, having no other place. With this I was quite content, because to me it was the greatest joy and comfort to behold one more church in which the Most Blessed Sacrament was adored. But my joy lasted only a little while; for when Mass was over, I chanced to look out into the court from a window, and saw all the wall in many places quite in ruins, to repair which would require the work of many days. O my God! when I beheld Thy Divine Majesty exposed in the streets, in so dangerous times as we now live in, on account of these Lutherans, what sorrow and dismay seized upon my heart! And then came before me all the difficulties raised by those who had so greatly opposed me; and I saw clearly they had much reason in doing so. It now seemed to me impossible to go on with what I had begun, for, as formerly, all things appeared to me so easy, seeing they were done for God, so now the temptation had such power, that I thought I never had received any favour from Him: my own weakness and baseness were alone present to me. Relying, therefore, on so miserable a support, what good success, thought I, could I hope for? Had I been alone, I think I could have borne up better; but the thought of my companions turning back again to their house, after all the opposition they had met with when they left it, seemed to me very hard. I also imagined that, having thus erred in the first of the new foundations, I had no right to expect our Lord to do anything for those which should follow; and a fear came on me immediately, lest what I had heard in prayer had been a delusion; and this was a still greater source of trouble and uneasiness, because I began to be extremely fearful lest the devil had deceived me.

"O my God!" she continues, as she reviews this terrible conflict, "what a grievous spectacle is the soul, which Thou art pleased to leave in such pain! Truly when I remember this and other afflictions which I suffered during these foundations, it appears to me that no account is to be made of bodily pains, though I have endured some which were very severe."

Yet the brave heart bore on alone. "I did not reveal my trouble to my companions, because I did not wish to add to the afflictions which they had already endured. In this anguish I passed a great part of the evening, till the Rector of the Society sent a father to visit me, and he animated and consoled me exceedingly. I did not tell him all my sorrows, but only that which I felt at finding ourselves in the street. I began to speak to him about hiring a house for us (cost what it might) wherein we might dwell till the other was repaired. I now began to take courage on beholding so many people coming to the church, and no one accused us of folly, which was a mercy of God; for had they reflected on our situation, they would have done quite right to take away the Most Blessed Sacrament from us. I wonder now that no one thought of doing this, and also at my own stupidity, in thinking that if that were done, all would be undone.

" In spite of all the diligence used in seeking a house, none could be found to let in the whole town; therefore I was in great trouble night and day, because though I had appointed men to watch and guard the Most Blessed Sacrament, yet I was fearful lest they might fall asleep; and so I arose in the night myself to watch it from a window, whence by the clear light of the moon I could see it very plainly. During all these days great multitudes came to the church; and, far from blaming us, their devotion increased the more to see our Lord again in a stable; and His Majesty (who is never weary of humbling Himself for our sake) appeared unwilling to remove from thence.

"About a week afterwards, a merchant who lived in a very good house, seeing our necessity, told us we might have the upper part of it, where we could dwell as in a house of our own.

"He had also a very large hall, with a gilded roof, and this he gave us for a church, and a lady who lived near the house we had bought, whose name was Doña Helen de Quiroga, a great servant of God, told us that she would help us, that so a chapel might be immediately prepared in which the Most Blessed Sacrament might be placed; and likewise, that she would so accommodate us, that we should live in enclosure. Other persons also liberally contributed to our support, but no one so bountifully as this lady.

"And now I began to feel more quiet and at rest, being able to keep perfect enclosure; so we began to recite our office.

"The good Prior took great pains in fitting up the house, and made all possible haste; but with all his labour it cost him two months to accomplish it. He repaired it so thoroughly, that the religious were able to live there with tolerable convenience for several years; and since that time our Lord has enabled us still further to improve it."

The Carmelites at Medina, like those at Avila, soon lived down the opposition which had arisen against them at their first arrival.

"The nuns," says S. Teresa, "continued to gain credit with the people, who were greatly delighted with them, and I think with reason, because all had but one object, which was, how each could best serve

our Lord. In every respect they observed the same
rules that are kept in the Convent of S. Joseph's
at Avila ; the constitutions are also the same. Our
Lord began to call some sisters to take the habit; and
the favours He granted them were so great, that I was
astonished thereat. May He be for ever blessed,
Amen, for He seeks only to be loved that so He may
grant us His love."

Amongst the chosen souls called by our Divine
Lord to fill the cloister of Medina del Campo, was
Geronima, the beloved child of the holy widow, Helen
de Quiroga, who had so zealously aided the foundation. Geronima had not fully completed her four-
teenth year when she received the habit of Mount
Carmel. Helen de Quiroga, who ever after the foundation of the convent at Medina was honoured with the
intimate friendship of S. Teresa, after a life of extraordinary sanctity in the world, having fulfilled her
duties in the education of her remaining children,
obtained the long desire of her heart, and was admitted into the Order of her friend and her child
in 1581, only one year before the death of the
former.

After the foregoing narrative of her second foundation, S. Teresa, pauses to dwell with overflowing
thankfulness on the interior sanctity which adorned
and consecrated the exterior building.

" As now these little dove-cots of the Blessed
Virgin our Lady began to fill, so His Divine Majesty
began also to show His greatness in these poor, weak
women, so strong in good desires and in disengagement from creatures; for this it is which, being joined
with purity of conscience, unites the soul most closely
with its Creator.

" I need not, indeed, have mentioned purity of conscience, for if the disengagement be real and sincere,

it seems to me to imply a careful endeavour never to offend God. And as all the discourses and meditations of these His faithful spouses relate to Him, so does His Majesty appear unwilling ever to depart from them. This is what I now see, and can affirm with truth. Let those fear who shall come after us and read these words; and if they see not what we now see, let them not ascribe it to the times, for at all times God is ever ready to bestow favours upon those who serve Him in earnest, and endeavour to discover and correct whatever imperfections may remain in them.

"The favours which our Lord bestows in these houses are very great, for there are few amongst our sisters whom He conducts by the way of ordinary meditation, the rest are raised to perfect contemplation, whilst some have been favoured with raptures; on others our Lord bestows graces of various kinds, such as revelations and visions, which evidently come from Him. There is now not one of our houses in which we may not find one or two, or even three of these favoured souls.

"I am well aware," adds the *Saint of Common Sense*, "that sanctity does not consist in all these things, neither is it my intention to praise these nuns, but to show how necessary and applicable are the remarks which I am about to make."

And here follow some of those wonderful instructions on the true nature of prayer and of interior perfection, in which S. Teresa gives us a fuller knowledge of herself than can be gained from any narrative of her exterior life.

"I have met with some," she says, "who seem to imagine that the essential point in prayer is the exercise of the understanding, and if they can keep their mind fixed on God, though by using great violence to themselves, they immediately consider themselves to be very spiritual persons, and if they experience involuntary distractions, or are obliged to turn their mind to anything else, even to things good and meritorious, they immediately become greatly afflicted, and fancy they are doing nothing.

"But the true proficiency of the soul consists, not in much thinking, but in much loving. And if you ask me how this love must be acquired, I answer, by resolving to do the Divine Will, and to suffer for God, and by so doing, and so suffering, when occasions for action and for suffering arise.

"Oh, how does divine charity *press* the heart of those who truly love the Lord, and know the desires of His heart! How little rest do they take if they can be of any use in advancing the welfare of a soul, and increasing her love of God; or if they can give her any comfort, or free her from any danger! How little do such souls look to their own interest or their own ease! And when they can do no good by their works, they endeavour to do something by their prayers, importuning our Lord in behalf of those numerous souls whom they grieve to see in danger of eternal destruction; and thus bewailing their lot, they sacrifice their own repose and pay no regard to their own happiness, considering only how they may best accomplish the will of God. And thus it is with obedience: it would be a strange thing if, when God clearly tells us to do something for Him, we should choose rather to stand gazing upon Him, because we could thus please ourselves most! This would indeed be a strange way of advancing in the love of God; to bind His hands, and compel Him to lead us onward in a way of our own choosing!

"O Lord, how far are Thy ways above our thoughts! And what dost Thou require of a soul, which is already determined to love Thee, and give herself entirely into

Thy hands, but that she should be obedient, that she should enquire in all things what most tends to Thy glory, and ardently desire to execute it? She has no need to seek out new paths, or to choose between them, for her will is now Thy will. Thou, O my Lord, takest upon Thyself the care of leading her in the path wherein she shall make the greatest progress. And though the superior may not take the trouble of guiding her in the way most advantageous to her, but may employ her only in those duties which he thinks will tend most to the good of the community, yet Thou, O my God, dost conduct her, disposing her and all her employments in such a manner, that (without understanding how) she finds herself making great spiritual progress, obeying with such fidelity every command of her superiors, as is matter of astonishment even to herself. Such a soul was a religious, with whom I spoke a few days ago, who by obedience had for fifteen years been so engaged in his duties and offices, that during all this period he did not remember to have had one day for himself. All that he could do was to steal some spare time in the day to devote to prayer, and to attend carefully to the purifying of his conscience. This was the most obedient soul I ever knew, and he even imprints this virtue on all with whom he converses. Our Lord has liberally rewarded him, for (without his knowing how) he enjoys that precious liberty of soul which the perfect possess, and in which consists all the happiness that can be hoped for in this life; for, desiring nothing, he possesses all things. Such souls neither fear nor covet anything on earth; afflictions do not disturb them, neither does pleasure elate them; nothing, in short, can rob them of their peace, because nothing can deprive them of God, on whom alone it depends; the fear of losing Him is the only thing which could disturb them. Everything else in this world is in their eyes as if it were not, because it neither gives nor takes away their joy. O blessed obedience ! blessed even in the distractions which it imposes, since the soul is thereby raised to so high a degree of perfection !

"Courage, then, my daughters, let there be no sadness : when obedience calls you to exterior employments (as, for example, into the kitchen, amidst the pots and dishes), remember that our Lord goes along with you, to help you both in your interior and exterior duties. I remember a religious once told me, that he had determined within himself always to do whatever his superiors should command him, no matter what trouble it might give him. One evening, being quite spent with labour, and not able to stand on his legs, he wished to rest himself. No sooner had he sat down than his superior came and found him, and bade him take a spade, and go dig in the garden. The good man said nothing, though so completely exhausted : he took his spade, and as he was going into the garden by a certain passage (which I saw many years after this was related to me, when I founded a house in that very town), our Lord appeared to him with His cross on His shoulders, and so faint and weary as to make him understand that what he then suffered was nothing in comparison with what his Saviour had endured.

"I believe that it is because the devil knows well there is no path which leads us sooner to the highest perfection than that of obedience, that he raises so many difficulties under the semblance of good to disgust us with it. Let this truth be well understood, and men will clearly see that the highest perfection does not consist in interior joys, nor in sublime raptures, nor in visions, nor in having the gift of prophecy, but in bringing our will into such conformity with the Will of God, that whatever we know He desires, that also shall we desire with our whole affection; receiving what is bitter as joyfully as what is sweet and pleasant, if only it be according to the Will of His Divine Majesty.

"I particularly wish it to be understood that the reason why obedience (in my opinion) is so speedy, and so sure a means of arriving at this happy state is, that in order so to master our own will as to be able to devote it wholly and sincerely to God, it must be subject to reason, and obedience is the shortest and most efficacious means of bringing it into this subjection. To attempt to effect this by arguments is never to come to a conclusion, and is a dangerous method withal : for nature and self-love will always have so many good reasons on the other side that we should never come to a conclusion, for that which our reason sees to be best, often appears to us foolish because we have no mind to do it.

"Our Lord so values this submission to superiors for His sake, that by exercising ourselves therein, and disengaging ourselves from self-love, we come, though painfully at first, to conform our will to the will of those who command us, by the help of our Lord, Who, because we subject our will and reason to others for His sake, gives us the mastery of our own will, which we are then enabled with perfect freedom to offer wholly to God, that He may unite it with His own, and that the fire of His love may descend from heaven and consume the sacrifice; we on our own part avoiding all that may be displeasing in His sight.

"All we have to do is thus to lay our will upon the altar, not suffering it, as far as in us lies, to be defiled by anything of earth.

"This," continues the Saint, "is the union which I

desire to see in you all, and not certain raptures, however sweet they may be, to which the name of union is given, and which indeed will often be granted, over and above, to those who possess the true union of which I have been speaking. But if these raptures leave us averse to obedience, and attached to our own will, they will, in my opinion, have united us to our own self-love, rather than to the will of God.

"One day spent in humility and self-knowledge, though at the cost of many afflictions and labours, I account to be a greater favour from our Lord than many days spent in prayer: the rather, that a true lover loves everywhere, and at all times thinks of his beloved. And here we must be upon our guard, that we may never neglect, in the performance of those external duties, which are imposed by obedience and charity, frequently to think of God and of our interior sanctification. And believe me, our spiritual progress does not depend upon the length of time which we spend in prayer; for when we fulfil with great perfection those duties to which we are called by charity and obedience, we often advance more in the love of God in a few moments thus employed, than in many long hours of consideration.

"All must come from His hand; may He be blessed for ever and ever!"

Thus was founded and built up in sanctity the second convent of the reform, which, like its predecessor at Avila, and most of the subsequent foundations of S. Teresa, was placed under the invocation of S. Joseph. When the Saint received from our Lord a command to write the history of her foundations, she would have omitted that of Medina del Campo, as containing nothing remarkable, when He enquired of her by an interior voice: "Seemeth it not to thee to have been full of miracles?"

The providential guidance which had led her to Medina, paved the way also for the execution of her great project of the foundation of a house of reformed friars.

She unfolded her plan confidentially to the good Prior Heredia, who had exerted himself so strenuously in behalf of the new foundation, in the hope of obtaining help from his prudence and long experience of the religious life which he had entered at the age of ten years, and inquired of him whether he knew of any, either in the Order or among the secular clergy, who would be able and willing to make trial of such a life. To her utter amazement, the venerable Prior, notwithstanding his sixty years, his long superiority, his delicate health, and his profession for half a century of the mitigated rule, at once offered himself as the first of her disciples.

She thought he was jesting, and told him so; "because, though he was always a good religious, recollected and studious, and a lover of his cell, yet I did not think he was a fit person to begin such an undertaking, or that he had sufficient strength and spirit to bear the rigour and severity requisite for such a life, for he was very delicate, and not accustomed to any austerities. But he assured me it was otherwise with him, and he certified to me that some time ago our Lord had called him to a stricter life, and also that he had determined to become a Carthusian, and that the fathers had told him they would receive him. With all this, however, I was not quite satisfied, though I was glad to hear it; and I entreated him to wait some time and exercise himself in those things which he would have to perform under a vow. He did so for a year, and during this period he met with so many troubles and false accusations as made it appear that our Lord wished to try him. And he bore all so well, and advanced so much in perfection, that I praised our Lord for it, because I thought He was thus disposing him for this undertaking."

Besides the persecutions which served to brace the strength and courage of this veteran soldier of Christ, he exercised himself in various corporal austerities, in preparation for the life to which he desired to devote himself, wearing a coarse woollen tunic in the greatest heat of summer, and spending many hours in prayer, wherein he was favoured with singular graces from our Lord.

Still the mind of S.Teresa was not entirely at rest. " I was not," she says, " fully satisfied with the Prior." She continued to pour forth fervent prayers to our Lord that He would be pleased to raise up fitting instruments for the work which He had inspired her to undertake, and not long after the conversation above recorded with the Prior of S. Anne's, another religious of the same Order brought with him as his companion, when he came to visit her, a young friar lately raised to the priesthood, named John of Matthias, known afterwards in Carmel by the name of Blessed John of the Cross, a name to which the Church has added the title of Saint. He was the son of poor but pious parents; his mother, a saintly woman, who became afterwards the intimate friend of S. Teresa, was now a widow, and residing at Medina, where her son had been trained in the college of the Jesuit Fathers. Having distinguished himself there by his proficiency in literature, rhetoric, and philosophy, John de Yépez consecrated himself to God at the age of one-and-twenty, in the presence of his happy mother, in the Order of Mount Carmel. He had lately returned from finishing his theological studies at Salamanca when he first became acquainted with S. Teresa, who felt no distrust of this second postulant sent to her by

Divine Providence. She seemed at once to recognise a spirit in unison with her own. " I gave thanks," she says, " to our Lord." She waited, however, for the young religious to give her an opening to speak upon the subject so near her heart, and when he had laid before her his desire to lead a life of greater solitude, and his conviction that God was calling him to a state of higher perfection, which he hoped to attain in the Carthusian Order, " My son," she said, with the authority and tenderness of a mother, " have patience, and go not to the Carthusians, for we are about to open a reformed house of our own Order, in which you will be able to satisfy all your desires of retirement, recollection, penance, and prayer, and will do great service to God and to His Blessed Mother." She then represented to him how much better he would be able to serve our Lord, and how much greater good he would be able to effect by promoting a reform of his own Order, than by forsaking it for another.

While Teresa spoke, our Lord brought vividly to the recollection of the young friar words which he had heard whilst yet a secular, and in uncertainty as to whither the will of God was calling him, " Thou shalt serve Me in an Order, the ancient perfection of which thou shalt aid Me to restore." He at once promised to assist Teresa in her undertaking, and to lay aside every other purpose, on one only condition, that there should be no unnecessary delay in the commencement of the work. Teresa was now quite ready to begin it, being provided, as she playfully said, with " a friar and a half," alluding to the lofty stature and noble presence of the Prior, and the insignificant and meagre aspect of S. John of the Cross, whom, with reference to his wisdom of speech, she was accustomed also to call her " little Seneca." A considerable time, how-

ever, still intervened before the work was begun,
either from the difficulty of finding a house, or because
the prudent foundress was in no haste to seek for
one, being desirous of a longer time to test the
strength and endurance of Father Antony.   She
therefore begged her new associates to remain at
Medina, preparing themselves for their work by
earnest prayer, until God should provide them with
a suitable dwelling.   In the meantime, she turned
her attention to the foundation of two other convents
of nuns.

CHAPTER XIV.

1567.

THE next application which Teresa received for a new
foundation was from one who seemed little likely to
interest himself in the formation of convents for contemplation.   Don Bernardin of Mendoza, brother of
the Bishop of Avila, was a young and gallant gentleman, whose life bore upon its surface few marks of
predestination, except a tender and chivalrous devotion
to the Blessed Mother of God.

Some business having brought him to Medina, he
went to visit the Mother Teresa, whom he held in
high esteem, not only from the public report of her
sanctity, but from the especial respect and affection
borne to her by the Bishop, his brother.   Don Bernardin urgently pressed her to make a foundation as
soon as possible near the fine and populous city of
Valladolid in Old Castile.   " He told me," she says,
" that he would willingly give me a house which
belonged to him near Valladolid, having a large vineyard and magnificent gardens attached to it, and

that he would put me in immediate possession if I would make the foundation at once. To say the truth, I was not very willing to establish a convent at the distance of three-quarters of a mile from the city. But the offer was made with so good a will, and to so good an end, that I was unwilling to refuse it or to deprive this young gentleman of the merit which he might derive from his generosity. Besides, I considered that it would be easy afterwards to exchange this house for one in Valladolid. Therefore I gratefully accepted the offer."

Don Bernardin, for a reason which the Saint afterwards understood, continued to urge the immediate foundation of the house, a desire which she was unable to gratify, as two other persons, whom she considered to have a superior claim, were at the same time calling her elsewhere.

The first of these was her old friend Doña Louisa de la Cerda, who now earnestly begged her to found a convent on one of her estates, at a place called Malagon. The other who asked her aid was Doña Eleanora Mascareña, formerly governess to Don Carlos, the son of Philip II. This lady begged her to come to Alcalà de Henarez, a city of New Castile, in order to instruct in religious observance the inmates of the convent, which had been erected there four years before by the venerable Mary of Jesus, whose intercourse with Teresa at Toledo has been already mentioned. This blessed woman was endowed with many excellent gifts. She was humble, penitent, fervent in prayer, and so keenly alive to the beauty of evangelical poverty, that our Lord had chosen her as His instrument to excite our Saint to found her houses without revenues. But it had not pleased Him to bestow upon her the qualities necessary for carrying out her own idea. She had been compelled to consent to the endowment of the convent which she had founded about a year after that of S. Joseph's at Avila, and she introduced into it a rigid and extraordinary way of life, which, not being tempered by the necessary sweetness and prudence, caused many of her subjects to lose their health, and made all very clearly perceive that it would be impossible long to persevere in the course which had been begun. They determined, therefore, to have recourse to the known prudence and wisdom of the Mother Teresa; and at their desire Doña Eleanora, at whose expense their convent had been founded, conveyed to the Saint their request that she should visit them.

Teresa agreed to meet Doña Eleanora at Madrid, and then to visit Alcalà on her way to Malagon. She had no sooner arrived at the Mascareña palace, accompanied by two religious from Avila, than the news of her presence spread through the city, and a bevy of ladies of Madrid assembled to gaze at her, some out of devotion, many out of mere curiosity. Not a few expected her to work a miracle before them, or hoped at least to see her in an ecstasy. So they gathered round her; one to ask the solution of a question of conscience, another to hear a prediction of the future. Earnestly as Teresa wished herself at home again, she managed with her usual address to elude the attacks of the fine ladies. Having replied with her wonted gentle courtesy to their greetings, and those of her noble hostess, she began to talk of *the beauty of the streets of Madrid*, and other such commonplace subjects, keeping the conversation so entirely in her own hands, that the poor ladies found it utterly impossible to introduce one of the weighty subjects which they had come prepared to discuss. Great was their mortification and confusion; most of them went away saying that the *Mother Teresa was doubtless a good religious, but certainly no Saint.* A few of greater discernment saw through the artifice by which she had contrived to shroud her sanctity under the veil of her humility. Of the same opinion as these last were the discalced nuns of S. Clare, with whom S. Teresa spent a fortnight during her stay at Madrid, at the earnest desire of their foundress, Doña Jane, sister of King Philip II. That princess, the religious, and especially the Abbess of the convent, who was a kinswoman of S. Francis Borgia, were filled with admiration at the marvellous simplicity of their saintly guest. "Blessed be God," said one of them, "who has consoled us by the sight of a Saint whom we may all imitate; she eats, sleeps, and speaks as we do, and converses with us without that reserve affected by some who pretend to spirituality. Her spirit is certainly the spirit of the Lord, for she is simple and sincere, and lives amongst us as He lived amongst men."

S. Teresa left Madrid with her two companions in the November of 1567 for Alcalà, accompanied by Doña Maria of Mendoza, sister of Don Bernardin, who made her travel in her carriage.

She was received by the religious of Alcalà as a messenger from Heaven. They consigned to her the keys of the convent, and presented themselves to her as her loving and obedient children. The venerable foundress surpassed them all in humility and submission; thus proving that, in whatever degree she might be wanting in some of the qualities requisite in a superioress, she was amply endowed with the essential graces of the religious life. S. Teresa spared no labour in forming these fervent souls to the true perfection of their state. She gave them the constitutions which had been drawn up for the use of S. Joseph's at Avila; and then, having completed her charitable work at Alcalà, proceeded to the foundation of her third convent at Malagon.

Doña Louisa de la Cerda' had provided a house and a sufficient maintenance for the religious of the new foundation. Teresa was very unwilling to depart from her purpose of founding in absolute poverty, but was convinced by the reasons of Doña Louisa, and of her confessor, Father Bañez, of the necessity of such a provision in a country place like Malagon, where the surrounding peasants would be incapable of supporting the nuns by their alms. The holy mother left Alcalà for Toledo just before the Lent of 1568. There she made the necessary arrangements for the foundation with Doña Louisa, and sent for four of her daughters from Avila, who, with her two companions, completed the number of six. They accompanied Doña Louisa to Malagon, which they reached about ten days before Palm Sunday, and were lodged in her castle. Until the convent should be built, they were to inhabit a house in the market-place, whither they were to remove on Palm Sunday. In the meantime, Teresa, accompanied by one of her sisters, the mayor, and the parish priest, went out to choose a site for the convent. They soon came to a place which seemed very suitable for the purpose. "No," said the Saint, "we must leave this site for the discalced Fathers of S. Francis, who are to make a foundation here." These words were verified a few years afterwards, to the no small amazement of those who remembered the prophecy. A little way out of the village they came to an olive garden. "We will go no farther," said Teresa, "for God has chosen this as the site of our convent." "On Palm Sunday," says the Saint, "all the people of the place came out in procession, and, putting on our veils and white mantles, we came to the church, whence the Most

Blessed Sacrament was taken to our monastery. This excited great devotion in the people."

Thus was founded the third monastery of discalced Carmelites, which bore, like the first two, the name of the glorious Patriarch S. Joseph.

S. Teresa remained there about two months, forming the new community to every practice of perfection. She tells us, that one day after Communion our Lord said to her that *He should be greatly served in that house.* The chronicles of the Order record the extraordinary life of penance and austerity of these holy religious, who seemed anxious thus to make up for the absence of that perfection of poverty which had characterized the former foundations of the reform.

S. Teresa was now pressed to open a house at Toledo, but she postponed doing so for a time. " My spirit," said she, " hurried me to go and found a house in Valladolid." She was impelled to this haste by the tidings of the unexpected death of Don Bernardin of Mendoza. " He fell so suddenly ill," writes the Saint, "that he was deprived of the use of his speech, and was unable therefore to make his confession, although he gave many proofs of contrition for his sins : he died in a very short time, at a great distance from the place where I then was. Our Lord told me that his salvation had been in great danger, that He had had mercy on him on account of the service rendered to His Blessed Mother, in giving that house to found a monastery of her Order ; but that he would not be delivered from Purgatory until the first Mass should be said there. The grievous sufferings of this soul were so continually present to me that, though I wished to found a house in Toledo, I would not begin for the present, but hurried on to the utmost of my power the foundation in Valladolid."

Some delay was, however, unavoidable, for the Saint was obliged to stop for some days on her way at S. Joseph's at Avila, and afterwards at S. Joseph's at Medina del Campo. During these few days which she spent at Avila an opening at last presented itself for the foundation of a house of discalced friars.

"A young gentleman of Avila," says the Saint, "named Don Raphael Mexia, with whom I had never before spoken, came to hear (I know not how) that I wished to found a monastery of discalced friars, and therefore he came and offered to give me a house which he possessed in a little village called Durvelo. There were few houses in the place; not above twenty, if I remember rightly; this house was inhabited by a farmer, who collected his rents. Though I judged what kind of a dwelling it must be, I praised our Lord, and, accepting the offer, thanked the gentleman much. He told me it was on the way to Medina del Campo, and that I must pass by it to go to Valladolid, so that I might then see the place. I answered that I would do so, and kept my word. I left Avila in the month of June, with only one companion (Antonia of the Holy Ghost), and Julian of Avila, the chaplain of S. Joseph's, the priest who assisted me in these journeys. Though we set off at daybreak, yet, not knowing the road, we missed our way; and, as the place was not much known, no one could direct us; and thus we walked on all that day in great trouble, for the sun was very hot, and when we thought we were near the place, we had as far again to travel. I shall always remember the fatigue and wandering of that day. We arrived there a little before night, and when we entered the house it was in such a state that we dared not remain there during the night, because the place was so exceedingly dirty, and there were also many reapers about. It had a tolerable hall, one

chamber, with a garret, and a little kitchen: this
building was all that was to compose our convent. I
thought that the hall might be converted into a
chapel, that the garret would do very well for a choir,
and the chamber for a dormitory. My companion,
though much better than myself and a great lover of
penance, could not endure the idea of establishing a
convent there, and therefore she said to me, ' Certainly, Mother, no soul, however fervent, could endure
such a place; speak no more about it.' Father
Julian, though at first of the same opinion, when I
told him my intentions did not oppose me. We
passed the night in the church, though, on account of
our great fatigue, we stood more in need of sleeping
than watching. When we arrived at Medina, I immediately spoke with F. Antonio, and described to him
exactly the place which we had seen, asking him if he
had courage to remain there for a time. I told him
he might be sure that God would soon provide something better, if only we would begin. I spoke thus
positively, because I seemed to have present before
me what our Lord has since done, and to have no
more doubt of it than now I see it before my eyes. I
told him also that he might be assured that neither
the former nor the present Provincial would give us a
license if they were to see us in a very fine house,
even if we could procure one; whereas, living in such
a small house, and in such an obscure village, no
notice would be taken of us. Our Lord had given
greater courage to him than to me, for he said he was
' willing to dwell, not only there, but even in a pig-
sty.' F. John of the Cross was of the same mind.
And now we wanted only the consent of the two
Fathers Provincial, which our Father-General had
made a condition of granting the license. I hoped in
our Lord to be able to obtain it, and therefore I spoke

to Father Antonio to take care to collect all he could for the house, and then departed with F. John of the Cross for the foundation of Valladolid."

Some necessary arrangements detained S. Teresa at Medina on her way. Full of charity as was her heart for the suffering soul which was thirsting for the first Mass at Valladolid, there was another Heart yearning over it with a love infinitely exceeding that of any creature, however saintly; another Eye, which neither the reformation of an Order, nor the care of the whole creation of God, could avert for a moment from that one point in the universe whence His banished one was stretching out his hands to Him. "Make haste," said the voice of the Good Shepherd, as Teresa knelt before His Tabernacle at Medina, "for that soul is suffering exceedingly."

"When I heard these words," she says, "I began my journey immediately, though without any preparation, and entered Valladolid on the Feast of S. Laurence. When I saw the house, I was exceedingly afflicted, because I perceived it would be madness for the nuns to remain there. It could not be rendered habitable without very great expense; and also, although there was much room for recreation in the beautiful garden, it could not fail to be very unhealthy, because a river ran close by it. Though exceedingly wearied with our journey, we wished to hear Mass in a monastery of our Order at the entrance of the city, which, as it was at a considerable distance, increased our fatigue. I did not, however, say anything to my companions, lest I should discourage them, for I had a belief, in the midst of my weakness, that our Lord would in some way provide for the accomplishment of what He had told me. Accordingly, I privately employed workmen to make partitions by means of which we might be able to observe enclosure, and so all that was of absolute necessity was accomplished."

S. Teresa employed the time which elapsed before the enclosure could be effected in instructing the young friar, who was to be the foundation-stone of the reform amongst his brethren, in the manner of life led by herself and her daughters.

"He" (S. John of the Cross), she says, "wished to be informed concerning our mortifications, the nature of our conversation, and of the recreations which we have all together, and which are used with such moderation, as serves only to discover the faults of the sisters, and to afford them a little relaxation to enable them the better to support the rigour of their rules. That father was so good, that I might have learnt much more from him than he from me; but this was not my design at that time, but only to show him after what manner we live."

S. John of the Cross, exercising at the same time the office of confessor to the little community, was able to observe the exact conformity between its exterior mode of life and its interior perfection.

Julian of Avila endeavoured in the meantime to procure a license from the ordinary. This license could not be immediately obtained; but on the following Sunday leave was given for Mass to be said in the place which had been prepard for a chapel; and there the Holy Sacrifice was accordingly offered. "I had no thought," says the Saint, "that then would be fulfilled what I had heard concerning that soul; for although I was told it would be at the *first Mass*, I took these words to mean that Mass at which the Blessed Sacrament would be exposed. When the priest came forward to give us Communion with the ciborium in his hand, at the moment I received the Sacred Host, that gentleman appeared to me standing at the side of the priest, with joined hands and a radiant and joyful countenance. He thanked me for having delivered him from Purgatory, and then ascended straightway into Heaven. It was a great joy to me when I first heard that he was in the way of salvation, for when I received the news of his sudden death, I was in a manner hopeless, fearing that his soul was lost, because, though he had many good qualities, another kind of death was (I thought) needed for such a life, for he was much given to the vanities of the world. True it is that he told my companions that he believed his death to be near. Great is the mercy of our Lord, and wonderfully acceptable to Him is any service rendered to His Blessed Mother. May He be praised and blessed by all men who thus rewards with eternal life and glory our mean and miserable actions, making those things great which are in themselves so worthless."

This marvellous event occurred on the the Feast of our Blessed Lady's Assumption, and the convent thus happily founded bore the title of *our Lady of Mount Carmel.*

The unhealthy position of the house soon told painfully upon its new inhabitants. The religious fell sick one after another, and Teresa's time and thoughts were devoted to the duties of infirmarian, till she was herself laid prostrate like the rest. Doña Mary of Mendoza, however, soon came to her assistance. She purchased another house in a healthy situation nearer the city, and gave it to the religious, in the place of that bestowed on them by her deceased brother.

They removed to their new abode on February 3, 1569, in solemn procession, accompanied by the Bishop of Avila, and all the clergy, secular and regular, of the city.

The Convent of Valladolid, under the superiority

of Mary Baptist (Mary of Ocampo), was distinguished even amongst the houses of the reform for the singular perfection of its inmates.

S. Teresa employs two chapters of her Book of Foundations in describing the extraordinary vocation of Casilda de Padilla, daughter of the Adelantado of Castile, who following the example of her brother and two elder sisters, renounced the splendid inheritance which fell to her by their consecration to religion, to devote herself to God in her thirteenth year in the Convent of Valladolid; and the saintly life and death of Beatrice Oñez, a kinswoman of Casilda (in Carmel, Beatrice of the Incarnation). Want of space alone withholds us from inserting entire this finished picture of a perfect religious by the hand of S. Teresa. The secret of its perfection is disclosed in the reply of Beatrice to one of the sisters who expressed surprise at her undisturbed tranquillity amidst the severest trials and sufferings. "The value of whatever we do, however small it may be, for the love of God is inestimable. We should not so much as turn our eyes except to please Him."

The palace of Doña Mary d'Acuna, the mother of Casilda, and herself a woman of great piety, was a nursery of Saints. Besides her three daughters and Beatrice Oñez, it gave shelter for a time to a young peasant girl, who afterwards, under the name of Stephania of the Apostles, entered the Convent of Valladolid as a lay sister, and, after a life of extraordinary purity and penance, died in the odour of sanctity, and was seen by her companions entering the glory of the Blessed. Another lay sister of Valladolid, Catharine of S. John the Evangelist, equalled Stephania in sanctity, and, like her, in the midst of a life of lowly service and unremitting labour, was favoured with the highest gifts of contemplation.

CHAPTER XV.

1568-1571.

TERESA was now free to begin her long-contemplated work. The cottage at Durvelo was as suitable a cradle for the new family of poverty as the hut of Rivo Torto two centuries before; and the spirit of the saintly youth and the noble-hearted old man, who were there to consecrate their lives to the renovation of their Order, was worthy of the days of S. Francis.

The approval of the Bishop of Avila, the diocesan, was readily given. The assent of the two Provincials was more difficult of attainment. F. Alonzo Gonzalez, the Provincial now in office, happened providentially to come to Valladolid at this time, and thus fell under the personal influence of the Saint, which so often proved irresistible.

"It pleased God," says she, "that the Provincial of our Order, Alonzo Gonzalez (from whom I was to obtain a license), should come here at this time. He was a good, simple old man, but irresolute in this matter. When I asked for the license, I gave him so many reasons for granting it, and insisted so much on the account he would have to render to God if he in any way hindered so good a work, that, His Divine Majesty so disposing him (because He willed that the request should be granted), he was greatly moved. Doña Mary de Mendoza, and the Bishop of Avila, her brother, who has ever favoured and protected us, coming thither at the same time, soon obtained his consent, as well as that of Father Angelo de Salazar, the former Provincial, from whom I feared greater opposition. As soon as we had obtained the consent of these Fathers, it seemed to me that nothing more

Q

was needed. We at once arranged that F. John of the Cross should go to the house, and make it in some sort habitable ; for I made all possible haste to begin, lest some obstacle should arise in the way. F. Antony had already collected a few necessary things, and we gave what little help we were able to afford."

S. John of the Cross took up his abode at Durvelo in the beginning of October. Having first adored the Blessed Sacrament in the parish church, he entered his poor dwelling, kissing the floor in the overflowing joy of his heart. He set to work to arrrange it according to the directions of the holy Mother, and adorned the rough walls with skulls and wooden crosses, made of branches of trees which he collected from the neighbouring woods. Night found him still so absorbed in his work that he had forgotten to provide himself with any food. He sent a boy to ask alms from some of the neighbouring peasants, and receiving a few dry crusts, he joyfully supped on this meagre fare after the labours of that happy day. Having risen before morning to pray, he laid on the rude altar the habit of the reform made by the hands of S. Teresa, blessed it, and having offered the Holy Sacrifice of the Mass, clothed himself therewith, girding himself with a leathern belt, his feet being entirely bare (by a rule subsequently made the fathers of the reform were directed to wear sandals).

"Our Lord had in His wisdom so disposed that, although not the first to offer himself to the work, S. John of the Cross should be the first to assume the habit of the reform, so that the structure of the restored temple of Carmel might rest upon one, of whom it has been truly said, that he was a *Cherub in wisdom, and a Seraph in love.*"

He remained alone for two months in a solitude which well represented the ancient hermitages of the desert.

The country people gathered round him, attracted at first by the strange novelty of his habit, and then lingered to hear the saving truths which flowed from his lips, and to pray in the little sanctuary which had so suddenly been raised in the midst of them.

In the meantime F. Antony had been busy on his quest, in which he had succeeded more entirely to his own satisfaction than to S. Teresa's.

"He came to me," she says, "at Valladolid, full of joy at the provision he had made. Scanty enough it was, but he told me that he had got together five hour-glasses, which made me laugh heartily. He said that as he wished to observe exact regularity as to hours, he had taken care to be well provided with hour-glasses.

"I think they had as yet nothing to sleep upon. There was some little delay in fitting up the house; for though they wished to make several alterations, they had no money. After this, F. Antony, with great joy, renounced his office of prior, and made profession of the primitive rule. I had wished him to try it first, but he would not, and went to his little house with the greatest contentment in the world. He told me that when he first saw that poor place it gave him very great interior joy, as he seemed to have given up the world altogether, and entirely to have left it behind him on entering that solitude. Neither to him nor to F. John did the house appear inconvenient, but rather they imagined that they were living in a paradise. O my God! how little do fine buildings and exterior delights contribute to interior joy!"

Father Antony took with him two companions from the monastery at Medina—a young brother named Joseph, who was preparing for holy orders, and a priest who desired to make trial of the primitive rule.

They arrived at Durvelo on the 27th of November, and passed the night in fervent prayer.

On the following morning, the first Sunday in Advent of the year 1568, the two priests, Antony and John, having said Mass, knelt before the B. Sacrament, together with B. Joseph, to renew their religious profession, renouncing all mitigations of the rule, which they vowed hereafter to observe in its primitive severity. F. Antony at the same time followed the example of the holy foundress of the reform by exchanging his ancient hereditary surname of *Heredia* for the sacred name of *Jesus*.

From this Advent Sunday dates the foundation of the Congregation of Discalced Friars, which took place under the Pontificate of S. Pius V., S. Charles Borromeo being at that time Cardinal Protector of the Order of Mount Carmel.

In the following Lent, S. Teresa, on her way to Toledo, paid a visit to "this little cave of Bethlehem," as she calls it.

"I came there one morning," she says, "when Father Antony of Jesus was sweeping the doorstep of the church with a cheerful countenance, such as he always has. 'What is this, Father?' said I, 'what has become of your dignity?' He replied in words which expressed his great interior joy: 'Evil were the days in which I enjoyed honours.' When I went into the church I was astonished to see the spirit which our Lord had infused into that house; and not only I myself, but two merchants also, friends of mine, who had come with me from Medina, could do nothing but weep at the crosses and skulls which covered the walls. Never shall I forget one little wooden cross placed over the holy water stoup, to which was fastened a picture of our Lord crucified, which excited greater devotion than if it had been a crucifix very elaborately carved. ' The attic, which formed the choir, was high enough towards the middle for the Fathers to recite their Office there; but to enter it they were obliged to stoop very low, as were those also who came to hear Mass.

"They had made two little hermitages on each side of the church, where they could not remain, except either sitting or lying down, and filled the inside with hay, because the place was very cold. Their heads, even in a reclining posture, almost touched the roof. Towards the altar were two little windows, and two stones served for pillows; here also were crosses and skulls. I understood that after Matins were over, they returned not to sleep, but continued in prayer, the gift of which they possessed in a sublime degree; and it happened many times when they went to Prime that their habits were covered with snow, and they perceived it not.

"They went about preaching in many neighbouring places, where the people were without any instruction, which was one reason why I was glad that a house should be established there, for I was told there was no monastery near to afford them spiritual help. In a short time the Fathers gained such a reputation as gave me the greatest consolation to hear of. They went to preach at a distance of six or eight miles, barefoot (for they wore no sandals then, though afterwards they were commanded to wear them), in the midst of the snow and cold; and when they had finished preaching and hearing confessions, they returned very late to their meal, but with such joy that all their sufferings seemed but little to them. As for food they had sufficient, for the people in all the neighbouring villages provided them with more than they wanted; and some neighbouring gentlemen who came to their church to confession were not slow to offer them better houses, and more conveniently situated.

"Among them was one Don Louis, of Toledo, who was lord of five villages. This gentleman had built a church to receive a picture of our Lady, worthy indeed of the veneration of the faithful."

To this sanctuary of our Lady at Mancera, a village not far distant from Durvelo, F. Antony of Jesus removed his little community at the earnest desire of Don Louis, who built them a house, and provided all things necessary for the service of the church and whose pious liberality to our Lady of Mount Carmel was afterwards rewarded by the vocation of his daughter and his eldest son, who both lived happy lives, and died happy deaths in her Order.

Whilst S. Teresa was busied in the foundation of Valladolid, she had been invited to open a house at Toledo—one of the most ancient and wealthy cities of Spain. She thus relates the circumstances which led to this request :—

"There lived in the city of Toledo an eminent merchant and great servant of God, whose name was Martin Ramirez. He would never marry, and led such a life as befits a good Catholic, for he was a man of great virtue and honesty. He had amassed his money in a lawful calling, with the intention of devoting it to some such work of charity as he should find to be most pleasing to our Lord."

This good man falling dangerously ill, was advised by his confessor, F. Hernandez, of the Society of Jesus, to devote his wealth to the foundation of a convent of Carmelite nuns.

Having no time to arrange the matter himself, Martin Ramirez left full powers to make the foundation with his brother, Alonzo, who, immediately after his death, wrote to the Saint, begging her to come as soon as possible to Toledo. Being at that time too much engaged in the foundation of Valladolid to be able to leave that place without some little delay, Teresa wrote to accept the foundation, promising to come to Toledo as soon as she should be at liberty. In the mean time she begged Doña Louisa de la Cerda, and her other friends at Toledo, to find a house and obtain the necessary license for the foundation. Great difficulties, as usual, arose, of which S. Teresa was duly informed by Alonzo Ramirez. She was in no way disconcerted thereby, considering, as she says in her answer to his letter, that things went remarkably well when her friends just escaped being stoned, as had nearly befallen them in the foundation of Avila. "I know by experience," she adds, "that the devil cannot endure these houses, and is sure to raise a persecution against them ; but God is all-powerful, and our infernal enemy is sure to come off with a broken head."

Thus, full of courage, and having visited Durvelo (as we have seen), and stayed for a short time at Avila on her way, Teresa arrived at Toledo on March 24, 1569. She took up her abode once more in the house of her beloved friend Doña Louisa, where, with her two companions, she lived in all the retirement that she could have enjoyed in her own convent. It might have been expected that few difficulties would have attended a foundation in so wealthy and populous a city as Toledo, especially as several rich and influential persons were interested in its success ; but seldom did Teresa meet with so many and such vexatious difficulties as in this her fifth foundation. Our Lord apparently intended to show that the progress of the reform depended upon Himself, and not upon the aid of man.

"I immediately began," says the Saint, "to treat

on the business of the foundation with Alonzo Ramirez; but a son-in-law of his, named Diego Ortiz, although a very good man, and one who had studied theology, was more attached to his own opinion than Alonzo, and would not therefore so soon listen to reason. They began to demand of me many conditions which I did not think proper to grant."

Moreover, no house could be found, and the Vicar-General who administered the affairs of the diocese (the archiepiscopal see being vacant) refused the necessary permission, though some of the most influential inhabitants of the city, both ecclesiastical and secular, did all in their power to obtain it.

"On the other hand," says S. Teresa, "I was able to conclude nothing with Alonzo Ramirez, on account of his son-in-law, so that at last we broke off the agreement altogether. I knew not what to do; for, as I had come to Toledo with no other purpose but to make a foundation, I saw that to go away without doing so would expose us to great ridicule and reproach. My principal concern was about the license from the Ordinary; for I doubted not that if we could once obtain this our Lord would provide for everything else, as He had done in other places. I resolved therefore to speak to the Vicar-General myself, and, going to a church near his house, I sent to ask him to speak to me. The matter had been dragging on for more than two months, and becoming more hopeless every day. When the Vicar-General appeared, I said to him that it seemed a very hard case that poor women who had come to Toledo, desiring only to live in strict enclosure, and to labour after their own perfection, should find others who were making none of these sacrifices, but passing their lives in ease and pleasure, oppose a purpose so praiseworthy, and so pleasing to God. By these and

many other arguments which I used with all freedom
and courage, our Lord enabled me so to move his
heart that before I left him he gave me the permission
required. I came away well pleased, thinking that I
now possessed everything, though in fact I had
nothing but three or four ducats, with which I immediately bought two pictures painted on linen (because
I had not one to place on the altar), two straw beds,
and two coverlets. As to a house, I knew of none,
and had nothing more to do now with Alonzo Ramirez.
Another merchant of this city, a friend of mine, who
had always led a single life and applied himself to
good works, especially to the relief of prisoners, told
me not to be troubled, for that he would find me a
house. He fell sick, however, and could not keep his
promise."

Our Lord sent His servant in a few days an unexpected helper.

" A very holy Franciscan," says she, " named
F. Martin of the Cross, who had spent some days at
Toledo, had asked a young penitent of his to offer to
do me any service in his power. This young man,
whose name was Andrada, and who was very poor, did
not seem likely to be able to help us much. One day
when I was hearing Mass in a church, he came to give
me the good father's message, assuring me that he
would do all in his power to serve me. I thanked
him; but my companions and I could not help laughing heartily at the assistance sent me by the holy
friar.

" Now, however, that I had a license, and no one to
help me to use it, I thought of the young man sent
me by F. Martin, and mentioned him to my companions, but they laughed much at me, telling me that
he would be sure to make the matter known. I
would not, however, listen to them, for, as he had

been sent by that servant of God, I was confident he would prove in some way useful, and that he had not been sent without a reason. So I sent for him, and told him what had passed, strictly enjoining him to secrecy, and desired him to look for a house, for the rent of which I would give him security. The money was to be provided by Alonzo d'Avila, who, as I have said, had fallen sick. The young man thought it would be very easy to find a house, and assured me that he should succeed in his search. So the next morning, being at Mass at the church of the Jesuits, he came to tell me that he had found a house, and, as it was very near, he had brought the keys with him that we might go and see it. We did so, and found it so convenient that we dwelt in it almost a year. Very often when I think of this foundation I am astonished at the ways of God; for two or three months several rich persons had been going all round Toledo seeking for a house, without being able to find one, and yet when this poor young man undertook the search, our Lord was pleased that he should find it at once. A monastery might have been erected without any trouble had I agreed with Alonzo Ramirez, but this was not to be, in order that the house might be founded in poverty and suffering.

"I ordered immediate possession should be taken of the house, lest any fresh difficulty should arise. Not long afterwards Andrada came to tell me that it would be empty that day, and that we might send in our furniture. I told him that there was little to move, for we had nothing but two straw beds and a coverlet, at which he seemed astonished. My answer did not please my companions, for they said that, as I had let him know we were so poor, he would, perhaps, be unwilling to help us. I did not heed this, nor did he take any notice of what I had said; for He who gave him the will to help us, continued it also for the accomplishment of the work.

"Nothing could surpass Andrada's diligence in preparing the house. We borrowed all that was necessary for saying Mass, and at nightfall we went to take possession of the house, carrying with us a little bell, such as is rung at the elevation (for we had no other), and thus we spent the night as quietly as possible, in making preparations; but I found no place proper for a chapel except a room which was entered through another little house adjoining, which we had also hired, but which was partly occupied by some women, to whom we dared not say anything, lest they should discover us." The noise made by the preparations in the chapel alarmed these good women, who began to clamour loudly against the foundation. A little money and the promise that another house should be found for them, brought them, however, to reason. The doors were secured, the room prepared for Mass; and thus another Church was dedicated to S. Joseph; the Blessed Sacrament was placed on the altar, and legal possession taken of the monastery on May 14, the Feast of S. Boniface.

On the day after the opening of the convent, an incident occurred which gave great consolation to Teresa. A child who was passing by stood still to look at the little chapel, and cried aloud: "Blessed be God! how beautiful and clean it looks." Greatly touched to hear that thanksgiving from those innocent lips, Teresa said to her companions, "I account myself well repaid for all the troubles that have attended this foundation by that little angel's one *glory to God.*"

To the vexatious opposition which she had already endured was added the trial of a greater degree of poverty than had been experienced in any former foundation.

It seems extraordinary that Doña Louisa, who had the power, and most certainly the will, to assist the friend whom she loved so well, should not have come forward to help her; but it would seem as if our Lord was not pleased that she should miss the privilege of poverty in the midst of this proud and luxurious city.

"For some days," says the Saint, "we were without any furniture but our two straw beds and coverlets. Our poverty was so great that we had not so much as a chip to broil a sprat with, till our Lord moved some one (I know not who) to place in the church a faggot of wood, whereby our wants were supplied. During the nights we felt the cold very much, though we covered ourselves as well as we could with our cloaks. It may seem strange that, coming from the house of a lady who loved me so much, we should have been left in such great poverty. I know no other reason for it except that our Lord wished us to learn from experience the manifold blessings of that virtue. It is true I asked for nothing, for I do not like to be troublesome to anybody; so she may not have thought of our necessities, for she had been so bountiful to us on former occasions that she would not have willingly neglected us now.

"Be this as it may, our state of destitution was a great blessing to us. When I look back upon the joy and consolation which filled our hearts, I cannot sufficiently admire the treasures which God conceals in the bosom of Holy Poverty. It was to us a time of sweet contemplation, though it lasted but a short time, for it was not long before our wants were more than supplied. And truly my sadness was then so great, that I seemed like one possessed of precious jewels, who has had them all stolen, and is thus left poor; so was I afflicted at the loss of my poverty, as were also my companions. When I asked them what made them sorrowful, they answered: 'What are we to do, Mother, for now it seems we are no longer poor?'

" From that time the desire of poverty has increased within me, and a certain contempt of temporal goods, the want of which brings with it such peace and content."

The person who came forward to the relief of the religious was Alonzo Ramirez himself. Finding that the convent had been established without him, and that the poor Carmelites were now in high esteem with the authorities, both ecclesiastical and secular, of the city, he once more proposed to build them a church and convent; limiting the troublesome conditions which he had at first imposed, to the reasonable request that he and his descendants should have a right of burial in the church of which he was to be founder.

A difficulty arose on this point, characteristic of the country and the age. The proud nobles of Toledo had no desire to monopolize the exercise of works of charity, but were highly indignant that one not belonging to their caste should enjoy any privilege attached to it.

It was very right and very suitable that a noble lady of the best blood of Castile should found a convent in their city. The strictness, and even extremity of its poverty, was, to religious, an honourable poverty, and, therefore, discreditable neither to her nor to them; neither did they see any reason why the wealthy merchant should not employ his wealth in the erection of a convent and church; but that a man who was not of illustrious, or even gentle birth, should pre-

sume to claim the right of sepulture there, thus arro-
gating to himself the position of a patron and founder,
was a presumption not to be endured. Such was the
feeling not only amongst seculars; the Vicar-General,
who had granted the license for the foundation, spoke
of withdrawing it on the plea that it had been given
for a house without revenue and without patron or
founder.

Teresa was in no small peplexity, but our Lord
solved it for her in prayer.

" Thou wilt act foolishly, my child," said He, "if
thou givest way to the maxims of the world. Look
upon Me, poor and despised. Are the great ones of
this world great before Me? Men are to be esteemed,
not for their lineage, but for their virtues." The
holy Mother immediately concluded her agreement
with Ramirez, who furnished money to build a new
monastery, to which the nuns removed in the following
year.

" In that church," says the Saint, " are many
Masses said, to the great consolation both of the nuns
and of the people. Had I paid attention to the vain
opinion of the world, it would have been impossible
to have established ourselves so conveniently, and we
should have done an injury to him who so freely
bestowed his charity on us."

Among the subjects who came to offer themselves
at Toledo was one who afterwards bore in religion the
name of *Anne of the Mother of God.* " She was about
forty years old," says S. Teresa, " and her whole life
had been spent in the service of His Divine Majesty:
and though no pleasures were wanting to her in her
state and in her own house, for she was single and
very rich, yet she chose the poverty and obedience of
a religious order, and so she came to speak to me on
the subject. She was very sickly; but when I saw a

soul so well disposed and determined, it seemed to me
a good beginning for the foundation, and accordingly
I admitted her. God was pleased to give her much
better health in her austerity and subjection than ever
she had in the midst of her liberty and pleasures;
but that which edified me most was, that before she
made her profession, she wished to give her large property to the convent in the way of alms. To this I would
not consent, telling her she might repent of this step, or
that we might not allow her to make her profession,
and then what would she do; the thing would appear
very hard to her. We should not of course have dismissed her without restoring her property, but I wished
so to place the case before her for two reasons; first,
lest anxiety on this point should become a source of
temptation to her; secondly, to test her disposition.
She answered me that were this to happen, she would
willingly beg her bread for the love of God, and I
could get no other answer from her. She has lived
very happily in religion ever since, and in much better
health than she had in the world." ·

During her stay at this time in Toledo the Saint
received a most blessed revelation from our Lord.

" One of our sisters," she says (it was Sister Petro-
nilla of S. Andrew), " fell dangerously ill, and after
receiving the last Sacraments, was so cheerful and
happy that she seemed already in Heaven, so that we
entreated her to recommend us to God and to those
Saints to whom we had a particular devotion. A
little while before she expired, I went to pray before
the Most Holy Sacrament, beseeching our Lord to
give her a happy death. I then came back to her cell
to stay with her, and on my entrance I saw our Lord
at the bed's head, with his arms outspread as if protecting her, and He said to me, *Be assured that in like
manner I will protect all the nuns who shall die in these*

monasteries, so that they shall not fear any temptation at the hour of death. By these words I was greatly comforted. A short time afterwards I spoke to her, when she said to me : *Mother, what great things I am about to see;* and with these words she expired like an Angel. I have observed that several of our sisters who have died since that time have evinced a deep repose and peace like that of profound contemplation, and have seemed to be free from all temptations.

"And thus," continues the Saint, "I hope, in the goodness of God, that He will grant us this favour through the merits of His Son, and of His glorious Mother whose habit we wear; wherefore, my daughters, let us endeavour to be true Carmelites, for our journey will soon be at an end; and did we but know the affliction which many endure at the hour of their death, and the snares and delusions with which the devil tempts them, we should highly esteem this favour."

About a fortnight after the foundation of the convent at Toledo, Teresa was called upon to establish another. "After we had finished fitting up the house," says she, "being weary with having to speak with workmen, and thinking all was now finished, I was sitting down to my meal on Whitsun Eve so full of joy, that I could scarcely eat at the thought that now on this festival I should have some time to converse with our Lord." She was not, however, to be left long at peace, being called to the grate to speak with a messenger from the Princess of Evoli, the wife of the Prince Ruy-Gomez de Silva, Chamberlain to Philip II.

Teresa had some time before received an application from this lady for a foundation at Pastrana, but had no expectation of being so soon called upon to begin it.

She was now informed that the Princess was waiting to meet her at Pastrana, having left Madrid for this express purpose.

To leave the foundation at Toledo thus in its very infancy seemed impracticable to the Saint, and no less so to her companions, who with one consent besought her to remain with them till the novices should be formed and regular observance established. She, therefore, determined to write a letter to the Princess, declining her offer, at least for the present; but first, according to her invariable practice, she went before the Tabernacle to consult our Lord.

He returned her this answer, " My daughter, fail not to go; it will be for more ends than this foundation, and take the rule and constitutions with thee." Teresa, who always thus tested the inspirations which she received in prayer, immediately laid the matter before her confessor, without acquainting him with the answer she had received; and, being advised by him on no account to refuse the proposal now made to her, she set off for Pastrana on Whit Monday in the carriage sent for her by the Princess, accompanied by Isabella of S. Paul and another religious from the Incarnation at Avila, both of whom had lately embraced the reform. They lodged at Madrid on their way, at a Franciscan convent, founded by Doña Eleanora de Mascareña, who lived in a house adjoining it. And now Teresa understood the meaning of our Lord's words, that she was going to Pastrana for another purpose than the foundation of a convent of nuns. Doña Eleanora informed her that there were two devout hermits at that time in Madrid who greatly desired to speak with her.

The first of these named Ambrose Mariano, of a noble Neapolitan family, had distinguished himself in almost every branch of secular and ecclesiastical learning, as well as in the profession of arms. He was a mathematician, a scholar, and a poet; having taken the degree of doctor both in theology and law, he was deputed to attend the Council of Trent, and was employed by the Fathers there in many weighty matters in several of the northern States of Europe. He afterwards entered the Order of the Knights of Malta, and fought with distinction at the battle of S. Quentin, 1557, and entering the town with the Spanish army after the victory, he drew his consecrated sword in defence of two young ladies who were threatened with insult by some of his companions in arms. A short time afterwards he was thrown into prison on a false accusation of murder. Being set at liberty by the discovery of the perjury of his accusers, who owed their lives to his generous intercession, he was appointed by Philip II. governor of the Prince of Salmone, and accompanied his pupil into Spain, where, having made the spiritual exercises of S. Ignatius under the Jesuit Fathers at Cordova, he came out of his retreat fully resolved to consecrate himself entirely to God. He joined a community of hermits, and persevered in leading a poor, humble, laborious, and penitent life, from 1562 till 1569. He had made several attempts to obtain an approval of the rule of this hermitage from the Pope, S. Pius V., but the holy pontiff objecting to the establishment of any new religious Order, he and his companions adopted the rule of S. Basil. At the time of S. Teresa's visit to Madrid, on her way to Pastrana, he with his companion, a poor, unlearned, but saintly man, named B. John of Misery, was also bound to the same place, to take possession of the site for a new hermitage, which had been offered to him by the Prince Ruy-Gomez.

S. Teresa now understood why our Lord had commanded her to take with her the rule and constitutions. She gave them to Mariano, who spent that night in reading them to his companion, B. John, translating from the Latin as he went along. He interrupted himself by exclaiming, in the joy of his heart, " B. John, we have found what we have been seeking so long.

" This is the rule which our Lord would have us to embrace. It is approved by the Church ; it has re-kindled the fervour of many, both men and women ; the foundress is a most holy soul. What more do we want ? Let us make our profession of this institute, for doubtless it is our way to Heaven." The joy of the Saint equalled that of her new postulant at the opportunity thus afforded of opening the second house of reformed friars, which she had been em-powered to found, at the hermitage which had been given by the Prince for the use of these holy men. She wrote immediately to the Bishop and the two Provincials for the necessary faculties, and, desiring Mariano to wait for the answers in Madrid, she went on herself to Pastrana.

Ambrose Mariano displayed the same heroism and energy in religion which had distinguished him in the world. Sometimes, however, the impetuosity of the soldier, and the independence of the solitary, gave no little trouble to the holy foundress, especially in the conflict which arose with the mitigated Carmes.

She complains in a letter to the General in 1575, of his impatience and self reliance.

" There have been no few contests amongst us, particularly between F. Mariano and myself ; " and again, in a letter to Mariano himself, she says : " May God keep you, father, notwithstanding all your faults, and make you a great saint." This prayer was granted, for F. Mariano ended a life of great austerity by a very holy death.

R 2

The Saint was received with great affection and respect by the Prince and Princess, who assigned her separate apartments in their palace, which she was obliged to occupy much longer than she expected, on account of delays in the preparation of the house intended for the nuns. It was not long before several events occurred which rendered her stay there extremely unpleasant. The Princess had brought with her from Madrid an Augustinian nun of Segovia, whom she had set her heart upon inducing Teresa to receive into her reform. The Saint steadily refused, on the ground that, except for some special cause, which she had no ground to believe existed in this case, she had determined never to receive a religious from another Order. This was quite enough to excite the anger of the Princess, who was not accustomed to be contradicted.

To satisfy her, Teresa wrote to ask the opinion of Father Bañez, with whose decision in the negative the Princess was obliged to appear content. But a fresh opportunity which arose of annoying the Saint, soon showed that her satisfaction was only apparent. By some means or other, she had discovered that Teresa had brought with her the manuscript of her life; and forthwith proceeded by every means of teazing, coaxing, and chiding, to gain a sight of it. Failing in her own attempts, she next brought her husband to her aid, whose just and honourable character would, she knew, have greater weight with their guest than her own. Teresa yielded at last, on the promise that the manuscript should be seen by none but the Prince and Princess. Whether from carelessness or design, the book got into the hands of some one of the household, and the contents were soon known throughout the palace. The Mother Teresa was censured, ridiculed, and slandered, as another sorceress, like Magdalen of the Cross, whose name was but too famous at that time in Spain.

These reports spread even to Madrid, where the witticisms of the Princess of Evoli on Teresa's book were circulated among the ladies of the Court, and in course of time led to its being sent for to be examined by the Inquisition.

S. Teresa passes over this petty persecution with these few words. " We lived here for three months, during which we endured many severe trials; the Princess, moreover, required of me many conditions not in accordance with the spirit of our Order. I resolved, therefore, to return without making any foundation, rather than agree to her wishes. But the Prince, by his prudence and moderation (which were very great), made his wife sensible of the injustice of her demands, and I also agreed to some things because I was anxious for the erection of the monastery of friars, knowing its importance, which was afterwards proved."

The Princess had desired that this convent should be erected in strict poverty, promising to support it by her alms; but S. Teresa saw too plainly the uncertainty of any help depending upon her to consent to this arrangement; she therefore required that a sufficient provision should be made for the religious, as had been the case in the foundation of Malagon.

F. Mariano and his companion now arrived with the license for the foundation, and S. Teresa sent for F. Antony of Jesus from Mancera to give them the habit. As he delayed to come, and F. Mariano was impatient, and S. Teresa no less so, to begin the foundation, she determined not to wait for him.

" I prepared," says she, "their habits and cloaks that they might take the habit immediately. About this time also I sent for some more subjects from the

Convent of Medina del Campo, for I had brought only two nuns with me. With them came a father named Balthasar of Jesus (in the world Balthasar de Nieto), who, though rather old, was a very good preacher; he came intending to become a discalced friar, for which I returned thanks to God.

"He gave the habit to F. Mariano and his companion, as lay brothers, because F. Mariano did not wish to be a priest, but to be admitted as an inferior; nor could I prevail on him to change his mind, though he afterwards received the priesthood at the command of our Father General.

"These two monasteries then being founded, and Father Antony of Jesus having also come, some novices entered who began to serve our Lord so fervently, that, if He please, I hope some one else will relate their virtues better than I can. As regards the nuns, their convent was founded here, to the great joy of the nobility; and the Princess took great care to make them happy, and to show them every kindness until the death of the Prince."

S. Teresa left Pastrana about the middle of July, 1569, for Toledo, where she seems to have remained some months.

The visitation of the Father General having failed, in consequence of the passive resistance of the Spanish friars, to effect the desired reform, two *Commissaries Apostolic* were empowered by Pope Pius V., in the beginning of the year 1570, at the request of the Catholic King, to visit the houses of the Order of Mount Carmel, the one in Andalusia, the other in Castile, and to establish such reforms as they should judge to be necessary. The two visitors, Peter Hernandez, Prior of the Convent of Talavera, and Francis de Vargas, Prior of S. Paul's at Cordova, were both Dominicans, distinguished for their learning, prudence and sanctity.   Hernandez, the commissary for Castile, determined to visit, in the first place, the convent of discalced friars at Pastrana, thinking probably that he should find less difficulty in reforming those convents which had need of it, if his authority were first acknowledged by those who were strictly observing the primitive rule.   In the beginning of Lent the Apostolic Visitor appeared at Pastrana with a companion of his Order.   They travelled on foot, preceded by a mule which carried their mantles and other necessaries.   Both religious and seculars were edified at this humble mode of travelling in a man venerable both by his years and his position, and invested with such high authority in the Church.

To the remarks of those who expressed their admiration, he replied, that, " being come to visit Saints, it befitted him not to travel like the profane."

In the convent he strictly followed the austere rule of the fathers, kept silence like them, was assiduous in his attendance in the choir, and shared their rigid Lenten fast on bread and water.   After a few days he called the fathers together in Chapter, and unfolded to them his commission.   He told them that, although in truth it did not extend to them who had already embraced so strict a reform, yet they might, if they should judge it expedient, acknowledge him for their superior,   as   he   had   authority   from   the Apostolic Nuncio to receive their submission.   The fathers, having consulted together, were all agreed on the great benefit which would arise to the reform from its being placed under subjection to the Apostolic Visitor, and they accordingly professed obedience to him, their example being followed by the nuns.

The opinion of Hernandez with regard to the reform may be gathered from his answer to a novice who manifested to him a temptation to leave the Order for one of greater austerity and perfection. The experienced religious saw through the deceit of the enemy, and quieted the troubled mind of the youth by these words : "From all that I have ever seen or read, I believe that there is not in the whole Church of God a monastery which exceeds this in austerity and perfection."

The benefit which accrued to the reform from its ready obedience to the Apostolic Visitor appears from the facilities which it obtained from him for its extension.

The number of subjects in Mancera and Pastrana had increased so rapidly, that a great desire arose for the foundation of a house near one of the universities, where the younger members of the institute might have fuller opportunities of cultivating their minds to the greater glory of God, and where their example might be the means of exciting the secular students to follow it by forsaking the world.

The faculties granted by the Father General for the foundation of houses of discalced friars extended only to two, which had been already founded, and although the Father Provincial, Alonzo Gonzalez, might have been willing to extend the permission, the jealousy of the reform, which was already arising in the Order, rendered it useless to apply to him, many of his best subjects having followed the example of F. Balthasar Nieto, and joined the ranks of the reform.

The fathers at Pastrana having no doubt conferred upon the matter with their holy Mother, had recourse to the Apostolic Visitor, who was furnished with the fullest authority, and who gladly gave faculties for the erection of their third convent at Alcalà de Henarez.

This house was opened on November 1, 1570, and the wisdom of the choice of the famous university of

Alcalà for the new foundation was proved by the speedy application of many of its most promising members for admission into the rising reform.

On the same day that the monastery of Alcalà was begun, S. Teresa founded another convent for nuns at the seat of the no less celebrated university of Salamanca, whither she had been invited by Father Martin Guttierez, the Rector of the Jesuit College in that city.

Having travelled through the greater part of a very cold night; the holy Mother, then more than usually weak in health, arrived at Salamanca on the Vigil of All Saints.

The approval of the Bishop, Don Gonzalez de Mendoza, had been readily obtained. This prelate had lately returned from attending the Council of Trent, where he had been remarked for his piety, learning, and ability. Having turned his attention especially to the regulation of religious communities, he was overjoyed at the prospect of the foundation in his episcopal city of a house which would be a model to the religious of his diocese of primitive regularity and perfection.

Being furnished with this approval, the holy Mother considered the convent, as she says, " already founded." She had, moreover, taken measures for the hire of a house in the occupation of some students, who were expected to vacate it without fail before the arrival of the religious. The following is her own graphic description of the misfortunes which awaited herself and her solitary companion when they reached Salamanca.

" On the Vigil of All Saints we arrived at Salamanca about the middle of the day. As soon as we reached the inn, I endeavoured to find out a man of that city whom I had previously requested to have the house ready for us. His name was Nicholas Guttierez, a great servant of God" (probably a kinsman of F. Guttierez), "who took a great deal of trouble about this foundation, and entered into the matter with much devotion and goodwill. When he came, he told me that the house was not empty, because he could not induce the students to depart. I told him how important it was that they should give up the house immediately, before it became known that I was in the town, because I was always afraid of some disturbance. He went to the owner of the house, and laboured so hard, that they left it that evening, and we entered it immediately. This was the first house I founded without the Most Blessed Sacrament being placed there, having hitherto supposed that possession was not taken till this was done; but I had now learnt that this was not necessary, which was a great consolation to me having had no time to prepare the church; for the students, having little or no regard for cleanliness, had left the house in such a state that we were obliged to work all that night to clean it.

"The next morning the first Mass was said." Thus was the seventh convent of the reform founded in a night, and under the invocation of S. Joseph. "I sent for more nuns," says the Saint, "from Medina del Campo. In the mean time my companion and I remained there alone on the night of All Saints. I tell you, sisters, that when I remember the fears of my companion, whose name was Mary of the Blessed Sacrament, a nun older than myself, and a great servant of God, I cannot help laughing. The house was very large and in great disorder, and contained many garrets. She could not help thinking of the students, because she imagined that as they were unwilling to leave the house, some of them might have hidden themselves in it, which they could, indeed, have very easily done. We shut ourselves up in a

room where there was some straw (which was the first
kind of furniture I always provided when founding a
house), because we thus had something to sleep on;
and that night we had borrowed two coverlets. The
next day the nuns of S. Elizabeth, who lived near us,
whom we imagined we had greatly displeased, lent us
coverlets also for our companions who were coming,
and gave us alms with great kindness and charity as
long as we remained in that house. When my companion found herself shut up in this room she seemed
somewhat more calm and quiet about the students,
though she did nothing but look around, first on one
side and then on the other, with much fear; and the
devil endeavoured to heighten her apprehensions of
danger, that so he might disturb me; for on account
of the weakness of my health at that time, a little
thing was sufficient to trouble me. I asked her what
she was looking at, since no one could enter our
chamber? She answered: 'I am thinking, Mother,
if I should die here, what would you do alone?' If
such a thing had happened, I should certainly have
been in a sad case. She did, indeed, make me muse
a little on the subject, and also made me afraid; for
dead bodies (though I do not fear them) always give
me a sort of sinking in my heart, even when not
alone. And as the continual ringing of the bells
increased my fear, for, as I have said, it was the night
before All Souls, the devil took the good opportunity
of making us waste our thoughts on mere trifles; for
when he perceives that we fear him not, he tries to
frighten us about something else. However, I
answered her quietly enough: 'When this happens,
sister, I will think of what I am to do; at present, let
me go to sleep.' As we had had two bad nights,
sleep soon quieted our fears, and the arrival of our
sisters the next day dispelled them altogether.

Amongst the religious whom S. Teresa sent for to Salamanca were Anne de Tapia (in religion, Anne of the Incarnation), who was appointed Prioress, and Anne of Jesus, who, though still in the noviciate, was, on account of her extraordinary perfection, made Mistress of Novices.

Agnes and Anne de Tapia, cousins of S. Teresa, were, it will be remembered, of the number of those chosen friends amongst whom the idea of the reform was first spoken of in S. Teresa's cell on the memorable Feast of the Assumption, of the year 1560. The two young sisters had been trained by the Saint to the life of perfection; they were with her at the foundation of S. Joseph's at Avila, and never wavered in their intention of embracing her reform. A short time before the foundation of the convent at Medina, S. Teresa gave to both the habit they had so long desired. A few days before that appointed for the clothing, Agnes was taken so seriously ill that it seemed but too likely that her holy purpose would be frustrated. S. Teresa had recourse to our Lord in earnest prayer, and received for answer, " She will not die ; I am keeping her for greater things." S. Teresa took the two sisters with her to the foundation of Medina del Campo, where she appointed Agnes Prioress, and Anne sub-Prioress. Agnes of Jesus justified the high opinion formed of her wisdom and prudence by S. Teresa, who was wont to say that she was better fitted than herself to govern a convent. She remained for ten years at the head of that at Medina, where she implanted the spirit of S. Joseph's at Avila.

Anne of the Incarnation, who was now removed to Salamanca, was no less distinguished than her holy sister for her gift of government. Her work seemed to be less the formation of novices than of foundresses, so great was the number of religious who were sent forth from Salamanca to govern other houses. S. Teresa would often say to her, "May God reward you, my dear daughter, for training such perfect religious for me." In order to spare the holy Mother any needless anxiety, she never wrote to her about any painful matter which she could possibly arrange herself. "No prioress," said Teresa, "does so much to lighten the burden of my office as Anne of the Incarnation. She never writes to me about the troubles which God sends her, but suffers them between herself and Him alone." In the midst of their arduous and responsible labours, prayer was the very life of those two blessed sisters. During the latter years of their lives the patience of both was perfected by intense bodily sufferings; and on the same Easter morning, the one at Salamanca and the other at Medina del Campo, they both entered into the joy of their Lord.

The early maturity in perfection attained by Anne of Jesus was a prelude of the great work which she was hereafter to accomplish for the Order, of which she became the foundress both in France and Flanders.

One of the confessors of our Saint relates, as having heard it from herself, that as she stood by the death-bed of one of her daughters at Salamanca, she saw our Divine Lord supporting the head of the dying sister with His own hands; and venturing, in the fulness of her joy, to ask Him to bestow a similar grace upon the rest, "I will grant it," replied He, "to all who shall strictly observe their rule." That the nuns of Salamanca did thus faithfully keep their rule, we may gather from the fact revealed by one of them, who died in 1623, to her companions, that all those who before that time had died in that house were in the eternal enjoyment of God.

About two months after the foundation at Salamanca, S. Teresa was invited by Francis Velasquez, treasurer to the Duke of Alva, and Teresa de Layz, his wife, to found another convent at Alva de Torrez. The holy Mother was at first unwilling to make another foundation in a small town like Alva, which was not likely to furnish alms sufficient to support the nuns, for whose maintenance the endowment of the house would therefore be necessary. She asked counsel, as usual, of F. Dominic Bañez, who advised her by no means to refuse the work to which God was calling her, since the endowment of the convent need be no impediment to the perfect observance of religious poverty by its inmates. In accordance with this advice, S. Teresa left Salamanca about the beginning of the year 1571, and established the foundation in the house of Velasquez on the Feast of the Conversion of S. Paul, under the title of the " Incarnation of our Lord." By the same generous benefactors a suitable monastery and church were afterwards erected on the spot, which was to enjoy the unspeakable privilege of receiving the mortal remains of our glorious Saint, who passed to her reward from that convent, and was buried in that church.

The following is one amongst many examples related in the Chronicles of the Order of the power of the prayers of His faithful spouses over the Heart of Jesus. The Saint was one day leaving Alva in haste, when one of the religious, named Catharine of the Holy Angels, who was suffering under some severe internal trial, besought her Mother to stay and speak with her. S. Teresa, being unable to delay her departure, the sister carried the trouble which she had been unable to unfold to her before the Blessed Sacrament; and in the course of half an hour the holy Mother and her companion returned on foot, their carriage having broken down on the way. Teresa recognized the sweet Providence of our Lord, who thus vouchsafes to console His children, and said, as she entered the cloister, " Send me Catharine of the Holy Angels, for it is she who has caused me to return."

The circumstances which led to the foundation of the house at Alva bore singular marks of Providential guidance. The pious founders had for many years been praying in vain for children. Teresa de Layz, who had a special devotion to the Apostle S. Andrew, addressed her request particularly to him. One day she heard a voice saying to her, "Wish not for children, or thou wilt lose thy soul." The good woman, conscious that her one motive for desiring children was that she might leave them behind her to praise God in her place, desisted not from her petition, saying to herself, " My desire for children is for so good an end that I do not see how I can be condemned for it." A vision was next vouchsafed to her to teach her the same lesson. She saw (whether sleeping or waking she knew not) a house, in the courtyard of which was a well under a corridor; near it was a verdant meadow full of beautiful flowers. By the well stood the Apostle S. Andrew, who, pointing to the flowers, said to her, " These are far holier children than those for whom thou art longing." Her long-cherished desire vanished from that moment from her heart, and she began to consult with her husband as to the foundation of a convent of nuns.

A short time afterwards Velasquez removed from Salamanca, where he at that time resided, to fill the office of treasurer to the Duke of Alva. When his wife went with him to take possession of the house which he had purchased at Alva, to her astonishment she recognized the very place which she had seen in her vision. There was the court, the well, the corridor, everything in fact which she had seen, except the flowery meadow and the Apostle S. Andrew. Seeing the hand of God visibly manifested here, Velasquez and Teresa determined to place their convent on that spot, and to this end purchased several adjacent houses.

The pious founders were very anxious that the future monastery should belong to some austere and penitential Institute, and, having long sought for such in vain, the devil had nearly persuaded them that they had made a mistake, and that they would do far better to arrange a marriage between the nephew of the husband and the niece of the wife, to make them the heirs of the principal part of their wealth, and leave the rest in alms for the benefit of their souls.

Not a fortnight after this arrangement had been made, the intended bridegroom was carried off by a sudden illness, before the solemnization of the marriage.

Velasquez and his wife saw the hand of the Lord in this chastisement, resumed their former intention, and, by the advice of a holy Franciscan friar, who made known to them the wonderful reform effected in the Order of Mount Carmel by S. Teresa, they wrote to beg her to accept the foundation.

Having left her daughters well established at Alva, the holy Mother returned to Salamanca, where her presence was still greatly needed.

Before she entered the convent, she remained, by the command of the F. Provincial, for some days in the palace of the Count de Monte Rey, where she healed two sick persons, the one by her touch, the other (a young daughter of the Count) by her prayers. Having remained for a short time at Salamanca, she proceeded to Medina del Campo to be present at the election of the new Prioress.

The Father Provincial was anxious that the choice of the Chapter should fall on a religious named Teresa de Quesada, formerly a nun of the Incarnation at Avila. The community, being well aware of her unfitness for the office, with the approbation of the Saint, re-elected Agnes of Jesus, who had been appointed Prioress at the foundation of the house, and of whose great sanctity and remarkable gift of government mention has been already made. The Provincial, though a prudent and religious man, was greatly disturbed and angered at the disregard paid to his recommendation, which he probably attributed to partiality on the part of Teresa for a kinswoman of her own. He commanded her, on pain of excommunication, to retire immediately with the newly-elected Prioress to Avila, and committed the government of the house to Teresa de Quesada. The holy Mother, regardless of the tears of her daughters, or of the evils which she foresaw from the choice of the Provincial, instantly obeyed his command, though no better means of transport could be obtained for herself and her companion than two mules belonging to a water-carrier. She returned to her beloved monastery of S. Joseph in great peace and contentment, and a short time afterwards received a visit there from the Apostolic Visitor, Peter Hernandez, who was most desirous to become acquainted with the mother of those holy religious whom he so highly esteemed.

Hernandez had already heard the praises of Teresa from the lips of his brother in religion, Father Dominic Bañez, but it was not till he saw her himself that he became convinced that there was no exaggeration in the report which he had received. He was hence-

S

forth accustomed to say that the Mother Teresa was a wonderful woman, and that she had shown the world that it was not impossible even for her feeble sex to attain to the most sublime degree of evangelical perfection.

Hernandez next proceeded, on his visitation, to Medina del Campo, where he heard of the disturbance occasioned by the Provincial's choice of Teresa de Quesada, the imprudence of which she had now manifested herself; for, weary of the primitive rule, of her office, her subjects, and herself, she resigned her charge, and returned to the Convent of the Incarnation, where she had been professed. The Father Visitor could think of no fitter means of settling the matter than the election of the holy Mother as arbitress, which was carried by the unanimous votes of the religious. Teresa, knowing how necessary her presence was at Medina, accepted the office, though sorely against her will. On her journey from Avila, she arrived with her companions at nightfall, on the banks of a river; it was so dark that the different members of the party could hardly see each other; and every one shrank from attempting the passage till reassured by the cheering words of their Mother. "We cannot remain here all night," she said, "in the open air; come, let us pass over, recommending ourselves to God; I will go first." The words were no sooner said, than a light, like that of a torch, appeared at a little distance, and continued to shine until the whole party had passed the perilous ford. Great was the joy of the nuns of Medina at the sight of their holy Mother, who, they felt assured, would soon set in order all their affairs, spiritual and temporal. They were not, however, to enjoy her presence long, for a far harder task awaited her elsewhere.

CHAPTER XVI.

1571–1574.

Two or three months after his visitation of Medina, Father Hernandez proceeded to Avila to visit the Convent of the Incarnation. He soon perceived the extreme necessity in which that house then stood of an experienced superioress to arrange its temporal affairs, and to revive the practice of regular observance. The convent had fallen into such great penury, that the nuns were destitute of the necessary means of support. The expenditure of the house so far exceeded its revenues, that many of the religious had determined to ask permission of their superiors to return to their homes, where they might at least be sure of their daily bread.

That such an idea should have been entertained for a moment by members of a community which had once numbered amongst its religious Teresa of Jesus, Jane Suarez, and the two blessed sisters, Agnes of Jesus, and Anne of the Incarnation, evinces a lamentable state of declension. The Visitor, compassionating the deplorable spiritual and temporal condition of this once highly-esteemed monastery, felt that the fittest remedy which he could apply to it would be the appointment of a superioress capable of remedying the evil.

With the consent and approbation, therefore, of the Superiors of the Order, he nominated Teresa Prioress of the Incarnation, that by the example of her sanctity she might raise the spiritual tone of the house, and by her prudence and extraordinary ability in matters of business, set in order their temporal affairs.

Great was the trouble of the holy Mother when

she received this obedience, which broke in upon the peace and tranquillity which she was enjoying with her children. She was well aware that the various houses so lately founded still stood in need of her counsels and her presence; her loving heart was wrung too at the thought of the sorrow of her children at S. Joseph's. And, in addition to her exceeding aversion to holding office or authority, she foresaw what would be the difficulty of governing nuns who professed a relaxed rule, and had now ceased to practise even the rule which they professed. She foresaw that every reasonable command would be accounted an extravagance; and that every endeavour to restore regular observance would be suspected as an attempt to introduce the practices of the reform.

In the anguish of her heart, she had recourse to her Divine Spouse, beseeching Him to make known to her His will, and to strengthen her to fulfil it.

He was not deaf to her entreaty.

"As I was praying one day," says she, "very fervently for a brother of mine, who was at the time in a position which I feared would prove perilous to his salvation, I said: 'O Lord, if I were to see a brother of Thine in such peril, what would I not do to help him!' And, indeed, it seemed to me, as I spoke, that I should count no labour or suffering too great for such an end. But our Lord said to me: 'Oh! my daughter, my daughter, the nuns of the Incarnation are my sisters, and thou delayest to help them! Now take courage, and consider that this is My will. Thou wilt not find the office so difficult as it now seems to thee; and whereas thou thinkest that the convents of the reform will suffer loss by thy absence, believe Me that by obeying Me thou wilt bring benefit to them all. Resist no longer, for I am all-powerful.'"

The fears of the Saint vanished at the words of our Lord, and she immediately prepared to obey the Father Visitor. On her arrival at Avila, she went first to her own Convent of S. Joseph's, both in order to console her children for her temporary absence from them, and to avoid the disturbance which she foresaw would arise on her sudden arrival amongst the religious of the Incarnation.

To judge by the excitement occasioned there by the news of her election, no easy task awaited her amongst her former sisters in religion. The nuns exclaimed loudly against the tyrannical measure of the Visitor in imposing a Superioress upon them against their own consent. They were fully persuaded that the new Prioress intended to force upon them the rule of the discalced Carmelites, a rule which they had never professed, nor ever intended to profess. The more insubordinate and lax members of the community dreaded her coming, in the conviction that she would close the doors at the fitting hour, restrict their visits to the parlour, and put a stop to that free intercourse with seculars which had led to so many abuses. In short, the nuns of the Incarnation, some from one reason and some from another, were fully determined not to accept the new Prioress, and to oppose her entrance by every means in their power. To this end some of them were not ashamed to ask assistance from certain gentlemen of Avila, who, to the no small reproach of the *City of Knights*, were not ashamed to promise it. The holy Mother was not ignorant of all these proceedings; but strong in her love of sufferings, and stronger still in her faith in the promise of her Lord, that great benefits should arise from her appointment, she prepared with calm courage for her difficult enterprise. She took the precaution, in case of any attempt being made to interfere with her own practice of the primitive rule, during her government of the convent, formally to renew her profession of it, and to renounce all mitigations, in the presence of the two priests, Gaspar Daza and Julian of Avila. Her next step was to direct that all the pensioners who were receiving their education in the convent should be immediately dismissed, lest they should be scandalised by the dissension and confusion which she foresaw would arise on her arrival.

Strange to say, notwithstanding the determination of the nuns to resist her authority, and the decrease of their already scanty revenues which must ensue, she was immediately obeyed. The Saint entered the Convent of the Incarnation in the month of October, 1571, accompanied by the Father Provincial, Angelo de Salazar, who had been recently reappointed to that office, and another religious of the Order. They came by the direction of the Apostolic Visitor, who apprehended some opposition from the nuns, who in fact were awaiting their new Prioress with a mind rather to insult than to obey her.

The Saint entered the house, holding in her hand an image of her beloved Patron, S. Joseph, which she was accustomed to carry with her to all her foundations. The Father Provincial gave immediate orders that all the religious should assemble in the outer chapel in Chapter. As soon as they were collected together, he read to them the patent of election from the Apostolical Visitor and the heads of the Provincial Chapter, appointing to the office of Prioress the Mother Teresa of Jesus there present. The words were no sooner uttered, than such a storm arose of protestations, reproaches, exclamations, and accusations, as if the unwelcome patent had been the death warrant of the community. The poor Father Provincial was fairly bewildered. Happily there were a few wise virgins amidst this company of distracted women. One of them, named Catherine de Castro, made her voice heard above the storm. "We love her, we choose her," said she, "Te Deum laudamus." Other voices now joined that of Catherine; and, regardless of the outcry, these few faithful religious raised the processional cross, and went forth to meet their new Mother. The other party resisted her entrance, so that the Father Provincial, with the help of his companion, was at last obliged to drag her by main force within the enclosure. The scene which followed defies description: one party, according to custom, chanting the Te Deum; the other giving vent to every term of hatred and contempt against their Prioress and against those who had intruded her within their walls. The Provincial could no longer restrain his indignation; he reproved, threatened, but all in vain: he had no power to stem the tumult. Probably he was now convinced, by the evidence of his own eyes and ears, of the necessity of a reform. There was but one peaceful spot in this scene of wild confusion; it was where Teresa knelt before the Blessed Sacrament, humbly beseeching her Beloved to calm the furious winds and hush the stormy sea. Then she arose and turned to speak to the nuns, declaring that she greatly pitied them for having such a Prioress placed over them; she next addressed the Provincial, excusing the excitement of his subjects on the ground of her own unworthiness. Some of the sisters had fainted away in the tumult of their feelings, and on the Saint gently touching them with her hand, they immediately recovered consciousness.

The irresistible power of meekness calmed these perturbed spirits for awhile; but Teresa was well aware that there was an under-current of discontent

ready to burst forth on the first opportunity. She
summoned her first Chapter. " Now is the time,"
said the malcontents, " for the reformer to declare
herself; now she will throw off the mask, declaim
against abuses, endeavour to introduce new customs,
and attempt to deprive us of our just liberties."
They assembled, therefore, with a full determination
to contradict her will and oppose her commands. As
they entered the chapter-room, however, a sight met
their eyes which quieted them in a moment. In the
place of the Prioress stood a beautiful statue of our
Blessed Lady, holding in her hands the keys of the
convent; and in the place of the Sub-Prioress, an
image of S. Joseph. The first glance of every nun,
as she entered the room, was at the seat of the de-
tested Prioress; and beholding in her place the Great
Mother and Protectress of their Order, they were
seized, as one of them afterwards confessed, with
terror and remorse.

When the religious had taken their places, the
holy Prioress chose for herself a low stool at the foot
of our Lady's image, and addressed to them the
following words, which are found in the appendix to
her letters :—

" My ladies, mothers, and sisters,—By the obedience which I owe to my superiors, our Lord has been
pleased to send me back to this house to exercise the
office of Prioress. I never thought of such a dignity,
because I knew I was far from deserving it. I was
grieved at my election, both because a charge was
thus given to me the duties of which I am unequal to
fulfil; and also because you have been deprived of
the right of election which belongs to you, so that a
Prioress has been imposed upon you against your own
will and pleasure—a Prioress, too, who would think
she had done great things could she only learn from

the least amongst you the virtues which are practised in this house. I come to serve and to please you in every way I can ; and I hope our Lord will assist me herein. With regard to everything else, the least amongst you is able to teach and correct me. You must then, my dear mothers and sisters, let me know what I can do for each one of you, for I shall be most willing to do what you ask, even were it to shed my blood for you. I am a daughter of this house, and your sister. I know the disposition and wants of all the religious here, or at least of the greater part of them. You have no reason, then, to fear being under the government of one who is wholly yours by so many titles. And though I have till now lived amongst my discalced nuns, and have been their Prioress, nevertheless I hope, through the goodness of our Lord, to be able to govern those who are not discalced. My desire is that we may serve the Lord with sweetness and humility, and that through our love of Him, to whom we are so much indebted, we may perform what our rules and constitutions command. I know our weakness is great ; but if we cannot attain to the exact fulfilment of all our obligations, let us at least cherish an ardent desire to fulfil them. Our Lord is compassionate, and He will give us strength, by little and little, to carry those desires and intentions into effect."

There was not a heart among the nuns of the Incarnation which did not melt at the words of the Saint, and at the touching sight of the sacred image of Mary standing in the place of their Prioress. They all submitted at once, and with their whole heart, to their legitimate Superioress, and to whatever reform she should see fit to introduce. The visible sanctity of Teresa, and the tender affection which she showed to all her subjects, without distinction, did much to confirm their good dispositions; but far more was effected by the fervour of her prayers. She tells us herself that, on the Octave of Pentecost, our Lord made known to her that the souls in that house should advance more and more in perfection, and it was afterwards revealed to her that the praises which they offered to God were counted worthy of being presented to Him by the hands of Mary.

Nor was it only spiritual blessings which Teresa brought with her when she entered that house in company with S. Joseph; he provided also for their urgent temporal necessities. In the distribution of these things also the holy Mother found means to evince her tender considerateness, and thus, by winning the hearts of the sisters to herself, to gain their souls for God. In a letter written to her brother Laurence in the preceding year, she says, " You must know that since our Lord has employed me in the foundation of these houses of His, I have become such a woman of business that I know a little of everything." Those amongst the religious of the Incarnation who had been accustomed to look upon the Saint as a visionary enthusiast, or, at best, an abstracted and austere contemplative, were no less astonished than touched by the ready presence of mind and minute solicitude with which she regulated the complicated affairs of the community, and supplied the most trifling wants of each of its members. For one, she provided a tunic; for another, a habit; carefully assigning to each whatever she stood in need of. Our Lord blessed the Convent of the Incarnation, as He had blessed the houses of Laban and of Potiphar, for the sake of His servants Jacob and Joseph; and the minds of the religious were soon relieved from the wearing anxiety concerning temporal matters, which had been one of their manifold causes of distraction.

Teresa sent to Valladolid for sister Isabella of the Cross, to aid her in the office of Sub-Prioress; and a few days after the first Chapter had been held, some of those who had been formerly most disaffected, said to the holy Mother, with all sincerity and goodwill, " Would it not be well, dear Mother, that your Reverence should take possession of the keys of the turns and of the parlours, and assign the various offices of the house to such and such of the sisters ?" naming the very persons whom Teresa had, in her own mind, fixed upon for those employments. Keeping her previous intention to herself, the holy Mother answered, " Since such is your wish, my good mothers, by all means let it be so." She was thus enabled to remove from the parlour and the grate those whose youth or indiscretion unfitted them for such a charge, and to confer the various offices of the house upon those most worthy to fill them, without incurring the odium of displacing the former officials.

The evil spirit had been cast out of the Convent of the Incarnation, but he was still busy among the secular friends of the nuns. One of them especially, a gentleman of one of the first families of Avila, finding that his frequent visits to the parlour would no longer be permitted, sent for the Prioress, and addressed her in terms of great insolence and violence. Teresa heard him with undisturbed patience and humility, and, when he had finished, answered him in a tone which caused the proud man to quail before her, and to report to his companions in the city that " the Mother Teresa was not to be trifled with," and that they had better make an end of their visits to the Incarnation.

The next and the greatest benefit which Teresa conferred upon that convent was the procuring for it a saintly confessor in the person of F. John of the

Cross, who, by the command of the Visitor Apostolic, left Pastrana to undertake the spiritual direction of the nuns. The parlour is still shown in that convent where the two Saints were found by one of the religious raised in ecstasy some considerable distance from the ground. This occurred on the Feast of the Blessed Trinity, when S. John had been discoursing to the Saint, as she knelt at his feet, on that Divine mystery. The same wonderful fact happened more than once in their conversations, so that Teresa was wont to say that she " could not speak of God with F. John of the Cross, because he was so full of Divine love, that he fell into raptures himself, and caused every one who conversed with him to do the same." Under such a Superioress and such a Director, the nuns of the Incarnation attained to so high a degree of perfection, as to differ in habit only from their sisters of the reform. This had been the fruit of the patience, as well as of the faith and charity of the Saint. An ancient and zealous religious came to her one day to complain of the failings of some of her companions. " Be not troubled, sister," said she gently, " be not troubled, for I can assure you that there are in this house more than fourteen most holy souls, for whose sake God looks upon it with complacency. Had there been as many at the time of the flood, the world would not have been destroyed." S. Teresa herself attributed this change entirely to the intervention of the Blessed Virgin. In a letter to Doña Mary of Mendoza, written in the March of this year, she says, "Assuredly there are here some great servants of God, and, thanks to my *Prioress* " (B. V. M.)," there is a great improvement in all."

In the additions to her life, S. Teresa thus relates our Blessed Lady's acceptance of the office committed to her by her faithful love. " On the vigil of S.

Sebastian, in the first year that I was Prioress of the Incarnation, while we were chanting the *Salve Regina,* I saw the Mother of God, surrounded by a great multitude of angels, approach the stall of the Prioress, which was occupied by a statue of our Lady of Mount Carmel. The image disappeared from my eyes, and our Blessed Mother took its place. I remained in ecstasy during the whole time of the *Salve.* I saw a great number of angels ranged above the stalls in the choir. The Blessed Virgin said to to me, ' Thou hast done well to place me here. I will be present at the praises sung by the religious of this convent in honour of my Son, and will offer them to Him.' "

In the second year of her government of the Convent of the Incarnation, our Divine Lord vouchsafed to the Saint that marvellous vision in which He espoused her to Himself. "On the octave of S. Martin," says she, " Father John of the Cross, when he gave me Holy Communion, divided the sacred particle between me and one of the sisters. It came into my mind that he did it to mortify me, because I had told him that I liked always to receive a large host, though I knew very well that I gained nothing by it, since our Lord is wholly contained in the smallest particle. Then our Lord said to Me, ' Fear not, my child, that anything can ever separate thee from me ; ' and showing Himself to me in the very interior of my soul, by a sensible vision, as He had often done before, He gave me His right had, and said to me, ' Behold this nail ! it is the sign and the pledge that from this day forth thou shalt be My spouse ; hitherto thou hast not deserved this name ; henceforth thou shalt take care of My honour ; not only beholding in Me thy Creator, thy King, and thy God, but regarding thyself as my veritable spouse. From this moment My honour is thine, and thy honour is Mine.' So powerful

was the effect of this grace, that in the holy transport with which I was carried away, I said to my
Divine Master: ' O Lord, either strengthen my weakness, or confer not upon me a favour, under the excess
of which my feeble nature sinks.' I have felt ever
since the admirable effects of this vision, to my exceeding shame and confusion, who have done nothing
to show my gratitude for so inestimable a blessing."
In the conclusion of the book of the *Interior Castle*,
S. Teresa treats of the ineffable mystery of these
spiritual espousals. "All that I can speak of it," she
says, "is that our Lord makes known in one moment to the soul what is the glory of heaven, in a
manner far more sublime than can be expressed by
any vision, or any other spiritual favour. If I may so
express myself, that which may be called the *spirit of
the soul*, becomes one thing with God. That great
God who is a Spirit, in order to show us how much He
loves us, has thus been pleased to give to certain souls
an experience of the extent of that love; and this in
order to excite us to give Him unceasing praise for
these marvels of His grace. He is pleased thus to unite
His infinite Majesty to a feeble creature in such an inseparable union as is figured by the indissoluble bond
of the Sacrament of marriage. Perhaps by these
words, *He who is united to God is one spirit with
Him*, S. Paul intended to describe that mystical
marriage which unites the soul inseparably with God.
. . . The soul which has attained to this state
never departs from that centre, where she is at rest
with God; neither is her peace ever disturbed, for she
receives it from Him who gave it to His apostles when
they were gathered together in His name. I have
often thought that those words of our Lord to His
disciples, *Peace be with you*; and those which He
spoke to Magdalen, *Go in peace*, must have an

effect far beyond what we understand by them. As with God, to speak is to do, these words, when addressed to souls duly prepared, doubtless deliver them from the trammels of the body, that so their spiritual nature may be capable of that celestial union with the uncreated Spirit. It is certain that when, for the love of God, we empty our souls of all affection for creatures, that great God immediately fills them with Himself. Therefore did our Lord Jesus Christ ask of the Eternal Father for His apostles, *that they might be one,* and *that, as His Father is in Him, and He in His Father, so they might be one in His Father and in Him.* What love, my sisters, can surpass this love? and what prevents us from sharing it, since our adorable Saviour adds, *And I pray not for them alone, but for them also who shall believe in Me through their word. . . . I am in them.* Oh, how true are these words! and how well does that soul understand them who has seen them accomplished in herself by this spiritual marriage! O my daughters, how well should we all understand them, if we did not render ourselves unworthy of them by our own fault, for the words of our Lord Jesus Christ, our King and God, are infallible! . . . When the soul has attained to this dwelling, in which God abides, she may be considered as the heaven of heavens, wherein He hath set up His throne; for as that centre moves not with the motion of the other heavens, so the soul is no longer subject to the movements which it formerly received from the impulses of its imagination and its various powers; so that they can neither harm it nor disturb its peace.

"But it must not be supposed that when God has vouchsafed so great a favour to any soul, it is thereby assured of its salvation, and certain never to fall. When I speak of its security, I mean only so long as

our Lord keeps His hand upon it, and as it refrains
from offending Him. I know at least that the person
of whom I am speaking, and who some years* ago
was raised to this state, does not account herself
secure; on the contrary, she walks with greater fear
than before, and more carefully avoids the slightest
offence against God. She has the most ardent desire
to labour for His service, but she is grieved and
ashamed to be able to do so little for Him who has
done so much for her.

"This inability is no small cross; nay, it is the
severest penance which she can endure. I
have said that, by this mystic alliance, the soul lives
in Jesus Christ, and Jesus Christ lives in the soul.
Now these are, as far as I can understand them, the
effects of this new life. The first is such a total
forgetfulness of self, that it seems as if that soul had
no longer any being, because so complete is the
transformation which has taken place within it, that it
no longer knows itself. That soul thinks neither of
life, nor honour, nor even of the happiness of heaven,
but is wholly occupied in promoting the glory of God.

"In the life of such a person we see the faithful
accomplishment of the words once spoken to her by
our Lord: 'Occupy thyself with My interests, and I
will take care of thine.' Without solicitude as to
what may befall her, she lives in such entire forgetfulness of self that she seems to have no longer any
being of her own, and desires to be nothing, except so
far as she may be able to increase, though in the
smallest degree, the honour and glory of God, for
which she would gladly lay down her life.

"Do not imagine, however, that such a person

---

* The Saint herself. She had received this grace in November
1572, and wrote these lines in November 1577.

ceases to eat or sleep, or neglects faithfully to fulfil all
the obligations of her state. What I have said relates
only to her interior. As to exterior works, let one
word suffice; far from fearing them, her only trouble
is to see that all which her strength permits her to do
for God is a mere nothing. No power on earth could
hinder her from performing to the utmost limit of her
strength, whatever she sees to be for the service of
our Lord.

"The second effect of this life in Jesus Christ is a
great desire for suffering; a desire, however, which is
free from all disquietude. So ardently do these souls
long for the accomplishment of the will of God in
them, that they are equally satisfied with whatever He
is pleased to appoint. Thus, if He wills that they
should suffer, they are very glad of it; if He wills it
not, they are not troubled as once they were wont to
be. If these souls should suffer persecution, they
experience great interior joy, and a peace far more
profound than they even felt before. Far from
cherishing a shadow of resentment against those who
injure or desire to injure them, they love them with a
specially tender affection. They are deeply moved if
they see them in any affliction, and there is nothing
which they would not do to alleviate their pain. They
recommend them heartily to God; nay, they would
willingly consent to be deprived of some of the graces
which they have received, and to see them transferred
to these persons, if so they might be brought to
desist from offending their Divine Master. But that
which most amazes me in these souls, is that ardently
desiring death, in order to enjoy the presence of our
Lord, and accounting the prolongation of this exile a
cruel martyrdom; yet so intense is their desire to
serve Him, to cause some to bless His name, to be
useful to some soul, that far from sighing for death,

T

they would fain live for many long years, and in the
midst of the greatest sufferings; too happy if at this
price they could procure for their Divine Master, even
in the least possible thing, a particle of the praise
which He deserves. Though they should have a
certainty of going straight from the prison of the
body to enjoy the vision of God, and though their
mind were filled with the thought of the glory of the
blessed, they would be moved by none of these things,
because they desire neither that vision nor that glory.
Their glory is to be able to do something for their
crucified Lord, especially when they consider how
many there are who offend Him, and how few who,
regardless of themselves, look simply to His honour.

"Do not suppose, my daughters, that the souls who
have attained to this close union with God are free
from imperfections, or even from indeliberate venial
sins. Our Lord gives them especial grace to preserve
them from deliberately offending Him, even venially.
As to mortal sins, consciously committed, they are
exempt from them; still they are never without fear,
especially when they see so many souls fall into
perdition, and read in Holy Scripture of the fall of
those who had been most favoured by God, such as
David and Solomon. Therefore, my sisters, let the
one among you who thinks she has the greatest
ground for security stand most in fear, according to
the words of David: *Blessed is the man who feareth
the Lord.*

"May our Divine Master ever keep us! Let us
earnestly ask this grace of Him, that we may never
offend Him: this is the greatest assurance which we
can have in this life.

"We are not to imagine that our Lord's design in
admitting a soul to this union with Himself is to overwhelm her with joy and consolation; for the most

signal favour which God can bestow upon us is to make our life like to the life of His Son on earth. Therefore, I hold it for certain that our Lord bestows upon us these graces in order to strengthen our weakness, and to enable us, after His own example, to endure great sufferings. Those who are nearest to Him, as His Blessed Mother and His glorious apostles, have had most to suffer.

" Whence did S. Paul derive strength for his excessive labours ? We see clearly in him the effect of those visions, and of that contemplation, which come from God, and not from a disordered imagination, or from the artifices of the spirit of darkness. After having received such great favours from on high, did he go and hide himself to enjoy in sweet repose the consolations which inundated his soul? On the contrary, he passed his days in the labour of the apostolate, and his nights in toiling for his daily bread.

" Who can say to what a degree a soul, in whom the Lord dwells in this especial manner, forgets her own repose, how little honours touch her, how far she is from desiring the smallest measure of esteem ! Walking continually hand in hand with her heavenly Bridegroom, how can she remember herself? Her sole thought is to please Him, and to find means whereby to show Him her love.

" This, my daughters, is the end of prayer, and the one end of this spiritual marriage is the continual production of works for the glory of God. Works, as I have already said, are the surest proof of the reality of this Divine favour.

" The company in which the soul now dwells gives her strength far greater than she ever had before. If, in the words of David, we become *holy with the holy,* who can doubt that the soul which has become one with the God of strength, by that supreme union of spirit with spirit, participates in His strength? Thence it is that the Saints drank in that courage which enabled them to suffer and to die for God.

"And let us also, my sisters, seek to enkindle within us this great zeal for the glory of God. Let us seek in the holy exercise of prayer, not spiritual sweetness, but apostolic strength for the service of our Divine Spouse. Do you know what it is that He desires most ardently of us? That our zeal, by every means within our reach, may strive to bring back souls to Him, that those souls may be saved, and may sing His praises throughout eternity."

We have extracted these passages not only for their exceeding beauty and sublimity, and the practical instruction they contain even for souls which will never attain this state of perfect union with God until they have been prepared for it by the fire of Purgatory; our chief reason for introducing them here is to present another picture of the Saint's interior life, painted by her own hand at a period when she had attained a union with her Divine Spouse, only lower than that conferred by the beatific vision. Let us keep this picture before us, as we follow her through the continually increasing labours, trials, and perplexities of the remaining ten years of her life; the fightings without, the fears within; the persecution of the good who were against her; the vacillation, or the rashness, or the obstinacy, or the other imperfections of the good who were on her side; the unceasing and distracting occupations, which might have seemed to render recollection impossible; the continual drag, and weary up-hill struggle, with languor and ill-health and increasing age; and we shall in some small measure realize the combination of perfect interior repose, with incessant exterior activity, which marked the last ten years of the life of Teresa of Jesus.

From this period, she tells us, her ecstasies and raptures became less frequent, and scarcely ever occurred in public. She had ever been accustomed to speak of them as *weaknesses*, and now she shows us how here, as always, humility is truth. "Formerly," says she, "a pious hymn, the first words of a sermon, or the sight of a holy picture, was enough to throw that soul into a rapture. Now, whether it be that she has found the place of her repose ; whether, after having seen so many wonders in that abode, she is no longer astonished at anything ; whether it be that her solitude has ceased in the company of her Divine Spouse ; or, for some other reason unknown to me, our Lord has no sooner received her into this dwelling, and shown her its beauties, than she loses that great weakness which was so painful and so habitual with her. This change perhaps arises from our Lord having so strengthened and enlarged that soul, as to render it capable of receiving such great favours without being overwhelmed by them."

In the beginning of the year 1561, our Lord had said to His servant Teresa, "Thou shalt see in thy lifetime a great increase of the Order of my Mother." It might have seemed that her appointment to be Prioress of the Incarnation would interfere with the fulfilment of this promise, but our Lord kept His word ; the reform continued to increase. In the year 1571 the discalced fathers founded a convent on the highest point of the Alto Mira, which divides the province of Toledo from that of Cuença. In the following year they penetrated into Andalusia, where the Convent of the Immaculate Conception at S. Juan á Porto, formerly occupied by friars of the Mitigation, was assigned to them.

The progress of the reform at this time doubtless owed much to the prayers of the holy Pope, S. Pius V., who died on May 1, 1572, and appeared to our Saint shortly after his decease, encouraging her to prosecute her glorious work, and promising her his assistance.

The fathers were invited into Andalusia by the Apostolic Visitor, Francis de Vargas, who showed himself no less zealous, and (as it would seem) somewhat less prudent, in protecting the reform, than the Visitor of Castile.

After Teresa had been for two years Prioress of the Incarnation, she was sent by F. Hernandez to arrange the affairs of the community of Salamanca, which she had been obliged reluctantly to leave still unprovided with a proper house. After much difficulty and delay, one was found and prepared, and possession was to be taken on Michaelmas-day, when it appeared that the chapel, which had been hastily finished, let in the rain at all sides. "I tell you, daughters," says the Saint, "that on this day I found myself very imperfect, for notice having been given of the opening of the church, I knew not what to do but to lament, and I begged our Lord, as if complaining, either not to command me to undertake such works or to provide a remedy for this necessity. The good man, Nicolas Guttierez, with his usual cheerfulness, as if nothing at all was the matter, told me very calmly not to trouble myself so much, for that God would provide a remedy. And so He did, for on S. Michael's day, when the people were coming, the weather began to clear, which excited in me great devotion, and I perceived how much better that blessed man had acted, by trusting in God, than I by my trouble." Such is the version given by the Saint's humility of occurrences related in a very different manner by the Mother Anne of Jesus, the Prioress of the convent. Seeing that the rain was falling in such torrents as to impede the removal of the religious from one house to another, and to interfere with the concourse of people which was expected to attend the sermon of a celebrated preacher, and the exposition of the Blessed Sacrament announced for the following day, Anne of Jesus, with two other sisters, came to the holy Mother, and said to her with great earnestness, " Your reverence sees that it is eight o'clock, and there is everything to be done; surely you might ask our Lord to stop the rain, so that we may have a dry place to prepare the altars." The Saint, affecting displeasure, replied, " If you think the thing so easy to obtain, ask for it yourself." M. Anne retired, fearing that she was really angry with her. Teresa, however, asked for the grace in the words given above, and her prayer was immediately granted. The Prioress had hardly left her, when she saw the sky become serene, and the stars shine out as if there had been no rain that day. " Your reverence," said she, " might as well have asked sooner for the rain to stop. Let us all go now and dry the church." Teresa could not refrain from laughing, and took refuge in her cell. The nuns made such haste in their preparation, that everything was ready by the following day, when the Blessed Sacrament was exposed with great solemnity.

" In none of the convents which our Lord has founded of this primitive rule," says the Saint, " have the nuns undergone greater troubles than in this, but they have borne them with the greatest joy. May His Divine Majesty grant that they may advance more and more ! for to have, or not to have, a house of our own matters little; rather it is a great pleasure to us to be in a house from which we may at any time be driven forth, for we remember that the Lord of the world had none. To be in a house not our own, has often happened to us, and I never noticed any of the nuns to be grieved at it. May His Divine Majesty grant that we may obtain the eternal mansions through His infinite goodness and mercy ! "

During her stay at this time at Salamanca, Teresa received the joyful tidings of the approaching return of her beloved brother Laurence from South America.

Laurence de Cepeda had left his country in the year 1540, to follow, like his two elder brothers, the profession of arms ; he was first made captain, and afterwards treasurer of the province of Quito. He married, in 1556, the excellent wife who has been noticed in one of the Saint's former letters. After a happy union of eleven years, God called this holy woman to Himself. Her last words to her husband are thus recorded by him :—

" She said twice to me that one day I should follow her, and that if I wished to be with her in glory, I must be a faithful Christian, and fervently serve our Lord." These words of his dying wife, and the counsels of his saintly sister, wrought so powerfully on the mind of Don Laurence, as to bring him to the decision referred to in the following letter, to abandon the high position which he held in Quito, and the almost fabulous wealth which, in the New World, was in those days at the command of persons in power, to return to Spain, in order to prepare his soul for death, and to train his children for a Christian life.

Letter to Jane d'Ahumada :—

" JESUS.

" May the Holy Spirit be with you, my dear sister ! These letters which I forward to you, will, I am sure, give you very great pleasure ; mine cannot be greater. I hope in the goodness of our Lord, that my brother's return will be the alleviation, or rather the termination, of your troubles. Intentions so holy as his cannot fail to receive a great blessing from God. Oh, how much better do I love to see my brothers living quietly at home, than engaged in those great employments which are never free from danger! Blessed be our Lord for His goodness to us!

"I repeat it, great has been my joy at the news of my brother's approaching return, especially on account of yourself and your husband. After all, some good comes of my letters. Do you see what are the purposes of God for Laurence de Cepeda? For my part, I believe that he thinks more of securing his children's salvation than of making a great fortune. O Jesus! how much do I owe Thee! how little do I serve Thee! I have no greater joy than to see brothers whom I love so dearly, illuminated by the light of grace, and determined to choose those things that are most profitable to their souls.

"Did not I tell you and John d'Ovalle to trust in our Lord, and that He would arrange everything? I say the same now: put all your affairs into the hands of our Divine Master, and He will do what is best for us. I say no more now, because I have written a great deal already, and besides it is late. It fills me with joy, I assure you, to think of the joy which you are about to receive. May our Lord give us that joy which alone is lasting, for all in this world passes away! I am very well, and very busy arranging the purchase of the house—the affair prospers well. My love to Beatrice.

" Ever yours,
" TERESA OF JESUS.

"October 19."

Before Teresa left Salamanca, two other foundations were offered to her; one at Segovia, the other at Veas. For the foundation at Segovia she had received an express command from our Lord. "It seemed to me," says she, "impossible to fulfil this command, for I could not do it without an order from my superiors, and I knew that the Apostolic Visitor had no desire that I should found any more houses at present. I saw likewise, that the three years not having expired, during which I had been commanded to remain at the Incarnation, he had reason for not wishing any more foundations to be made till then. While thinking on this matter, our Lord told me to ask his leave, for that he would grant it. He was then at Salamanca, and I wrote to him accordingly, to say that, as he knew I was under a command of our Most Reverend Father General, whenever an opportunity should present itself in any place of founding a monastery, not to let it slip; and that I was now requested to found a monastery with the consent of the city and the Bishop of Segovia, with which request, with the permission of his reverence, I would gladly comply.

"These words I made use of to discharge my conscience, and then rested very well content and satisfied with whatever he should command, and I told him also I thought he would do God a service by consenting to the foundation. It plainly appeared that such was our Lord's pleasure, for the Commissary Apostolic immediately commanded and empowered me to found a monastery in that place, at which I wondered, considering what I knew of him in similar cases."

The approbation of the Apostolic Visitor having been so readily obtained, the Saint wrote to an intimate friend of hers, Doña Anna Ximenes, begging her to hire a house for the nuns; "for I had not," says she, "a farthing to buy one, and I thought that, if possession was once taken, our Lord would not fail to provide one for us."

Hearing that everything was ready at Segovia, S. Teresa left Salamanca, accompanied by S. John of the Cross, Julian of Avila, and a pious gentleman named Antony Gaytan, who had offered his services to assist her on her journeys. She took with her Isabella of Jesus, a cousin of Doña Anna, and Mary of Jesus, both natives of Segovia. "Don Antony Gaytan," says the Saint, "was a man of prayer, and our Lord has shown him so many favours, that what to others appears impossible, seems easy and delightful to him; such are all the labours to be endured in these foundations. It clearly appears that God chooses both him and F. Julian of Avila, who assisted at the first foundation, for this work. For the sake of such companions, I believe our Lord made everything prosper with me; their discourse on the road was always on God."

S. Teresa, when she undertook this journey, was enduring great affliction both of mind and body. "I had a fever upon me," she says; "loss of appetite, and many other corporal afflictions, beside the interior suffering of aridity and extreme darkness of soul, it being our Lord's will that there should be no foundation without some affliction."

The Saint and her companions left Salamanca on March 18, 1574, and were received with great affection by the pious widow, Doña Anna. She was not accustomed to lose time, so on the following day, being the feast of her great patron, S. Joseph, possession was taken of the new convent, which was dedicated to him. The first Mass was celebrated by S. John of the Cross.

One of the Canons of Segovia, happening to pass by the little chapel, and being much edified by its modest and devout appearance, asked permission also to celebrate the Divine Sacrifice there, when he was interrupted by the Vicar-General, who, in great wrath that the chapel should have been opened without his permission, forbade the Canon to say his Mass, stripped the altar of all its ornaments, and gave orders to a priest who accompanied him to consume the Blessed Sacrament. The nuns were concealed behind the grille; Julian of Avila hid himself under the stair-case; S. John of the Cross, who was the only person visible, barely escaped being sent to prison.

S. Teresa, in the quiet consciousness that she had obtained the permission of the Bishop before she left Salamanca, smiled within herself at the disturbance made by the Vicar-General. She sent to ask her never-failing friends, the fathers of the Society of Jesus, to explain the matter to him, and show him that his jurisdiction had been in no way interfered with. Some gentlemen of the place, relations of Isabella of Jesus, also interposed in behalf of the nuns, and the Vicar-General, at last, though with considerable reluctance, withdrew his opposition so far as to allow Mass to be said in the church, though he still forbade the Blessed Sacrament to be placed there.

This matter being settled, Teresa had next to take measures for the removal of the nuns from Pastrana to the new foundation.

We have heard enough of the treatment endured by the holy Mother before the foundation at Pastrana from the Princess of Evoli, to be in some measure prepared for the extravagances committed by that lady on the death of her pious and reasonable husband. " The Princess," says S. Teresa, " took great care to make the nuns happy, and to show them every kindness, until the death of the Prince; but after that event, the devil (or perhaps our Lord permitted it, and His Divine Majesty knows why) contrived that the Princess, in a sudden fit of passion for the death of her husband, should become a nun in our monastery."

This resolution on the part of the Princess was so sudden and ill-considered, that she insisted upon being clothed in Madrid by Father Mariano, who had assisted her husband in his last agony; and without listening to any advice, or stopping to arrange any of the weighty affairs which depended upon her, she entered the convent in the middle of the night.

The Prioress, the prudent and holy Mother Isabella of S. Dominic, in consternation at the sudden metamorphosis, exclaimed, " The Princess a nun ! I give up the house for lost." During the new postulant's brief month of religion, the Prioress and the nuns had ample material for merit. Mother Isabella at last, having tried every milder means, said to her, " If your Excellency continues to behave in such a manner, rest assured that we will leave the monastery and go elsewhere to observe our primitive rule."

This resolution was now carried into effect. S. Teresa prevailed upon the superiors to remove the community to Segovia. " The Princess," says she, " because the Prioress would not give her all the liberties she wished, took such a dislike to her, and to all of us, and even after she had taken off the habit and retired to her own house, still troubled the poor nuns so much, that I endeavoured by every means in my power to have the monastery removed."

At their departure from Pastrana, the nuns not only gave up everything which they had received from the Princess, but they took with them to Segovia some novices whom, at her desire, they had received without portion. They carried away nothing but their beds, and some little furniture which they had brought with them. " The whole place," says S. Teresa, "was in grief at their departure; as for me, I was very glad that an end was put to their troubles, and that they were restored to peace. Doubtless it was not the will of God that a convent should be established in that place."

On the day on which these sisters were expected at Segovia, the holy Mother said to the religious there, " Sisters, let us pray hard for the nuns who are coming from Pastrana, for they are in great peril." On their arrival, it appeared that they had been in great danger of being drowned in passing a river; a danger from which her prayers had doubtless delivered them. S. Teresa remained six months at Segovia, arranging the affairs of the house, and training its inmates to religious perfection.

Amongst the first to receive the habit in that place were the holy widow, Doña Anna de Ximenes, and her daughter. With the portion brought by these ladies, a suitable house was purchased; but before the nuns could be removed thither, Teresa was obliged to leave them, in order to be present at the Chapter to be held at Avila at the termination of her three years of office.

Before her departure from Segovia she was favoured by a vision of S. Albert, the author of the primitive Carmelite rule, to whom she had earnestly commended the interests of her reform. He made known to her that it would be necessary for its stability that it should be separated from the control of the Superiors of the Mitigation.

CHAPTER XVII.

1574.

The holy Mother arrived at Avila just in time for the opening of the Chapter. Though she had been absent for a year, owing to her necessary occupations in the foundations of Salamanca and Segovia, the religious of the Incarnation felt so strongly the benefits which they had derived from her two years of superiority, that they unanimously re-elected her. Teresa was, however, most reluctant to be longer separated from her own children, and the Provincial refused to confirm the election.

Her daughters at S. Joseph were but too glad to be able to claim her for themselves, and their united voices compelled her once more to assume the government of her first and best-loved foundation. She was not, however, left there long in peace, being soon called upon to found a house at Veas.

When at Salamanca, the holy Mother had received a letter from a lady of Veas, named Doña Catharine of Sandoval and Godinez, and other pious persons of that place, requesting her to come and found a monastery there, for they had already a house ready, and they wanted nothing but her presence for the foundation. "I asked," says she, "certain questions of the messenger, and he gave me a good account of the country, and justly so, for it is very pleasant, and the temperature is good. But considering its great distance, it seemed to me foolish to go there, especially as I could not do so without leave from the Commissary Apostolic, who I knew was an enemy (or at least no friend) to any more monasteries being

founded at that time.   I resolved, therefore, to answer
that I could not make the foundation, without saying
anything further.   But I thought afterwards that, as
the Commissary Apostolic was then at Salamanca, it
would not be well to act without his advice, on
account of the command laid upon me by our Most
Reverend Father-General, that I should not omit any
opportunity of founding monasteries.   When he had
read the letters, he sent me word that it would not be
well to discourage those persons, with whose devotion
he was much edified; and that I should send them
word that as soon as they had obtained a license from
the council of the Knights of S. James, the Superiors
of the place, I would hasten to found a monastery;
adding that I might be assured they would not be
able to obtain leave, for he knew several persons who
had for many years tried in vain to procure such a
license from the Knights.   In a word, I was not to
return them an unsatisfactory answer.   I sometimes
think on this matter, and how, when our Lord wills
anything to be done, it comes to pass without our
perceiving that we are the instruments, as was the
case with Father Peter Hernandez, the Commissary
Apostolic; for thus, when they obtained the license,
he could not deny his permission."

The Saint gives the following account of the conversion of Catharine de Sandoval.   " There lived in
the town of Veas a gentleman called Sancho Roderick
de Sandoval, of noble descent and great wealth; his
wife was a lady named Doña Catharine.   Amongst
other children whom our Lord gave them were two
daughters, who were the foundresses of this monastery.
The elder was named Catharine, and the younger
Mary.   The former was fourteen years old when our
Lord called her to His service.   Before that time, she
was very far from abandoning the world; nay, she

had so high an esteem of herself that when her father wished her to marry, she rejected every one whom he proposed as greatly her inferior. Being one day in her chamber, she accidentally happened to read the title that was placed above a crucifix. While she was reading it, our Lord wonderfully changed her. She had been considering a proposed alliance which was considered very honourable to her, and she said within herself: "What a little thing contents my father, who thinks it good enough for me to marry a Mayorazgo !* I intend the honour of my family to begin in me." She had, however, no inclination to marry, as it seemed to her a mean thing to be subject to any one ; nor did she know whence her pride arose. But our Lord knows well how to bring good out of evil. May His Majesty be blessed for ever ! When she read the title, she seemed to have received a sudden light in her soul, to understand the truth, as if the sun should shine in a dark room ; and with this light she fixed her eyes on our Lord hanging on the Cross, and shedding His Blood; and she then considered how ill He was treated, His profound humility, and how different a path she was treading in her pride.

"In these considerations she remained for some time, as our Lord held her in a rapture, wherein He gave her a true knowledge of her own great misery, and a desire that all men should know it also. She was then seized with so ardent a desire of suffering for God, that she longed even for martyrdom, and this was joined with such a deep sense of humility and hatred of herself, that if she could have done so without offending God, she would have been content to be esteemed a notorious sinner, that so all might abhor her. She thus began to despise herself, being

---

* The eldest son of a noble house.

U

filled with the desire of doing penance, which afterwards she carried into effect. She made a vow of poverty and chastity on the spot, and was so desirous of being subject to another, that for that end she would have been glad to have been transported as a slave to the country of the Moors."

From that moment Catharine gave herself to a life of austere penance and unremitting charity, in which she was joined by her younger sister.

Soon afterwards she was favoured with a remarkable vision, which, nearly twenty years afterwards, she related to S. Teresa. "She told me," says the Saint, "that she went to bed one night, desiring to discover the most perfect religious Order on earth, in order that she might enter it; and she dreamt that she was going along a very narrow path, in the greatest peril of falling down deep precipices, which lay on each side of her, when a person in the dress of a discalced friar said to her, 'Sister, come along with me.' He took her to a convent, in which were many nuns, and where she saw no light, except that which came from the candles in their hands. She inquired to what Order they belonged. All were silent; but they lifted up their veils, and, smiling, showed her their happy countenances. The Prioress took her by the hand, and said, 'My child, I wish you to be here,' showing her at the same time the rule and constitutions."

From this time, 1565, Catharine persevered in her purpose to enter religion in the Order which had been thus revealed to her; and after many years of painful trial, arising from the opposition of friends, and long and severe illness, from which she was at last miraculously restored, she ascertained from one of the Jesuit fathers that the vision which she had seen had reference to the new Carmelite reform.

In the Lent of 1575, permission having been with great difficulty obtained from the Knights of S. James for the foundation, S. Teresa began her journey to Veas, with Mother Anne of Jesus, whom she summoned from Salamanca to undertake the government of the new convent.

As the travellers were passing the high mountain peak of the Sierra Morena, they lost their way and came to a point where it seemed equally perilous to advance or to recede. The Saint enjoined her daughters to recommend themselves to God and S. Joseph in a strait where human aid seemed hopeless. A voice, as from the highest peak, answered them : "Stay where you are; if you pass on you will be dashed down the precipice." The muleteers instantly stopped, and asked the friendly voice to point out to them the way of safety. They were directed along a path so precipitous, that nothing short of a miracle could have enabled them to follow it. When the fearful passage had been safely made, some of the party wished to go in search of their benefactor. "I do not know," said S. Teresa to the nuns, as the men set off upon their search, "why we have let them go; for it was my Father, S. Joseph, whom assuredly they will not find." In fact, they returned, after a fruitless search, and from that moment the mules travelled with such rapidity, that the muleteers swore they went rather like birds than beasts ; as if the rugged rocks had been changed into a smooth and easy road. On February 18, the party reached the entrance of Veas, where the principal citizens, who had come forth on horseback to do them honour, brought them in triumph to the church, where the priests in their cottas were waiting for them ; and preceded by the Cross, and accompanied by the two ladies of Sandoval and other nobility of the place, they were conducted in procession to the house of Doña Catharine. As soon as she was alone with the nuns, they raised their veils, and the joy of that faithful and long-suffering heart was full, for she recognised the faces she had seen in her vision. She knelt at once at the feet of M. Anne of Jesus, who pointed out S. Teresa to her, saying, "It is to our Mother, lady, that you owe obedience." "This is our Mother Foundress, doubtless," replied Doña Catharine, "but it is your reverence whom God has given us to be our Prioress." She recognised also the friar who had guided her in her dream, in the person of the venerable Brother John of Misery, the companion of Father Mariano, who, on his way from Castile to Seville, had come to meet the holy Mother at Veas.

The convent of *S. Joseph the Deliverer* was founded on the Feast of S. Matthias, in the house of the ladies of Sandoval, who on the same day received the religious habit, with the names of Catharine and Mary of Jesus. So generous and perfect was their abandonment of the world, that they made a full and free gift of their wealth to the convent, without the slightest condition. "But what will you do," said the holy Mother, "if we should refuse after all to profess you, and drive you out into the street?" "We will serve your reverences as portresses," said they; "and if you will not give us anything to eat, we will ask alms for the love of God."

S. Teresa remained for three months at Veas, where she gave the habit to four other novices. This convent, under the direction of its holy Prioress, became one of the most remarkable in the Order for religious fervour.

During her stay in Veas, S. Teresa was informed by her old friend and benefactor, the Bishop of Avila, that the Inquisition had desired an inquiry to be made concerning her history of her own life. This inquiry had originated, as is supposed, in the rumours which had been set afloat in Madrid, by the indiscreet curiosity of the Princess of Evoli. The humility of the Saint immediately took alarm, and her old fears of being deluded returned upon her. She was consoled and strengthened by her beloved daughter, Anne of Jesus, and a mightier Comforter was at hand. The next day, after Holy Communion, she said to Mother Anne : " My daughter, thank God with me, for when I received our Lord to-day, He consoled me saying: ' Trouble not thyself, for this cause is mine.' "

It was at Veas that Teresa first became acquainted with one who was to exercise so powerful an influence both over herself and her reform. Jerome Gracian (in religion, *of the Mother of God*) was the son of Don Diego Gracian de Alderete, who had been successively secretary to Charles V. and Philip II., and was one of the most eminent men of his time for learning, wisdom, and virtue. Of his mother, Doña Jane Dantisco, S. Teresa, who knew her intimately, says : " I have known few women equal to her in excellence."

The son of these parents was worthy of them. At the age of seven-and-twenty, when he left the world, Jerome Gracian was already one of the most remarkable men of his time, as a man of letters, a theologian, and an orator. His birth, his merit, his learning, his renown, the singular gift of fascination by which he gained such an influence over all who came within its sphere, his own and his father's favour with Philip II. opened the way to his attainment of the highest ecclesiastical dignities, when he turned his back upon them all to take up the Cross of Christ.

S. Teresa thus narrates his vocation to Carmel. " A Father of our Order of Discalced Friars came to

see me at Veas, whose name was F. Jerome Gracian,
of the Mother of God. He had taken the habit a few
years before when at the University of Alcalá; he
was a man of very great learning, judgment, and
modesty, and during all his life was so distinguished
for his virtues, that it seems our Lady had chosen him
for the good of this primitive Order. When he was
at Alcalá, he was very far from thinking of taking our
habit, though fully purposed to become a religious.
His parents, however, had other intentions for him,
on account of their being in high favour with the King,
and by reason of their son's distinguished abilities.
His father (who was the King's secretary) desired that
he should study the law; but although then very
young, he disliked the thought of such a life so much,
that by his tears he obtained leave to devote himself
to the study of divinity. He made an attempt, as
soon as he had taken his doctor's degree, to enter
the Society of Jesus, but, for some reason or other,
his admission was postponed by the superiors, and he
finally relinquished the design. He told me that all
his pleasures and amusements served but to torment
him, because he thought this was not the safe way to
Heaven. He constantly observed fixed hours of
prayer, and his recollection and modesty were very
great.

"In process of time an intimate friend of his (in
religion B. John of Jesus) entered our monastery at
Pastrana. I know not whether it was a letter from
this religious on the excellence and antiquity of our
Order, or some other cause, which gave him an inclination for it. He began to take such great pleasure
in reading anything connected with our Lady's Order,
and in verifying what he read by the testimony of
grave authors, that he often felt a scruple at inter-
rupting his study of other things, by his continual

reading of our history, to which he also devoted his hours of recreation. Oh, the wisdom and the power of God! How vain are the efforts of men to elude His will! Our Lord knew well what great need we had of such a man to carry on the work which His Divine Majesty had begun. I often praise Him for the favour He has shown us herein; for if I had asked His Divine Majesty for a person to regulate all the affairs of our reform, I could not have fixed upon one equal to him whom He gave us. May He be blessed for ever!

"Being then far from the intention of taking this habit, F. Gracian was requested to go to Pastrana, to speak with the Prioress there about the admission of a postulant. How wonderfully does our Lord order things! For had he gone thither resolved to take the habit, he would perhaps have met with so many to oppose him, that he would never have accomplished his design.

"But the Blessed Virgin, our Lady (to whom he is exceedingly devout), wished to reward him by the gift of her habit. She was unwilling that one who so greatly desired to serve her should want an opportunity of carrying his design into execution; for she is ever wont to bestow favours on those who desire to place themselves under her protection.

"When only a child at Madrid, F. Gracian often paid his devotions to an image of our Lady, which he was accustomed to call his *Beloved*. She obtained for him from her Son that purity in which he always lived. He told me once that she sometimes appeared to him with her eyes filled with tears on account of the offences committed against her Son. Hence arose within him an impetuous desire for the welfare of souls, and an intense sorrow whenever he saw God offended. He is so strongly impressed with this desire

of doing good to souls that no labour seems great to
him, if thereby he can benefit any one. This I have
seen myself in the many troubles which he has
endured.

" The Blessed Virgin then brought him to Pastrana,
as he thought, to procure the habit for another; but
our Lord was waiting there to bestow it on himself.
O! how wonderful are the secrets of God! And how
sweetly (without our wishing or intending it) does He
dispose us for receiving His favours! Thus did He
repay this man for the good works which he had done,
and for the good example he had given, and the great
desire he had of serving His glorious Mother; for
assuredly His Majesty will always repay such desires
by bestowing wonderful graces!

" On his arrival at Pastrana, F. Gracian went to
speak with the Prioress (M. Isabella of S. Dominic)
about the admission of the postulant, little supposing
that she would treat with our Lord about his own
entrance into the Order. As soon as she saw him, his
demeanour pleased her much, insomuch that she and
all the nuns earnestly besought our Lord not to suffer
him to go away without taking the habit. The Prioress herself is a very great servant of God, and hence
I think her prayer alone would be heard by His
Divine Majesty—how much more the prayers of so
many devout souls that were living there! They all
took up the matter very earnestly; and with fasting,
disciplines, and prayers, they continually besought
His Divine Majesty, till at length He was pleased to
grant this favour.

" When F. Gracian went to the monastery of friars
and saw so much devotion and such opportunities of
serving our Lord, and, above all, that it was the Order
of his glorious Mother, whom he desired so much to
serve, his heart began to be moved not to return to

the world again. And though the devil suggested many difficulties and in particular the grief which this step would cause his parents, who loved him much, and hoped that he would be of great use to their children (for they had many), yet leaving this care to God, for whose sake he abandoned all things, he determined now to become a devout servant of our Lady, and to take her habit; and accordingly it was given to him, to the joy of all, especially of the Prioress and nuns, who gave great thanks and praise to our Lord.

" He spent his year of probation with such humility, that he seemed to be the lowest of the novices. At one time his virtue was especially tried, for, as the Prior was then absent, a Superior was appointed who was very young and without learning, abilities, or prudence for governing ; neither had he any experience, as he had been only lately admitted into the Order. It was a very strange thing to see how he governed the religious, and the mortifications which he imposed on them ; every time I think on the subject, I am astonished how they could have borne with him ; the Divine Spirit alone could have enabled them to endure this trouble. But it was afterwards discovered that he was extremely subject to melancholy, so that wherever he went (even as a subject), he gave trouble ; how much more when he was in command ; for this melancholy had gained great power over him. He is, nevertheless, a good religious, and God sometimes allows the error to happen of putting such persons in authority, in order to perfect the obedience of those He loves ; and so it was here.

" In recompense for this trial, God bestowed a very wonderful light in matters of obedience on F. Jerome, that so he might hereafter teach this virtue to his subjects, as one who had made so good a beginning in the exercise of it. And that he might not want experience in everything necessary for our government, he had most grievous temptations three months before his profession; but (like a brave captain who was one day to lead the sons of our Lady) he manfully defended himself against them; and the more the devil pressed him to take off the habit, so much the more did he resolve to cling to it, and to bind himself to it by the vows. He gave me a treatise which he wrote during those violent temptations, from which I derived great edification, seing clearly the strength which had been given him by God.

"It may seem strange that he should have communicated to me so many particulars concerning his soul, but our Lord allowed it, that I might insert them here, to the end He might be praised in His creatures, for I know that neither to his confessor nor to any one else had he revealed so much. Perhaps he thought (on account of my age and of what he had heard of me) that I had some experience in these matters.

"For the most part," continues the Saint, "those who speak with him love him (which is a special favour from our Lord), and he is also extremely beloved by all his inferiors, both men and women. For though he is very exact in leaving no fault unpunished, having a regard for the welfare of the Order, yet he does everything with such sweetness and mildness, that it seems no one can complain of him.

"I have been very short, that should these words ever come to be read by him, they may not displease him, but I could not say less than I have said, nor forbear mentioning one who has been so great an instrument in the restoration of our primitive rule. For, though he was not the first who began it, yet the time has been when, but for my confidence in our Lord's goodness, I could sometimes have been angry that the work had been begun before. I speak of the houses of the friars, for as regards the nuns, they have up to this time always gone on well; but the houses of the friars, though they did not go on badly, had within them the principle of dissolution, because, having no Provincial of their own, they were governed by the fathers of the mitigated rule. Those who were able to govern (such as F. Antony of Jesus, who began the reform) were not approved nor supported, neither had particular constitutions been given them by the most Reverend Father General. The prior of each house did as he thought fit; and, until the time when the reform came to have Superiors of its own, this was an occasion of great troubles; for some were of one opinion, others of another, and this state of things often gave me much pain. All this, however, our Lord remedied by means of F. Jerome of the Mother of God; for he was made Commissary Apostolic, and received authority over all the friars and nuns of the discalced Order. He also drew up constitutions for the friars (the nuns had received theirs already from our most Reverend Father), by virtue of his Apostolic authority; being fitted for the work by the great gifts which he had received from our Lord. The first time that he visited the fathers, he put everything in such excellent order, that it was quite clear he was assisted by His Divine Majesty, and that our Lady had chosen him for the good of her Order."

F. Gracian had accompanied F. Mariano into Andalusia, on the invitation of the Visitor Apostolic, F. Vargas, to aid him in the work of reform.

Whether because he was weary of the struggle with the Andalusians, or that he considered that they would be more amenable to one of their own Order, Vargas delegated his powers as Visitor Apostolic to this young religious, who had not yet reached the age of thirty;

thus placing the fathers of the Mitigation under his control.

F. Gracian's first measures were most prudent and conciliating. He restored to the mitigated Carmelites the monastery at S. Juan á Porto, which had been taken from them, and sent back to them several subjects who had joined the reform. Having no house of their own in Andalusia, the two fathers, Gracian and Mariano, took up their abode at the Convent of the Mitigation in Seville, where they were residing at the time the former met S. Teresa at Veas.

The holy Mother ascertained for the first time, in a conversation with F. Gracian, that Veas belonged to the province of Andalusia. She was much disquieted at the information, having received express orders from the Father General to make no foundation in that part of Spain. He had himself experienced the difficulty of dealing with the Andalusians, and was well aware of the want of sympathy, or rather the antipathy, which existed between the fitful and fiery people of the south and the calm and steadfast Castilians.

"I had always," says Teresa, "refused to make any foundation in Andalusia, and if I had known that Veas belonged to that province, I would never have gone thither; but the mistake arose from the fact that, though the town is not in Andalusia, it is subject to it." F. Gracian, whose authority was not derived from the General, gave himself no trouble about the matter, but took advantage of the mistake to exert his authority as Visitor of Andalusia to induce her to make a foundation at Seville.

"Your reverence," said he, "being now in Andalusia, is my subject, and in future must execute whatever we may judge most for the Divine service." Teresa was no way unwilling to be under obedience to one for whom she had already conceived so high an opinion, and he gave her an occasion of exercising a most heroic act of obedience. She was at this time contemplating a foundation in Caravaca, and another in Madrid. F. Gracian pressed her to lay both these aside for the present, and to found a convent at once at Seville, the capital of Andalusia.

He bade her, however, first to consult God on the subject.

Having done so, she told him that our Lord had given her to understand that it would be best to make the foundation at Madrid first. " I am of opinion, nevertheless," replied Father Gracian, " that you had better go first to Seville." The Saint made no reply, but immediately began her preparations for the journey, and chose the religious who were to accompany her. In a few days, F. Gracian, in admiration at her prompt obedience, said to her, " It is not at all impossible that I may have been mistaken in my opinion; how is it that you immediately determined to follow it against a positive revelation ?"

" I cannot be deceived," replied Teresa, " in obeying my superiors. I may be deceived as to the truth of a revelation." F. Gracian was so much struck by this answer, that he obliged the Saint once more to consult our Lord, who, on this occasion, replied : " You have done well to obey. Your reform, as well as the foundation at Madrid, will gain by it. Go to Seville ; the house will be founded, but you will have much to suffer."

At this time the Saint, as she relates in the following words, was placed by our Lord Himself under the direction of F. Gracian.

" I saw our Lord in the form under which He is wont to appear to me. On his right side was F. Gracian, and I myself was on His left. He took both our right hands, and joining them in His own, said to me : ' This is he whom I will have to stand to thee in My place as long as thou shalt live, and I will have you both to agree in all things, for such is My will.'

" I felt so great an assurance that this vision came from God, that I did not hesitate to obey it, though I felt a great repugnance to leave two of my confessors whose direction I had long followed, especially one of them whom I greatly reverenced and loved. So I determined to do all that my Divine Master told me, and faithfully to follow in all things, for the rest of my life, the direction of F. Gracian, unless it should be in any matter visibly contrary to the law of God; and this I am certain will never happen, for, from certain things which he has said to me, I believe that he has bound himself by the same vow which I have taken myself, to do always that which is most perfect."

In the following Whitsuntide, the Saint was favoured by a glorious vision of the Holy Ghost, in the visible form of a dove, by which she felt her love of God sensibly increased. "I felt," she says, "within my soul the most intense desire to make some return for this signal grace, and it came into my mind that the most acceptable thing that I could do for that Divine Spirit, would be to bind myself by vow to the obedience which I had already determined to pay to F. Gracian. I felt the most intense repugnance to do this, and again the greatest anguish that I should shrink from doing anything which I had an opportunity of doing for God.

" Except the agony which I felt at leaving my father's house to enter religion, no other act of my life, not even my profession, cost me so much as this.

" After a brief struggle, our Lord gave me strength to overcome myself, and I knelt down and promised to follow the will of F. Gracian all my life long, provided it should not be against the will of God, nor against that of other superiors whom I might be bound to obey. I promised besides never to conceal from him any of my sins, or any of my faults, a thing to which we are not bound with regard to our superiors : in short, to consider him in all things, interior and exterior, as holding to me the place of God Himself. Then I felt as if I had done something great for the Holy Ghost; at least, I had done my best to please Him, and I felt a satisfaction and joy which I have never since lost. I thought that I was going to bind myself with a chain, and I have been far more free than ever I was before. I am well assured that our Lord will grant F. Gracian fresh supplies of grace, of which I shall have my share, and light to direct me in all things. May He be blessed for having created one in whom I could feel such confidence as to dare to make such a vow ! "

CHAPTER XVIII.

1575, 1576.

F. Gracian left Veas for Madrid to meet the Papal Nuncio, by whose authority he was created Provincial of the reform; and S. Teresa, with six religious, accompanied by Julian of Avila and Antony Gaytan, set off on her journey to Seville. "With our utmost haste," says the Saint, "we were unable to reach Seville till the Thursday after Pentecost. The heat was excessive, and though we halted at mid-day, we were in a kind of purgatory. My companions were so holy, that they thought it sweet to suffer something for God, and if I had taken them into the land of the Turks, they would have had strength, I doubt not, or rather God would have given them strength, to suffer all torments for His love. For as I had to take them to so distant a foundation, I had chosen such as were most perfect in prayer and mortification."

The most remarkable amongst these saintly sisters was Mary of S. Joseph, afterwards Prioress of Seville (in the world, Mary of Salazar), whose vocation to religion dates from S. Teresa's stay in the palace of her kinswoman, Doña Louisa de la Cerda, at Toledo. She had received the habit of Mount Carmel at the foundation of the convent at Malagon in 1568.

The journey to Seville was full of disasters. S. Teresa was attacked on the Vigil of Pentecost with a violent fever, aggravated by the intense heat, and the whole party narrowly escaped drowning in crossing the Guadalquivir. They hastened to reach Cordova early in the morning to be able to hear Mass quietly. "After many vexatious delays, we arrived," says the Saint, "at the church where F. Julian d'Avila was to say Mass. We found it full of people assembled on account of the festival, for it was dedicated to the Holy Ghost. A sermon was also to be preached. When I perceived this, I was greatly troubled; and, in my judgment, it would have been better to have departed without hearing Mass than to have got ourselves into such a crowd. F. Julian thought otherwise; and, as he was a theologian, we followed his opinion, otherwise the rest of my companions would perhaps have followed mine, which would have been quite wrong. We alighted near the church; and though no one could see our faces, our veils being down, the sight of those veils, together with our sandals and white mantles, was enough to cause curiosity and emotion among the people. A sudden palpitation of the heart, occasioned by fear of the crowd, quite took away my fever. When we got into the church, a good man met us, and made way for us through the crowd. I begged of him to conduct us to some little chapel, and he did so, locking the door upon us until he came again to take us out of the church. A few days afterwards this good man came to Seville, and told one of our fathers that, in recompense, as he believed, for the good office he had done us, an unexpected inheritance had fallen to him. What I tell you, daughters, may seem to you a mere trifle, but to me it was one of the severest mortifications of my life; for the excitement of the people at the sight of us was no less than if we had been so many bulls driven in for a bull-fight."

The misfortunes on the way were but preliminary to the trials which awaited the Saint at Seville. She was directed to a small and damp house hired by F. Mariano. Teresa had anticipated no difficulties in this foundation, having been assured both by F. Gracian and F. Mariano that the Archbishop was most favourable to the reform, and would gladly sanction the establishment of a convent in the city; she had therefore omitted, as unnecessary, the usual preliminary of asking the license of the Diocesan. On her arrival, however, she found that the Archbishop was wholly averse to the foundation of a convent without endowment. "This was the same," says the Saint, "as saying that no convent should be founded at all; for though I had accepted endowments for poor places, where the nuns could not otherwise be supported, I would never have consented to do this in so wealthy a city as Seville. On the other hand I had not a farthing left from the expenses of our journey; and we had brought nothing with us but our habits, some tunics, and some cloth which had covered the waggons. We, were even obliged to borrow money to pay the drivers.

In this state of things the foundation seemed impossible. At length, after many entreaties from F. Mariano, the Archbishop gave leave for Mass to be said on the Feast of the Most Holy Trinity (May 29, 1575). But he would suffer no bell to be rung. Thus matters continued for about a fortnight, and I determined, if I could obtain permission from the Father Visitor, to return to Veas with my nuns for the foundation of Caravaca. At length it pleased God that the Archbishop should come and visit me, when I represented to him that he was dealing hardly with us. He listened to my reasons, and granted me all that I desired, and from that day he has never ceased to favour us."

The Saint's troubles at Seville were not, however, over, and they were aggravated by great interior trials, which made them harder to bear. "No one could have imagined," says she, "that in so wealthy and populous a city as Seville, I should have had more trouble and difficulty in founding a house than in any other place; so much so that I sometimes thought we were not meant to have a monastery in this city. I know not if it be in this part of the world that the devils, as I have heard, have greater power, by the permission of God, to tempt people than in other places; for here they assailed me so dreadfully that during all my life I never knew myself to be so pusillanimous and so cowardly as I was in Seville. Sometimes I hardly knew myself. Not that I had lost confidence in our Lord, but my nature was so different from what it was wont to be, that I plainly perceived He had withdrawn His hand from me, to convince me that whatever courage I once had was not my own."

Severer trials, however, than any connected with the foundation of Seville were now impending. We

have neither space nor inclination to enter into the long
and grievous history of the internal conflict in the
Carmelite Order which for five years together threatened to crush S. Teresa's reform. She has left the
following sketch of it in the book of her Foundations,
to which we shall only add from time to time such
notices as bear upon her personal history.

" After the convent at Seville was established, the
foundations were discontinued for more than four
years, on account of the great persecutions which at
that time suddenly arose against our discalced friars
and nuns; for, although they had before suffered
many, yet not to such a degree as now, for these trials
were near putting an end to our reform. The devil
hereby showed his envy at our good beginning, which
our Lord, by its ultimate success, proved to be His
own work.

" The discalced fathers, and especially the Superiors,
suffered much on account of the serious accusations
and contradictions which they endured from almost
all the fathers of the mitigated rule. These had so
prejudiced our Most Reverend Father General, that
(although he was a very holy man, and had himself
given leave for the foundation of all the monasteries,
except that of S. Joseph's in Avila, which was the
first, and which was erected by the authority of the
Pope) he insisted that the discalced fathers should
proceed no further (to the houses of the nuns he was
always favourable) ; and because I had assisted them,
they made him displeased with me, which was the
greatest affliction I suffered in these foundations,
though I had to endure many. For, on the one hand,
my learned confessors and directors would not consent
to my desisting from undertakings which I clearly
saw would do our Lord some service, and also increase
our Order; and, on the other, to go against what I

x 2

perceived was the wish of the Father General, was indeed a kind of death to me; for, besides the duty I owed him as my Superior, I loved him tenderly, as I had reason to do. The truth is, that however much I might have desired to please him in this matter, I could not, because of the authority of the Apostolical Visitors whom I was bound to obey. About this time the Pope's Nuncio died, who was a holy man, a great lover of virtue, and a sincere friend to the discalced fathers. Another succeeded him, who it seems was sent by God to exercise us in sufferings. He was in some way related to the Pope, and, though doubtless a great servant of God, he was entirely in favour of the fathers of the mitigated rule; and according to the information which he received from them concerning us, he came to the conclusion that it was better that the reform should proceed no further; and accordingly he began to execute his plans with extreme rigour, condemning, imprisoning, and banishing all those who he supposed might resist him. Those who suffered most were F. Antony of Jesus, who founded the first convent of discalced fathers, and F. Jerome Gracian, whom the late Nuncio had made Apostolic Visitor of the fathers of the mitigated rule. With these, and with F. Mariano of S. Benedict, he was displeased the most; he forbade them, under pain of heavy censures, to undertake or manage any business. It was clear that all this trouble came from God, and that His Majesty permitted it for some greater good, and that the virtues of these fathers might become better known, as indeed came to pass. He appointed a father of the mitigated rule to visit the monasteries, both of friars and nuns; and had what he imagined of us been true, this would have been a great affliction to us; as it was, we suffered exceedingly, as may be seen in the narratives of those who write better than I do. I only just touch on these points, in order that the nuns who come after us may understand how much they are bound to advance in perfection, since what they find so easy has cost those now living very dear; some of them having suffered at that time heavy accusations, which afflicted me much more acutely than what I endured myself, which was rather a source of pleasure to me. It seemed that I was the cause of all this trouble, and that if I had been thrown into the sea, like Jonas, the tempest would have ceased. God be praised, who ever defends the truth: and so it happened now: for when our Catholic king Don Philip heard what had taken place, and was informed of the life and virtues of the discalced fathers, he took up our cause so favourably, that he would not allow the Nuncio alone to judge it, but appointed four others in addition, wise and prudent men, three of whom were religious, to examine the case. One of them was Peter Hernandez, a very holy man, and very prudent and learned: he had been Apostolic Commissary and Visitor of the fathers both of the mitigated and discalced rule in the province of Castile. He well knew the truth, and the manner of life of both, which was all that we desired; and thus, seeing the king had appointed him our judge, I considered the business as already finished, as by the mercy of God it is now. May His Majesty grant that it may tend to His honour and glory! Although many great men in the kingdom and many bishops had taken pains to acquaint the Nuncio with the truth, yet all would have availed but little, if God had not made use of the king as His instrument."

The mitigated Carmes had been long pouring their grievances into the ear of the Father General, who, conceiving that the Apostolic Visitors had exceeded their powers, and infringed upon his authority, obtained from the new Pope, Gregory XIII., in August, 1574, a revocation of their commission. Philip II. was known to be so favourable to the reform, that Rossi did not venture immediately to use the power thus obtained against it; and the Nuncio, Hormaneto, by virtue of the very extensive powers entrusted to him, confirmed the two Visitors in their office, and confirmed at the same time the delegation of the authority of Vargas to F. Gracian. The zeal of Nicolas Hormaneto in the cause of ecclesiastical reform had drawn upon him from his adversaries the ironical sobriquet of *the reformer of the world.* He had been Vicar-General of Milan under S. Charles Borromeo, who highly esteemed him, and employed him in the great work of reform in his diocese; he had also assisted Cardinal Pole, in his brief work in England, especially in the purification of the universities from the heresies with which they were infected.

A still heavier blow was struck at the reform in the General Chapter of the Order held at Placencia in the spring of 1575, which passed a decree annulling all that had been done by the Vicars Apostolical in its favour. All the monasteries in Andalusia were to be dissolved, as well as all those in Castile which had not been founded by the authority of the General. A Portuguese Carme, named Tostado, was appointed by the General as his Vicar, to carry out the decrees of the Council.

His instructions were to treat the discalced Carmes with great external deference; but to scatter them among the convents of the Mitigation, by which they would in fact be absorbed and neutralised. S. Teresa, notwithstanding the F. General's former experience of her saintliness and prudence, had incurred his displeasure by her foundations in Andalusia, which had

associated her in his mind with the supposed con-
tumacy of the Fathers Gracian and Mariano. A
peremptory order was conveyed to her by F. Angelo
Salazar, the Provincial of Castile, to refrain from
making any new foundations, and to make choice of
one of her convents as her future place of abode,
which she was not to leave on any pretext whatsoever.
What were the feelings of the Saint on receiving this
command the following letter to the F. General will
show :—

"Jesus. The Grace of the Holy Spirit be ever
with your Reverence! Amen.

"Since my arrival at Seville, I have written to
your Reverence three or four times. I did not write
again because our fathers who came from the Chapter
told me you were not at Rome, but had gone to visit
the convents at Mantua. Thanks be to God for the
success of that affair! In my letters I gave your
Reverence an account of the three convents that have
been founded this year, viz. at Veas, Caravaca, and
Seville. In these places you have religious, who are
indeed great servants of God. The first two are
endowed, but the latter is founded in poverty. At
present we have no house of our own here; but I
hope in our Lord we shall soon have one. I do not
give you a particular account of each of these foundations, because I am certain that some of my
former letters will, by this time, have reached your
Reverence.

"In one of them I observed what a difference there
is between hearing the discalced fathers speak (I
mean F. Gracian and F. Mariano), and hearing their
enemies speak of them. These fathers are certainly
the true children of your Reverence; and, I may say,
that in every spiritual point they yield to none of those

who boast so much of being your children. As they
have asked me to beg your Reverence to receive them
again into your favour (for they themselves dare not
write to you), I entreated you with all possible earnestness to do so in the letters which I wrote you; now
I renew my entreaties. I trust you will grant me this
favour, for the love of our Lord. Believe what I say,
for I have no reason to induce me not to speak the
truth. Besides, I think I should offend God were I
to conceal this matter from you: and even though I
should not thereby offend Him, I should consider it
a great crime and baseness to conceal anything from
a father whom I love so tenderly. When we shall
appear before the tribunal of God, you will see what
you owe to your true daughter, Teresa of Jesus. This
is the only thing that consoles me in the matter, for
I believe some will be found who may tell you
differently. But those who are unprejudiced must
acknowledge that I speak the truth, and this I will do
as long as I live.

" I have already written to your Reverence respecting the commission which F. Gracian received from
the Nuncio, and how he was sent for by him. You
must know that he has been confirmed in his office
of Visitor of our fathers and sisters, and likewise of
the mitigated Carmes of the province of Andalusia.
I am confident that he has done all in his power to
avoid accepting the latter office, though report says
the contrary. But I tell you the truth, neither does
his brother the secretary wish him to accept it, because
it is always attended with great trouble. But as it
was a matter already settled, if those fathers had
taken my advice, all would have been amicably arranged, as between brothers, without offence to any
one. I have done all I could to make them agree, as
was but fitting, for those fathers have helped us much

since we have been here. I have also found here, as
I told your Reverence, persons of great talent and
learning. I wish we could have such as these in our
province of Castile. I am very fond of making a
virtue of necessity, as the saying is ; and for this
reason I should have wished that those persons,
before they undertook to make any opposition, had
considered whether there was any probability of their
succeeding in it.   On the other hand, I do not
wonder at their opposition, for they are tired of so
many visitations and changes which have taken place
in these last few years on account of our sins. God
grant we may know how to profit by them, for His
Majesty thereby tries us much !   However, as the
Visitor is now of the same Order, the visitation will
not be considered in the light of a reflection upon
it.   I trust in God that, if your Reverence will but
show some kindness to this father, all the affair
will prosper well ; for then every one will know that
he is in your favour. He has taken the liberty of
writing to your Reverence, since he is very anxious to
be at peace with you, and not to give you any pain,
because he considers himself to be one of your
obedient sons.

"I once more beg of your Reverence for the love
of our Lord and His glorious Mother, whom you love
so tenderly, and whom F. Gracian also loves (for he
entered our Order for her sake), I beg of you to
answer his letter with mildness, and to forget what
has passed, even though he should have been in
fault, and to receive him again as your child and
subject, for he is indeed an obedient son.   I beg the
same for poor F. Mariano, who sometimes does not
know how to explain himself. Hence I should not
be surprised if he has written things to your Reverence
different from what he had in his thoughts, for want

of knowing how to express his meaning, for he positively declares that he never had any intention of displeasing you either by word or deed. As the devil gains a great deal by making people take things in a wrong sense, so he has employed all his art to make these two fathers, contrary to their intention, appear in the wrong.

" But your Reverence should consider how natural it is for children to err, and for parents to pardon and forget the faults of their children. For the love of God, then, I beg of your Reverence to grant me this favour. It is necessary for many reasons, which you may not know so well in Italy as I do here; and though we poor women are not fit persons to give good advice, still sometimes we hit the mark as well as a man. I cannot see what harm can come from receiving these poor men into favour again; on the contrary, you may (as I said) derive a great deal of good from so doing, whereas I see none that can be gained by refusing lovingly to receive those who would willingly cast themselves at your feet, were they near your Reverence. God does not fail to pardon us, however guilty : imitate Him, then, on this occasion, and make it known that you are glad that one of your own children and subjects has undertaken the reform of the Order, and that in return you are glad to pardon him, if in anything he has offended you.

"If there were many to whom this commission could have been given, well and good; but as it seems there is no religious so fit for the office as this father is (and I am sure if you saw him you would be of the same opinion), why does your Reverence not show us that you are glad to have such a man under your obedience ? Why should you not wish all the world to know that the reform (if it should prosper) was effected through your means and by your advice? It is certain that if your Reverence is known to approve this reform, all difficulties will vanish.

"I could say much more respecting this matter. But I beseech our Lord to make you understand how necessary that is which I have already said, for it is now some time since you have paid any attention to my words. I am quite certain that if I fall into any mistake, my intention at least is sincere.

"F. Antony of Jesus is here: he could not help coming. Although he has begun to defend himself like the other fathers, he now writes to your Reverence, and perhaps may be more fortunate than I have been in receiving an answer. I trust your Reverence will form a right judgment about all I tell you. As to the rest, may our Lord order everything how and as He pleases and sees best!

"I have heard of the decree of the General Chapter, which forbids me to leave the house which I may choose as my abode. The Provincial F. Angelo had sent the news to F. Ulloa, with a command to notify the decree to me. He thought this would trouble me, for those fathers in procuring such a decree had the intention of giving me pain; and on this account he kept the document in his hands, not venturing to show it to me for more than a month.

"But as I had been informed of the matter during that time from another quarter, I induced him to mention it to me.

"I assure your Reverence in all sincerity that, as far as regards myself, it would have given me great pleasure and content had you sent this command to me by letter, signifying that feeling compassion for me on account of the numerous labours and sufferings which I have endured in these foundations (and your

Reverence knows well that I have but little strength)
you had commanded me to take some rest as a recompense for what I had suffered. Knowing from
whom such a command came, I should have felt great
consolation in my repose.

"But the sincere esteem I have for your Reverence makes me feel, on the other hand, that this
command is somewhat rigorous, because it was sent
to me as to one who had been very disobedient. So
at least F. Angelo had represented it to the whole
Court before I knew anything of the matter.
Every one thought it too great a restraint upon me;
and he informed me himself that I might obtain a
remedy by writing to the Pope, as if it were not in
fact a great relief to me; and even though it had
been a great affliction, never should I have dreamt of
disobeying your Reverence, for God forbid that I
should ever seek any pleasure against your will. I
can truly assure you (and our Lord is my witness)
that if I have had any comfort in the labours, dis-
quiets, afflictions, and distractions which I have
endured, it was in the thought that I was doing your
will and giving you pleasure; and hence I hope that
I shall now also receive the same comfort from ful-
filling the command of your Reverence.

"I wished to obey your order immediately, but as
Christmas was near, and the journey so long, my
desire was not granted, as my director knew it was
not the wish of your Reverence to hazard my health;
and so I am still here; not however with the intention of always remaining in this house, but only till
the winter is over, for I do not feel at home with the
people of Andalusia.

"I humbly beg of your Reverence not to forget
to write to me, wherever I may be; but as I have
nothing now to occupy me (which indeed is a great

comfort to me), I fear you will forget me, though I shall endeavour to prevent this, for however tired your Reverence may be of hearing from me, I shall not cease to write to you for my own comfort.

"People never imagined here, nor do they yet believe, that the Council and the Pope's brief could take from superiors the power of commanding religious to go from one house to another for the good of the Order, and for affairs which may arise connected with it. I do not mention this for my own sake, as I am now good for nothing, for if I knew I could thereby afford your Reverence the least pleasure, I would willingly remain all my life not only in the same house (for I am glad indeed to enjoy a little quiet and repose), but even in a prison. This I say in order to take away any scruples which your Reverence may have with regard to the past, for though furnished with your *Letters Patent*, I never would go to any place to found a monastery (and it is clear I could not leave my convent for any other cause) without a command or written permission from my superior. When I went to Veas and Caravaca, it was by the order of F. Angelo, and F. Gracian commanded me to come here, for he had then the same commission from the Nuncio that he has now, though he did not make use of it.

"How can F. Angelo say then that I have come here as an Apostate or excommunicated person? May God forgive him! Your Reverence knows well, and can testify that I have always endeavoured to befriend him with you, and to please him in all things that were not displeasing to God, and yet he never would be friends with me.

"It would have been much better had he turned against F. Valdemoro, who, being Prior of Avila, drove the discalced fathers from the Convent of the

Incarnation, to the great scandal of the people. The convent was in such a good state as to make one praise God for it, and yet he treated the poor nuns so ill, that it was a pity to behold the great trouble they had to endure. They wrote to me to excuse the Prior, and they took all the blame upon themselves. The fathers have, however, returned, and I am informed the Nuncio has forbidden all other Carmes to hear the confessions of the sisters.

"The troubles of the poor religious have afflicted me exceedingly, for they gave them nothing but bread, and they are still in trouble, and I feel much for them. May our Lord provide a remedy for all these evils, and preserve your Reverence many years! I am told that the General of the Dominicans is coming here. Would to God that you were here also! My joy would then be complete, though I should on the other hand feel for you on account of the fatigue to which you would be exposed from the journey. Thus I am content to wait for my consolation in that eternity which will have no end, where your Reverence will know how greatly you are indebted to me.

"May our Lord grant in His mercy that I may one day arrive there! I earnestly recommend myself to the prayers of those reverend fathers who accompany you. The religious of this house, the daughters of your Reverence, beg your blessing, and I ask the same favour for myself.

"Your Reverence's unworthy daughter and subject,

"TERESA OF JESUS.

"From Seville."

The other directions of the Chapter could not be carried out in the face of a King and a Nuncio so determined as Philip and Hormaneto. By the latter,

F. Gracian was appointed Superior of all the houses of the reform throughout Spain, and Visitor of those of the Mitigation in Andalusia.

The foundation of Seville had advanced little further in the Lent of 1576 than when S. Teresa arrived there in the preceding spring.

She had no prospect of buying a house, no money for the purchase, and no person to stand security for her should she attempt to borrow any. Those who had induced F. Gracian to send for religious of the reform, on the strength of the numerous vocations which were already to flock into the Order, now held back. The ladies of this wealthy and luxurious city were terrified at the severity of the rule. The time was approaching for Teresa's return to Castile, and though deeply concerned at leaving her daughters in so unsettled a position, she saw no use in prolonging her stay, perceiving, as she said, that she was doing nothing at Seville.

Many fervent prayers, meantime, were offered to our Lord; many pious processions made to implore our Lady and S. Joseph not to let the holy Mother depart till a house should be found for her children.

Help came at last, and once more, as in a former strait, by the hand of that devout Christian and noble-hearted gentleman, Laurence of Cepeda, who, with his brother, Peter of Ahumada, his three sons, and his little daughter Teresa, arrived at Seville in the preceding August, where, to his great joy, he had found his holy sister ready to greet him. By his exertions, and at his own personal inconvenience and risk—for, by some mistake with regard to the purchase, he had been on the point of being thrown into prison—the house was at last secured; but, before possession was taken, the patience of Teresa was exercised by a new trial. A certain postulant had

been so strongly recommended as to draw from her
the remark, " If this good soul does not work miracles
before she dies, your reputation for wisdom will
perish."

The supposed saint, having been crossed in her
desire to practise certain private devotions, gave way
to such sadness and discontent, as proved to the
religious that she was in no way suited for their institute. She had no sooner left the convent than she
felt herself bound in conscience to denounce the nuns
to the holy Inquisition. Among other practices which
her hypochondriacal humour had misinterpreted, was
the manifestation of conscience to the Prioress.

She asserted that the nuns went to confession to
one another. This and other graver slanders she
carried to a confessor, who unfortunately listened to
her, and, moreover, carried the tale from one cloistered
monastery to another, on the plea of consulting the
learned religious of various Orders upon the subject.
The consequence was that one morning, when F.
Gracian came to visit the holy Mother, he found a
train of horsemen at the door, and was informed on
enquiry that they were in attendance on the ministers
of the Holy Office who were engaged in the convent
in examining the supposed crimes of the religious.
The above-mentioned priest was standing with a sad
and solemn countenance at the door, waiting to see
the nuns carried forth to the prisons of the Inquisition.

F. Gracian anxiously summoned Teresa, whom he
found even more calm and bright than usual; and,
smiling at his face of consternation, she consoled him
by the assurance that God would never suffer the reputation of His servants to be stained by so black a
calumny! and that He had Himself told her not to
fear, for that " these clouds should pass away." And,

in fact, in a few hours the Inquisitors sent for the priest who had accused them, and severely reproved him, saying that if he had not maliciously invented the slander, he had at least shown himself incapable of the direction of consciences.

With a view to her fuller justification, the holy Mother was advised to send a narrative of her life, and a statement of her manner of prayer, to a learned and pious Jesuit, F. Roderick Alvarez, by whom both were approved and transmitted to the Inquisitors.

"By this means," says her biographer, " the Lord was pleased that the holiness of Mother Teresa and the virtuous lives of her religious should come to be better known and held in higher reputation." In a letter to her niece, Mother M. Baptist (Mary of Ocampo), S. Teresa says : " I assure you that of all the persecutions we have had to endure, none can bear the least comparison with what we have suffered at Seville.

"When you know what has taken place, you will see I have reason for what I say, and that it will be a mercy of God if we escape safely from these troubles, as at present we have every reason to hope we shall do. Blessed be our Lord, who can bring good out of everything ! As for me, I have experienced a wonderful consolation in the midst of all these sufferings. If my brother had not been here, we could have done nothing. He has suffered much in our cause, but with so much courage and generosity that we cannot sufficiently praise and thank our Lord. Our sisters have reason to love him, for in all this trouble he alone has stood our friend. He is at present in hiding on our account, for he was near being dragged to the town prison, which is a kind of hell, and all this without any sort of justice.

"An exorbitant demand was made upon us, and he

Y

was to suffer as our security. We hope to get this matter righted by an appeal to the Court.

" As to my brother, he was glad to suffer something for God. He is now staying at the Convent of the Carmes with our father. Though troubles and vexations have rained upon him like hail, he feels our sufferings far more than his own, for which reason I conceal them from him as much as I can. To form an idea of them, recall to mind what I wrote to you before of the falsehoods which that novice had published about us; this is nothing in comparison to what she has said since. I must tell you that in the midst of all the calumnies, by a special grace of God, my soul has been full of consolation. Notwithstanding all the evils which I saw might result to our houses, my heart was filled with joy. What blessed things are peace of conscience and liberty of soul ! "

In the midst of all her trials at this time, Teresa was greatly consoled by the perfect sympathy and harmony which subsisted between her brother Laurence and her sister Jane, who, with her good husband John of Ovalle, had come to Seville to meet him. Of Teresa, the little daughter of Laurence of Cepeda, whom she always mentions under her pet name of *Teresita*, she thus writes to F. Gracian : " We have consulted one of the best theologians of the Company of Jesus about our little Teresa ; he tells us that it has been decided by the Council of Trent that a girl under the age of twelve cannot receive the religious habit, but that she may be brought up in a convent. Teresita is here with her habit already, to her father's great joy ; you would say she is the familiar spirit of the house. All the nuns are delighted with her. There is something really angelic in her disposition, and she enlivens our recreations by her wonderful tales of the Indians and the sea, which she tells much better than

I could do myself. I am so glad to see that our sisters do not consider her a trouble. God has bestowed on her a great grace, and she ought to be very grateful to *you* for it. I believe it will be for God's service that this soul should be brought up far from the vanities of the world."

About a month after the nuns were settled in their new convent, the Blessed Sacrament was placed there on the Feast of the Ascension by the Archbishop himself, who carried it in solemn procession, accompanied by the secular clergy, religious orders, confraternities, and principal nobility of the place, designing by this public demonstration to make amends to the religious for the calumnies and persecutions which they had endured. When Teresa knelt to ask his pastoral benediction, to her great confusion the Archbishop, in the presence of all the people, knelt to ask hers in return, thus testifying the high estimation in which he held her, and the work which she had begun.

Before her departure from Seville, S. Teresa sent Mother Anne of S. Albert to found the convent at Caravaca. An application had been made some time before for this foundation by three noble ladies, who devoted themselves and their wealth to the work.

S. Teresa left Seville on June 4, and before taking up her abode at Toledo, visited Malagon and Avila, whence she had been directed by our Lord to take with her as her inseparable companion that holy servant of God, Sister Anne of S. Bartholomew, who had received the religious habit at Avila in the year 1570, and was the first lay sister of the reform. S. Teresa's original intention had been that all the sisters should be equal; but finding that the duties of the choir were interrupted by the necessary household occupations, she decided upon the admission of a cer-

tain number of lay sisters. Anne of S. Bartholomew,
in the midst of her labours, attained to a high degree
of contemplation. S. Teresa observing that in the
fervour of her prayer she neglected to take the necessary repose, gave her an obedience to interrupt her
contemplation at the common signal, and go to rest
with the other sisters. On the night when she had
received this command, she was, as usual, rapt in
prayer when the bell rang. She immediately broke
off, saying to our Lord with all simplicity : " Lord, 1
have no permission to stay any longer with Thee ;
suffer me to go and sleep as I am commanded to do."
She went to bed, and she, who usually was unable to
close her eyes, slept soundly till the awakening bell
in the morning, when she found our Lord still present,
as if waiting for her rising, in token of His acceptance
of her ready obedience.

By command of her confessor, this holy sister
wrote an account of her own life, in which she says :
" I remember that, when I was a child, I used often
to say to our Lord : ' My God, if I could live with a
Saint I should lead a better life ! ' and yet," she adds,
" though I have lived with such a great Saint as
Mother Teresa, I have never followed her example ! "
On the other hand, S. Teresa would often say : " O
Anne, Anne, you have the works of a Saint and I
have the reputation of one ! " After the death of S.
Teresa, Anne of S. Bartholomew accompanied Anne
of Jesus into France, and having, by the command of
her Superiors, received the veil of a choir sister, she
was sent into Flanders, where she founded the Carmelite convent at Antwerp.

Teresa took with her from Seville her beloved niece
Teresita, and she speaks in her first letter from Malagon to Mary of S. Joseph of the child's sadness at
leaving her *Mothers* at Seville.

She reached Toledo in the beginning of July, leaving F. Gracian busy in his visitation of Andalusia.

Angelo of Salazar, the Provincial of Castile, had summoned a Chapter of that province in the preceding May, to carry out the decrees of the Chapter of Placencia. To this assembly he invited only the Priors of Mancera and Pastrana, and the Rector of Alcalà, accounting the rest of the discalced fathers to be excommunicated.

F. Gracian, on the other hand, assembled a Chapter of the discalced friars at Almodovar, to make the regulations requisite in the present posture of affairs.

CHAPTER XIX.

1576—1579.

IN her quiet cell at Toledo, Teresa's heart vibrated with every movement of the conflict which now agitated the reform. We can trace its history in the letters which she wrote at this period, especially in those to Father Gracian and Mariano, and to the Prioress of Seville. It was her great desire that F. Gracian should be relieved from his thankless office of Visitor of the mitigation, and be free to attend exclusively to the religious of the reform, and that measures should be taken to procure from the Father General, or, failing him, from the Pope, the erection of the reform as a separate province, subject only to the General. In the mean time she advises that the mitigated friar should be treated with all gentleness consistent with the needful exercise of authority. There was no fear of F. Gracian erring on the side of severity, save when, from lack of firmness, he was at times influenced by the Fathers Mariano and Antony

of Jesus. S. Teresa was, as she says, at continual
warfare with the former, now for excessive harshness
towards his opponents, and again for rash confidence
in their professions of friendship.

S. Teresa writes on September 20, 1576, to Father
Gracian at Almodovar : " Our fathers bring me good
tidings from the Chapter, and I am delighted to hear
how well everything has gone on there. Glory be to
God ! Assuredly, my Reverend Father, you cannot
escape this time receiving great commendation. All
is the work of God's hand, and prayers, as you say,
have doubtless had much to do with it. I rejoice to
hear that a *zelator* has been appointed for the houses :
this is a most excellent and useful measure. I have
recommended him to insist particularly on manual
labour, which is a matter of the utmost importance.
. . . He also spoke much to me of the plan which is
in agitation to obtain from our Most Reverend Father
General the erection of a separate province, and to
use every means in our power for the attainment of
this object. It is indeed a miserable thing to be at
warfare with the Superior of the Order. For the love
of God, Reverend Father, do not delay to send deputies to Rome. Do not look upon this as a mere acces-
sory, for it is the principal point. If nothing but
money is wanted, God will send it to us. If the
Prior of Peñuela is in such favour with the Father
General it would be well to send him with F. Mariano.
If nothing can be obtained from the General, then let
them apply to the Pope. But the first plan would be
far best ; and there will never be a better time than
the present, considering the good feeling entertained
towards us by the Nuncio, and his present state. I
cannot see what we are waiting for ; we are all content-
ing ourselves with a precarious position, and losing a
most favourable opportunity of placing the reform on

a permanent footing." . . . She writes again : " The letters which your paternity wrote to F. Mariano, and which he sent me to read, have given me great joy. It is a history which has led me to pour forth praises to our Lord. I know not where your head gathers so much skill and genius. Blessed be He who has bestowed it on you ! It is plain that it is His work : therefore, dear Father, keep always in mind that it is a grace from God, and have no confidence in yourself." Again, with regard to his visitation in Andalusia : " If God had not shown me by His light that all the good we do emanates from Him, revealing to me at the same time how little we can do by ourselves, I confess that I should be tempted to take a little pride in your success in Andalusia. May His name be praised and blessed for ever ! Amen ! What I admire most is the great tranquillity with which you do every-thing, and your talent for changing enemies into friends, and making them the authors, or rather the executors, of the good which you wish to introduce." In her letters written during the time of this conflict, Teresa was obliged to use the precaution of giving feigned names to the principal persons of whom she is writing ; thus our Divine Lord bears the name of *Joseph ;* F. Gracian is called sometimes *Paul,* some-times *Eliseus ;* the Saint herself sometimes *Angela,* sometimes *Laurencia ;* the Nuncio is *Methusalem ;* and the Inquisitors, *Angels,* &c. &c. In this letter she says playfully : " I do not think that all which *Paul* now endures equals the terror which he experienced at the visitation of the *Angels* "—referring to the visit of the Inquisitors to the convent at Seville.

On the Vigil of All Saints she writes : " I took the habit on All Souls Day ; pray to God to make me a good Carmelite nun : better late than never."

The departure of the deputies for Rome was still

delayed. S. Teresa writes to F. John of Jesus de
Roca, one of the leading fathers of the reform : " I
must tell you that I have very little power in this
matter. I have been long urging it, and I have not
yet been able even to get a letter written to him who
ought to be addressed " (apparently the General).
" I had hoped, as I was led to expect, that the departure of the deputies would have been arranged at
Almodovar."

To F. Mariano she writes : " I am surprised that
you should have so much confidence in our fathers of
the mitigation : I am far from sharing it. With regard
to Father Valdemoro " (Prior of the mitigated Carmes
of Avila), " I do not think him at all disposed to do
us good ; and if he appears friendly to us, it is only
to penetrate our designs, and to give notice of them
to his friends." Again : " I have had a visit to-day
from the good Valdemoro. I believe he speaks truth
in professing friendship for us just now ; it is for his
own interest. He talks to me of how S. Paul persecuted the Christians, and of what he did afterwards.
Let him do for God the tenth part of what S. Paul did,
and we will forgive him for what he has done, and
for what he may still do against us.

" He begs me to ask you to receive his brother.
The only thing which I think we can do in return for
his friendship is to recommend him to God. . . . .
May God give him health better than his intentions !
After all, there are twelve hours in the day, and
perhaps he may be changed ! "

F. Antony of Jesus was a source of no less uneasiness to the Saint than F. Mariano, on account of his
great deficiency in the gift of government, whereby
he was perpetually embroiling matters in the convents which he was deputed to visit. Many a time
was she reminded of her thoughts when the good

old man offered himself ten years before as the first postulant of her reform : "I was not altogether satisfied with the Prior." Yet he it was, and not F. Gracian, or S. John of the Cross, who, having been her first fellow-worker, was to have the privilege of ministering at her death-bed, and bidding that glorious spirit depart to its God.

F. Antony of Jesus, in his visitation of one of the convents, had disturbed the minds of the nuns by making a number of new regulations, against which S. Teresa appeals to F. Gracian.

"Believe me, Reverend Father," says she, "that these houses are going on very well, and have no need to be burdened with new ceremonies: everything which is added is a fresh load for religious to bear. I beseech you in the name of charity not to forget this. The Visitor's duty is to insist on the exact observation of the constitutions, and to require nothing more: the nuns will do well if they keep these."

F. John of Jesus seems to have fallen into the same fault in his visitation of another convent, and again the watchful mother enters her protest.

"You see, Reverend Father, the burden which this father has imposed upon the religious by the multitude of rules which he has drawn up in his visitation. The things which my nuns most fear, is to see certain hard and austere Superiors lay upon them a yoke which can only serve to discourage and crush them under its weight. It is a very strange thing that some people think they have not visited a monastery until they have made a number of new regulations, whereas this is to destroy all the benefit of a visitation. With regard to recreation, for instance, if there is to be no recreation on days of Communion, is it not plain that priests who say Mass daily ought never to have any recreation at all? But if they are dispensed from this rule, is it just to impose it upon others who are younger, and therefore have greater need of recreation? This father writes to me that as this house has never been visited, he had been obliged to use this severity. I will hope that he did not act without reason, but I have been so tired with only reading the multitude of regulations which he has made, that I know not what would have become of me if I had been obliged to keep them. Believe me, Father, our rule is not to be interpreted by such austere persons: it is quite sufficiently austere in itself."

In the February, 1576, S. Teresa writes to her brother Laurence that her mind has been relieved with regard to the manuscript of her life which had been sent for by the Inquisition. " I have received," says she, " good news of my papers. The Grand Inquisitor, contrary to his custom, has read them himself, no doubt because he had heard them praised. He told Doña Louisa de la Cerda that there was no work for the Inquisition in these papers; for, that far from being injurious, they contained many excellent things. He also expressed surprise that I had not founded a convent in Madrid. This prelate, Don Gaspar de Quiroga, who has just been made Archbishop of Toledo, is very favourable to our reform."

S. Teresa finished the book of her life in 1566. In November, 1577, she finished her *Interior Castle*, which she had begun on the Feast of the Holy Trinity in the same year at Toledo. Not the least wonderful thing connected with that wonderful book is the fact of its having been composed at a time of such intense mental anxiety. S. Teresa teaches us, in the passages which we have extracted from it, the secret of that peace surpassing all understanding which springs from theclose union of the soul with God, and her words bear a twofold weight when taken in connection with the time at which they were written.

At Toledo S. Teresa also continued the history of her foundations, by the direction of F. Gracian, to whom she writes in October, 1576 : "I am now about to continue the narrative of the *Foundations*. *Joseph* (our Divine Lord) has told me that this book will do good to many souls, and if He helps me I believe it will. But independently of this command, I had determined to continue the narrative simply in obedience to your injunction."

S. Teresa had begun this book in 1573 at Salamanca by the direction of her Confessor F. Jerome Ripalda, the Rector of the Jesuits' College in that city. The persecution which had now set in against the reform led her to believe that the foundation of Caravaca was to be her last, and she writes on November 14, 1575 : "I have written the last page to-day in the monastery of S. Joseph at Toledo. This book is at last finished, and I beg of my Superiors to strike out whatever may be ill said, and perhaps that will be what I consider to be said best. I have finished this work by command of our Father Gracian, Visitor Apostolic of the Carmes and Carmelites of the primitive rule and Visitor of the mitigated Carmes in Andalusia. May this book bring honour and glory to our Lord Jesus Christ, Who reigns and shall reign for ever and ever ! Amen. I beseech, in the name of God, my sons and my daughters who shall read these pages to recommend me to our Lord, that He may have mercy upon me and deliver me from the pains of Purgatory, which I may have deserved, and grant me the enjoyment of His Divine Presence. As this book will not be put into your hands during my life, it is just that at least after my death, if you should be permitted to read it, I should receive some reward for the labour which it has cost me, and for the exceeding desire which I have had in writing it to give some consolation to your souls."

The death of the Nuncio, in June, 1577, fell like a thunderbolt on the reform. As notwithstanding S. Teresa's urgent remonstrances no vigorous measures had been taken for the establishment of a separate province, it was left at the mercy of his successor, who came strongly prepossessed against it by the mitigated Carmes, and resolved to root it up as a dangerous novelty.

The mission of Philip Sega is a lesson on the mischief which may be done by excellent people, with the best intentions, and a fresh chapter in the history of persecutions inflicted by the good on their betters.

The new Nuncio was a near kinsman of the recently elected Pope, Gregory XIII., and was honourably distinguished both for his learning and piety. Like his predecessor, he was an intimate friend of the great ecclesiastical reformer S. Charles Borromeo, who, it is said, used to ask him to tell him his faults. His love of holy poverty is recorded in his epitaph, and yet this friend of holy poverty and confidant of S. Charles had allowed himself to be so strongly prejudiced against S. Teresa and her reform, that he came to Spain fully determined to sacrifice it to what he accounted the general good of the Order. Of S. Teresa he scrupled not to affirm that she was a restless, disobedient, and contumacious woman, who, under pretext of devotion, had invented pernicious doctrines; who was accustomed to leave her cloister, contrary to the command of the Council of Trent, and to set herself up for a teacher in the Church, in direct opposition to the precept of S. Paul.

The opinions of the new Nuncio were soon known in Spain, and the Vicar-General Tostado, who had been prevented by Hormaneto from exercising his powers, now declared open warfare against the reform. He forbade the foundation of any new house, or the reception of any new novices, by which means he hoped gradually to destroy the already existing foundations. Moreover, he claimed submission from all the Superiors of the reform. F. Gracian, foreseeing the tempest that was impending, had hastened to Madrid, on the news of the late Nuncio's death, to resign the commission which he had received from him; but it being the opinion of the most learned doctors of Salamanca and Alcalá that his powers did not expire with the life of him from whom he had received them, he was compelled to retain his office.

In the month of September of this year, S. Teresa was sent to the Convent of S. Joseph's, at Avila, to make arrangements for placing it under the jurisdiction of the Order, our Lord having made known to her that the reason for which it had been subjected to that of the Bishop no longer existed, and that its discipline and religious perfection would suffer were it to continue in its isolated position. Her personal influence was needed to reconcile the good Bishop of Avila to the loss of a community in which he had ever been so deeply interested, and to induce the nuns to forego his fatherly care.

The matter was at length arranged, subject to only one condition on the part of the Bishop, viz., that he should have the privilege of sepulture in their chapel, and that S. Teresa herself should also be buried there.

From Avila S. Teresa writes the following letter to the King, craving protection from a calumny brought against F. Gracian, which was afterwards rendered harmless by the retractation of both the accusers :—

" September 13, 1577.

"Jesus. The grace of the Holy Spirit be ever with your Majesty. Amen.

" I have heard that a memorial has been presented to your Majesty against the Rev. F. Gracian. This stratagem of the devil and his ministers has indeed terrified me, because, not content with defaming the character of this great servant of God (and he is truly such, for he gives edification to all of us, and when-ever he visits our monasteries, he fills the religious with renewed fervour), his enemies are now striving to injure those houses in which our Lord is so devoutly served.

" For this purpose they have made use of two Carmelite friars ; one of whom was a servant in our monastery before he took the habit ; but he conducted himself in such a way more than once, as plainly to show us he possessed but little judgment. The enemies of F. Gracian have induced others who are opposed to him, because (as Visitor) he has the power of punishing them, to sign such foolish charges against the nuns, that I should certainly laugh at them, were I not fearful lest the devil might be able to draw some evil from them. Such accusations, if true, would be monstrous, considering the habit we wear.

" I beseech your Majesty, then, for the love of God, not to allow such scandalous charges to be brought before a court of justice, because the world might be inclined to believe that we had done something to give occasion for them, even though our innocence should be proved, and our reform, hitherto so blessed by the Divine goodness, would be seriously injured by the least stain of this kind. Your Majesty would be able to form a judgment in the matter, should you be pleased to read the attestation which F. Gracian has thought proper to draw up respecting these monasteries. It includes the testimony of several persons of great weight and holiness, who have had communications with the nuns. Moreover, since the motive by which these are influenced who have written the memorial can easily be discovered, I beseech your Majesty to examine the matter, because the honour and glory of God are concerned; for if our enemies should see that some attention is paid to their charges, they will not hesitate, in order to prevent a visitation, to accuse as a heretic whoever shall undertake to make it; and, where there is no fear of God, there would be no difficulty in finding false testimony.

"I sympathize deeply with the sufferings of this servant of God, which he endures with such patience and perfection; and this induces me to beseech your Majesty to take him under your protection, so as to remove the cause of these dangers, for he belongs to a family that is extremely attached to your Majesty: independently of this consideration, he has great merit of his own. I consider him to be a man sent to us by God and our Blessed Lady, for whom he has a most tender devotion. Our Lord led him to our Order, that he might be an assistance to me, for, as I have now laboured alone for more than seventeen years, my weak health will not allow me to endure much more. I beg of your Majesty to pardon me, for having entered so fully into this matter, but the great respect which I have for your Majesty emboldened me to do so: for I considered that as our Lord endured my indiscreet complaints, so also would your Majesty. May God be pleased to hear all the prayers of the religious of our reform that your

Majesty may have a long life ; for we have no other protector on earth. I remain your Majesty's unworthy servant and subject,

"TERESA OF JESUS."

During the Christmas festival of 1577 the patience of S. Teresa was exercised by the effects of a painful accident, which befel her, as she says herself, by the agency of the devil. As she was ascending the steps which led to the choir before Compline with a candle in her hand, she was suddenly thrown down by a violent blow, and fell from the top to the bottom with such violence that the religious who hastened to assist her expected to find her dead. When they raised her they found that her arm was broken. A woman was sent for who was skilled in surgery, but being ill at the time, she did not arrive till the end of the month of April. As the Saint foresaw that the operation would be painful, to spare the religious the suffering of witnessing it, she sent them to the choir to pray for her. In the meantime, after the rough fashion of surgery in those days, the woman and her companion went to work so violently to set the broken limb that the bones were dislocated. Teresa uttered not a cry, but contemplated the violence with which our Lord was stretched on the Cross, and when the sisters returned from the chapel she told them with a smile that she would have been very sorry to have missed this opportunity of suffering something for Him.

One of the first enterprises of F. Tostado under shelter of the patronage of the new Nuncio, was directed against the nuns of the Incarnation, who had once more ventured to elect S. Teresa as their Prioress. The Provincial of the mitigated Carmes, F. John of S. Magdalen, by the direction of F. Tostado, "came" (says S. Teresa in a letter to the Prioress of Seville) "to preside at the election of the Prioress. Such a scene followed as was never seen before. He threatened the religious who should give me their votes with excommunication. Nevertheless, undismayed by his threats, fifty-five religious voted for me as if he had never said a word. As the Provincial received each separate suffrage, he poured forth his malediction on the religious who presented it, and declaring her excommunicated, he struck the paper with his fist, tore it, and threw it into the fire. The nuns have been excommunicated now for nearly a fortnight; they cannot hear Mass, nor enter the choir during office, nor speak to any one, even to their confessor or relations. What is still more singular, on the day following this stormy election, the Provincial summoned them to begin another. They replied that they had no election to make, for they had already made it. He excommunicated them again, and having assembled the forty-four nuns who had not voted for me, he caused them to make another election, and sent the *procès-verbal* to F. Tostado for confirmation. The confirmation has already arrived, but the religious are firm in their opposition, and declare they will only acknowledge the Prioress elected by the minority, as Vice-Prioress. Theologians say that they are not excommunicated, and that the mitigated Carmes have gone against the decree of the Council of Trent, which ordains that elections be made by the plurality of votes. The religious who voted for me sent word to F. Tostado that they will have me for Prioress: he replied that *he will not have me*, adding, that if I choose to go to the Incarnation to recollect myself, I may, but that he will never endure me as Prioress.

"I know not how all this will end, but matters stand thus now; every one is surprised and grieved.

z

I would willingly pardon those who have elected me,
if they would leave me in peace, for I have no desire
to be in the midst of this Babylon, especially with my
weak health, which has never been good in that house.
May God order everything for His greater glory, and
deliver me from that office ! "

The religious of the Incarnation at last yielded to
the advice of the Saint, and accepted the Prioress who
had been imposed upon them; and towards the end
of November, the Nuncio, at the King's desire, withdrew the censures under which they had been laid.
But on the very same occasion, their two confessors,
S. John of the Cross and his companion, were violently
carried away and imprisoned ; their papers were seized,
and it was on this occasion that the precious series of
letters from S. Teresa to S. John of the Cross perished.
Before the search began, S. John destroyed the letters,
tearing up some, and actually swallowing others. His
place of imprisonment was for a long time concealed.
S. Teresa writes of his *enchantment*, as if he lay in
durance like an imprisoned knight of romance under
the power of some wicked magician.

He had, in fact, been removed from the convent at
Avila to that of the mitigated Carmes at Toledo ; so
that for nearly a year he was close to her without her
eing aware of it.

Of the heroic virtues practised by S. John during
his imprisonment, the following narrative was furnished at the process for his Beatification, by one of
the religious who guarded him :—" I knew F. John of
the Cross when he was imprisoned in our convent at
Toledo, when he had every kind of opportunity of
practising virtue. Indeed, I was fully persuaded that
he was even then a real Saint, for, in the midst of all
his sufferings, he always evinced such a deep humility
and such heroic courage, that, far from being depressed

by the ill-treatment which he endured, he preserved such an evenness of soul under it all, as showed the perfection of his love and his firm confidence in the Divine mercy. He was so grateful also, that it seemed as if he did not know how to show his thankfulness for any little service that I was able to render to him. He showed his love of suffering by his unvarying patience under it, never did the slightest word of murmur or resentment against any person whomsoever escape him."

The same witness gives the following account of his captivity :—"By the permission of our Lord, he was seized by the fathers of the Observance in the city of Avila, where he was confessor to the nuns of the Incarnation, who are subject to the Order, and thence he was brought to Toledo, where he was shut up in a very dark dungeon. The religious who guarded him having been removed, the Prior intrusted the care of him to me. I found his health broken by the great suffering which he endured from his close imprisonment, but he never complained. Touched with compassion at the sight of his patience, I sometimes left the door open that he might take a little air in the adjoining corridor, and I left him alone that he might be in greater freedom. I could only do this at the time that the religious retired to rest at mid-day, and when I began to fear that some of them were coming, I used to warn him that it was time to retire, when he would embrace me, and thank me with joined hands for the charity which I showed him."

In his prison of Toledo S. John of the Cross enjoyed Divine favours which made his captivity sweet to him, and, though so reserved in speech that he made them known to few during his lifetime, we may gather from his works that our Lord at that time rewarded his courage and his love by the closest union with Himself.

CHAPTER XX.

1578, 1579.

THE Vicar-General, Tostado, was compelled by royal authority to leave Spain in November 1577, and carried his grievances to Rome, but the reform gained little by his absence, as the Nuncio took matters into his own hands, and insisted on the immediate submission of all its members to the Superiors of the mitigation. In the March of 1578, a subject of considerable importance both from character and position was added to its ranks in the person of Nicolas Doria, of the illustrious Genoese house of that name, who, having been sent to Spain on some affairs of the republic, received a vocation first to the priesthood and then to the Order of Mount Carmel. That he should have had the courage and generosity, having already attained middle age, to join what must then have seemed a forlorn hope, certainly bespeaks a character deserving the high terms of commendation in which S. Teresa writes of him :—" It would seem," she says, " that our Lord had called him to the assistance of our Order. The others who might have aided us were shortly afterwards exiled or imprisoned; but as he was new in religion, little notice was taken of him, so that God made use of him for our assistance. He was so prudent and wary that he remained at Madrid in the convent of the mitigated fathers, on pretext of other business, and such was his subtilty and dexterity that they never found out that he was managing ours; so they let him stay. I often corresponded with him when I was in the Convent of S. Joseph's at Avila, and we concerted together what was most expedient to be done, to his great consolation. Hence may be seen the necessity to which our Order was then reduced, since, for want of good men such account was made of me." In the following year, when matters seemed darker still, she writes to F. Gracian :—" F. Nicolas spent three or four days with me at Avila. Great has been my consolation to see that you will at last have some one with whom you may take counsel concerning the affairs of the Order, who will be able to help you, for it has been a great pain to me to see that there are so few amongst us from whom you can receive assistance. F. Nicolas certainly seems to me to be a man of sense and judgment, and a true servant of God, although he has not that extraordinary grace and sweetness which our Lord has given to *Paul*, for there are few on whom He bestows so many graces at once. . . . Therefore, Reverend Father, place confidence in him, for, if I mistake not, great benefits will arise therefrom." In another letter she says :— " You will never have anything to suffer from F. Nicolas." The vision of the future was mercifully veiled from the eyes of the Saint. It was not till she beheld it from Heaven that she knew the sufferings which were to be inflicted upon her beloved and venerated Father by the self-opiniated obstinacy of one whom, notwithstanding his many excellences, F. Bouix characterizes as *the hard Genoese*. " He sacrificed F. Gracian," says he, " because he was incapable of understanding him," and on the same false testimony on which he and his associates had previously condemned S. John of the Cross. The decision of the Apostolic See reversed the sentence upon both.

On October 15, 1578, S. Teresa writes to F. Gracian, on receiving intelligence of the death of the Father-General Rossi : " The news which I have just heard of the death of our Father-General Rossi has given me great pain, and I have not been able to refrain from weeping bitterly. It grieves me to think of all the trouble we have given him, which certainly he did not deserve. If we had gone straight to him, all our difficulties would have been removed. May God forgive those who have always hindered it, as but for them I could have prevailed with you, although you have not paid much attention to what I have said upon this subject. May God turn all to our greater good!" She proceeds to say that she would no longer advise sending deputies to Rome. "I have just seen my brother Laurence, who commends himself to your prayers. We are all agreed here that now our Father-General is dead, it is no longer expedient to send any of our religious to Rome. First, because their journey could not be kept secret, and they would probably be taken by the mitigated fathers before they could leave Castile; and secondly, because they are not sufficiently conversant with affairs at Rome, and having no longer our Father-General to look to, they might be taken in the streets as fugitives; and if we have not been able to liberate F. John of the Cross, who was close at hand, what could we do for them there?"

Early in the year 1579, a malignant accusation was made against F. Gracian and the nuns of Seville, which touched even S. Teresa herself. The Prioress, Mary of S. Joseph, was deposed, and the whole community subjected to a persecution the severity of which may be gathered from the following letter, overflowing with maternal affection, which was addressed to them by S. Teresa :—

"January 31, 1579.

"Jesus. The grace of the Holy Spirit be with you, my daughters and sisters!

"Be assured that I never loved you so much as I

do now, neither have you ever had such an occasion for returning thanks to our Lord as you have now; for He bestows a great favour upon you by making you taste something of the bitterness of His Cross, and of that abandonment which He felt when He hung upon it. Happy was the day on which you entered Seville, where such opportunities for acquiring merit have been prepared for you! I really envy your happiness; and to tell you the truth, when I heard of all these changes which were told me without any exaggeration, but above all, when I heard that they wished to drive you out of your house, and other particulars of the same kind, so far from being afflicted at these trials, I felt the greatest interior joy to see that, without making you cross the seas, our Lord wished to show you the mines of eternal treasures with which His Majesty desires to enrich your souls, that so you may distribute them to those around you.

"I trust in His mercy that He will help you to bear your troubles, without offending Him in anything. Be not discouraged if you feel them somewhat too sensibly; for our Lord permits this in order to show you that you are not so strong as you supposed when you were so desirous of suffering. Courage, my daughters, courage! Remember that God does not send us greater troubles than we can bear, and that His Majesty is ever with the afflicted; since then this is certainly the truth, you have nothing to fear; rather should you hope in His mercy that the truth will be in time discovered; then will be known by what artifices the devil has caused these trials which you now endure.

"Pray, pray, my sisters; and prove your humility and obedience by your submission, and especially by that of your late Prioress, to the newly appointed Superioress. Oh! what a favourable opportunity you now have for gathering the fruits of those generous resolutions which you have made to serve our Lord! Remember that He often wills to try us, in order to see if our works agree with our words. Do credit to your sisters, the daughters of Mary, by your patient endurance of this terrible persecution.

"If you will help yourselves, our good Jesus will help you; and though He may sometimes sleep upon the waters, yet when the storm is fiercest He commands the winds to be still. He wishes us to invoke His assistance, and He loves us to such a degree that He is always seeking for means to advance us in holiness. May His Name be blessed for ever! Amen. Amen. Amen.

"All the religious of our houses continually pray for you; this encourages me to hope in the goodness of God that your troubles will soon be at an end. Therefore, be of good cheer, considering that whatever you suffer for so good a God is but little, for One too who has endured so much for us. Remember you have not as yet shed your blood for Him; that you are living among your sisters, and not at Algiers. Leave it all to your Spouse, and you will soon behold the sea swallow up all our enemies, just as it swallowed up Pharaoh and his army, and delivered the people of God. Then shall we desire fresh sufferings and new troubles, considering the great advantages which we have already gained from past afflictions. I have received your letter, and I am sorry that you have burnt what you wrote, because it might have been useful to us on this occasion. You need not, according to the opinion of learned men in these parts, have given up my letters, but it is of little consequence. Would to God that all the faults which they say have been committed were laid to my charge, though indeed I have felt the trouble of those who have suffered so unjustly as if they had been my own. But that which grieved

me most was to find that in the statement drawn up
by the command of the Father-Provincial, certain
things were asserted which I knew to be exceedingly
false, because I was then on the spot. For the love of
our Lord, examine strictly, and inquire if any of the
sisters gave their depositions through fear or passion ;
for so long as God is not offended, all the rest is
nothing. But to tell lies to the prejudice of our
neighbour, this it is which wounds my heart. I cannot imagine how people can do such things, since
every one knows the candour and virtue with which
F. Gracian conversed with us, and the great profit we
derived from his instructions, and how much he helped
us to advance in the service of our Lord. This being
the truth, it is a great crime to publish such accusations, even with regard to matters of little consequence.
Charitably remind the sisters of the fault they have
committed. May the Most Holy Trinity remain with
you and preserve you ! Amen.

"All the sisters tenderly commend themselves to
you. They hope that when the clouds have been
scattered, Sister S. Francis will give them an account
of everything which has happened. Remember me
to good Sister Gabriella, and beg of her to be content.
She must have felt great pain in beholding Mother
S. Joseph so treated. I pity Sister S. Jerome, if her
desires are sincere ; if they are not, I should have
more compassion for her than for all the rest.

"I should have felt much more pleasure in speaking with Señor Garcia Alvarez than in writing ; but
I will not write to him now, because I cannot say what
I wish in a letter. Remember me to all the sisters,
to whom you may show this letter.

" Your unworthy Servant,

" TERESA OF JESUS."

On receiving the command of the Nuncio to submit to the authority of the mitigated friars, the leaders of the reform, with F. Gracian at their head, adopted the imprudent measure of assembling a second Chapter at Almodovar to erect an independent Province and elect a Provincial on their own authority. The following letter from S. Teresa to F. Gracian will show how urgently she endeavoured to dissuade him from this step :—

"To the Rev. Father Jerome Gracian of the Mother of God.

"Jesus be with your Reverence!

"My Father, after the departure of the Prior of Mancera, I spoke to Master Daza and Doctor Rueda, concerning your intention of making a separate Province for our reformed Carmelites, because I should not wish your Reverence to do anything which people might take hold of, and blame you for. Even should the undertaking succeed, this would give me more pain than any reverse which might befall us without our fault. They both agreed that the project would be very difficult of execution unless your Reverence had a particular commission, empowering you to establish the Province. Doctor Rueda, especially, urges this point very strongly; and I pay great deference to his opinion, because I see that what he recommends always succeeds : he is a very learned man. He says, the election of a Provincial being a matter of jurisdiction, is a very difficult point, because the choice belongs either to the General or to the Pope. Hence the thing cannot be done, for the votes would be null and void. He adds, that the attempt would give an opportunity to the others to apply to the Pope, and to proclaim that you were about to withdraw us from our obedience, by appointing Superiors when you had not the power to do so. He also adds that this undertaking would be misinterpreted ; and he is confident that you would have more trouble in obtaining the confirmation of a Provincial so appointed, than in obtaining the erection of a separate Province from the Pope. If the king were to write to his ambassador at Rome, the Pope would gladly grant leave, for this could easily be done ; particularly if it were represented to his Holiness with what severity our fathers of the reform have been treated. If any one would speak to the king on the subject, his Majesty, I am sure, would willingly write to his ambassador, and this would be of great assistance to the reform ; for when the other fathers see that the king interests himself in our behalf, they will have more respect for us, and will have less hope to destroy the reform.

" It would be well, I think, if your Reverence were to mention the matter to Father Chaves (when you give him the letter which I sent by the Prior), for he is a very prudent man : and if he would only make use of the influence he possesses with the king, he would perhaps obtain the favour ; and being by this means furnished with the letters from the king, fathers deputed by you might hasten to Rome on the subject. And even should no such letters be obtained, I should still wish them to go by all means ; for Doctor Rueda says that the right way to manage this business is to apply directly either to the Pope or to the General. I am confident that if F. Padilla had united with us in representing the matter to the king, we should before now have accomplished our desire. Your Reverence may yet be able to speak to him, or to the Archbishop on the subject ; for if the Provincial after he has been chosen must be confirmed, and the election and confirmation be afterwards approved by the king, it would be better to secure his approbation before proceeding to the election. If we should not succeed, we shall at least be spared the affront which we should sustain by failing to obtain a confirmation of the election, which would be a disgrace to us ; and the character of your Reverence might suffer if you should attempt what you are not able to do, and thus incur the reproach of being wanting in judgment.

" The Doctor says that if the Visitor of the Dominicans or of any other Order were to make this election, there would not be so much said about it as if our Priors were to undertake it themselves, for, as I have before said, there is the greatest delicacy and danger in meddling with matters of jurisdiction, and it is of the utmost importance that our Superior be appointed by legitimate authority. In fact, I lose all courage when I seem to foresee that they will have some cause to throw all the fault upon you ; whereas I should not fear did they blame you without reason, but, on the contrary, should be animated to greater courage thereby. On this account I have been anxious to write this letter to you, in order that your Reverence may consider well what you are about to do. Do you know what I have been thinking ? It is this, that perhaps our Father-General will turn against us the letters which I have written to him (though there was nothing but good in them), and may show them to the Cardinals. These thoughts suggested to me the propriety of not writing to him again until we have seen the result : it would be also well should an opportunity present itself to offer some token of gratitude to the Nuncio. I perceived, Father, that when you were at Madrid you did a great deal in a day, hence I think that by speaking to different persons and interesting the ladies whom you know at Court in the matter, and by prevailing on F. Antony to induce the duchess to use her influence, you might do a great deal towards obtaining this favour from the king, who is very desirous that the reform should be maintained. F. Mariano, who often speaks with the king, might give him an account of the present state of things, and beg his protection: he could also remind his Majesty how long that little Saint, F. John of the Cross, has been detained in prison. I know the king listens to every one, and I cannot imagine why this matter has not been told to his Majesty, and why F. Mariano, especially, has not entreated him to set this father at liberty. But what need have I to say all this to you? and what nonsense am I writing to your Reverence, yet you bear with my foolishness! I assure you I am greatly troubled at not being able to do myself what I advise others to do. The king is now going to a great distance: I only wish he could do something before his departure. May God bring it to pass, for He can do it!"

The remonstrances of the Saint were unhappily disregarded, as were also those of S. John of the Cross, who, having been delivered from his captivity by the miraculous intervention of our Blessed Lady, hastened to the Chapter at Almodovar. The playful sweetness of S. Teresa's reply to the letter in which F. Gracian notified his adherence to his own judgment, is a model of obedience and humility under a very trying mortification.

"Jesus be with your Paternity!

"My Father *and Superior*, as you say,—I cannot help laughing whenever I think of your letter, at the serious way in which you remind me that I am not to judge my Superior. Oh! my dear Father, you have

little occasion to swear even like a Saint, far less *like
a waggoner*, for I am perfectly convinced of this.
When God gives to any one such zeal for souls as He
has given to you, will He deprive him of it with regard
to the souls of his subjects? I will say no more on
the subject now; except to remind you that you have
given me permission to judge you and to tell you
freely what I think.

"Yesterday, on April 25, just at night-fall, your
mother arrived, thanks be to God, in perfect health.
I have passed many happy moments with her. I love
her better and better every day, and understand more
of her goodness and wisdom."

Doña Jane Dantisco, the mother of F. Gracian, came
to Avila to bring her daughter Mary, on her way to
enter the noviciate at Valladolid. Another sister,
Isabella, had been previously clothed at Toledo.

"I am equally delighted," continues the Saint,
"with our new religious. I cannot tell you how happy
she seems; one would think she had been here all
her life. I hope God will do great things for her.
She has an excellent understanding and great quick-
ness."

S. Teresa delighted in the society of young people,
whose brightness and innocence were congenial with
the freshness and simplicity of her own spirit; and
she was prepared to give to F. Gracian's young sister
a place in her heart beside her beloved Teresita, who
was now growing in perfection at Avila under the
care of the religious of S. Joseph.

In another letter to F. Gracian the Saint speaks of
the consolation which she hoped hereafter to find in
his sister's society. "I have been already thinking
what a comfort my child Mary of S. Joseph (her name
in religion) will be to me. She writes beautifully, has

great talent and great cheerfulness, which would aid
me to carry my burden. God perhaps will grant me
this consolation after her profession. After all, young
people do not greatly delight in the company of old
ones ;* and I wonder, my dear Father, that you are
not tired of me."

It is hard to imagine S. Teresa an old woman, such
wonderful brightness and elasticity appears in every
line of her writing ; yet she says in another letter:
" I am very old and very weary ; " and the constant
anxiety, and strain of continual letter-writing, during
her residence at Toledo, had told upon her physical
strength, and added to her usual maladies a painful
nervous affection, which produced a constant wearing
noise in the head, often compelling her to use another
hand to write for her.

CHAPTER XXI.

1579.

THE Fathers assembled at Almodovar elected as their
Provincial F. Antony of Jesus, and then, with
singular inconsistency, sent a deputation to the
Nuncio to explain the reason of their conduct, and to
ask him to confirm the election. As might have been
expected, he considered the whole proceeding as an
infringement of his authority, annulled the acts of
the Chapter, and inflicted the severest penalties upon
its principal members. On the Vigil of All Saints
he excommunicated the Fathers Gracian, Antony of
Jesus, and Mariano, and imprisoned them in three
separate convents in Madrid. S. Teresa was directed
to make that of Toledo her place of imprisonment.

* At the date of this letter the Saint was in her 65th year.

The news of the disastrous Chapter of Almodovar crushed for a moment the firm spirit of S. Teresa. Her faithful companion, Anne of S. Bartholomew, relates that for a whole day she ate nothing. S. Ignatius Loyola, when meditating on what circumstance would give him the greatest pain, declared that he would be reconciled to the destruction of his Order by a quarter of an hour's recollection. Perhaps he had not taken into account the additional anguish of seeing it perish by the imprudence of its own children. Be this as it may, the brightness of Teresa's spirit was overcast for a whole day. When her loving daughter came at last to beg her to eat, she came down to the refectory at her desire and sat down to table. Then, as Mother Anne relates, she saw our Lord tenderly approach His sorrowing servant, and taking bread in His hands, He said to her, " Eat, my child, for I see that thou hast suffered much ; be of good courage, for so it must be." The cloud instantly passed away ; and from that moment Teresa was, as usual, the light and life and strength of all around her.

She writes to F. John of Jesus and to F. Mariano of a gracious revelation made to her at this time as to the issue of the struggle.

" To F. Mariano.

" May the grace of the Holy Spirit be with your soul !

" Your letter, my dear F. Mariano, has given me great pain by informing me of the proceedings of the Nuncio, of the arrival of F. John of Jesus very sorrowful at Madrid, and of the sadness of you all at my imprisonment. God be for ever praised ! as such is His holy will. And now that I see the world and hell rise up against my children, I have such an

assurance that our Lord and my holy Father S. Joseph
will undertake our cause, that from this very day, my
dearest Father, you may account yourself not the
vanquished but the victor. Lucifer desires nothing
better than .to see this little flock of our Lady dis-
persed and destroyed, but it shall not be as he
thinks; on.the contrary, my dear son, those who now
persecute us will declare themselves in our favour.
Therefore let your tears be changed into joy. As for
me, what wrings my heart in these events is that my
sons have to suffer; that they are living in dispersion
and under persecution because of a sinful woman like
myself. This it is which makes me sigh and weep.
As to the rest, I believe victory to be certain, inasmuch as our cause is the cause of God. Be pleased
to tell F. John of Jesus to return to Valladolid to
the house of Doña Mary de Mendoza, and not to leave
it till he hears from me. For you, Reverend Father,
take this letter from me to the king without a moment's loss of time. Make known to him the state
of our affairs, of which I also inform him in my letter,
and you will see how he will take things to heart for
the glory of God. Behave with great humility to
the king, and do not show a shadow of resentment
against those who have done so much to deserve it.
It befits us to show great patience in all things. I
say this that you may be on your guard; in this way
things will be smoothed. As to the letter to the
Nuncio, give the king time to reply before you deliver
it, and you will see, my dear Father, what will take
place. Be full of confidence, and do not give way
to the weakness of saying, *we cannot endure this any
longer :* for *we can do all things in Jesus Christ.*
Be full then of faith, for it is faith which enables us
to do great works for God. I say this that henceforth we may learn to hope in him. Go to the

Princess of Pastrana for me, and tell her that I have punctually accomplished what she asked of me. Tell her not to be troubled at my imprisonment, for I deserve something much worse; and that we shall soon meet again. I leave all other matters till I see you. My companion begs you to tell B. John to paint for her the S. Joseph which he ·promised her. Let him do it, for I should like to see the world full of devotion towards my Father S. Joseph. My health of body is very good just now; not so my spiritual health, because instead of penance, there has been nothing but indulgence. I grieve to be in this state. Pray to God for me, Father, and ask him to make me good. May that Divine Master be blessed in all things, and for all things, and may He give you His grace and His Spirit!

"TERESA OF JESUS."

The letter to F. John of Jesus, written on the same day, reveals the ground of the Saint's extraordinary confidence as to the happy issue of the present trial.

"Jesus, Mary, and Joseph be in the soul of my Father John of Jesus!

"I received your Reverence's letter in this prison, where I am now filled with the greatest delight, because I endure all my troubles for my God and for my Order. That which grieves me, my Father, is the affliction your Reverence feels; this it is that troubles me. Do not, however, my son, be troubled, nor any one else, since I may say, like another Paul, though not his equal in sanctity, that prisons, labours, persecutions, torments, ignominies, and insults for my Saviour and for my Order are to me delights and favours.

"I never knew myself to be more free from troubles than I am now. It belongs to God to help the afflicted and imprisoned with his favour and assistance. I give my God a thousand thanks, and it is fitting that we should all thank Him for the favour He has done me by this imprisonment. My son and Father, can there be a greater delight or sweetness than in suffering for our good God? When were the Saints at the height of their joy, but when they were suffering for their God and Saviour. This is the most secure and certain path that leads to God, since the cross should be our joy and delight. Let us then, my Father, seek the cross; let us desire the cross; let us embrace afflictions; and whenever we shall have none, woe to the Carmelite Order, woe to us. You tell me in your letter how the Nuncio has given orders, that no more convents of our Order should be founded, and that those already erected must be suppressed by desire of the Father-General. You also mention that the Nuncio is exceedingly angry with me, and considers me a troublesome woman and of a roving disposition; that the world is against me and my sons, who hide themselves in the rocks of the mountains, and the most retired places, in order not to be found and taken. This is what I lament—what I feel—what grieves me—that, for such a sinner and wicked nun as I am, my sons should endure so many persecutions and afflictions, and should be abandoned by all men, but not by God. For of this I am certain He will not forsake us, nor abandon those who love him so tenderly.

"But in order that you, my son, and the rest of your brothers may rejoice, I will tell you something very consoling; but this must be in confidence between myself, your Reverence, and F. Mariano, for I should be grieved if others knew it. You must know then, my Father, how a certain nun of this house, being in prayer on the Vigil of the Feast of

2 A 2

my Father S. Joseph, he appeared to her in company with the Blessed Virgin and her Son; and she noticed how they stood asking for the reformation (of the Order); and our Lord told her that many, both in hell and on earth, rejoiced greatly to see, as they supposed, the Order dissolved, but that, when the Nuncio commanded its dissolution, God confirmed it. He told her to have recourse to the king, who in everything would be to her and her sons as a father. Our Lady and S. Joseph said the same, and several other things not fit to be mentioned in a letter. She was also told that within twenty days I should be delivered from prison, God so willing. Let us then all rejoice, for from this day forward the reform will continue to advance more and more.

" What your Reverence should do is to continue in the house of Doña Mary de Mendoza till you hear again from me. F. Mariano must go and present this letter to the king and another to the Duchess of Pastrana. I hope your Reverence will not leave the house lest you should be apprehended, for we shall soon see ourselves at liberty. I am well and strong, thank God! My companion is indisposed. Recommend us to God, and say a Mass of thanksgiving in honour of my Father S. Joseph. Do not write to me till I tell you. May God make you a holy and perfect religious !

" TERESA OF JESUS."

S. Teresa's letter to the king has been unhappily lost. It did not produce any immediate effect, for Philip had been much annoyed at the want of promptness and decision shown by F. Gracian at the first arrival of the new Nuncio. The Archbishop had reproached him at having no more courage than a fly. This irresolution, however, probably proceeded not from want of courage, a defect which is hardly conceivable in one so deeply venerated by S. Teresa. It seems to have arisen from exceeding delicacy of conscience, joined to that morbid sensitiveness which often accompanies high genius. Jerome Gracian was a man of genius, no less than of sanctity; this was the secret of the fascination by which he swayed the minds of men; this it was which kept him lonely in the midst of them, longing for sympathy, and yet shrinking from the approach of uncongenial spirits. This also it was which led him to seek refuge in the prompt decision of harder and coarser minds, from the responsibility of reconciling difficulties which were visible only to his keener perception; and thus (as in the case of the Chapter at Almodovar) to terminate a long period of irresolution by some act of fatal rashness.

From the time of the death of Hormancto he seems to have been haunted by a doubt of the validity of his commission; and the excommunication pronounced against him by Sega weighed most painfully upon his mind. S. Teresa often scolds him for his excessive depression and scrupulosity. "I had a great mind, my dear Father, to write a long reply to your melancholy and desponding letter, but all these letters which I enclose have left me no time to write any more, and I am glad of it, for my head is nearly worn out already. As to the first point, my dear Paul is very simple to indulge in so many scruples. Be pleased to tell him so. To you, my dear Father, I have nothing to say. All theologians declare that your conscience may be in perfect security until the brief has been notified to you: they add that it would be perfect folly to place yourself now in the hands of the Nuncio. . . . For pity's sake, do not thus forecast the future. God will turn everything to good.

Keep yourself in concealment as much as you can :
this is my one subject of anxiety. If, with so many
to care for you, you give way to this despondency,
what would have become of you if you had had to go
through what has befallen F. John of the Cross."

Again, she writes : " May the Holy Spirit be with
you, my Reverend Father, and bring you off victorious
from this conflict ! In our days there are few against
whom our Lord permits the world and the devil to
wage such furious warfare. May his name be blessed,
who has been pleased that you should merit so much,
and in so many ways at once ! Notwithstanding the
sensibility of nature, reason, I assure you, shows us
very plainly how much cause we have to rejoice. I
am at peace now that I know you are convinced that
you are not touched by the excommunication. For
my part, I never thought for a single moment that
you were."

Again, during his visitation : " Your conscience, my
dear Father, is not one fitted to arrange matters on
which there are contrary opinions. You torment
yourself when there is no reason for it, as you have
been doing now. Leave people to settle their own
debates. You have quite enough to do in running so
many risks without tormenting yourself with scruples.
I assure you that my greatest trouble, in the midst of
all this disturbance, is the fear that you may not be
relieved from the office of Visitor. But if it shall
please our Divine Master still to lay it upon you, He
will take care of you as He has hitherto done. . . .

" I envy the souls whom you are leading forward in
the path of perfection, while I, to my sorrow, do
nothing but eat and sleep, and talk about our dear
brothers, the mitigated Carmes, who are continually
giving me occasion for it. . . . Allow me to say,
Reverend Father, that I do not see the benefit of

your thus going from village to village. You are surrounded by so many dangers, that I think you are over-bold thus to go from one place to another, while there are souls to be saved everywhere."

The excessive severity of the Nuncio at last roused Philip to so royal a remonstrance that Sega thought it prudent to propose to share his responsibility with four assessors appointed by the king. Of these two were Dominicans, one of them being Peter Hernandez, then Provincial of the Dominican Order in Castile, formerly Apostolic Visitor of the Carmes in that Province, who had ever shown himself a true and devoted friend of the reform. " Since the appointment," writes S. Teresa, " of those two venerable and beloved Dominican Fathers as Assessors to the Nuncio, I have not had the smallest anxiety about our affairs. I know them well, and am assured that four such Assessors as have been named will regulate everything for the honour and glory of God, which is our only desire."

The authority and judgment of his four colleagues at last dispelled the prejudices of the Nuncio, who, being a good and upright man, was grieved at his past injustice, and took measures at once to remedy the evil which it had occasioned. His first act was to withdraw the discalced fathers from the jurisdiction of the Provincials of the mitigation, and to place them under a prelate of their own, entitled the Vicar-General of the discalced. F. Angelo de Salazar, so long Provincial of Castile, and now Prior of the Carmes at Valladolid, was appointed to this office on April 1, 1579. The first use which the new Vicar-General made of his authority was to leave the holy Mother at full liberty to go whithersoever she would. In concert with the king he instituted an immediate inquiry into the accusations brought against F. Gracian and the Carmelites at Seville, by which their innocence was triumphantly established. Mother Mary of S. Joseph, after an ineffectual opposition on her own part, was once more placed at the head of the convent. Father Angelo de Salazar soon afterwards took F. Gracian for his companion and secretary, and intrusted the government of the reform entirely to him. S. Teresa writes thus to F. Gracian on April 15, from Avila.

" May the Holy Ghost repay you for the consolation which your letter has given me by the hopes which it holds out that I shall see you soon ! For the love of our Lord, so arrange your work and your journey that you may be able to come to me. For if it is hard to be deprived of happiness which we have left off hoping for, it is harder still to be deprived of that which we had looked to enjoy. I believe that our Divine Master's glory will be promoted by our meeting. In the joy which this hope has shed over my soul, I have accepted with resignation the choice of our new Superior. God grant that he may not enjoy his authority long ; not that I mean, in any way, that I wish him to be deprived of it by death. After all, he is by far the most prudent among the mitigated Carmes. He will be full of consideration for us, and with his discretion will fully understand what ought to be the end of his mission. In some respects this nomination is far less favourable to the other fathers than to us. If we were perfect, we ought to desire nothing better than the present Nuncio, who has given us so many occasions of merit." S. Teresa's first use of her liberty was to go with her companion, the Venerable Anne of S. Bartholomew, to her beloved home of S. Joseph's at Avila, that monastery being nearest to Madrid, and therefore most convenient for her residence during the important affairs now under negotiation. It was at this time that she received the revelation which she has thus solemnly recorded.

"Being at S. Joseph's in Avila on the Vigil of Pentecost, in the hermitage of Nazareth, considering a great favour our Lord had bestowed on me on that day about twenty years before, a strong impulse and fervour of spirit seized me and threw me into a rapture. In this state I heard from our Lord what I will now relate. He bade me tell the discalced fathers from Him that they should endeavour to observe four things, which, while they observed, this Order, would go on increasing, but, if they failed to do so, they would then know that they had fallen away from the perfection of their primitive rule. The first was : *That the Superiors should all be united.* The second : *That though it might be necessary to have many convents, yet in each there should be but few friars.* The third : *That they should converse but little with seculars, and that little only for the good of their souls;* and the fourth : *That they should teach more by works than by words.* This was in the year 1579, and for greater confirmation of the truth I hereby affix my name—

"TERESA OF JESUS."

S. Teresa was occupied by the command of her Superior for some months of the year 1579 in visiting the convents of Valladolid, Salamanca, and Malagon. In the latter place she was attacked by paralysis and confined for two months in her bed, her sufferings being alleviated by the tender affection of her children and by witnessing their religious perfection.

Meanwhile the Nuncio and his four assistants had come to the conclusion that the measure most expedient for the welfare of the reform would be its permanent establishment as an independent Province under a Provincial of its own. The king's approbation having been obtained, the next step was to send deputies to Rome to lay the measure before the Holy Father. Father John of Jesus de Roca and Father Diego of the Holy Trinity were appointed to this mission. For fear of being intercepted by the adverse party, the two deputies were to travel in secular dresses, and accordingly Father John of Jesus appeared at Malagon, to ask S. Teresa's parting blessing, in the array of a gallant cavalier. The expenses of this journey were defrayed by the liberal contributions of various houses of the reform; and S. Teresa thus writes to Mother Anne of Jesus, the Prioress of Veas, to thank her for the noble generosity which she had shown on this occasion, and for the support which she had been to her through all the past trial. This is one of the few letters which remain to us addressed by the Saint to the daughter who is said most nearly to have resembled her.

" Jesus.

" May the Holy Spirit be ever in your soul !

" My dearest Daughter—My Daughter and my Crown,—I cannot sufficiently thank God for the favour which He has shown us in calling you to our Order : for, as when He brought out the Children of Israel from the captivity of Egypt, He caused a pillar to go before them to guide and enlighten them during the night, and to shelter them from the heat during the day, so has it pleased Him to show forth the might of His arm with regard to our Order ; and He has made you, my dear daughter, to be this pillar to guide, to enlighten, and to defend us. Nothing could have been more wisely conceived or more happily executed than all that you have done for our religious, who are now setting off for Rome. It is plain that God is in your soul from the grace and the greatness of all that you do. May the Lord, to Whose glory alone you look, reward you and bring our affairs to a happy conclusion!" It is remarkable that the severest reproof which is to be found in any of S. Teresa's letters is addressed to this same religious. Great must have been her confidence in the perfection of one whom she could venture thus fearlessly to praise, and unsparingly to blame. But she was addressing Anne of Jesus, to whose sanctity S. John of the Cross bore witness, saying that he felt when in her company as if in the presence of a Seraph; so great were also her natural gifts that it used to be said of her that she was fit to govern a kingdom.

CHAPTER XXII.

1580.

WHEN S. Teresa was at Toledo, at the beginning of the troubles affecting the reform, an application had been made to her for the foundation of a convent at Villanueva. But the poverty of the place and the heat of the persecution obliged the Saint to delay granting the request, which came from four sisters of noble birth, who had been attracted to Villanueva by the fame of the sanctity of the celebrated penitent, Catharine of Cardona. Not having health to emulate her austerities, they associated with themselves five other pious maidens, four of whom were also sisters, thus forming a community of Tertiaries who wore the scapular of our Lady of Mount Carmel, and awaited in humility, patience, and poverty the day when they should be admitted to the full privileges of the Order.

"When I was at Toledo, in 1576," says S. Teresa, "a priest came to me, bringing letters from the municipality of Villanueva de la Xara, desiring me to receive into our Order a community of nine persons, who for some years had lived together near the hermitage of the glorious S. Anne; and that with such recollection and sanctity as to induce the people of the place to endeavour to further their desires of becoming religious. The parish priest of Villanueva also wrote to me on their behalf: his name was Augustin de Ervias; a very pious and learned man. It appeared to me impossible to admit them, for various reasons. First, because having been so long accustomed to their own way of living, it would be very difficult to them to accommodate themselves to ours; secondly, because they had hardly any means of support, and the town, having little more than a thousand inhabitants, would be able to afford little assistance in the way of alms; and, although the municipality offered to support them, they could not (it seemed to me) promise anything lasting; thirdly, they had no house; fourthly, Villanueva is at some considerable distance from our other monasteries. Again, though I was told they were very excellent persons, yet, as I had not seen them, I could not judge if they possessed the qualities requisite in our convent, and so I determined to refuse the foundation altogether. But before I gave my answer, I wished to speak with my confessor, Doctor Valasquez, Canon and Professor of Theology in Toledo, a very learned and virtuous man, who is now Bishop of Osma. When he had read the letters, and understood the matter, he told me not to give a decided refusal, but to return a courteous answer; because, as God had united so many hearts together in the same design, He perhaps willed to be served thereby. So I gave such an answer as neither absolutely accepted nor positively rejected the proposal."

In the year 1579, F. Antony of Jesus retired from the troubles of the time to the monastery of our Lady of Succour, which is about three leagues from the town of Villanueva, whither he went occasionally to preach, and there becoming acquainted with these holy women, he took their wishes very much to heart, and wrote to urge S. Teresa to admit them into the Order.

The monastery of our Lady of Succour had been founded on the site of a grotto, long inhabited by the Blessed Catharine of Cardona, who, at eight years old, had devoted herself to a life of austere penance, to deliver the soul of her father from the sufferings of Purgatory, and afterwards left the court of Philip II. to live the life of a hermit in this cavern, where she practised austerities equal in severity to those of the fathers of the desert, and died there in the odour of sanctity in the habit of Mount Carmel.

Finding that his letters had not succeeded in convincing S. Teresa of the practicability of the work which he wished her to undertake, F. Antony, in company with the Prior of our Lady of Succour, went to Malagon to try the effect of a personal interview.

"The Father Prior," says the Saint, "came to speak to me on the matter, giving me an account of what could be done for the house; and telling me that, when it was founded, Dr. Ervias would, with the permission of the Holy See, give 300 ducats as an endowment from a benefice which he held. This offer made me uncertain what to do, for though it could not be depended on till the foundation should be made, it would have been sufficient, together with what little they already possessed; however, I gave

the Father Prior many reasons why it was not wise to
admit them, and in my judgment they were good
reasons. I also begged that he and F. Antony would
consider the matter well, and so I left it to their
conscience, thinking I had already said enough to
put a stop to the undertaking. After he departed, I
considered how bent he was on the plan, and that
he might perhaps persuade our present Superior (F.
Angelo de Salazar) to admit them. I therefore wrote
to F. Angelo immediately, desiring him not to grant
the licence, and giving him my reasons for the request.
He answered that he would not think of doing so
without my approbation.

" About six weeks (or perhaps a little more) had
passed away, and I began to consider the matter as
quite at an end, when there came a messenger with
letters from the municipality of Villanueva, promising
to provide for the support of the convent. Dr. Ervias
also engaged to perform what he had promised. I
received letters also from the Prior and F. Antony,
pressing me to admit the foundation ; but I was
afraid to do so, lest some difficulty might arise in
attempting to blend these people with our own religious, and likewise because I saw no certainty of
their support, for there was no security that the
assistance offered by the town would be continued.
All this caused me to fall into great perplexity.
Afterwards I discovered it was from the devil; because, although our Lord has usually given me courage, I was then so great a coward that I seemed to
have no confidence at all in Him. But the prayers of
those holy souls at length prevailed.

" One day after Communion, when I was recommending the matter to God, being disposed to return
a favourable answer by the fear lest I might put an
obstacle to the progress of some souls towards perfec-

tion ; and all my desire being to find out some means
whereby our Lord may be more perfectly praised and
served, His Majesty gave me a sharp reproof, saying :
' With what treasures have all the houses been
founded which have been hitherto begun ? Do not
hesitate to make this foundation, for it will greatly
advance My glory and the good of souls.' How
powerful are the words of God ; for the understanding not only apprehends them, but is thereby enlightened to know the truth, and the will is disposed
to desire to execute them ; and so it happened to me,
for I was not only delighted to found the monastery,
but it seemed to me that I had done wrong in waiting,
and in being so wedded to human reason, as I have
seen how far what his Majesty has done for this holy
Order exceeds our reason. Having resolved then to
admit this foundation, it appeared necessary for me
to go with the nuns who were to remain in the house,
for many reasons which presented themselves to me,
although I was greatly opposed to the journey, having
arrived very unwell at Malagon, and being so still.
But knowing now that God would thereby be served,
I wrote to my Superior to command me to do what
he thought most perfect. He sent me the licence for
the foundation, commanding me to go, and to take
with me such nuns as I thought most suitable for the
work. This made me very solicitous to choose such
as could live with those who were already there.
Having recommended the matter earnestly to our
Lord, I took two from the monastery of S. Joseph's
in Toledo, of whom one was to be the Prioress, and
two from Malagon, one of whom was to be Sub-
Prioress. The choice of these sisters having been
fervently recommended to God, proved by His blessing of Great service to His Divine Majesty. His
special aid was needed in this foundation, which was

necessarily attended with greater difficulties than those begun by our own sisters alone.

"F. Antony of Jesus and the Prior came for us, being sent by the people of Villanueva, and we left Malagon on the Saturday before Quinquagesima Sunday, being February 13, 1580. God was pleased to give us such fine weather, and to give me such good health, that it seemed as if I had never been ill. I wondered greatly at this, and considered how important it is not to be deterred by weak health or other obstacles when opportunities of serving God present themselves, since He is able to turn our weakness into strength, and our sickness into health; and, when He does it not, it is because He sees that suffering is better for us; for why are life and health given us, save to lose them in the service of so great a King and Lord; and with our eyes fixed on His honour and glory to forget ourselves? Believe me, sisters, you will never go wrong by following this road. I confess to you that my wickedness and weakness have often made me doubt and fear; but I remember not, ever since our Lord gave me the habit of a discalced Carmelite, nor for some years before, that I have ever followed any other rule of conduct. By His mercy alone He has given me grace to overcome these temptations, and to devote myself without flinching to whatever I considered was most to His honour, however difficult it might be. I clearly perceive my co-operation was worth very little; but God desires no more than such a single resolution on our part to do the thing Himself for us.

"May He be ever blessed and praised! Amen."

On her way to Villanueva, S. Teresa visited the sanctuary of our Lady of Succour, where she was favoured by a vision of the B. Catherine of Cardona.

"We had to pass by the monastery of our Lady of Succour, mentioned before, which is nine miles from Villanueva; and there we had to stay and give notice that we were come, for so we had agreed to do, and it was fit that I should in all things obey those fathers with whom we travelled. The house stands in the midst of a delightful solitude, and when we were near to it, the religious came forth to receive their Prior with great solemnity; and the sight of them as they came forth bare-footed, with their poor cloaks of coarse cloth, excited great devotion in us all. I was greatly moved, for I seemed to be living in the blessed times of our primitive fathers. They seemed at that time to be so many white odoriferous flowers, and such I believe they are before God, for He is truly served by them. They entered the church singing the *Te Deum* with voices whose weakness showed their mortification. The passage to the church is underground, as if through a grotto, representing that of our Father Elias. As I entered it, I experienced such great interior joy, as would have repaid me for a much longer journey, though I grieved much for the death of the Blessed Catharine of Cardona, by whose means God had founded this house, because I had not deserved to see her, though I so greatly desired it.

"One day, after I had communicated in that holy church, a rapture came upon me which took away my senses. In it this holy woman was represented to me (by an intellectual vision) as a glorified body. Some angels were with her, and she told me 'not to grow weary, but to endeavour to go on with these foundations.'

"We arrived at Villanueva on the first Sunday in Lent, being the Vigil of S. Peter's Chair and the Feast of S. Barbatus, in the year 1580. On the same day the Blessed Sacrament was placed at High Mass

2 B

in the church of the glorious S. Anne. The whole of
the town council came forth to receive us, with Dr.
Ervias and some others. We alighted at the parish
church, which was at a considerable distance from
S. Anne's.

"The joy of the people was so great, that it gave
me exceeding consolation to behold with what pleasure they received the Order of the Blessed Virgin
our Lady. We heard the bells ring at a great
distance; and as soon as we entered the church the
Te Deum was intoned, the Canons taking one verse
and the choir another. The Most Blessed Sacrament
was placed on one car, and our Lady's image on
another, with crosses and standards, and thus the
procession went forward with great solemnity: we
walked in the middle, in our veils and white cloaks,
next to the Most Blessed Sacrament; next came our
discalced fathers in great numbers from the monastery;
then the Franciscan fathers (for they had a monastery
in the town), and with them a Dominican friar; and
though he was alone, I was much pleased to see that
habit there.

"As the distance was very great, several altars
were erected on the way, at which the procession
stopped, singing hymns in honour of our Lady of
Mount Carmel. The sight of all these people thus
vieing with each other in praising our Lord, borne in
triumph before them, and the honour which for His
sake was paid to seven poor little Carmelite nuns,
filled us with the tenderest feelings of devotion. But
at the same time I thought as I walked along, to
my great confusion, that had they treated me
according to my deserts, they would all have turned
against me.

"I have thus given you, sisters, a long account of
the honour here shown to the habit of our Lady, that

you may praise our Lord, and beseech Him that He may turn this foundation to His honour.

"I am, however, more delighted when in founding monasteries I suffer many persecutions and troubles, and these I more joyfully recount to you. True it is that those sisters who lived there before we came had endured a great deal for about six years after they entered the house of the glorious S. Anne, besides their poverty, and the trouble they endured in pro-curing means of subsistence, for they never liked to ask alms, lest the people might think they came there to be supported by them. I will not speak of their severe penances, their long fasts, their scanty meals, their poor beds, and the smallness of their house, which was most inconvenient, considering how strict was their enclosure. But their greatest affliction (as they told me) was their ardent desire to receive our holy habit; and this desire tormented them day and night exceedingly, because they thought it would never be fulfilled; and thus all their prayers and tears were offered to God for this intention; and, when any new difficulty arose in the way, they were extremely afflicted, and increased their penances. Out of their earnings, and by stinting themselves in food, they paid the messengers who were sent to me; thus proving to those who were in any way able to relieve them, that they could maintain themselves in their poverty. I was convinced, after I had spoken to them and observed their sanctity, that their prayers and tears had been instrumental in gaining admittance into the Order; and I esteemed such souls a greater gain to us than if they had brought us great revenues; and I feel assured that this house will advance greatly in perfection. When we arrived, they were all standing at the door, each wearing the same dress in which she entered the house, for they never wished

to assume any religious habit till they could receive
ours. Though what they wore was very modest, its
poverty and their extremely pale and ascetic looks
showed how severe had been the mortification of their
life. They received us with many tears of great joy,
which were proved to be sincere by the love with which
they served our Lady, their great virtue, humility, and
obedience to the Prioress, and to all who came to found
the monastery; they could not do enough to please
us. All their fear was lest we should be driven away
by the sight of their poverty and small inconvenient
house. No one of them ever commanded the rest,
but each one did what she could, with all humility and
love. The two eldest managed all necessary business;
the others never spoke with any one. They slept but
little, being obliged to work for their food, and in
order to make time for prayer, in which they spent
many hours, and on festivals the whole day. They
were directed by the works of F. Louis of Granada
and F. Peter of Alcantara. They spent much of their
time in reciting the Divine Office as well as they could
(only one knew how to read well), and their Breviaries
were not uniform, some of them being old Roman
office books given them by priests who no longer used
them; and as they could not read well, they spent
many hours over it, and no doubt made many mis-
takes; but God accepted their good intentions, and
they said their Office in a place where they could not
be heard by the people outside. When F. Antony of
Jesus became acquainted with them, he told them to
say only the Office of our Lady.

"They had an oven, where they baked their bread;
and everything was done with as much order in the
house as if they had a Superioress. All this made
me praise our Lord the more; and the more I conversed with them, the more pleased I was that I had

come. I would not have neglected to console these sisters for any trials which it might have brought upon me. My companions, who were to remain with them, told me that at first they felt some reluctance to do so ; but when they discovered their virtues, it was their greatest joy to live with them, for they loved them exceedingly. How great is the power of holiness and virtue ! It is true that those who came thither, whatever difficulties and labours they might have to endure, would have borne them all patiently by our Lord's assistance, because they desired to suffer in His service ; and that sister who finds not in herself this desire, let her not esteem herself a true discalced Carmelite, since our desires should not be for ease and rest, but for suffering, that so we may in some measure imitate our true Spouse. May His Majesty be pleased to give us grace to do so ! Amen ! "

During her stay at Villanueva an accident befell the holy Mother, by which the arm, from the fracture of which she had already suffered so much, was broken a second time. This accident was followed by a very dangerous abscess, insomuch that, as Anne of S. Bartholomew informs us, her life was despaired of. It pleased God, however, to deliver her from this peril by the breaking of the abscess.

After remaining a month at Villanueva, S. Teresa began her journey to Toledo, but, before she left them she called her daughters together, and said to them : " My children, be of good courage, for you will have great need of it on account of the destitution and poverty in which I leave you, which moves me to great sorrow and compassion. On the other hand, great is my consolation and my confidence in the promise of our Lord, who has pledged His word that those who perfectly observe their obligations shall be provided, by His mercy, with all things needful for them, and in His name I promise it to you. But if you have not courage to remain here, tell me so plainly, and I will take you with me." There was but one reply from those faithful hearts, that they were ready to persevere unto death, not there only, but amongst the Moors, should it be her pleasure to leave them there.

CHAPTER XXIII.

1580, 1581.

S. Teresa left Villanueva on March 20, and arrived at Toledo about Palm Sunday. On the Thursday in Holy Week she was attacked by paralysis, and by such acute pain in the heart, accompanied with fever, that in her letters to F. Gracian and the Prioress of Seville, she says that she thought she was about to die. Before she had fully recovered, she received a command from the Vicar-General to go to Valladolid to meet the Bishop of Palencia, who was desirous to establish a convent in that city, to which he had been recently translated from Avila. The holy Mother left Toledo after the Feast of Corpus Christi, and arrived at Segovia before June 26. On that day, while she was at work, with the other religious at recreation, her beloved brother, Laurence of Cepeda, who died almost suddenly on that day, appeared to her. The Saint changed countenance for a moment, and then, without uttering a word, put down her work and hastened to the choir, followed by the nuns, to commend the departed spirit to our Lord. She had no sooner knelt before the Blessed Sacrament than our Lord vouchsafed to assure her that her brother had been a very short time in Purgatory, and was now enjoying the eternal bliss of Heaven. The religious had observed her sudden change of countenance, and besought their mother to make known its cause, when she related to them the vision which she had seen.

Laurence of Cepeda, since his return from America, had been living in devout retirement, on an estate called Serna, which he had purchased in the neighbourhood of Avila. The following letters to his second son, then in America, and to the Prioress of Seville, of which house he had been such a great benefactor, describe the last years and the death of this holy man.

" To Don Laurence of Cepeda.

" May the grace of the Holy Ghost be with you, my son.

" You may well believe with what pain I write the bad news which I have to send you. But as you must necessarily hear it from others, who perhaps will not be able to tell you all the consoling facts which lighten the great trouble, I think it is best you should hear it from me. If we consider well the miseries of this life, we ought to rejoice at the happiness of those who are already with God. My son, it has pleased our Divine Master to take to Himself, two days after the feast of S. John, my good brother Laurence of Cepeda, your father. He died of the breaking of a blood-vessel, which took him from us in a few hours, but he had confessed and communicated on the Feast of S. John, and from what I know of his life I believe it was a favour on the part of our Divine Lord not to give him a longer time. I am sure that such was the state of his soul, that his Divine Master found him ready, since for a long time past he had lived in continual preparation for that last hour. About a week before his death, he wrote to me that he had a very little time to live, though he knew not precisely which day would be his last. He died like a saint, commending himself to God; so that we have reason to believe that he was a very short time in Purgatory, if he has been there at all. All his life long, as you know, he had been a great servant of God; but for the last few years he had been so entirely devoted to Him, that he could not bear to speak of any worldly things, nor to converse with any but those who spoke to him of our Lord. Everything else was a weariness to him, under which I was often obliged to console him. In order to enjoy greater solitude he had retired to his country house at Serna, where he died, or rather where he began to live. If I could write you certain particulars of his interior life, you would see how much you are indebted to God for having given you such a father, and how strictly you are obliged so to live, as to prove yourself worthy to be his son. But I cannot speak of these things in a letter. Take comfort from what I have said, and be assured that, in the place where your father now is, he can do you more good than when he was still on earth. This separation has been very painful to me, and no less to the good Teresita of Jesus, your sister; but she has shown what virtue God has given her, by bearing this blow like an Angel as she is. I may add that she is an excellent religious, and very happy in her vocation. I hope in the goodness of God that she will be like her father."

July 4, 1580.

" To Mother Mary of S. Joseph, Prioress of Seville.

" Jesus. The Holy Spirit be with your Reverence !
" My Mother,—It seems our Lord does not wish me to remain long without afflictions, for you must know that he has been pleased to call to Himself His good

friend and servant, Laurence de Cepeda. He died after an illness of six hours from the breaking of a blood-vessel. Two days before, he had received the Most Blessed Sacrament. He died in his perfect senses, recommending himself very devoutly to our Lord. I hope in the goodness of God that he is now in the enjoyment of eternal glory, for he always lived in such a way as to have no other care but to serve Him; everything else was a weariness to him; and on this account he retired to his country house, which was about a league from Avila, in order to avoid the noise and gaiety of the world.

" His prayer was continual, for he always kept himself in the presence of God; hence His Majesty filled his soul with so many graces and favours, that sometimes I have been quite astonished at them. He had a great attraction to penance, and would have practised greater austerities than I thought fit for him. He gave me an account of all his interior life, and paid wonderful attention to all I said to him. This I think arose from the great affection which he bore me. I now return such affection by rejoicing that he has left this miserable life, and is now in a place of repose. This I say, not for the sake of saying it, but I assure you when I think of his happiness I feel great joy. I grieve much for his children, but I hope God will provide for them through the prayers of their father.

" I have written thus fully to your Reverence, because I know you will be grieved to hear of his death, and this account may help to console you all, for he certainly deserves to be regretted by all the sisters. It was wonderful to see what he felt on hearing of your afflictions, for great was the love he had for your house. Now is the time to repay that love by recommending his soul to God, on condition, however, that, if he should not stand in need of your prayers (as I think he does not, considering the life he led), they may be applied to those souls who have greater need of them, in order that they may be relieved thereby.

" I must tell you that a short time before his death he wrote to me at S. Joseph's Convent in Segovia, where I now am, and which is eleven leagues from Avila. In that letter he said many things with regard to the shortness of life, which quite astonished me. As then, my daughter, it is certain that everything passes quickly away, we ought continually to be thinking of a good death, rather than of the means how we are to live. Since I must still remain in this world, God grant that I may serve Him in something. I am four years older than my brother was, and yet God has been pleased that I should survive him. I have now quite recovered from my last illness, though I still have my usual indispositions, especially a pain in my head.

" 'Tell Roderick Alvarez that his letter just came when I wanted it, for it speaks of the great advantage of afflictions. Tell him also that I think God works miracles through him even during his life; what then will He do after his death ! I have just heard that the Moriscos of Seville are conspiring together to get possession of the city. What a fine opportunity you will all have of becoming martyrs ! Inquire if the report be true, and order the M. Sub-Prioress to send me an account of every particular. I was very much pleased to hear that she is in good health, and grieved to hear that you are ill. For the love of God take great care of yourself. I have been told a good remedy for your malady, viz., dog-roses beaten to powder, when they are dry, about half an ounce should be taken every morning. But ask the doctor about it. Let me beg of you not to be so long again without writing to me. Remember me very kindly to all the sisters, and especially to sister S. Francis. Mother-Prioress and all the community here send their regards. It must seem to you very delightful to be among standards and the tumults of war. God grant that you may know how to turn all the strange things which you must see to your spiritual profit. It is very necessary, however, for you to be on your guard, lest you should be distracted by them. I am very anxious you should all become saints.

" What would you say if the foundation in Portugal were to come to pass ? Don Teutonio, Archbishop of Evora, informs me that the town is not more than forty leagues from this place. I should feel great comfort were the foundation begun. Since God spares my life, I desire to do something for His honour and glory ; and as I have not long to live, I will not spend my time so idly as I have done in past years, during which I suffered so much in my interior. As to other things, what I have done is not worth speaking about. Beg of our Lord to give me strength, that I may employ my time in doing something for His glory.

" I have already told you, that you may show this letter to F. Gregory. I hope he will consider it as addressed to himself, for I certainly do love him in our Lord, and I have a great desire to see him. My brother died on the Sunday after the Feast of S. John. May His Majesty watch over you, and make you what I desire you to be !

" Your Reverence's servant,

" TERESA OF JESUS."

From the letters addressed by S. Teresa to her brother it appears that she directed him in the spiritual life. She encourages him under the fears and scruples by which he was afflicted; reproves him for an imprudent vow which he had made never to commit a venial sin, and directs him to get it commuted; replies to various questions on spiritual subjects, assigning to him different exercises of mortification, and prescribing rules with regard to his method of prayer. Such was the high estimation in which Laurence held his sister, that he wished to oblige himself by a promise to obey her in the direction of his soul. S. Teresa, however, would not allow him to do more than apply to her for counsel. Besides the above-mentioned revelation of his eternal happiness, the Saint was favoured with another blessed vision regarding him at Holy Communion. As she approached the altar, she saw the glorious S. Joseph on one side, and her blessed brother on the other, accompanying her with lighted candles.

Laurence de Cepeda left his sister executrix of his will, in which he signified his desire to be buried in the church of her convent at Avila, leaving a portion of his wealth for the building of a chapel there, in honour of the holy martyr S. Laurence.

On her arrival at Valladolid the holy Mother again fell dangerously ill; her recovery was retarded by the press of business which now fell upon her, and which was greatly increased by the cares brought upon her by her brother's will. "Oh! my children," she writes to the Prioress and religious at Avila, "what trouble and weariness do these temporal goods bring with them. I have always thought so, and now I know it by experience. In my opinion all the labours and anxieties which I have endured in all our foundations have fallen far short of what I am now enduring on this account: it may be that my illness makes me feel the burden heavier."

Francis, the eldest son of Laurence of Cepeda, soon

after the death of his father, expressed his desire to enter religion, and received the habit of Mount Carmel; but apparently his was not a true vocation, for a few months afterwards the Saint writes of the sudden change which had taken place in his mind, and not long afterwards she writes to his brother in America of his approaching marriage. " Don Francis," she says, " has always hitherto been very virtuous, and I hope in the mercy of God that he will continue so for the future, for he is a very good Christian." Teresita had received the religious habit at S. Joseph's at Avila.

The foundation at Palencia was an occasion of some anxiety to Teresa. Mary Baptist, her niece, the Prioress of Valladolid, with her usual promptness and energy, urged her greatly to the undertaking. " Yet," says the Saint, she could not persuade me, for I saw no prospect of success, because the monastery was to be founded in poverty; and I was told that, as the town was very poor, the nuns would not receive sufficient support. I was about a year considering this foundation, as well as that of Burgos, and at first I was not so averse to it, but many difficulties afterwards presented themselves to my mind, though it was for this object alone that I had come to Valladolid. I know not whether it was the weakness left by my illness, or the devil who desired to hinder the good which was afterwards done there.

" The truth is, I am astonished and afflicted (and often I have complained thereof to our Lord) to see how the poor soul participates in the infirmity of the body, which it seems must follow its laws, and be subject to all its necessities and trials. It appears to me that one of the greatest troubles and miseries of life is the want of noble courage to bring the body into subjection; for though pain and sickness be trouble-

some, yet I account this as nothing, when the soul
can rise above them in the might of her love, praising
God for them, and receiving them as gifts from His
hand. But on the one hand to be suffering, and on
the other to be able to do nothing, is a terrible thing,
especially for a soul that has an ardent desire to find
no rest, either interior or exterior, on earth, but to
employ herself entirely in the service of her great
God. In this case there is no other remedy but patience
and the acknowledgment of our misery, and perfect
resignation of ourselves to the will of God, that He
may dispose of us as He pleases, and how He pleases.
I was in this state, though beginning to get well, but
my weakness was so great that I had lost the confidence God usually gave me in beginning these foundations. Everything seemed impossible to me, and
I greatly needed some one to encourage me; for some
increased my fears instead of diminishing them, and
others failed to cure my cowardice."

Our Lord sent S. Teresa the encouragement she
needed in the person of F. Ripalda, of the Society
of Jesus, who happened to come to Valladolid at this
time.

" He was," says she, " a great servant of God, and
one who had been my confessor for some time. I told
him my difficulty, and that I wished him, as in the
place of God, to declare his opinion. He greatly encouraged me, and told me that my cowardice proceeded
from old age; but I clearly saw that it was not so, for
I am now older, and yet am not in the same state of
discouragement. He must have known it himself,
but he said so only to reprove me for my cowardice,
and show me that it did not come from God. I had
nothing either for this foundation of Palencia or for
that of Burgos: but this was no hindrance, for so I
was accustomed to begin. He told me that I should

not on any account refuse the foundation of Palencia. F. Balthasar Alvarez, Provincial of the Society, had told me the same in Toledo, but then I was well. Now the devil, or (as I have said) my illness, held me so fast, that though I was more inclined to the foundation, I was still afraid to proceed. The Prioress of Valladolid helped me as much as she could, because she was very anxious for the foundation of Palencia; but when she saw me so cold, she began to fear also. Until the true Sun shone upon me the words of His servants were insufficient to encourage me, and hence it may be seen that it is not I who do anything in these foundations, but He who is all-powerful.

" One day, after I had communicated, being still in these doubts, and undetermined what to do, I asked our Lord to enlighten me, that I might do His Will in all things, for my coldness was not so great as ever to fail in this desire. Our Lord said to me, as if in reproof; ' Of what art thou afraid? When have I been wanting to thee? I am the same now that I have ever been. Do not neglect to make these two foundations." O great God! how different are Thy words from those of men! I became so resolute and courageous, that all the world would not have been able to hinder me. I set to work immediately, and our Lord also began to afford me the means.

" I chose two nuns for the foundation whose means enabled me to purchase a house ; and although I was told that it was impossible to live in Palencia upon alms, yet it was the same to me as if it had not been said, for to found a monastery with endowment was, I clearly saw, not then possible ; and since God had commanded me to found the monastery, I was assured that His Majesty would provide for it. Thus, although I had not yet quite recovered, I determined to go, though the weather was still cold, for I left

Valladolid on the Feast of the Holy Innocents, in the year 1580. A gentleman of Palencia lent us a house of his which he had hired until S. John's day. I wrote to a Canon of that same city, who I was assured was a servant of God (for, as we have seen in the other foundations, our Lord selects some one in every place to assist us, because he sees the little I can do myself). I wrote to this Canon, entreating him with all possible secrecy to get the house free for us, without telling the person who lived in it for what purpose we wanted it. The Canon, whose name was Reynoso, managed the business so well, that he not only had the house ready for us, but provided beds and many other conveniences, of which we stood in great need, for the cold was excessive; and the day before was so foggy, that we could scarcely see one another. It is true, we took little rest till we had fitted up a place for saying Mass the next day, before any one could know we had arrived. And in these foundations I have always found this to be the best course; for, if we begin to take opinions, the devil raises a disturbance, which, though he may not prevent the foundation, hinders and delays it. And so in the morning at day-break Mass was said.

"I had brought with me five nuns, and a lay-sister (Anne of S. Bartholomew) who had been my companion for a long time; and so great a servant of God is she, and so discreet, that she can be of greater assistance to me than all the rest of the nuns. I was much pleased that the house was founded on the Feast of King David, to whom I have a great devotion. I sent word early in the morning to the Bishop, who did not know that we had arrived. He presently paid us a visit, and, with the great kindness which he had always shown us, said he would supply us with bread, and he ordered his steward to provide us with many other necessaries. The Order is so much in-debted to him, that it is bound to recommend him to our Lord, living or dead.

" The joy was great which all the people showed at the establishment of this convent. The knowledge that the Bishop greatly approved it was much in our favour, for he was exceedingly beloved in the city; but the people of Palencia seemed to exceed in nobility and generosity of mind any whom I have seen else-where; and so I rejoice daily more and more at the foundation of this house."

The next step was to found a permanent house for the religious. A church dedicated to our Lady, and much frequented by the people, was bestowed upon them by the Bishop; and S. Teresa resolved upon the purchase of two houses adjoining it. After consider-able difficulty and opposition, the matter was so far arranged as to want only another security in addition to that of Canon Reynoso for the purchase. The Canon went in search of the Vicar-General, "to whom," says S. Teresa, "we are much indebted. He met him in the street, and the Vicar-General asked him whither he was going. The Canon replied that he was going to ask him to sign an agreement. He laughed, and said : "Do you ask me to become security for so large a sum ?" and immediately, while sitting on his mule, he signed the deed—a thing very wonderful in these our times. I cannot leave off praising the charity which I found in Palencia. The truth is, it seemed to me to resemble that of the Primitive Church, and to be very unusual in this age of the world. We had no revenue, and the people were to provide us with food; and yet they were not only not offended, but they considered it a very great favour shown them by God; and they said the truth, if we rightly consider the matter, for to have only one

2 c

church more where the Most Blessed Sacrament is reserved would be an exceeding favour.

" May He be for ever blessed ! Amen."

When the monastery was finished and the nuns ready to enter it, the Bishop wished them to proceed thither with great solemnity on some day within the Octave of Corpus Christi, and he came over himself from Valladolid for the occasion. The Chapter, the different Orders, and almost the whole city, assembled together with excellent music. " We all went in procession from the house where we dwelt, in our white cloaks and veils, to a parish that was near the house of our Lady, where we were met by an image to which the people had great devotion. The Most Blessed Sacrament was then placed in the church with great solemnity, joy, and devotion. The nuns were with us who had come for the foundation of Soria, and we all carried candles in our hands. I believe our Lord was exceedingly praised that day by the people of the place. May He always be thus praised by His creatures ! Amen."

CHAPTER XXIV.

1581.

WHILE S. Teresa was occupied in the foundation of Palencia, the long-expected brief was granted at Rome for the erection of the reform into a separate Province, on June 22, 1580. The following is her own account of the conclusion of this long trial :—

" When I was at Palencia, it pleased God to make a separation between the fathers of the reform and those of the mitigation, each division forming a Province of its own ; and this was one of the most joyful events which could have taken place, and the most conducive to our peace and quiet. At the request of our Catholic king, Don Philip, who has always greatly favoured us, a very ample brief was obtained from Rome, by virtue of which a Chapter was convened for this purpose at Alcalà, by the Rev. John de las Cuevas, of the Dominican Order, Prior of Talavera, who was appointed by the Pope, and nominated also by his Majesty, and who was a very holy and discreet person, as such an office required. The king defrayed all expenses of the Chapter, and by his command the university favoured it greatly. The Chapter was held in a convent of our Order which bears the name of S. Cyril of the Discalced, and all proceeded with remarkable peace and concord. It is needless for me to mention here what passed at this Chapter. Our Lord was thus pleased to finish this important business to the honour and glory of His glorious Mother, who is the Lady and Patroness of our Order. This separation has given me the greatest pleasure and consolation which I could receive in this life; for during more than twenty-five years the Order has had to endure more troubles, persecutions, and afflictions than I have space to relate. Our Lord only knows them, and he that knows not the troubles which have been endured cannot conceive the joy of my heart at seeing them thus concluded, and my intense desire that all the world should praise our Lord for it. Let us also recommend to Him our holy king, Don Philip, by whose means God has brought this work to so happy a conclusion; for the devil had already exerted his craft so well, that, but for the king, our cause would have been lost.

"And now we are all in peace, reformed and mitigated, having no one to disturb us in the service of our Lord, wherefore, brethren and sisters, since His

Majesty has heard our prayers, let us make haste to
serve Him. Let the living (who have been eye-
witnesses of all this trial) consider the favours He has
shown us, and from what troubles and cares He has
freed us; and, for the love of God, let not those who
shall come after us, when they find everything smooth
and easy, fall short in any degree of the perfection to
which they are called. Let not that be said of them
which is said of certain Orders, that their beginning
was commendable. Since this is our beginning, let
us strive generously always to advance from good to
better. Consider, my daughters, how, by means of
very small breaches, the devil is continually preparing
the way for greater.

"Never let it be said, 'There is no harm in this,'
or, 'These are extremes.' Oh, my daughters, we
ought to regard as of great importance everything
which impedes our progress in the service of God.
For the love of our Lord, I beseech you to remember
how soon everything passes away; what a favour our
Lord has bestowed on us in calling us to this Order;
and the great punishment they will have to endure
who shall introduce any relaxation; and ever place
before your eyes those holy Prophets from whom we
have descended, for we have many Saints in Heaven
who have worn the habit. Let us cherish, by the
Divine assistance, the holy presumption of aspiring to
become what they were. The conflict, sisters, will
last but for a short time, while the reward is eternal.
Let us despise those things which are earthly, and
seek only after those which are in Heaven, that so we
may more and more love and serve our Lord, who shall
be hereafter our living Beatitude. Amen, Amen. To
Him be benediction, praise, and thanksgiving!"

The work before the Chapter was the establishment of a separate Province for the reform, the

election of the Provincial and his Council, and the examination and confirmation of the constitutions which had been drawn up by F. Gracian, as Apostolic Visitor, for the friars, and by S. Teresa for the nuns. F. de las Cuevas relied on the former for the preparation for all the matters to be decided, and especially for everything connected with the government of the nuns. The following extracts from S. Teresa's letters to F. Gracian, previous to the opening of the Chapter, will give her judgment on the various subjects under discussion :—

" I know not, Reverend Father, why you should not speak your mind as to what regards us, the nuns of the reform. In my letter to the Commissary-Apostolic I have expressed myself so strongly on the benefit which we have received from your visitations (which was the simple truth), that you may speak with full liberty. You will do us a favour thereby, for which we shall be deeply grateful. It is a duty which you owe to our sisters, in return for all the tears which this struggle has cost them. Indeed, I would not have any one but you and F. Nicolas to meddle with the subject. It is not necessary that our constitutions, or anything relating to us, should be brought before the Chapter. These points were always arranged between F. Peter Hermandez and myself. Some of the things which I have set down may seem to you of very little importance, but I consider them so necessary that I would not have one omitted. I may claim to have a voice in the Chapter with regard to all that affects the nuns. I have seen many things, apparently of little importance, the occasion of much injury to them.

" I see plainly that, in this first election, it is most important in every respect that you should be chosen Provincial, and I have said so to the Father Commissary.

"But should F. Nicolas be elected, you, as his companion, might afford him the assistance of your experience, and of your knowledge of our religious, both friars and nuns. I have told the Commissary that we know from experience that *Macarius* (F. Antony of Jesus) has not the qualities requisite for this office, adding that this was also the opinion of F. Hermandez, who, but for this, would gladly have put him in authority. I have also pointed out F. John of Jesus, that I might not seem to think of no one but you two, but I have said, at the same time, that I do not believe that he has the gift of government, though, if he had one of you for his companion, he might be able to fill the office, because, as I believe, he is a man of sense, who would take advice. If you were with him, he would follow yours exactly, and so he would govern well, but I am quite sure he will not get the votes. May the Lord, who has done so much for us, direct this election to His greater glory!

"If you should be made Provincial, try to have F. Nicolas for your companion. As F. Bartholomew is in such bad health he cannot abstain, and some will make unfavourable remarks upon him. At all events, in the beginning, it will be very useful to have F. Nicolas with you, for his advice will be always worth having. After having borne so patiently as you have done so many troublesome people, it will be a relief to you to be with one from whom you will never have anything to suffer. Say everything that is kind from me to F. Bartholomew. I am sure that, in his state of health, he must be worn out by your habit of never taking any rest. It is enough to kill yourself and any one who may be with you. I often think how ill you used to look in Holy Week. For the love of God, do not preach so continually this Lent, nor eat those miserable fishes. Though you may not perceive it at first, excess of labour on one side, and bad food on the other, will not fail to do you harm, and then come temptations. . . . I have given F. Mariano a long lecture on the temptation, which he tells me he feels, to vote for *Macarius*. I do not understand that man upon this point, but I do not intend to enter upon it with any one but you. Therefore, keep what I have written upon it to yourself, for this is of the utmost importance. Do not fail to have recourse to F. Nicolas, and let the Capitular Fathers be well convinced that you do not seek the office for yourself. I do not see, for my part, how any of them can in conscience vote for any but one of you two. . . . If any change is to be made in the constitutions of the nuns, do not specify of what their shoes are to be made, but say simply that they may wear shoes, or there would be no end to their scruples. I should advise, if you think proper, that the rule made by F. Hermandez should be abolished, which forbids us to eat eggs in Lent, and bread at collation. I could never persuade him not to put in these two articles. With regard to fasting, it is sufficient to observe the law of the Church, without imposing another in addition. It is a source of scruples to the religious, and hurts the health of many, who think that they have strength to do both, and, in fact, have it not. . . . Our constitutions say *that the religious are to live on alms, and cannot possess revenues.* As many of our houses are endowed, it would be well either to omit this article, or that the Father Commissary should declare that, as it is permitted by the Council of Trent, the Carmelites may possess revenues. . . . I have been much moved by what you say in your letter, that you will always be on the side of the nuns. At least, you will always be their true father, as you are assuredly bound to be.

If you were to live for ever, and they were always to be governed by you, many of our requests to the Chapter might be omitted. Oh! how earnestly do they pray that you may remain Provincial; nothing else in the world, I believe, would content them. May God, my Father, preserve you to your children! They all commend themselves to your prayers, and I the most earnestly of them all.

" These are the memorials which have been sent me by the nuns; when I have received the rest I will send them to you. I do not know whether they are now satisfactory, but it is quite clear that it was necessary for me to see them first, as your Reverence wisely directed. That of your friend, Mother Isabel of S. Dominic, was the only one which required no correction. . . . It is, in my opinion, of the utmost importance that it should be established by rule, that the confessors of our religious should not be their Superiors. So essential a point do I hold this to be in our Order, that, though I agree with you in thinking it of great importance that they should be directed by religious, I should prefer to forego this advantage, and to leave things as they are, rather than to see each confessor become the Superior of the house to which he is attached. There are serious evils attending such an arrangement, as I will tell you when we meet. On this point I beseech you attend to me. . . . For the same reason, and for many others, it is equally necessary that the nuns should not be subject to the Priors. If one among them should be wanting in discretion, he might order things which would cause a great deal of confusion. As we shall never have any one like F. Gracian to govern us, and as we must consider the future, the great experience which we have acquired makes it our duty to avoid all dangers of this kind. The greatest benefit which the Fathers of the Chapter can confer upon our religious is to establish a rule that the only relation in which the confessor shall stand towards them is that of hearing their confessions, and that he shall not converse with them out of the confessional. To preserve the recollection of the house, it is sufficient for him, as confessor to report its state to the Provincial. . . . The infraction of this rule, and the reception of too great a number of religious, are the two things which I have always most feared, as likely to do us the greatest harm. Therefore, Reverend Father, I beg of you to spare no pains to make these two points in our institutions firm and unchangeable. I expect this favour from you. Pray give many kind messages from me to F. Antony of Jesus, and tell him that the letter which I wrote to him was not one of those which are answered by silence, and that as I seem to have been addressing one who is deaf and dumb I will write to him no more. Add that he sends F. Mariano away well satisfied with his endeavours to procure for the religious a more sufficient supply of food than the Priors are accustomed to give them. I declare to you, Reverend Father, that, if this be not remedied in all our houses, we shall see what will come of it. The Capitular Fathers ought to impose it upon the Priors as an obedience to give proper food to their subjects. God will never fail to send them what is necessary. If they give little to their religious, He will give little to them. For the love of God, Reverend Father, take care that there be all fitting cleanliness in the beds and table-linen of the friars, whatever expense it may entail. For want of cleanliness is a terrible thing. I am decidedly of opinion that this ought to be ruled by a constitution, and, indeed, being what they are, I doubt whether a constitution will be sufficient. . . . Now, as to the desire which you express to me, not to be elected or confirmed by the Chapter, I am writing on this subject to the Father Commissary. If I have myself desired to see you at liberty, I see clearly that that desire sprang rather from the great affection which I bear you in our Lord, than from regard to the good of the Order. From that affection arises the natural sensibility which causes me to suffer so much, when I see that all our fathers do not understand what they owe you, and what labour you have endured for the reform. Hence it is that I cannot bear to hear a word said against you: it is a thing which I cannot endure. And yet, after having weighed all this, the general good compels me to desire that this burden should be laid upon you. God avert, my Father, from our houses so great a misfortune as that of being deprived of your care? Our discalced Carmelites require a government which will regulate the most minute details, and a Superior who can take in both sides of a question. They are the servants of our Lord, and he will watch over them."

On March 4 F. Gracian was elected Provincial. He immediately appointed three Vicars-Provincial, and gave to S. Teresa an authority over all the convents of the nuns, subordinate only to his own.

In a letter written on Good Friday S. Teresa thus expresses her joy at the good news of this election, which she had just received from him :—" May our adorable Lord reward you, my Reverend Father, for the good tidings contained in your letter, and especially for sending me the printed brief! I only want now to see the constitutions printed also; and God, I doubt not, will grant us this favour. I know how much labour it must have cost you to obtain this brief, to set all things in order, and to bring all things to such a happy termination. May He who has enabled you to do it be eternally blessed! It seems to me a dream. If we had had nothing to do but to wish for it, we never could have imagined any conclusion nearly approaching that which God has wrought in our favour. May He be blessed for ever! As I do not understand Latin, I have not been able to read the brief. I am waiting till the end of this Holy Season for some one to be kind enough to explain it to me. Yesterday your packet was brought to me, and fearing, if I read too much, my head would not be strong enough for the Tenebræ, from which, on account of our small number, I could not be absent, I only read your letters. Be pleased to tell me whither you are going when you leave Madrid. A thousand things may happen which may make it necessary that I should know where you are. . . . I have one request to make to you, which shall be my Easter gift. Some time ago, to console F. John of the Cross, for all he had to suffer in Andalusia, I promised him, that if it should please our Lord to give us a separate Province, I would do all in my power to bring him here. He now claims my promise, and expresses his fear of being elected Prior of Baeza. He writes to me to beg you not to confirm his election. If it be a thing in your power, it will be but just to grant him this consolation, for he has been over-whelmed with suffering. . . . As to the dear nuns who are with me, they do not know how sufficiently to express their delight at having you for their father. Their joy is as perfect as any joy on earth can be. May God one day give us the possession of that which will never end, and may He, Reverend Father, grant you a blessed Easter!"

CHAPTER XXV.

1581, 1582.

BEFORE S. Teresa left Palencia, she received a letter from Don Alonzo Velasquez, Bishop of Osma, begging her to make a foundation at Soria, a small town in his diocese. This Prelate had been Canon of Toledo during the time of her residence in that city; he had been her ordinary confessor there, and had afforded her great consolation and support under the afflictions which then weighed heavily upon her. His veneration for his holy penitent was unbounded, and he was no sooner raised to the episcopal see of Osma, than he seized an opportunity afforded him by the pious liberality of a noble lady, Beatrice of Beaumonte, to establish a convent of the reform. He wrote to the Saint, earnestly begging her to come in person to found the house, offering, on his own part, a church, and, on the part of Doña Beatrice, a convenient house for the convent.

Teresa was full of joy at receiving such an application from one whom she so greatly loved and revered. She immediately prepared for the journey, and chose Catherine of Christ, one of the holiest of her religious, to accompany her as Superioress of the new foundation. F. Gracian was somewhat doubtful of the prudence of this choice, and represented that Catharine could not write, and had no knowledge of business. "Content you, Father," replied the Saint, "Catharine of Christ knows well how to love God; she is a great Saint, and adorned with high perfection, and she wants nothing else to enable her to govern well."

S. Teresa and her daughters were warmly welcomed

both by the Bishop and by Doña Beatrice, and on
the day after their arrival, F. Nicolas Doria, who
accompanied them, said Mass in the new convent on
June 3, 1581.

On the following Feast of the Assumption the holy
Mother gave the habit to two novices; and thus was
established the convent of Soria, so peacefully and
happily as to cause some little uneasiness to the Saint.
" I am afraid of this foundation," said she, " because
it has been made with so much ease, and without
any contradiction."

Troubles and calamities arose afterwards, which
satisfied her mind that the devil thought the work
sufficiently successful to give him uneasiness. In a
letter written to the Prioress, to thank her for some
charitable help afforded to the sisters at Avila, then
in great necessity, after congratulating the religious
of Soria upon the mutual peace and charity which
reigned among them, she congratulates them still
more on having been unjustly evil spoken of. " Oh,
how thankful ought we to be for this," she says, " for
hitherto in this foundation there has been little opportunity for merit ! "

If the journey to Soria had been prosperous, and
the foundation without difficulty, the religious had
trials enough to endure in their journey home, which
was undertaken under the care of a good Prebendary
of Palencia, named Ribera, F. Nicolas Doria being
needed elsewhere.

" I did not wish," says S. Teresa, " any one else to
travel with me, except my companion (Anne of S.
Bartholomew), who, by her diligence, was enough for
me ; and the less noise there is the better able I am
to travel. But on this occasion I paid for my easy
and pleasant journey to Soria, because, though our
guide knew the way to Segovia, he knew not the

waggon-road, so that he led us through places where we were often obliged to alight, and sometimes to go along narrow paths where our waggon seemed suspended between craggy precipices. If we took guides of the country, they directed us as far as they knew the way was good; but when we came into a bad road, left us, saying, *they had some business to attend to.* Before we could find any inn, we had suffered much from the heat, and the waggon was often in danger of being upset. I was very sorry for the good Prebendary who travelled with us, for, though we had been told we were going right, we were continually obliged to return again : but his virtue was so deeply rooted, that he appeared not at all displeased, which I greatly admired, and praised our Lord for it, for where virtue is solid, events can affect us but little. I praise our Lord for delivering us from the road."

They reached S. Joseph's at Segovia on the Vigil of St. Bartholomew. "Our nuns," says the Saint, "had been uneasy at my long absence: but, as the road was so bad, it was with the greatest difficulty that we got along. They caressed us much, for God never sends me any trouble which He does not immediately reward. I rested there above eight days; and because this foundation had been finished without any trouble, I made light of this, considering it to be nothing.

" I left Soria with pleasure, because I hope, through the mercy of God, He will always be served by those who live there as He is served now. May He be blessed and praised for ever and ever ! Amen. Thanks be to God ! "

A trial which had pressed heavily on the heart of S. Teresa for some time past was the unsatisfactory state of her first foundation at Avila. She writes to Mary of S. Joseph in November, 1581 :—" Your last

letter was a great joy to me, which is indeed no new
thing, for I am accustomed to receive from your letters
a consolation which makes up to me for the pain and
anxiety which come to me from so many others. If
you love me well, I assure you that I return your love,
and like you to tell me that you love me. Oh ! how true
it is that our poor human nature looks for a return,
and this cannot be wrong, since our Lord Himself
looks for it from us. And though there is an infinite
distance between the love we owe to Him, who has so
many claims to our service, and that which belongs to
feeble creatures, nevertheless it is an advantage to us
to resemble Him in anything, if it be only in this. I
wrote you a long letter from Soria, which I am afraid
F. Nicolas did not send you ; in it I said that we had
prayed so much in all our convents for you and your
daughters, that far from being surprised that you are
now enjoying such peace, and are so good and virtuous, I am astonished that you have not become
Saints fit for canonization ; for we never ceased during that terrible tempest to ask the help of the Al-
mighty for you, and to beseech Him to restore you to
tranquillity. Now, my dear Mother, as you are enjoying the sweets of repose, you are bound to pray for
those who are still in the heat of the battle, especially
for this convent of S. Joseph's at Avila, which is truly
in need of prayers, and which has just elected me
Prioress, as a remedy for the necessities in which they
are. What a burden for a person of my age, overwhelmed with infirmities and occupations, to be
charged with the government of a house in the state to
which this is reduced ! I do not know if you have
heard that a certain gentleman, lately deceased, has
left a sum of money to this convent, of which it will
not obtain possession for some time to come, so that
the only effect produced at present by the legacy has

been to stop the supply of alms formerly received from the city. This has embarrassed us much, the more so as the house is already loaded with debt, so that I know not what will become of it. Pray for me, my dear daughter, for nature is weak, and sometimes gets weary of suffering, especially of being Prioress when there are so many troublesome matters to arrange. But if God be glorified by it, I shall esteem myself very happy, and account all my troubles as less than nothing."

In one of S. Teresa's letters to F. Gracian, before the opening of the Chapter at Alcalà, she alludes to a more serious evil which had befallen the convent at Avila than any difficulties with regard to money. Under the rule of an incompetent Prioress, an inexperienced confessor, and the too easy government of F. Angelo de Salazar, the nuns of S. Joseph had fallen far short of the state of perfection in which their holy foundress had left them. They had sent up certain petitions to the Chapter, which F. Gracian had wisely ordered to be first laid before S. Teresa. "Your Reverence," says she, "has done well to require that these papers should be first sent to me. The things demanded by the religious of Avila are such, that if they were granted, there would be little difference between them and the nuns of the Incarnation. I am amazed to see what the devil has already done, and it is the confessor who is almost wholly in fault. He has always had an idea that all the religious ought to eat meat, and this is one of the permissions which they ask. Is it not wonderful? I have been much grieved to see that this convent has fallen so far below its primitive perfection, and foresee that there will be much difficulty in restoring it to its former fervour, though it contains some excellent religious. This is not all. They have asked F. Angelo de Salazar, that

some of them who are not in good health may keep
something to eat in their cells; and they ask it in
such a way that I should not be surprised if it were
granted them. Thus it is that regular observance gradually falls to the ground." It was to remedy these
evils, both spiritual and temporal, that S. Teresa, as
formerly in the case of the convent of the Incarnation,
received an obedience from F. Gracian, to undertake
the government of the convent of S. Joseph, which
the Prioress, Mary of Christ, a good religious, though
an inefficient superioress, was thankful to deliver over
into her hands. Her election seems to have taken
place some time in October, for on the 26th of that
month she writes to F. Gracian: "I am very well
now, and have just become a great Prioress." In the
letter to the Prioress of Seville just quoted, which
was written on November 8, she speaks of the consolation which she feels in the piety and affection of
her niece Teresita, who has not forgotten her old tenderness for her mothers at Seville. "You would be
charmed, my dear Mother, to see her now; with all
her great liveliness, she has become very learned in
the science of the Saints. Pray to God, I beseech
you, still to give her His grace. In this world we can
never be without fear. We continually implore our
Lord to watch over her; may He be for ever blessed
for having left her to me!"

The government of the holy Mother soon restored
her beloved convent to its original fervour, and the
blessing of our Lord which she brought with her,
relieved it also from its temporal embarrassments.
Anne of S. Bartholomew relates that at this period
she frequently saw her countenance radiant with
celestial light, and that on one occasion especially,
when she was holding Chapter, she saw our Adorable Redeemer standing beside her, and the glory

2 D

diffused from His Divine Person seemed to encircle hers.

On January 15, 1582, Anne of Jesus, accompanied by several religious, under the care of F. John of the Cross, was sent by S. Teresa to make a foundation at Granada. The holy mother had been earnestly entreated by M. Anne of Jesus to make this foundation herself, but this was rendered impossible by the necessity of proceeding at once to Burgos; and she replied, "It is not the Will of our Lord that I should found a house at Granada, since He calls me elsewhere, but have no fear but that this foundation will prosper well. It is the Will of God that Mother Anne should be the foundress, and He will assist and uphold her in her undertaking."

S. Teresa remained at S. Joseph's till after the Festival at Christmas, purposing to return thither from Burgos for the profession of Teresita, and probably expecting that the summons which she was awaiting from our Lord was to find her there. But of this, her last earthly desire, she was to make a sacrifice to Him.

Just twenty years ago she had planted this Paradise of our Lord, which she had now weeded and beautified for Him anew. What had become of those who had laboured with her there? Francis de Salcedo had gone before her to his rest, having testified by his last will his undying interest in the convent of S. Joseph. It was a legacy from this good man which had proved, for the time, an embarrassment rather than a relief to the religious.

Master Daza was still the oracle of Avila, and the estimation in which the Holy Mother held his judgment is proved by her quoting it to F. Gracian on the subject of the Chapter of Almodovar. In one of her letters to the Bishop of Avila, before his removal to

Palencia, she asks him to bestow a vacant canonry on the good ecclesiastic, as on one who had well deserved this favour at his hands, and who, she seems to think, had been somewhat unaccountably passed over. " After all, my Lord," she says, " everybody is not obliged to love you after the same fashion as your poor Carmelites, who ask for nothing but your love, and that God may long preserve you to them."

The faithful Guiomar d'Ulloa, after vainly taxing her feeble health in an attempt to bear the rigour of the reformed rule, had found her vocation to be the patient endurance of sickness and solitude. Her heart was still at S. Joseph's, but, says the saint, " she seldom comes to see us, for she is very ill."

John of Ovalle and Jane of Ahumada had experienced severe reverses of fortune in the twenty years which had elapsed since the foundation of S. Joseph's. Teresa's letters to her sister are full of tender sympathy for these common-place yet wearing trials, and she writes ever and anon to solicit aid for her from her brother Laurence, who seems, like herself, to have been the general counsellor and helper in all family distresses. " If you can spare John of Ovalle the money wherewith to buy some sheep, you will do a charitable deed." These pious parents had one child only besides Gonzales, who did not long survive her who had once recalled him to life. Beatrice d'Ahumada struggled for many years with a vocation which mastered her at last, as she prayed before the tomb of S. Teresa. " You may do what you will, and say what you like, Beatrice," the Saint had said to her one day, " you will die a Carmelite after all." And so she did, and a Carmelite worthy to be the niece of S. Teresa. She became the brightest flower of the Convent of Alva, where her holy parents, having given their last and dearest offering to God, now rest beside both their children, in the chapel which they had endowed with their inheritance, and which contains the priceless treasure of the relics of S. Teresa.

———◦◦———

CHAPTER XXVI.

1582.

IT was often said of our Saint by her contemporaries, that *Teresa of Jesus could do anything ;* and doubtless she would have said the same herself, only adding, " Yet not I, but Christ who dwelleth in me." In his deposition in the process of her canonization, Julian of Avila bears the following testimony to her heroic constancy :—" I conversed with her, heard her confessions, and administered Holy Communion to her for twenty years, more or less ; and in all her foundations, until God called her to Himself, I always accompanied and served her. . . . Neither labours, nor contradictions, nor hindrances, nor opposition, nor many other things which it would be too long to relate, ever diminished, in the smallest degree, the fervour of that charity with which she offered every one of her actions to God. She might truly have said with S. Paul, ' What shall separate me from the love of Christ ?' I can affirm, as an eye-witness, that nothing, either adverse or prosperous, whether to health, or honour, or life, or anything else whatsoever, ever delayed her for a moment in the work of her foundations, being fully persuaded, as she was, that she should never be left without the aid of our Lord."

The following was one of the maxims in which S. Teresa expressed her immovable confidence in God :—

"It is not in the power of the whole world to undo what God has done, nor cause anything to be left undone which He wills to be done." She feared nothing but to offend God. Certain influential persons having once threatened, if she would not consent to something which they asked, to withdraw their assistance from a work in which she was engaged, she answered quietly, "In order to obtain your request, you must tell me that I shall perhaps sin in refusing it : where there is no fear of sin, I fear nothing else."

This heroism, springing from the intensity of her love of God, was at no time more gloriously manifested than in her last foundation at Burgos, in which, under the pressure of sickness and age, she contended with obstacles, seemingly insurmountable, with a courage no less invincible than that which had impelled her childish steps, just sixty years before, to seek martyrdom amongst the Moors.

The foundation of Burgos had been long contemplated. In the year 1557, S. Teresa had been requested by a religious of the Society of Jesus, to found a house in that city, the capital of Old Castile, and about twelve leagues distant from Palencia. A devout and noble lady of the place, named Catharine of Tolosa, the widowed mother of seven children, four of whom had already entered the reform, and all of whom, together with herself, eventually consecrated themselves to God in religion, generously offered a sufficient endowment for the house. The troubles which then agitated the reform rendered it impossible at that time to undertake the work proposed; and we have seen how, even when peace was restored, S. Teresa shrank, for a time, from attempting either this foundation or that of Palencia. We have seen also how a word from our Lord dispelled the cloud which hung over her.

Two daughters of Doña Catharine of Tolosa received the religious habit at Palencia, and S. Teresa then gave to their mother, who brought them thither, a promise that, as soon as the foundation of Soria should be concluded, she would proceed at once to Burgos.

The consent of the Archbishop, who was a native of Avila, and who had just been translated from the Bishopric of the Canaries to the Archdiocese of Burgos, had been obtained at S. Teresa's request, by her faithful friend the Bishop of Palencia. The Archbishop's reply to his application had been most gracious. "He would grant it," he said, "with all his heart;" "For even when he was Bishop of the Canaries," says S. Teresa, "he had desired to have a monastery of our Order, knowing well how fervently our Lord is served by our sisters : he also said that he had seen one of our monasteries in the place where he was born, and that he knew me well. The Bishop accordingly told me I need not wait for a written licence, for that his Grace highly approved the undertaking ; and that as the Council of Trent does not state that the licence must be in writing, I might consider the matter as already approved and settled by his verbal consent.

" The Archbishop wrote to me, assuring me that he heartily desired that I should come to Burgos. At the same time he wrote to the Bishop of Palencia, placing the management of the affair in his hands, and informing him that it was absolutely necessary to obtain the consent of the city of Burgos. His advice was that I should go thither, and try first to obtain this consent, the refusal of which, however, would in no way prevent him granting us leave. He said that he gave this advice because, having been at Avila at the time of the foundation of the monastery of

S. Joseph, he remembered that great uproar and opposition had taken place there, and that, therefore, he wished to prevent the like from happening again : adding, that in case of the consent of the city being refused, the convent must be endowed.

" The Bishop of Palencia naturally considered the matter settled, and, accordingly, sent me word that I should go to Burgos as soon as possible. But I thought I perceived some want of courage in the Archbishop ; and when I wrote to him, I thanked his Grace for the favour which he had done me, but at the same time I intimated that I thought it better to make the foundation without the consent of the city, than against it, which might raise some opposition to his Grace.

" I seemed to foresee that we could rely but little on the Archbishop, in case we should meet with any opposition to our procuring the licence. I also foresaw difficulties on account of the different opinions which usually arise on such matters. I therefore wrote to the Bishop of Palencia, begging him to let things rest for the present, winter being close at hand, and my infirmities so great that I should hardly be able to endure the cold of Burgos.

" I did not allude to my doubts about the Archbishop, because the Bishop had been already displeased by his making difficulties after having formerly displayed such goodwill in the matter ; and I did not wish to cause any disagreement between friends. I therefore left Soria for Avila, little thinking then that I should so soon go to Burgos; my presence in the monastery of S. Joseph at Avila being very necessary at that time."

The work of the foundation of Burgos was meanwhile advancing in other hands. "There lived," says S. Teresa, "in the city of Burgos, a devout widow, named Catharine de Tolosa, a native of Biscay; to recount her virtues of penance, prayer, and alms-deeds, her charity, prudence, and courage, would take too long a time. Some four years ago she had placed two daughters in our monastery at Valladolid, waiting to place two others in that of Palencia, as soon as it should be founded, and I received them from her hands before I left that city. All the four succeeded well (having been educated by such a mother); indeed, they seemed to me to be so many angels; she gave them good portions, as she is exceed-ingly wealthy, and no less liberal than rich. When we were in Palencia, we considered the Archbishop's licence as certain, so that there seemed no occasion to take any further precautions; accordingly I requested the lady to look out for a hired house, in order to establish the convent, and to have a grate and a turn put up at my expense, without intending her to be at any expense herself. She desired this foundation so much, that she acutely felt any delay; so after I had returned to Avila, then thinking, as I say, nothing about the matter, she was not idle, and thinking nothing was wanting but the consent of the city, she endeavoured to procure it without saying a word to any one. She managed the matter so well, that the licence was obtained from the magistrates and sent to the Archbishop in writing. Doña Catharine, when she had taken the first steps in the business, wrote to tell me how it was going on, but I took it for a joke, knowing with what difficulty poor monasteries without endowment are admitted, and because I neither knew nor suspected that she would pledge herself as she did.

"One day within the Octave of S. Martin, I was recommending the matter to our Lord, and thinking what I should do if the licence were granted, since it appeared impossible for me to go to Burgos with so many infirmities, which are always increased by cold, the weather being then very severe. It seemed to me rashness to undertake such a long journey, having but just returned from one so rough as that from Soria; nor did I believe the Father Provincial would let me go. So I began to think that the Prioress of Palencia might go instead, for, everything being made smooth, there seemed to be no prospect of much difficulty. While I was thus musing, and quite determined not to go, our Lord spoke these words to me, whereby I understood that leave had been granted:—'Do not regard this cold, for I am the True Heat: the devil employs all his power to hinder this foundation; use your power for My sake that it may be accomplished, and neglect not to go in person, for you will be of great service.'

"On hearing these words I altered my mind; for, though nature sometimes shows repugnance in difficult undertakings, yet never have I lost my resolution to suffer for this great God; and I always beseech Him not to notice these feelings of weakness, but to command me whatever He shall please, since, by His assistance, I·shall not fail to do it. There was then deep snow, but that which discouraged me most was my want of health; for if I had had that, it appeared as if I could despise every difficulty. This, my great infirmity, often afflicted me in this foundation. The cold was afterwards so little (at least that which I suffered), that truly I felt it no more than I had done at Toledo. Our Lord, who faithfully kept His word in this matter, had given me to understand that I should meet with great opposition, and I knew not from whom nor whence, for Catharine de Tolosa told me she had secured the house in which she lived for us, and the city was favourable, as was also the Arch-bishop; and hence I could not imagine whence the opposition would come which the devils were to raise, for I never had the least doubt but that the words I heard were from God. He, however, gives greater light to superiors; for when I wrote on the subject to our Father Provincial, he did not hinder me from going, but asked me if I had the Archbishop's licence in writing. I told him that they had written to me from Burgos, that the matter had been settled with him, that leave had been granted by the city, and that, as the Archbishop had given his approval on that condition, his sanction could not be doubted.

"The Father Provincial wished to accompany us to this foundation, partly because he was not then occupied, having finished preaching the Advent, partly because he had to visit Soria, which he had not seen since its foundation, and partly in order to take care of me on the journey, for the season was extremely cold, and I was old and infirm, and he thought my life still of some little importance."

The holy Mother was accompanied also by her beloved Teresita. Several of her letters about this time express a tender anxiety concerning the health of this cherished child.

"I think," she writes to F. Gracian, "that I must take my little Teresa with me, and the doctor thinks I shall do wisely. She grieves so bitterly at the thought of my departure that I do not think it right to leave her. Her heart is sad, and if anything were to happen, I do not know what she would do."

It would seem as if the child's loving heart had been overshadowed by a presentiment of that separation, the approach of which had certainly been revealed to S. Teresa. A few days afterwards she writes again—

"My niece Teresita is already better; I think we may now feel easy about her."

To Teresita's brother Laurence she writes, a few days afterwards, of her great desire to be professed, adding: "Do you know who is my greatest consolation? Our little Sister Teresa of Jesus. She is already a woman formed, and grows daily in excellence. You may well follow her counsels. The letter which she has written to you rejoices my heart. It is truly God who speaks by her, and she faithfully practises all she says. May that God uphold her with His hand! She is an occasion of edification to us all; and to all her other merits, she unites such sound sense as will render her capable of any work for God. Do not fail to write to her, for she is very much neglected in her solitude. When I remember all the affection which her father bore her, and his tender care for her, it grieves me to see that nobody thinks of her now. Don Francis, indeed, loves her well, but this is all that he can do."

In the same letter S. Teresa congratulates her nephew Laurence on his marriage, and asks assistance for the convent of S. Joseph's at Avila, and for her sister Jane d'Ahumada, then struggling with great pecuniary difficulties.

"The only one," she says, "who wants no money seems to be myself. Only pray to God that He would accomplish His Holy Will in me, and make great Saints of you all. Everything else quickly passes away. . . . Remember, my son, that, as you bear the name of so good a father, you are bound to follow his example."

The journey to Burgos was one of great difficulty, and even danger.

"The company of our Father Provincial was certainly," says S. Teresa, "a special Providence of God; for the roads were in such a state on account of the heavy rains, that it was quite necessary for him and his companion to go forward and examine by which way we could pass, and to help to pull the waggons out of the ruts, especially between Palencia and Burgos, where it required great courage to go forward. But the truth is, our Lord had told me we might go, and bade me not to fear, for He would be with us, though I did not mention this to our Father Provincial; but it consoled me in all the great afflictions and dangers which befell us, and especially in the passage near Burgos called the *Bridges*, where the water had overflowed so much, and in so many places, that the bridges could not be seen, nor could we tell whither we were going, for everything around seemed to be water, and very deep it was on both sides.

"Indeed, it seemed great rashness to pass that way, and especially with the waggons, for, had they swerved ever so little on either side, they would have been lost; and one of them was on the point of being swallowed up. We had, indeed, taken a guide from an inn that was near, who knew this passage; still the danger was imminent. And we had great difficulties as to our night's lodging, for we could not make the usual day's journey on account of the badness of the roads. The waggons often stuck in the mire, so that we were obliged to take the horses from one to pull out another. Our fathers had to arrange all this; and their trouble was the greater, as we chanced to meet with young drivers who were very careless. But the company of the Father Provincial was a great comfort, for he took care of everything; and he was also so cheerful, that nothing seemed to trouble him, and what would have seemed great to another appeared little to him; but at the Bridges even he seemed afraid. And who would not have feared on entering into a world of waters without a path, or without a boat? Though our Lord had strengthened me, yet I could not help feeling afraid: what then must my companions have felt? We were eight in all; two who were to return with me, five who were to remain at Burgos (four being choir-nuns, and one a lay sister). They all went to confession before passing the Bridges, and having asked my blessing, went on repeating the Creed. In order to comfort them, I showed no fear, but spoke cheerfully to them thus : ' Courage, my daughters ; what greater happiness can you wish, than, if need be, here to become martyrs for the love of our Lord? Let me alone, for I will go first; and if I be drowned, I earnestly beseech you not to pass on, but return back to the inn.' It pleased our Lord, that by my going first, I secured a passage for the rest.

"I had a violent sore throat, which attacked me on my journey to Valladolid; nor could I shake off the fever; so that I was in great suffering, which made me less sensible than I should otherwise have been of the dangers of this journey. The malady has continued till now, which is the end of June ; and though not so violent, yet it is very painful. All were well pleased when the danger was passed, and took pleasure in looking back upon it afterwards. Suffering through obedience is a great and beautiful thing, especially when practised as it is by these nuns.

" By this terrible road we at length reached Burgos. The Father Provincial wished us first to visit a holy crucifix, which is held in great veneration in that city, to recommend the foundation to our Lord, as also to wait for nightfall, for it was yet too early to enter Burgos. It was on a Friday, January 26, being the day after the Conversion of S. Paul. We had determined to open the house immediately, and I had letters with me from many eminent persons, begging their friends and relations to assist us ; and

so they did, for on the following day they all came to
see, as also the magistrates of the city, who told
us they in no way regretted having granted the
licence, but were exceedingly rejoiced at our coming,
desiring to know in what way they could serve me.
As our only fear had been with regard to the city,
we now considered everything settled, and, under
cover of the darkness and the heavy rain, we reached
the house of the good Catharine de Tolosa without
observation.   We had intended to acquaint the
Archbishop immediately of our arrival, in order that
the first Mass might be said as soon as possible, as I
was accustomed to do in most places; but the heavy
rain prevented us from doing so here.   That night we
rested very well, being most kindly entertained by
that holy lady; but having stood by a great fire to
dry our clothes, though the chimney was large, I
became so ill, that the next morning I could not lift
up my head: so my bed was brought close to a
window, before which a curtain was hung; and I spoke,
though with great difficulty, to those whom I was
obliged to see on business through a grille fixed in
the window.

" Early in the morning the Father Provincial went
to ask the Archbishop's blessing, thinking there was
nothing else to be done.   He found him so much
changed, and so greatly displeased at my coming, as
if it had been without his leave, and he had never
been consulted on the matter.   He told the Father
how exceedingly angry he was with me.   And yet he
admitted that he had commanded me to come, but
said he only meant that I should come alone to settle
the business with him, not that I should come with
so many nuns.   God deliver us from the displeasure the
Archbishop fell into when he was told that the business
had already been settled with the city, as he had

requested himself, and that nothing more remained to be done, for that the Bishop of Palencia had told me that nothing further was necessary, believing that the Archbishop desired the foundation, and that the only doubt was as to the consent of the city. All that we said, however, was of little use. But it was plainly God's will that the house should be founded, for, as his Grace said afterwards, had we informed him of our coming at first he would have forbidden it.

"At last he dismissed the Father Provincial with this answer, that on no account would he grant us leave unless we had a revenue and a house of our own, and that it would be better for us to return. The roads were indeed excellent, and the weather beautiful for another journey! Oh! my Lord, how certain is he to be repaid with a great affliction who does Thee some service! and what a precious reward it is to those who truly love Thee, if we could only understand its real value! But we did not wish for it just then. The Archbishop told us also, that the money which was to purchase a house and serve as an endowment must not be taken from any portions which might be brought in by the religious. Now an endowment could not be obtained in any other way, times being as they were. Still I was confident that all was for the best, and that these were impediments put in the way by the devil in order to prevent the foundation, which God would not fail to prosper.

"The Provincial returned very cheerful, for he was not at all disturbed by the Archbishop's answer, God so ordaining, that he might not reprove me for not having procured the licence in writing, as he had advised me to do. One of our friends advised us to ask the Archbishop's leave for Mass to be said in the house, in order to avoid our going through the streets, which were very dirty, in our sandals. The

house in which we were had a very good convenient
hall, which for more than ten years had been used by
the Society of Jesus as a church, when they first came
to Burgos ; we accordingly considered that this place
would do very well for us till we should have a house
of our own, but the Archbishop could never be persuaded to allow us to hear Mass in it, though two
Canons begged of his Grace to grant us this favour.
All that we could obtain from him was, that when we
should have a revenue we might make a foundation
there till a house should be purchased ; and that,
moreover, we must give security that we would purchase one and would remove thither. We soon obtained
security, and Catharine de Tolosa was ready to answer
for the endowment.

" More than three weeks were thus spent ; and in
the mean time we never heard Mass except on Festivals very early in the morning, and I was very ill all
the time with a burning fever. But Catharine was
so kind to us that she entertained us all for a month
in her own house, as if she had been the mother of us
all. We were placed in an apartment by ourselves
where we could be quiet and recollected.

" The Father Provincial and his companions lodged
in a house of one of his friends, named Doctor Manso,
who was Canon of the Cathedral. Our good Father
was greatly disturbed at all these delays, and yet he
did not like to leave us.

" The endowment and security having been settled,
the Archbishop said the documents must be given to
his secretary, who would immediately arrange the
business. The devil did not fail to interfere herein ;
for after we had considered everything, and thought
there was no further obstacle, and almost a month
had been spent in prevailing on the Archbishop to be
content with what had been done, the secretary sent

me a note, saying that leave would not be granted until we had a house of our own; that the Archbishop did not wish us to make a foundation where we were, because the place was damp and the street noisy : he raised I know not how many difficulties about the endowment, which, he said, was not sufficiently secure (as if the business had only then begun), although it had been in agitation for more than a month. When the Father Provincial heard this, he was much displeased, and so were we all; for, to purchase a site for a monastery every one knew required time. He was also grieved to see us obliged to go out to hear Mass for (though the church was not a great distance, and we heard Mass in a chapel where no one could see us), both to his Reverence and to ourselves, it was the greatest trial we had to endure.

" At this time we had all but determined to return home. But I could not endure this thought, when I remembered what our Lord had said to me, viz., *That I should labour for His sake;* and so I felt assured that the work would be accomplished; and should have felt no further trouble about it, but that the sadness of our Father Provincial troubled me, and I was sorry he had come with us. Being in this affliction, and my companions in still greater, though their trouble did not disturb me so much as that of our Father, our Lord said these words to me, one day when I was in prayer :—' Now, Teresa, be firm.' I immediately endeavoured more earnestly to persuade the Father Provincial to depart and leave us (and His Majesty had already put the thought into his mind), for it was now Lent, and he was engaged to preach. He and some friends prevailed on certain persons to give us some rooms in the hospital of the Conception, where the most Blessed Sacrament was reserved, and where also Mass was said every day. . . . The

2 E

hospital was at a great distance from Doña Catharine's house ; but she came to see us almost daily, and sent us everything we wanted. She had much to suffer for her kindness, for people spread all manner of reports against her, which, had she not been a most courageous soul, would have been sufficient to make her give up everything. It troubled me much to see what she suffered, because, although she generally concealed it, yet at other times she was unable to do so, especially when it touched her conscience. So great was her perfection, that, under all her great provocations, she was never heard to utter any word offensive to God. They said she would go to hell ; and that, having children, it was wonderful how she could act as she did. She did everything by the advice of learned and spiritual persons ; for even though she had desired to do otherwise, I would not, for anything in the world, have allowed her to do a thing which she ought not to have done, to bring about the foundation of a thousand monasteries, far less for the sake of one. She answered all with such prudence, and with such patience, that it appeared evident God had taught her the art of satisfying some, and of bearing with others, and that He gave her courage to endure everything.

" After the departure of the Father Provincial I felt more at ease, for, as I have said, his affliction was my greatest trouble. He left directions with me to purchase a house—a thing very difficult to effect, for hitherto none could be found to suit us. Our friends all agreed not to speak a word on the subject to the Archbishop until we should have a house of our own. His Grace always said he desired this foundation more earnestly than any one else, and I believe it, for he is a good Christian, who would say nothing but the truth. In his actions, however, he did not manifest such a desire, because he required things which were impossible according to our means. All this was but a scheme of the devil, to prevent the foundation. But, O Lord! how plainly do we see Thou art All-powerful! The same means which he took to ruin our work, were used by Thee for its accomplishment. May Thy name be for ever blessed!"

At last, on the vigil of S. Joseph, a suitable house was found; and while the holy Mother was considering about the purchase of it, our Lord said to her, "Why do you stay for money?" The sisters had earnestly begged S. Joseph to give them a house before his Feast, and their prayer was granted.

"It was evident," says S. Teresa, "that our Lord had kept this house for Himself, for we found almost everything ready fitted for us. When I saw how everything was, as it were, made for us, it seemed to me a dream that all had been accomplished so quickly. Oh! how well has our Lord repaid us for all we suffered, by bringing us to such a delightful place!—for so it is with respect to the garden, the prospect, and the water. May He be for ever blessed! Amen.

"The Archbishop was immediately informed of what had passed, and was much pleased that we had succeeded so well, thinking that his pertinacity had been the cause of it; and so it had. I wrote to tell his Grace how much pleased I was that he was satisfied, and that I would make haste to fit up the house, that so he might grant me all the favours I wanted. Having sent this letter, I made haste to the house, having had an intimation that our entrance might be delayed till certain papers should be drawn up. We went accordingly, though the tenant was in the house (and there was some trouble in getting him out), and took possession of one of the apartments.

"I was immediately told that the Archbishop was

2 E 2

highly offended with me for so doing. I endeavoured
to pacify him as well as I could; and being a good
man, though sometimes angry, his displeasure soon
passed away. He was displeased also when he heard
that we had put up a grate and a turn without his
leave. I wrote to him, stating I did not wish to
act independently, but that in religious houses these
things were necessary; and that I had not attempted
so much as to set up a cross, which was the truth.
But in spite of all the good-will which he expressed
towards us, he would not grant us the license. He
came to see the house, and was much pleased with it,
expressing great kindness for us, and giving us good
hope that he would grant the license when certain
writings should be drawn up, on the part of Catharine
de Tolosa. Doctor Manso, a friend of our Father
Provincial, who was very intimate with the Archbishop, watched an opportunity to induce him to
grant us the license without further delay, for he was
much troubled to see us so situated; because, though
in the house in which we were there was a chapel,
the Archbishop would not allow Mass to be said there;
so on Festivals and Sundays we were obliged for a
whole month to go and hear Mass in a church which,
happily, was near at hand. There seems to have
been no other cause for the Archbishop's refusal,
except that our Lord wished us to suffer. I did not
feel this trial so much, but there was a nun who
trembled, when passing through the streets, with the
pain it caused her. Oh, how impossible it is to relate
how much Catharine de Tolosa suffered at that time!
But she bore everything with such patience as astonished me; and she was unwearied in her charity
to us. She furnished all things necessary for the
house, such as beds and many other things, for she
had plenty of these at home; and she would rather

her own house should want something than that we should need anything. Some others who have founded monasteries for us have given much more wealth, but not one has ever endured the tenth part of what she has suffered; and but for her children, she would have given us all she had : and so anxious was she to see the foundation accomplished, that whatever she did for this object seemed but little to her.

"When I saw delay upon delay, I wrote to the Bishop of Palencia, begging him to write again to the Archbishop. He was exceedingly displeased with his Grace, for he considered what the Archbishop did to us as done to himself, and the greatest wonder was that the Archbishop never imagined he had wronged us in anything. The Bishop of Palencia sent me an open letter to the Archbishop, which had I given to him, would have ruined everything. Accordingly, Dr. Manso, who was my confessor and adviser, would not allow me to present it; for though it was very courteous, it told his Grace some truths, which, considering the Archbishop's temper, would only have made him more angry, for he was already not well pleased at some things the Bishop had told him, though once they were great friends. He complained to me, that as by the death of our Lord those became friends who were enemies before, so I had made enemies of those who were once friends, the Bishop of Palencia and himself. I answered him that thereby he might see what kind of person I was. To my thinking, I had acted with the greatest caution, in order that they might not fall out with each other. I therefore requested the Bishop again, using the best arguments I could think of, to write another milder letter to his Grace, representing to him the service he might do our Lord thereby. He did what I asked, which was no small effort; for when he saw it would be doing

God a service and me a kindness (for indeed he had
always been kind to me), he wrote again, though he
told me at the same time that nothing which he had
hitherto done for the Order had cost him so much as
writing that letter. It proved so effectual, that the
Archbishop at last granted us the license. It came one
day when the sisters were feeling more than usually discouraged, and Catharine de Tolosa fairly out of heart;
but it seems our Lord wished us to be most depressed
just at the time when He was about to console us; for
I, who had never lost hope, felt almost hopeless the
evening before.

" Blessed and praised be His holy Name, for ever
and ever ! Amen.

" The Archbishop gave Doctor Manso leave to say
Mass the next day, and to place the Blessed Sacrament in the church; and so he said the first Mass;
high Mass being celebrated by the Father Prior of
S. Paul, who was a Dominican (to which Order ours
is much indebted, as also to the Society of Jesus).
All our friends were exceedingly glad, and almost the
whole city likewise, for the people were much grieved
to see us so ill treated; the conduct of the Archbishop seeming to them so unjust, that often I was
more troubled at what I heard against him, than at
what I suffered from him. The joy of the good
Catharine de Tolosa and of all the sisters was so
great as to excite devotion in me, and I said to our
Lord, " What do these servants of Thine desire, but
to serve Thee and to become prisoners for Thy sake ? "
No one who has not experienced it can understand
the pleasure which we feel when, in a new foundation,
we find ourselves in an enclosure which no secular
can enter; for however much we may love them, it is
a far greater pleasure to us to be alone with God. As
fishes which have been drawn out of a river cannot

live except they be thrown in again, those souls who are accustomed to quench their thirst in the pure waters of their Spouse, pant and faint when they are drawn out by the nets of the world, and cannot truly live till they return to their native element. This I observed in all the sisters; and I know by experience that those nuns who desire to go abroad among seculars, or to converse much with them, have either never found that living water of which our Lord spoke to the Samaritan woman, or their Spouse has hid Himself from them; and that most justly, since they are not content with Him alone. This, I fear arises from one of two causes: either because they have not embraced their state solely for God, or because, after they have entered it, they do not appreciate the great favour which God has bestowed upon them in choosing them for Himself, and delivering them from being subject to a mortal man who too often brings them to a premature death; and God grant he may not also cause the death of their souls! Oh! my Spouse, true God and true Man, is such a favour as this to be undervalued by us? Let us thank Him, my sisters, for what He has done for us, and never let us be tired of praising so great a King and Lord, Who has prepared for us a kingdom that will never pass away, to reward us for these slight and passing sufferings, and those, too, accompanied by a thousand consolations. May He be blessed for ever! Amen."

CHAPTER XXVII.

1582.

AFTER the happy conclusion of the foundation of Burgos, the new convent was threatened with destruction by the sudden swelling of the rapid river Alanzor, on which the city is built. S. Teresa was ill at the time, and the peril is thus described by her tender nurse, Anne of S. Bartholomew :—

" I remember that our holy Mother was suffering one day from great faintness, and I could get nothing for her but a mouthful of bread steeped in water. Our house was built just outside the city by the side of the river, which had so far overflowed its banks, that no one could get at us to bring us any assistance, nor could we go out to seek it. The waters raged with such violence that the house, which was very old, shook as if it were about to fall. Our Mother's cell was the worst in the house ; you could see the stars through the roof, and the cold, which was most acute in that city, pierced through the crevices of the broken walls. The river had swelled to such a degree, that the waters reached the first floor of the house. We carried the Blessed Sacrament upstairs, and recited the Litanies continually, expecting every moment to be swallowed up. We remained in this great peril without being able to get any rest, or to take the smallest mouthful of food, because all our little store was buried beneath the waters. Our trouble was so great, that we never thought of getting anything for our Mother to eat. At last she said to me : ' My child, I am fainting ; see if you can find me a little bread, if it be but a single mouthful.' My heart ached to hear her. At last one of the novices waded waist-deep in the water, and got us a loaf of bread ; and a piece of this was all we could give our Saint in her urgent need. Our destruction would have been inevitable, but that our Lord sent two men to our aid. They swam to the house, and diving under the water, broke open the doors to let it out of the rooms. It left such a quantity of stones behind it as filled more than eight carts. Our holy Mother's room shook as if it must fall, and the cold, as I said, was so intense that we took our two coverlets, and put one over and the other under her in the bed—a thing she would never have permitted if she had been aware of it. I stayed near her, and when she called me I pretended that I had just risen, and she said to me, ' My child, you have come very quickly.' "

It was the belief of the Archbishop and of many others in the city, that it had been saved from destruction by the presence of S. Teresa.

The holy Mother was now anxious to return to Avila, and yet reluctant to leave her daughters at Burgos unprovided with subjects, or with temporal support, for, in consideration for the family difficulties of Doña Catharine of Tolosa, who had treated them with such noble generosity, they had formally renounced their claim to the endowment which she had made in their favour, reserving only the portions of her three daughters. One day, after Communion, our Lord tranquillised the fears of His servant by these words : " Why dost thou doubt and fear ? This is all provided for. Thou mayst depart in peace."

In obedience to these words, S. Teresa left Burgos in the beginning of August, 1582. On the 3rd of· that month she arrived at Palencia, whence she proceeded to Valladolid. From that place she writes, on September 1, to F. Gracian, who suddenly, and to her regret, had left Castile for Andalusia. This is her last letter to him, and perhaps the presentiment that they were not to meet again on earth throws a shade of sadness over it. She had been grieved also by hearing him blamed; "a thing," she says in one of her former letters, "which I cannot bear." It is remarkable that the very accusation, which was afterwards brought against him by his enemies, of acting without counsel, and keeping those capable of advising him at a distance, is noticed here.

"JESUS.

"May the grace of the Holy Spirit be with your Reverence!

"My Father,—The pleasure of often hearing from you, great as it is, cannot make up to me for your absence, though I have heard with much joy that you are well, and that the air of Seville agrees with you. God grant that your health may improve more and more! I have received all your letters. The reasons which determined you to go do not seem to me sufficient. You might have arranged all that was necessary here. It would have been but two months longer for the monasteries of Andalusia to wait, and in that time you might have regulated everything relating to our houses in Castile. I know not why, but I am so much grieved at your departure in these circumstances, that I have no heart to write to you. Therefore I have not written to you before; nor should I write to you to-day, were I not absolutely obliged to do so. . . . . My niece Teresa is well; but what was her grief when she learned that you were not coming!" (probably to her profession) : "we took care to keep it from her until now. For one reason I am glad of it, that she may learn how little right we have to depend upon anything but God. This reflection has not been without its use to myself. I sent you, Reverend Father, a letter which F. Antony of Jesus has written

to me. He is friendly with me again, and indeed he
has always been so in heart; and if he will but communicate with me, all will go well. And even though
he should feel some displeasure against you and me,
this will be no reason for sending another to Rome
in his place" (on the affairs of the Order). "I am
surprised that you should have thought of such a
thing, and no less so that you should think of establishing a house at Rome, when you have not subjects
enough for your convents in this country. The absence
of F. Nicolas, now at Rome, is a great loss to you.
It seems to me impossible that you can do everything
alone. F. John Cuevas, with whom I have spoken on
the subject several times, said so to me the other day.
He has the greatest esteem for you, and the most
ardent desire that you should succeed in your office of
Provincial. I was quite touched by his attachment to
you. He added that you were acting against certain
regulations, which prescribe that, in the absence of
his companion, the Father Provincial shall choose
another: I am not sure whether he did not say, with
the consent of the Priors and of the Province. Moses,
continued he, chose—I do not remember how many
men he said—to govern the people of Israel under
him. I represented to him that you had no one whom
you could choose, and that you had hardly Superiors
enough for your monasteries. He replied that this
office was of far greater importance. Since my arrival
in this place I have been told that your Reverence is
accused of not liking to have persons of merit and
capacity near you. Though I am persuaded that you
have no thought of the kind, I think it best before
the meeting of the Chapter, to give you warning of
what is said, that you may be on your guard, lest you
do anything which may give occasion to such a suspicion. For the love of God, be careful on this point,

and, above all, take care how you preach in Andalusia. I have never liked you to stay long in that country. What you have told me of the persecutions which some have suffered there, have so much increased my fear that the like may befall you, that I cease not to pray to God not to suffer such a misfortune to happen in my days. You say well that the devil never sleeps, and we ought always to be on our guard against his devices."

The Saint goes on to speak of a matter which had given her great uneasiness with regard to the convent of Salamanca, the Prioress there having set her heart upon the purchase of a new house, which, in S. Teresa's judgment, was a very imprudent step.

"The affair of Salamanca has cost me many anxious moments. On account of Teresa's profession, I cannot go thither at present, for I could not take her with me, far less could I leave her here. I have, therefore, hired the house for a year longer, in order to satisfy the Prioress, in which I hope I may have succeeded. This Prioress acts like a true woman; she negotiates the matter as if you had given her full permission to do so, telling F. Augustine, on one hand, that all she does is by my direction, and on the other, giving me to understand that this father is following your orders. There is some snare of the devil here which I cannot unravel, for I do not believe her to be capable of falsehood. I would willingly believe that her great desire to purchase this house has somewhat disturbed her judgment. . . . . Allow me, Father, to give you a piece of advice; and that is, never to trust to any women, however religious and holy they may be, when you see they have set their hearts upon anything; for the desire of carrying their point will cause them to invent a hundred bad reasons, which they think unanswerable. It would be far better for our sisters of Salamanca to buy a small house, like poor people, and there establish themselves in humility, than to run into debt to purchase a large one. If anything, Reverend Father, would console me for your absence just now, it is that you are out of the way of this terrible entanglement, for I would rather bear the pain of it alone than share it with you."

The last of S. Teresa's letters which remains to us was written to the Prioress of Soria, on September 15, when she was just on the point of starting from Valladolid. "I am so overwhelmed with business, that my head turns. May God direct it all to His glory! Amen. . . . I can say no more now, because we are just setting off for Medina del Campo. My health is as usual." The postscript of this letter mentions the Saint's arrival at Medina del Campo, having time only to say that the journey from Valladolid had been prosperous.

S. Teresa had long been aware of her approaching death. Eight years before, the year had been revealed to her in which she should be released, and she had marked the date down on a page of her Breviary. When she left Segovia for the last time, she told some of her daughters, as she took leave of them, that they should see her no more in this life, and that her departure was at hand. The Prioress of Medina, Agnes of Jesus, said to her one day, " Is not your Reverence now fifty-nine ? " and Teresa, having answered in the affirmative, was heard by a novice present saying to herself, " From fifty-nine to sixty-eight." During her illness at Salamanca, in 1579, she said to the doctor, who was recommending various remedies, that she had it in her mind to take no more medicine, and being asked why, she replied, " For the four years which I have to live it is not worth while." It is said

also that she had foretold to the Duchess of Alva that
she should die in that city. With these thoughts in
her mind, we may imagine with what tenderness she
took leave of the religious of the convents which she
was now visiting for the last time, and how deeply her
last counsels sank into their hearts. The sisters at
Burgos remarked the especial affection with which she
bade them farewell, and, contrary to her custom,
allowed them to kiss her hand. The nuns of Valladolid
have happily preserved the words which she addressed
to them on her departure from that house, three weeks
before her death. " My daughters, I leave you full
of consolation at the perfection of your house, and
the poverty and mutual charity which I have seen
among you. If you continue in this course, God will
greatly bless you. Let each of you endeavour so to
live as not to fall short by one hair's breadth of anything which belongs to religious perfection. Never
go through the duties of your state simply from custom, but endeavour daily to make heroic acts, and
continually to rise to higher perfection. Always
cherish great desires, for from these you will derive
great profit, even though you should never have an
opportunity of carrying them into execution."

On her arrival at Medina, the holy Mother found
F. Antony of Jesus, who was then Vicar Provincial of
Castile, waiting for her with a message from the
Duchess of Alva, who earnestly desired to see her, in
order to receive advice and consolation under some
spiritual trial. S. Teresa, as we have seen, had reasons
for desiring to proceed at once to Avila, but she received the communication from F. Antony as a message
from our Lord, and perhaps recognised in it the veri-
fication of the intimation which she had long ago
received that she was to die at Alva. The Duchess of
Alva had sent an easy carriage, that the journey might

be less distressing to her already enfeebled frame. But it would seem that on the 19th, when she left Medina, the Saint had been already attacked by her last fatal malady; for on arriving at a little village near Pegnaranda, she fainted away. "We were obliged to pass the night at that place," says the venerable M. Anne of S. Bartholomew, "and the Saint feeling very weak, said to me, 'My child, give me something to eat, for I am sinking.' I had nothing but a few dried figs, which I gave her, and she ate one, though she was very feverish. At the same time I gave four reals to a woman to get me two eggs at whatever price they might be; but she came back and told me that none were to be had even for money. I looked at the Saint, who seemed nearly dead, and began to weep. It would be difficult to say what I then felt. My heart seemed ready to burst when I found I could do nothing to relieve her. But she consoled me herself. 'Be not grieved, my child,' said she, 'for these figs are very good, and more than many poor people can get. It is God who permits all these things.'"

On the following day, the Vigil of S. Matthew, they stopped to dine at another miserable village, where nothing could be found but some herbs cooked with onions, which the Saint could scarcely swallow. She arrived at 6 o'clock at Alva, where the Prioress and religious, seeing her state of exhaustion, obliged her to go to bed immediately. "God help me, my children," she said; "how weary I feel! I have not gone to bed so early for twenty years past. I bless God that I have come to you to be nursed."

The physicians who were summoned judged her sickness to be mortal. Yet she arose as usual the following morning to Mass, and having received Holy Communion, she visited all parts of the convent, and took part in the exercises of the day as far as her

weakness would allow. She remained in the same
state for about another week. Though scarcely able
to rise from weakness and the extremity of the fever,
she daily recited her office, and daily received Holy
Communion. But on the Feast of S. Michael her
strength failed her; she was obliged to go to bed after
Holy Communion, and asked to be placed in an infirmary
on another floor, in which there was a grille looking
upon the high altar of the church, whence she could
hear Mass.

All her daughters watched over her with affectionate
care, and most of all her inseparable companion, Anne
of S. Bartholomew, who, in the extremity of her
affliction, could scarcely bear to leave her for a
moment. The Saint received all their care as if she
had been a stranger who had no sort of claim upon
their charity. The Duchess of Alva came to visit
her, accounting it a privilege to be allowed to share
with the religious the office of watching and waiting
upon her.

The Saint passed the whole night between the 1st
and 2nd of October in prayer. In the morning she
called Anne of S. Bartholomew, and told her plainly
that the hour of her departure was at hand, and that
she had not revealed it to her before for fear of afflicting
her.

" Her words," says the venerable Mother, " pierced
my heart, both because she was to die at Alva, because
I was to survive her whom I loved so well, and who
loved me in return, and because, seeing her to be so
closely united to our Lord, I felt great consolation in
living so near to her."

The nuns then called to mind certain extraordinary
phenomena which they had observed just before her
arrival. A bright light had been seen over the cell
in which she afterwards expired, and in other parts

of the convent, and sweet but mournful voices heard, the meaning of which they now understood but too well. Three days before her death the holy Mother sent for F. Antony of Jesus to hear her confession, and to strengthen her in her last agony. Having heard her confession, the venerable old man besought her earnestly, in the presence of her children, that since she was so necessary to the Order she would entreat our Lord to grant her a longer life. But she replied that she was no longer needed in this world, and that the time ordained by God for her departure was come.

F. Antony was still in the room when the Saint was suddenly seized with a fainting fit, which looked like death. The physician, having been hastily called, ordered that she should immediately be removed to the room in which she had been before, on account of the cold of that in which she was now lying. Some medicines were administered, which she took with a smile that marked her sense of their inutility. It was then proposed that cupping-glasses should be applied —a painful and useless remedy, to which, with her habitual desire of suffering, she submitted with joy.

On October 3, at five o'clock in the evening, she asked to receive the Holy Viaticum. She could no longer move except by the help of two religious. Whilst waiting for the priest to bring her the Blessed Sacrament, she joined her hands, as if in supplication, and thus addressed the weeping nuns who were gathered round her bed: "My daughters and my sisters, I beseech you, for the love of God, faithfully to observe the rule and constitutions of our Order; to practise them with all perfection, and to be obedient to your superiors." Then she added, "Forget the bad example which this unfaithful religious has set you, and forgive it." She was answered only by sighs and tears.

2 F

As soon as the priest entered with the Holy Viaticum, she, who had been unable to move in her bed without the help of two of her daughters, sprang up with wonderful agility, as if she would have thrown herself from it, to adore her present God. Her face shone suddenly with so glorious a light and so unearthly a beauty, that those who stood around could scarcely endure its lustre, and the love of her full heart broke forth in words like these : " O Lord, the hour is come at last that I have looked for through all these long, long years. Yes, it is time that I should come to Thee. It is time, my Lord and my Love, that I should depart hence. Let Thy most holy will be done. The end of that weary exile is come at last, and my soul rejoices in Thee, Whom it has desired so ardently and so long." Then she thanked God that He had made her a child of the Catholic Church, and in the bosom of that Church had given her grace to die ; repeating many times, over and over again, " After all, O Lord, I am a child of the Church,"—a thought which seemed to fill her with unspeakable joy. She then besought God to pardon her sins, and asked her companions to pray for her, adding that she hoped to be saved by the merits of Jesus Christ.

After the ceremony was over, the religious asked her to speak to them some words of edification ; but she simply recommended them, from time to time, perfectly to observe their rule and constitutions, and faithfully to obey their superiors. Her most frequent ejaculations were these words of the *Miserere :* " Sacrificium Deo spiritus contribulatus ; cor contritum et humiliatum Deus non despicies. Ne projicias me a facie tuâ, et Spiritum Sanctum tuum ne auferas a me. Cor mundum crea in me, Deus." The verse which was most frequently on her lips was the following : " Cor contritum et humiliatum Deus non despicies."

She continued repeating these words as long as she retained the power of speech.

At nine o'clock she received the Sacrament of Extreme Unction, joining in the Psalm and responding to the Litanies' and prayers. She then once more thanked God for having made her a child of the Church. F. Antony of Jesus asked her if she would desire to be buried at Avila. This question seemed to displease her, and she answered quickly, "Ought I to have a will of my own?" adding with touching humility, "Will they not give me a corner of earth here?" That night was passed in intense suffering, and in the continual repetition of her accustomed loving ejaculations. On the 4th, which was the Festival of S. Francis of Assisi, at about seven o'clock in the morning, the Saint turned upon her left side, and remained in that posture with a crucifix grasped tightly in her hand, for the fourteen remaining hours of her life. Her countenance was inflamed, and she seemed absorbed in the loving contemplation of God.

"For the last two days," says M. Anne of S. Bartholomew, "I had not left her for a single moment, because it was a consolation to her to see me near her bed. I asked the other religious for anything she wanted. I was in such deep sorrow that, on the day she died, I could not utter a single word. On that day, as I knew she was very fond of having everything clean about her, I changed all her linen,* even to her coifs and her sleeves, which seemed to please her greatly, for she looked at me and smiled, and thanked me by a sign. The beauty of that soul was manifested in all she did. In the evening, F. Antony ordered me to go and take some nourishment. I went; but when the Saint saw me leave her cell, she became uneasy,

---

* Linen was permitted to be worn in time of sickness.

looking from one side to another, as if for me. The
Father asked her if she wished me to come back.
She made a sign of assent, and he sent for me. As
soon as she saw me she smiled, took my hands in
hers, and caressed me tenderly, and then laid her
head in my arms. I held her thus till she had breathed
her last. I was more dead than alive. She seemed
so inflamed with the love of her Divine Spouse as to
be longing for the moment of her deliverance from the
prison of the body, that she might go to enjoy His
sacred presence.

"Our Lord is so good that, seeing how little
patience I had to endure this cross, He appeared to
me standing at the foot of the Saint's bed, in the
midst of a company of Angels and Saints, as if He
had come to take her with Him to Heaven. That
most glorious vision lasted for about the space of a
Credo, and made an immediate change in my heart. I
asked pardon of our Lord for my want of resignation,
and said to Him, 'Now, O my God, that I have seen
the glory which Thou hast prepared for this holy soul,
I would not that, for my consolation, Thou shouldst
leave her a moment longer upon earth.' I had
hardly finished these words, when the Saint expired,
and went like a pure dove to enjoy the vision of her
God."

It is related in the acts of her canonization, that
at the moment of the death of S. Teresa, some of
the religious present heard a noise as of a great
number of persons entering her cell, and ranging
themselves round her bed, and that it was their belief
that these heavenly visitants were the ten thousand
martyrs who, in one of her visions, had promised to
be present at her death, and to carry her to Heaven.
Another religious had seen a white dove issue from
her mouth as her holy soul departed.

S. Teresa revealed to Mother Catharine of Jesus, Prioress of Veas, that her death had been occasioned rather by an ecstasy of love than by any natural cause. Though it took place on October 4, her Festival is observed on the 15th, in consequence of the suppression of the ten intervening days at the reform of the calendar by Pope Gregory XIII.

The Saint died in the sixty-eighth year of her age, the forty-eighth of her religious profession, and the twenty-first since the establishment of her reform.

At the moment of her death, her countenance assumed a beauty even greater than it had worn in youth. The wrinkles disappeared which had been left on it by age and care, her complexion became white as alabaster, and her limbs flexible as those of a child.

Her body diffused a fragrance which filled the whole convent, and to which no natural scent could be compared. This fragrance had sometimes been perceptible even during life. On the following day the body of the Saint, which had been neither opened nor embalmed, was laid in her religious habit on a bier, over which was thrown a covering of cloth of gold; and thus was verified the vision which she related when, at the age of twenty, she had recovered from her death-like swoon. All the city crowded to the ceremony of her burial. The holy body, by the desire of Teresa Layz, the foundress of the convent, who feared that it might one day be removed, was placed in a very deep grave, and covered with chalk, stones, and bricks, in sufficient quantity to form the foundation of a solid building.

The Saint appeared to several persons immediately after her decease—amongst others to Catharine of Jesus, foundress of Veas, at the moment before Communion, telling her she was enjoying the presence of

God, and that she would be more useful to the Order in Heaven than she had been on earth. She appeared also to the faithful Anne of S. Bartholomew, who could hardly tear herself away from Alva, to return at the command of her Superiors to Avila.

"Do as you are commanded, my child," said the Saint, "and go to Avila."

Nine months after the interment of the holy body, which still continued to exhale the same miraculous fragrance, the Father Provincial determined upon its exhumation, in order to examine into the state of the precious remains, and to inter them with greater solemnity.

For fear of exciting any opposition on the part of the Duke and Duchess of Alva, who regarded them as the dearest treasure of their city, F. Gracian, with one companion, laboured secretly at his task. After toiling for four hours, they found the body of the Saint, which, though covered with the moss and earth, which had penetrated through crevices in the coffin, lay before them as perfect and as beautiful as on the day when it was buried nine months before, and diffusing a fragrance which moved all present to tears, at the glory thus manifested by our Lord in the relics of His Saints.

Another miraculous circumstance, which filled all the spectators with wonder, was the presence of a very sweet oil which flowed from the body, and bathed the earth around, and the cloths which were brought to absorb it.

In November, 1585, the body of S. Teresa was removed to the convent of S. Joseph at Avila, and having been juridically examined by the Bishop of that city, on January 1 of the following year it was brought back to Alva, where Pope Sixtus V., in 1589, decreed that it should remain, though portions of her relics also enrich various sanctuaries in Spain and throughout Christendom.

Miracles were multiplied at the tomb of the Saint, and the publication of her works in 1588, by the care of the Venerable Mother Anne of Jesus, increased the unanimous desire felt throughout Spain for her canonization. In 1614, Paul V. decreed her beatification; and on March 12, 1622, Gregory XV. solemnly inscribed the name of Teresa in the Catalogue of the Saints on the same day with that of her countryman, S. Isidore, and of her three glorious contemporaries, S. Francis Xavier, S. Ignatius, and S. Philip.

In 1627, Urban VIII. constituted her Patroness of all Spain, and made her Mass and Office of precept, which had hitherto been only of devotion. They were raised to the double rite by Clement IX. in 1668.

We have followed from her cradle to her grave, from her baptism to her canonization, this chosen vessel of grace—Saint, Virgin, and Confessor; Martyr in will, by the Moorish scimitar; Martyr in deed, by the lingering death of Divine love inflicted by the Seraph's lance; teacher of Doctors, Mother of Saints; the friend of God, the bride of the Lamb, the familiar companion of the Three Persons of the Most Holy Trinity;—and as we stood by her dying bed, listening for some glorious revelation from Paradise, some faint echo of the song of the hundred and forty - four thousand who follow the Lamb whithersoever He goeth, what was it that we heard?

The penitential breathings of the *Miserere;* the humble appeal to the heart of Jesus: "After all, O Lord, I am a child of the Church."

As her life lies traced out before her, in that awful perspective which anticipates to the dying the revelation of the particular judgment, on what does her failing vision rest?

On none of those things which we have gazed upon in wondering admiration. Not on the wonderful works which she had wrought for God; the "*paradises*," filled with pure and saintly souls, which, at her bidding, had blossomed for Him amid the wastes of Carmel; not on the hours of ecstatic prayer, in which He had espoused her to Himself; not on the marvellous *transverberation* of her heart, or the more marvellous vow which followed it; not on the sick restored by her touch to health, or the dead awakened by her prayer; not on the spiritually dead raised to the life of grace, or the dry bones of a whole Order, prostrate in sloth and tepidity, which, at her voice, had arisen to stand upon their feet in the full stature and beauty of religious perfection: not even upon the three vows, so fervently made, so faithfully kept, which had nailed her to the Cross with Jesus.

Farther and deeper still reaches the gaze of the dying Christian, till it rests on the font in the parish church at Avila, where her soul had been washed in the Blood of Jesus, that *Fountain of the Saviour* whence had been drawn all the streams of the marvellous spiritual life by which she had made glad the city of God. "After all, O Lord, I am a child of the Church." She pleads for pardon and acceptance in words which belong equally to every baptized infant, who departs with his chrism robe still wet from the life-giving font; to every returning penitent, for whom the Angel of penance has descended once more, even at the eleventh hour, to stir its healing waters. *O woman, great is thy faith!* greater still is thy humility!

Saint, Doctor, Confessor, and Martyr, laden with miraculous gifts, illuminated by marvellous revelations, in a measure, perhaps, never surpassed, and seldom equalled in the hierarchy of the Blessed. What strengthened her woman's heart, and steadied her woman's head, to walk unfaltering under such a weight of glory? Her dying words give us the answer. She was *" a child of the Church."* In all and through all, before all and beneath all, she was a simple, humble Catholic Christian. No foundation but the Rock of Peter could have borne so lofty a superstructure, and by no hand but the hand of that wise Master-builder has such a superstructure ever been raised.

Feast of the Patronage of S. Joseph, 1865.

NOTES.

A.

"MYSTICAL THEOLOGY is a supernatural, infused, experimental knowledge of God, which not only endows the soul with a vivid illumination with regard to God and the things of God, but also unites it to Him, and enkindles it with His love.

"It is called *mystical*, that is to say, secret, hidden, mysterious, because it makes known to the soul the most profound and secret mysteries which are hidden in God. It is so called, also, because it is very difficult, and often even impossible, for a soul to express in mortal language the sublime truths thus revealed to it by God. S. Paul tells us that he had heard *secret words which it is not granted to man to utter*, 2 Cor. xii. 4.

"It is *supernatural*, that is to say, infinitely above the reach of our nature, and eternally inaccessible to the natural faculties of our souls. Consequently, it comes from God, and not from our own efforts; it is not learnt, but inspired. It is directly infused, not acquired by our labour.

"It is *experimental*, that is to say, it possesses, by an intimate union of love, the Divine Object which it contemplates. And this is its supreme prerogative which separates it infinitely from all other sciences, not excepting even that of dogmatic theology. In fact, whatever be the science upon which our intellect is exercised here below, it is only by means of a certain light that we discern its object, and the properties belonging to it; but the object of that science remains external to the mind. It is not thus with mystical theology, which not only raises the soul to God who is its Object, but unites it intimately with Him. The soul possesses Him, enjoys Him, is penetrated with His light, and enkindled with His love.

"The end of mystical theology is to lead the soul by a holy life to the union of perfect charity with God. Its last stage is the full possession of God in Heaven, the intuitive vision of Him.

"Mystical theology being a supernatural and infused science, the soul cannot rise to it by its own powers, but it may dispose itself thereto. It so prepares itself, according to spiritual writers, by an absolute death to the life of the senses, in order to live only the life of the spirit, and by a courageous and faithful perseverance in ordinary mental prayer. This is the teaching of S. Dionysius, the prince of mystical doctors, in his treatise on this subject, addressed to S. Timothy : ' For thee, my dear son, exercise thyself with persevering fervour in 'mystical contemplation ; ascend courageously above the senses, above the sphere of intellectual operations, above all that can be perceived by sense or thought, above all things that are, and all things that are not ; and as far as is permitted to our weakness, you shall rise, after an incomprehensible manner, to union with Him who is above all being and above all knowledge. By this sincere, spontaneous, and absolute abandonment of thyself, and of all things besides, thou shalt attain at last to this supernatural light of Divine darkness.'

" This teaching of S. Dionysius is confirmed by that of S. Gregory, in his book of *Morals.* ' The soul,' says that great Pope, 'cannot rise to contemplation until it has been purified from the desire of human glory, and from all satisfaction in carnal concupiscence.'

" When the disposition of the soul is such that it desires nothing but God, He magnifies His goodness towards her ; and as He has raised the regenerate human race to the privilege of the intuitive vision of Himself, He vouchsafes to these faithful souls, thus thirsting for His love, the foretaste and the first-fruits of the life of Heaven. He opens to them the sanctuary of mystical theology, which is, as it were, the portal nearest to His glory : there, by some rays of ever-increasing brightness, He prepares by degrees and familiarizes them to the clear vision of Himself, in which they shall look face to face upon His Divinity. By some sparks of His love of still increasing intensity, He gradually enkindles and transforms them till He receives them into the Divine furnace of His charity. He prepares them, in short, by a union begun on earth for that consummate union with Him in Heaven, in which He shall be *All in all.*

" What are the effects of this infused and experimental knowledge of God ? It acts upon the whole soul, illuminating the understanding by a supernatural light, and inflaming the heart by the fire of Divine love. But the brightness of that light and the intensity and ardour of that love have different degrees, and these degrees are distinguished by different names in mystical theology. It is of these that S. Teresa has treated so admirably.

" Thus much may suffice to give an idea of the sublime and incomparable excellence of mystical theology. To assign to that science its due place, the Catholic has only to remember that it is not only the science of the Saints, but that it is also the school of sanctity ; that it is at once the fruitful mother of heroic virtues, and a sublime experiment, a Divine apprenticeship of the intuitive vision of God, a beginning and a foretaste of eternal beatitude. Then, in union with all the sublimest intellects and greatest teachers, and with all the Saints of the Church he will bow reverently before mystical theology as the Queen of all the sciences." —Note by P. Bouix to his translation of the *Life of S. Teresa.*

B.

The works of S. Teresa which remain to us are the following :—

The second *Book of her Life,* written between the years 1562 and 1566, by the desire of one of her confessors, F. Garcia of Toledo, of the Order of S. Dominic. In this narrative she has probably incorporated the first history of her life, written in 1561 and 1562, by the command of F. Ibañez, no portion of which remains. The *Additions* to her *Life* relate various signal graces conferred on the Saint from 1570 to 1579.

The Way of Perfection, written between 1562 and 1566.

The Book of the Foundations, begun by the command of our Divine Lord Himself, in 1573, and finished in 1582.

The Interior Castle, written in 1577 by the command of Don Alonzo Velasquez, Canon of Toledo, afterwards Bishop of Osma and Archbishop of Compostella.

The Conceptions of Divine Love, on certain words of the Book of Canticles, written in 1577 or 1578. A few chapters, previously copied by some other hand, alone remain of this work, which was burnt by the Saint in obedience to one of her confessors, who made ample amends to the Church for the loss of so rich a treasure by the act of heroic humility and obedience elicited by his ill-advised command.

Exclamations of a Soul to her God, written in 1579.

Constitutions of the Reform.

Admonitions to her Religious.

Method of Visiting the Convents of Discalced Nuns.

Various Hymns, called in Spanish *Glosa.*

Letters, ranging from 1560 to 1582.

C.

The following particulars exhibit the pedigree of the Houses of English Teresians traced to our wonderful Saint herself. The venerable Mother Anne of Jesus, whom S. Teresa on first beholding recognized by a prophetic instinct as her coadjutrix in the great work of the reform of Mount Carmel, twenty-two years after the death of the Saint, left Spain with five other religious to found houses of the Order in France. The venerable Mother Anne of S. Bartholomew, the constant companion of S. Teresa in all her foundations, accompanied these holy adventurers. After establishing in that country several convents of the Reform, Anne of Jesus and Anne of S. Bartholomew, with a few other sisters, pressed forward into the Low Countries for the same purpose, in which they succeeded beyond their expectations. In 1619 Mother Anne of Jesus was prioress of a convent in Brussels, and Mother Anne of S. Bartholomew held the same office in a convent in Antwerp. This convent is called to this day the House of the *Spanish* Teresians. One of the religious chosen for the foundation of this convent, was Anne of the Ascension, an *Englishwoman*, whose family name was Worsley. Her father, an English Catholic gentleman, had accompanied Philip II. into Spain and the Low Countries, after the death of Queen Mary. This holy religious had been most particularly instructed in the spirit of S. Teresa by Mother Anne of S. Bartholomew, who loved her very tenderly, and took most special care of her during the years spent under her guidance, teaching her even the least customs and observances of the Order, as the venerable Mother herself had seen them practised by S. Teresa.

In 1619 Lady Mary Lovell, in her zeal for the sanctification of her own countrywomen, furnished the means necessary for the foundation of a House of *English* Teresians at Antwerp. To this foundation was sent Mother Anne of the Ascension, who remained Prioress for twenty-five years. Under her holy guidance this English house became a most flourishing community, many noble and wealthy English young ladies took refuge there, from the persecutions and troubles at home, in the poverty and peace of Carmel. In 1644 Mother Anne of the Ascension received as novices, Margaret and Ursula Mostyn, whose future sanctity she foretold. Two Foundations for English Carmelites were made from this House. In 1648 one was made at Lierre ; in 1678 another was made in Hoogstraet. In the Convent of Lierre. Mother Margaret of Jesus

(Mostyn) held the office of Prioress until her holy death in 1679 at the age of fifty-four. Her sister, Mother Ursula of All Saints, was chosen to succeed her. She also died in the odour of sanctity in 1700. Under such superiors this Convent gained the name of the *Reliquary of Saints*, from the extraordinary sanctity of its inmates, as the lives of the sisters written at that time amply testify.

In 1794, the troubles of the Continent and the lawlessness of the French Revolution obliged the religious of the three convents above mentioned to take refuge in their own native country. The Carmelites from Hoogstraet spent several years in England, and afterwards settled at Valognes, in France. The religious of the English House of Antwerp finally settled at Llanherne, in Cornwall. Those of the Convent of Lierre had but a few hours' notice of the approach of the French. They exhumed the bodies of their venerable Mothers, the two Mostyns, and with nothing but these holy relics fled to Dunkirk, whence they sailed next morning for England, their church plate, vestments, paintings, books, &c., were all carefully preserved by the townspeople, who were greatly distressed at their departure. After remaining a few days in London, they were invited to St. Helens, Auckland, where they at first settled. Afterwards they removed to Cocken Hall, near Durham, where they remained for more than twenty years. Finally, in 1830, they removed to their present convent at Darlington.

·VYMAN AND SONS, PRINTERS, GREAT QUEEN STREET, LONDON, W.C.